About the Author

M LeRoy Lombard, was born in San Fernando, CA in March of 1972. When he turned three, his family moved to Hereford, Texas, then later to the Fort Worth area. His father owned and operated an automotive repair shop, and his mother was the bookkeeper. As soon as he became old enough, he would help at the family shop, sweeping and collecting trash. While growing up, his mother would read books to the family, either in the car on road trips, or at home on Friday evenings. Developing a love for books, several books became his favorite over the years. "Where the Red Fern Grows" was one he loved in grade school, because it was very descriptive and helped to emerse the reader in the story's surroundings. He also loved "The Best Christmas Pageant Ever" because of its situational humor. These two books helped to develop Lombard as a writer years later, attempting to emulate the writing styles. He also loved the Chronicles of Narnia series, which deleloped Lombard's love for adventure in an other-worldly environment. Lombard started writing short stories, poems, and silly songs for his wife when they were first dating. Later he added special writings for his sons as well as some to help the family keep a positive outlook while going through some series health issues. In 2014, Lombard suffered a serious aortic aneurism that required an emergency valve replacement surgery. While in recovery, Lombard dedicated his time to writing his first novel. Through the encouragement of his family, he decided to continue writing as a way to channel his anxiety in a healthier direction.

DEDICATION

To my beautiful wife, Lisa, who has for over twenty years been my princess. You've also been my "Olivia", the queen of my castle, and my lady-in-waiting. So much in one package! Also, to my boys, Josef and Nikolaus, whose traits and personalities can be found in many of the characters in this book [but mostly the arguing archers]. Thanks for adding humor and wit to my life. Thank you all three for enduring listening to this book as it progressed through the writing process. Love you all!.

M Le Roy Lombard

BETROTHED

Published by M LeRoy Lombard

ISBN: 978-1-964452-42-5 (Paperback)
ISBN: 978-1-964452-43-2 (Hardback)
ISBN: 978-1-964452-44-9 (E-book)

Library of Congress Control Number: 2025901741

Table of Contents

CHAPTER 1

It was a time of peace, yet a time of strange uncertainty for the kingdom of Nadeau. Nestled beside the Andjety mountains, it was a wealthy kingdom comprised largely of farmland. The city of Nadeau, of which the kingdom was named, sat at the very far west of the kingdom, along the coastline. Merchant ships lined the piers with their sails and riggings reaching high into the sky. The palace sat at the north of the city, with towers peaking at every corner of the citadel. The square had a multitude of markets and bazaars, with a stage set in the middle to allow the royal guard to make public announcements in the hearing of the people.

The rest of the kingdom jetted out east, beyond the two mountains, and spilled out into a valley of farmland. From one side of the kingdom to the other would take four days on horseback, six days by carriage, and no one knows how long if you walked it by foot. In fact, if you chose to walk from the farthest east of the kingdom, to the west towards the city of Nadeau, you most likely would be robbed, kidnapped, killed, or perhaps all three. The middle part of the kingdom, directly beneath the Andjety mountains, was considered the most treacherous part of the kingdom where thieves and marauders hid out and hunted wayward travellers.

Three days' ride from the capital city, towards the plains and past the mountains, lay a small farm village called Pachenthou. Pachenthou was settled mostly by farmers whose farms surrounded the village. But the village itself centred around the local pub, where the menfolk would gather on certain nights, spin yarns and drink rum or ale.

Balen was a local farmer that spent almost every night in the pub, though he rarely drank. He was an older man, with brown hair salted with grey and a bald spot in the middle of his scalp. He was of stocky build, not like a farmer from ploughing fields, but rather like one who had once trained as a soldier. His facial features told of one who had seen his fair share of misfortune, though his demeanour was kind and serene. The local towns people accepted him as one of their own, a farmer by trade.

Each night he would sit in the pub and listen to the town gossip. He kept himself aware of the events that trickled down from Nadeau to their village. He seldom interacted. It was as if he was waiting for some specific news to reach the town, but never did. He would sometimes sit at a table in the middle of the room and listen to multiple conversations in the pub, or he would stand at the bar and converse with the owner of the pub about news that was being chatted about the town.

One night, as Balen stood at the bar of the pub, two royal envoys burst through the door. This was strange, since there was nothing in the village or the surrounding area to interest the crown. All conversations within the pub ceased and all eyes were fixed on the official men. The two strangers were dressed in royal blue and red, each wearing an official insignia indicating they represented the king. The first man was fortyish in age. He obviously appeared experienced as an envoy. The second man was young and appeared rather new to how an envoy would normally carry himself. The envoys approached the bar and laid a royal letter from the king down on the bar opposite the owner.

"His majesty, King Malcom the Merciful, has ordered that any, every and all villages upon which his royal envoys stop, must supply such envoys with whatever provisions that are necessary and will be compensated at twice the cost of the provisions provided." At that declaration, the younger of the envoys dropped a velvet bag on the counter which gave out a clattering sound from the gold coins inside. Curious whisperings softly filtered throughout the room.

"Your generosity is gratefully accepted," the owner of the pub answered the men, standing behind the bar and eyeing the velvet bag. "What do you gentlemen require?" The young envoy laid a list on the bar and loosened the ties to the moneybag. The older envoy looked about the room, scoping out the pub's occupants. "Three meals prepared right away," the young envoy demanded. "A room of which to spend the night, with only one exterior entrance, on the ground floor. Three meals for breakfast ready to go at first light."

"Three meals?" the owner asked. "There is another with the two of you?" "In the carriage," the older envoy quietly replied.

"She will not be coming inside," the young envoy mistakenly interjected. The older envoy glared indiscreetly at his companion.

"She?" Balen piped up. "You have a woman you are escorting?"

"Affairs of state have little concern for farmers," the older envoy retorted. "Who we are… or are not escorting… is an official matter." The envoy turned his body away from Balen to show the conversation was over. Balen took a step backwards as to leave the bar when the envoy turned back around to study Balen's face.

"Do I know you?" the envoy asked, stopping Balen. The owner of the pub, who by now had grabbed the envoys' list in his hand, glanced up at Balen and then back down to the list. The younger envoy suddenly took an interest in Balen as well.

"I don't know," Balen answered. "It would stand to reason that if I knew you, you would know me. But it doesn't seem that we are aware of each other." The older envoy turned to slouch over the bar.

"Even been to Nadeau?" the older envoy asked. "The capital city?" "Yes," Balen answered, eyeing the younger envoy.

"Were you ever placed in public stocks?" the older envoy asked, with a half-smile on his face.

"No," Balen answered coolly. "I have never had that pleasure." The younger envoy chuckled at his response, then forced himself to stop when the other envoy did not laugh. "If it be a room you men be needing," the owner broke in, "I can give you the one around back. It is secluded from the rest of the inn. The only way into the room is through the outer door. But… uh…" The owner hesitated.

"What's the problem?" the young envoy asked. "What's wrong with the room?" "There nothing be wrong with the room. I just feel a little uneasy knowing that two men are sharing a room with a strange woman… Unless I know the circumstances, you see." By this time, the older man had pulled a gold coin from the bag and placed it between his first two fingers. He looked at his apprentice and nodded. "Would you feel better to know that neither of us are sleeping in the room?" the young envoy explained. "The room is for the young lady and we plan to sleep outside in the carriage."

"A lady!" Balen exclaimed. The younger man's face showed embarrassment that twice he unwittingly divulged confidential information. The older envoy tapped the coin on the counter three times and leaned close to Balen's ear.

"None of your affair!" the envoy whispered, posturing so as to intimidate Balen through his mystique.

"I know, I know," Balen conceded, showing no signs of intimidation. "Affairs of state."

"We'll get you three your suppers within the hour," the owner reassured the envoys. "Your other requests will be prepared by morning." The owner reached behind the desk and pulled out a large brass key and placed it on the bar. "The key to the room." The older envoy picked up the key from the bar and handed it to the other.

"Rolf, please show our… guest… to her room and stand guard outside her door till I return."

"Sir?" the young envoy asked a bit confused.

"I will relieve you of your post within the hour." He stared at his young companion for a few seconds until the envoy understood that he was being dismissed to care for their mystery friend. The young man turned to the door and exited outside to the carriage without looking over his shoulder.

Balen retreated from the bar and sat at a table nearest the middle of the room. The older envoy stood at the bar, surveying the people in the pub, while tapping the coin on the counter again. All the conversations in the room began to filter to new conversations. After a few minutes, the envoy, deciding everything was safe, retreated to the same table as Balen.

"Letting the young do the heavy lifting?" Balen teased.

"What are you doing here, Balen?" the envoy inquired. Balen turned his head to see who all was within hearing distance.

"He's rather young, isn't he, Rodrick?" Balen remarked. "Is he your apprentice?"

"I haven't seen you in over ten years, and the last place I would expect to see you… is in a peasant village in the middle of nowhere."

"Right," Balen countered. "The last place I'd expect to see any of you from the palace." He quickly changed topics to satisfy his curiosity. "Who's in the carriage? Or, by now I should ask, who's in the private room."

"Sorry, Balen. It is of the utmost secrecy."

"A royal envoy," Balen described, "travelling from the far east of the kingdom, on their way back to the palace, transporting a mystery woman of whom they cannot speak. I smell a scandal."

"It's nothing like that," Rodrick assured him, leaning forward in his chair towards Balen.

"Then… what is it like?" Balen demanded.

Rodrick sat back in his chair, still clinging to the gold coin. He nervously twirled the coin between his two fingers, occasionally tapping it on the table. "Why did you leave the royal court?" he asked.

"You know why I left. King Malcolm might be a merciful king, but his son, Prince Henry, is completely intolerable."

"Go on," Rodrick prodded his friend, who showed great reluctance. "Tell me the whole story, and I'll tell you who is being guarded by my young apprentice." "Well," Balen continued, "when Queen Luella died, the king was heartbroken. No one could blame him. She was beautiful, intelligent and disarming. I think the entire kingdom mourned her death. Even the townspeople in this village celebrate her birthday with an annual festival."

"And the king blamed his son for her death," Rodrick interjected.

"I don't believe the king consciously believes his son is the cause of her death. I mean, she did die giving birth to Prince Henry, but I think the king mostly mourned her loss and had no one to guide him through his grief. The late queen's Ladies as well as many palace servants, raised the prince, and the king had very little to do with his son.

This caused the prince to grow up with every privilege a young boy could imagine, but without guidance or discipline. It was a mixture for disaster."

"I had heard rumours about the prince playing cruel pranks on the palace servants, causing them to be punished by the king."

"That is true," Balen recounted. "He would also steal from the royal treasury and sneak crown jewels or gold and silver relics into the church offertory, causing distress between both the church and state treasurers."

"I remember when that came to light," Rodrick responded.

"Anyway, by the time, the prince reached the age of fifteen, and I could foresee nothing but problems under his authority. King Malcom the Merciful is a wonderful king, but Prince Henry is cruel and heartless. The king could see it, but never did anything to stop his own son. That is why we left.

"We?" Rodrick asked.

"That was ten years ago," Balen answered, deliberately ignoring his inquiry. "Well," Rodrick continued, "now the prince is nearing twenty-five. Do you know what that means?"

Balen thought for a moment. "The prince is due to be inaugurated as king," he answered.

"Yes. And that is why we were sent to the furthest eastern part of the kingdom." "Because the prince must be married in order to take the throne," Balen realised. "According to Nadeauan law," Rodrick reminded Balen, "the prince may only take

the throne after being wed. He is to marry a common maiden, from among the people, to rule alongside him, to represent the people."

"That is who you have with you." Balen's eyes opened wide with excitement. "The future queen of Nadeau." He started to stand, but Rodrick grabbed his arm to keep him in his seat.

"Wait! There's more, though." Both surveyed the room to see if their conversation was being overheard. "You mentioned that you believed that the king knew about his son's unscrupulous activities?"

"Yes," Balen answered.

"That the king never did anything to correct his son?"

"Yes."

"The fact is," Rodrick announced, "the king has done something that will prevent the prince from taking the throne on his twenty-fifth birthday."

"What is that?"

"Well, you know how the king holds the privilege of choosing the bride to be given to his son on the day of his inauguration?"

"Yes. I assume that the king gave you explicit instructions of who she was and where to find her."

"Oh. Explicit is right. In more ways than one."

"What do you mean?" Balen asked, rather puzzled at the envoy's response. "Let's just say, when the prince sees his new bride, he will not be happy one bit." Balen sat quietly contemplating what the envoy meant. "In what way?" he asked. "Well, all I can say is," Rodrick looked towards the door and then back at Balen,

lowering his voice. "There will be no wedding on the prince's birthday." "What?"

"And… the king will not be abdicating his throne any time soon."

"Why?" Balen asked. "Is she a bastard?"

"No, no!" Rodrick reassured. "The maiden is of noble birth."

"A princess?"

"Nobility—not royalty."

"Who is she?" Balen asked.

"She is the daughter of Lord Weatherly."

"I do not know them," Balen admitted.

"You wouldn't. The king awarded him the title about six years ago, to govern a village at the furthest most eastern point in the kingdom."

"Okay," Balen listened, waiting for the story to unravel.

"Well, about three months ago, Lord Weatherly and his wife were tragically killed." "Killed?" Balen asked.

"Murdered," Rodrick clarified. "leaving their only child, a daughter, all by herself. When the king heard about it a few weeks ago, he dispatched Rolf and I to find her and bring her back to the palace to be given to Prince Henry as a bride."

"So, why do you think this maiden would offend the prince? Is she unappealing?" "Ho!" Rodrick huffed. "She is adorable! Intelligent, witty and disarming.She is very much like the late queen in almost every respect."

"Well?" Balen asked, not understanding why the prince would be so offended— aside from being completely incompatible with an intelligent, beautiful and witty young woman.

"The two of us arrived a week and a half ago in the village of the Weatherly's," Rodrick recounted. "We searched for their daughter in every house, boarding room and pub. Finally, after we seemed to turn over every pebble in the village, we found her picking wild flowers by a secluded stream where she had been hiding since her parents'

death."

"Who killed her parents?" Balen asked.

"Andjety marauders… from the nearby mountains," Rodrick responded. "At any rate, when we discovered her and realised who she was… Well, Rolf and I knew right away that the king had chosen her as a pawn to prevent his son from taking the throne."

"The king?" Balen shockingly asked. "King Malcolm the Merciful… using people as pawns to further his own interests?"

"There is more to the king than always being merciful."

"If this betrothal between the prince and this maiden does not take, how will the fallout affect the kingdom?" The envoy raised both hands in a gesture of uncertainty. "If there is no wedding," Balen continued, "what will become of the lady?"

"It is a most curious of circumstances the king has devised. The prince is not at liberty to decline betrothal to the maiden. However, he can choose to put off his coronation and be wed at a later time. But, he will not be allowed to take the throne from his father until he is fully married. That is the law. But, on Prince Henry's birthday, not only will he officially be inaugurated as the crowned prince--she also will be inaugurated as the crowned princess, equal in power to the prince."

"Most curious, indeed," Balen answered.

"I, myself, am anxious to see how it plays out." Rodrick stood from his chair and walked over to the bar. "Where are those meals, sir?" he called to the owner.

"They are ready, sir." The owner replied, producing three plates of food on a wooden tray. "Shall I carry them to the room for you?"

"That won't be necessary," Rodrick replied. "I can manage." The envoy took the tray from the owner and headed for the door. "Nice to catch up, Balen," he called out from across the room. As he left the pub, the owner grabbed the open bag of money from the bar and set it on a table behind him. He counted every coin.

"Eleven gold coins!" he exclaimed. "That is five times the value of the food, room, and provisions they requested."

"True," Balen remarked. "However, I think the envoy was supposed to leave twelve." The owner glanced at Balen. "He left with one in his hand."

CHAPTER 2

Four days after the envoys arrived in Nadeau, the people assembled to celebrate Prince Henry's twenty-fifth birthday and, with it, his coronation. Most of the city gathered around the front palace wall to catch a glimpse of King Malcolm the Merciful and his son, Prince Henry. People gathered from many of the surrounding villages to also witness the inauguration of their new king. But more than anything else, the people were anxious to see who the new queen would be.

King Malcom the Merciful had married a beautiful young maiden the same year of his inauguration from a village in the eastern part of the kingdom. His marriage was part of a long-standing tradition to marry a maiden from the kingdom, who was at least sixteen years old, to represent the people to the king.

Malcom the Merciful's late wife was Luella. She was graceful, poised and beautiful. From the time she was a child, her whole village loved her. It was as if Luella was destined to marry the new king, Malcom. Luella had blond hair, fair skin and sparkling brown eyes that would grab your attention the moment you laid eyes on her. Her face was lightly sprinkled with freckles that gave her an eternal youthful appearance. Her frame was slender and tall and she always carried herself with dignity. When she died in giving birth to Prince Henry, the nation mourned for her greater than any past queen or past king. When Prince Henry became a lad and showed himself to be an obnoxious tyrant, the kingdom mourned even greater that his mother wasn't there to temper her son and pass on her loving disposition. Twenty-five years after Luella's death, the nation was anxious to know who would be the next queen. There was much hoping and anticipation for the wife of Prince Henry to be similar to his mother, Luella. Many believed that if King Malcom the Merciful chose a wife for his son that matched closely to his own wife in character, she might save the kingdom from the cruelty of the new monarch.

For almost ten years, the kingdom's subjects prayed for what they coined as, Palace balance. The villages began to paint symbols on their houses and barns of a straight line centred over a triangle, representing balance.

As the festivities were in wait to commence and the streets became crowded with subjects cheering for the king and the soon-to-be crowned prince, the palace became a frenzy with nobles, dignitaries and servants scrambling to serve them food and refreshments.

Prince Henry, dressed in his royal blue garnache and covered from his shoulders to the floor with a bright red herigaut, entered the main ball room with his armour-bearer and sparring companion, Pitt, walking at his right and two steps behind him. Prince Henry, dressed in his royal blue garnache and covered from his shoulders to the floor with a bright red herigaut, entered the main ball room. His armour-bearer and sparring companion, Pitt, walked at his right side, and two steps behind him. As they entered, the royal caller announced their presence.

"His Royal Majesty, and future king, Prince Henry of Nadeau." The entire room ceased their mingling, turned to the door of which Henry and Pitt stood and began applauding. Henry did a slight bow, acknowledging the approbation, then sauntered to the middle of the room so as to take his place as the centre of attention. Pitt kept to his right side, standing slightly behind him. Henry would turn his head so as to make the occasional comment to Pitt regarding his estimation of each dignitary that paid his respect.

"Lord Attenburough," Henry nodded to the noble. "To say he is overweight," he whispered over his shoulder, "is to say that a stocky man is painfully thin." Pitt chuckled and responded, "Your majesty."

"Lord Goodwyn," the prince acknowledged. "Wealthy due do his ill report of garnered taxes I'd assume."

"Your majesty," Pitt responded.

"Lady Gossette," Henry greeted. "A lady of few talents, but many noble friends— mainly the ones which burns and itches."

"Oh! Your majesty, sire!" Pitt playfully scolded. As the line of congratulants began to diminish, a loud fanfare was played by four trumpeters.

"Lords and ladies," the royal caller announced. "Welcomed guests of the Nadeau aristocracy! His Royal Excellency and Esteemed Sovereign—King Malcolm the Merciful!" The entire room roused with ecstatic applause. The king entered through his private entrance from the west wall, adjacent to his private chamber. His arms were raised, welcoming the fanfare and gestures of adoration, waving at distinct people.

The king was a tall man compared to many of his contemporaries of other nations. His face carried an expression of authority, yet kindness, and with a hint of painful experience. His hair was thick and silvery white. He sported a bushy white beard that extended at least an inch past his chin. His eyebrows were also bushy. His moustache was well manicured and trimmed close to his lip.

As the king reached the centre of the room, he reached out and placed his hand on Prince Henry's shoulder as a gesture of good will. Henry despised his father and could not accept such a gesture of kindness. As inconspicuous as he could, Henry turned his body so as to force his father's hand to slide off his shoulder.

Over the clatter of applause, the king leaned over and reassured his son of his intentions.

"I'm just wanting to show my support of your special day, my lad."

"I am happy that the day has come for me to take possession of the throne," the prince asserted. "Now I can be done with you being my father and my king." His eyes burned with resentment as they stared into his father's.

"Have I been so horrible at either?" the king inquired.

"You might be a hero to your subjects, but I know what you are as a father." The king stepped to one side, away from his son, and continued to wave at the applauding congregants. As the adulation began subsiding, the king gave a brief address to the people.

"People of Nadeau, I welcome you to this long-anticipated occasion. The coronation of my son as the future king of Nadeau." The people cheered again. "If you will join me upon the palace balcony. It would do me great pleasure if you would stand beside me and my son as I address the kingdom." The nobility within the ballroom applauded again as they all moved as one assembly through the French doors that opened onto the balcony. As the doors swung open and the Cryer announced to the public that the king was about to commence the coronation, the streets erupted with cheering, clapping, people beating sticks against any king of metal or wood that would produce a noise. The king stood at the very front of the balcony—dead centre. The king held up both hands to call for silence. The people quieted down to listen to their beloved king make what seemed to be his last and final address before he abdicated to his son.

"My dear people of Nadeau," the king announced. "It has been my honour and privilege to govern over you these past thirty years. During this time, we as a people have endured hardship, famine, wars and even tragedy. It was on my birthday thirty years ago that my father abdicated the throne and I became your king. And it was twenty-eight years ago that this nation of ours was struck by the worst famine in more than five hundred years. Our crops dried up and turned to dust. There was no money in your pockets to pay your required taxes. Your children began to starve. Even your cattle and sheep were thirsting for water. So, I, as your king, decided to lay a hold on all collecting of taxes. Furthermore, I opened the royal treasury and sent dignitaries to purchase grain and produce from kingdoms the other side of the sea. For three years, you ate the food you couldn't grow and bread you couldn't purchase. And why? Because I am your king and you are my people—my responsibility. And praise be! We have all made it through.

We survived together, the ugly realities of hardship and famine."

"However, twenty-one years ago, we experienced violent attacks from the Andjety nomads down from the mountains. They came and attacked our villages, burned our crops and left men, women and children dead or disfigured. It was because of this that your villages sent elders from your villages to inform the palace of the goings on. Upon hearing the news, I sent a band of elite swordsmen and archers to go and avenge the blood of our people. The fighting was fierce, but our valiant heroes were successful and beat back the forces of the Andjety people. We encounter them on occasion, but most of the time, we are at peace as a nation."

"Much of my success as your king, I admit, was due to the influence of my wife, Queen Luella of Nadeau!She inspired me to be a better king. He insisted that I not collect any taxes during the time of famine. She insisted that I open the treasury and purchase aid to send to the people of Nadeau that were suffering most from the drought. She was the reason your king was given the title, "Merciful", because she inspired me to be merciful and understanding as she was merciful, loving, tender-hearted and gracious. Tragically, she died twenty-five years ago today."

"But it is for this reason we are all gathered together on this most auspicious occasion. As tradition would have it, as I enter the years that I should abdicate the throne to my son, I am appointed with the duty to provide a bride for the soon-to-be crowned prince. A maiden taken from amongst her people to be a guide, an advisor and help her husband be the good king he is destined to be."

"Many of my subjects have worried about my son taking the throne. Yes, I have heard the whisperings, the rumours of fear and concern. I have seen the symbols painted on the sides of houses and barns. You are wanting my son to be wed to a maiden who will help shape him as a king. One who will temper his selfishness and arrogance. I believe I have found the perfect bride, for a boy who would not only want to be a man, but will one day become your king."

"People of Nadeau… I present to you—Henry of Nadeau!"

The people cheered as the king placed a royal crown upon the head of the prince. "With this crown, may you rule your people with compassion and justice. May you consider those hurting and in need, and vanquish those of hatred and war. I now pronounce you—Prince Henry of Nadeau!"

"But now, I know more than the coronation of my son, you have come out today to lay eyes upon the future queen of Nadeau. Therefore—people of Nadeau… It is my honour to present to you—Audrianna of Nadeau!"

The people in the streets become ecstatic all over again, cheering—banging sticks— and clanging metal objects to show their approval. The noblemen and ladies moved to either side of the balcony to make room for the princess. As the nobility turned around to greet the betrothed bride of the prince, their eyes met her—

Adrianna stood facing the king and prince, dressed in a petite, red and yellow silk ballgown, that hung from her shoulders, down to the floor. A beautiful necklace of gold hung around her neck. A sheer veil covered her head and draped down the backside of her to the floor. Two ladies in Waiting stood next to her, one on either side. She was beautiful in almost every detail, with the exception that even through her veil, one could see her cheeks were stained with tear marks. Her eyes still red and puffy, she wore an expression of fear on her face. And she stood, from head to toe, at the height of four foot, three inches. The patrons on the balcony gasped loudly in horror. Henry abruptly turned to face his armour-bearer, Pitt.

"He brought me a child to wed!" he exclaimed disgustedly.

"She's only eight years old!" people began to whisper.

"No! Ten, maybe," others said.

"She is adorable."

"The prince can't marry a child!"

"What has the king done?"

"Surely this is a joke."

The king waited to let the nobles on the balcony take in the sight of a child bride being given to his son. He then walked down the aisle way and held out his hand to the child. Audrianna reached out with her trembling hand and placed it in the king's. Malcolm led the little girl to the edge of the balcony for the entire kingdom to view her. He stood behind her and placed his hands on both her shoulders.

"People of Nadeau! You see before you a child. A little girl, no older than ten years of age. Nadeau law prohibits any man from marrying a maiden younger than sixteen. The prince cannot marry a girl of such tender years. So, is the problem with the law, or with the child? Clearly, the problem is with the child. My son is twenty-five this day and old enough to take the throne. However, I do not feel that the kingdom is safe under his current level of maturity. So, is the problem with the kingdom, or with the tender maturity of the prince? Clearly, both the prince and the princess have an amount of maturing to do. I propose that we wait another six years, until the princess, Audrianna, is sixteen, and let's see if Prince Henry's maturity rises to the same level as his betrothed. Six years! I, King Malcolm the Merciful, have spoken!" At that final proclamation, the crowds that filled the streets applauded their approval. Prince Henry ran up to the king.

"No, father," he protested. "I am twenty-five! I have a right to the throne." "Oh, but you don't," the king refuted. "I have legal right to choose whatever maiden I desire to betroth you to. The only stipulation is that she be an unwed virgin. I think it is safe to say she qualifies as a legitimate bride. Now, you are not allowed to take the throne without being married. And since you cannot marry her for another six years—YOU MUST WAIT!" At that, the king approached little Audrianna. "Please kneel, my dear." Audrianna knelt on the soft pillow the ladies-in-waiting placed at her feet. The king was handed a tiara, and he proudly and carefully placed it upon her head. "With this crown, I pronounce you—Princess Audrianna of Nadeau!" Again, the crowd cheered!

CHAPTER 3

As the sun set and palace lamps were lit, festivities continued in full swing throughout the city. All through the night, talented artists played their musical instruments in the market square by the light of the street lamps. Singers and bards shared their choruses in honour of the prince and his newly betrothed. Songs were also sung in honour of Malcolm the Merciful and in honour of the memory of Queen Luella who died twentyfive years that very day.

Soon, young Audrianna was led by her ladies-in-waiting, to her new private chamber on the same floor as the royal family. They brought Audrianna to her dressing room and began to dismantle her royal ballroom dress. It required two of them to remove her cape, fold it properly and place it in a special trunk at the end of her bed.

"Wasn't that a lovely party, Your Highness?" they asked the crowned princess. They could see that Audrianna was quiet and unresponsive and they tried their best to cheer her up. While in the presence of the king and the prince, it was not their place to speak to the princess except when spoken to.

"Yes," was her quiet, melancholy answer.

The third lady-in-waiting began the meticulous task of unlacing the back of her dress. The first two, having put the cape away, began to unbutton the princess's tightly bound sleeves. The trail of buttons on each arm started at the cuff and led all the way past her elbow. Eighttiny buttons on each arm were difficult to unfasten and they seemed like eighty to the ladies undressing the princess.

"You were so pretty in your royal gown, Your Highness," the other lady-in-waiting remarked. Audrianna didn't answer. She stood expressionless in front of the large mirror over her dressing table, except for the occasional tear that welled up in her emerald-green eyes and trickled down her cheek. After the laces were loosed and the sleeves unbuttoned, the three ladies-in-waiting lifted the gown over Audrianna's head, then folded it properly and placed it on top of the cape. Next was the bustier, a tightly laced corset, under the main dress and over the body-length undergarment.

"What village is Your Highness from?" the third lady-in-waiting asked the princess, attempting to change subjects since her betrothal seemed to be a source of sorrow.

Audrianna remained silent. As the bustier around Audrianna's middle was loosed, she let out an irrepressible sigh. As cumbersome as her ballroom dress felt, her bustier was the most uncomfortable of her ensemble.

"Feel better, Your Highness?" the first lady-in-waiting remarked, hearing her sigh in relief.24

"Yes, thank you," she answered, this time with a half-smile.

"Bustiers often make it hard to breathe. Right, Your Highness?"

"Yes, they do," Audrianna agreed, scratching her stomach with both hands. She looked up in the faces of her ladies-in-waiting, this time with a full smile.

"Oh, Your Highness! There's the smile we all knew she had!" the princess's smile beamed even wider. For the first time her green eyes twinkled.

"You can call me, Audrianna," she offered.

"Oh no, Your Highness!" the second lady-in-waiting exclaimed. "It ain't proper for us to speak to Your Highness so commonly. It ain't our place. Even His Majesty Prince Henry must refer to Your Highness as 'Your Highness.'"

"Really?" Audrianna asked in amazement. "The law requires the prince to be nice to me?"

"I wouldn't go so far as to expect His Majesty to be nice to Your Highness," the second Lady in Waiting corrected. "His Majesty just has to follow proper protocol, as does Your Highness."

"As do we," The third Lady in Waiting remarked.

"So, I call the prince, 'Your Majesty'..." Audrianna clarified. "What do I call the king?"

"Your Highness can either say, 'Your Majesty' or 'Your Excellency.'" The third Lady in Waiting summarised. "'Your Majesty' can apply to either the king or the prince. But, 'Your Excellency' only applies to the king. No one is more excellent than the king."

As they talked, one of the ladies-in-waiting began unbuttoning Audrianna's white undergarment. The thick cotton jumper had a string of buttons from behind her neck, all the way down to the small of her back. The first lady unbuttoned the back, while the other two pulled Audrianna's arms out of the sleeves and slid the undergarment downwards to the floor, allowing her to step out of the garment. Being fully undressed, the second Lady in Waiting brought Audrianna a thick sleeping gown, which was placed over her head, and drawn down to her ankles. Audrianna pushed her arms through its long, oversized sleeves, and two of the ladies-in-waiting tied the cuffs around her wrists to keep her hands free.

"Shall I unpin your hair, Your Highness," one of the ladies-in-waiting asked. "You will sleep much better if your hair be let down and then brushed out."

"Yes, please," Audrianna agreed enthusiastically, sitting herself in front of the large mirror. The royal hairdresser had braided her hair, and wrapped it in a bun so tight, that she felt like her ears were higher on her head. As the three ladies pulled out every pin and unbraided her hair, the princess's long brown hair draped around her head, down to her waist. The ladies became excited with the length and beauty of her hair. This was their first day to be assigned to the princess. In preparation for the coronation, only the royal hairdresser, the palace dressmakers, and the castle guards had access to the young maiden. The ladies-in-waiting each quickly snatched up brushes and took turns brushing out her silky hair.

"Your Highness's hair is so beautiful!" one of the ladies remarked. "Has Your

Highness been growing it out her whole life?"

"No. My father wanted a son, so he kept my hair short until I was four. My mother broke the news to him that I was a girl, and that my hair should grow out because I would always be a girl. He was so heartbroken, he never cut my hair again." They all laughed and Audrianna giggled. The ladies traded turns brushing her hair. One of the ladies-inwaiting walked to the far side of the room and poured water into a porcelain bowl. She dipped a fluffy white cloth into the water, rung it out and carried it back to the princess.

She then began to wash the tear stains off the princess's face with the cool cloth, and continued cleaning down to the bottom side of her neck. The lady doing the brushing, draped Audrianna's hair over her arm and lifted it up so the lady washing could clean the backside of the princess's neck. Audrianna felt refreshed, and her heart was a little more at peace.

"Now, is Your Highness ready for bed?" one of the ladies-in-waiting asked.

"Yes," she nodded. Audrianna stood up from the chair and walked over to her bed.

Two of the ladies walked on either side of the bed and simultaneously pulled the comforter and top satin sheet back so the princess could climb in. She stood next to the bed and paused. The top of the mattress came to the middle of her chest. She couldn't climb in on her own, and looking around, Audrianna didn't see a step stool to help her climb in. As she considered how to get into bed, the third lady-in-waiting picked her up and plopped her in the middle of the bed, closely in front of her four large pillows.

Audrianna let out a giggle as she bounced on the mattress.

"Does Your Highness require anything else before she sleeps?" one of the ladies asked.

"Umm…" the princess hesitated to ask. "If I need to… do something… in the middle of the night… where… do I find… the chamber pot?" Now it was the ladies turn to let out a giggle.

"Forgive us, Your Highness!" one of the ladies begged. "Your Highness's question caught us off guard. There is a chamber pot under Your Highness's bed, like there was in her last room in the tower."

"Okay," Audrianna answered, a little annoyed how often they called her, Your

Highness. "But, if I get out of bed, how will I get back in without help? The bed it too tall, and I am too short."

"Just ask one of us for help, Your Highness."

"Where can I find you again?" the princess asked.

"Oh. We'll be in the room with Your Highness all night?" Audrianna's eyes opened wide in surprise.

"You're going to stay in the room with me all night? All three of you?"

"Yes, Your Highness," all three chorused.

"But… But, where will you sleep? There's only one bed."

"We sleep on mats near the door, Your Highness," one of the ladies assured her.

"You don't have rooms of your own? Or a house or family you go home to?"

"No, Your Highness. We are 'ladies-in-waiting'. Our duty is to stay with Your

Highness and to serve her needs all day, every day."

"So, you are slaves?" Audrianna asked in surprise.

"Oh, no, Your Highness!" the first lady-in-waiting answered.

"There are no slaves
in Nadeau."

"No, Your Highness!" the second lady-in-waiting reassured the princess. "Your
Highness would have to travel past the Andjety mountains to find slaves."

"We three were given the honourto serve Your Highness!" the third lady announced.

"It is a rare privilege that very few maidens in all of Nadeau are permitted."

"I don't think sleeping on the floor is much of a privilege," Audrianna replied. She then quickly surveyed the size of her bed in comparison to the four of them. "Look at my bed. I hardly take up any space on it. Why don't we all share the bed?"

"No, Your Highness!" they all three emphatically chorused.

"That ain't proper for us, Your Highness," one of the ladies-in-waiting answered.

"We'd get in a lot of trouble if they caught either one of us in possession or using something that belonged to Your Highness."

"Even if I, the one who owns the bed, invited you three to join me?"

"It ain't our place, Your Highness."

"I hate all this, 'my place' and 'what's proper' stuff. I don't like being a princess where I'm supposed to look down on everybody."

"Begging your pardon, Your Highness," the third lady-in-waiting answered. "Your Highness shouldn't be ashamed about propriety. Your Highness might not like looking down on us people, but we people like to have a king and queen that we can look up to and revere."

"Oh," Audrianna thoughtfully considered the words of the lady-in-waiting. "So, what's your name?" she asked the third lady-in-waiting.

"My name, You Highness, is Rozelle."

"And yours?" Audrianna asked, looking at the first lady-in-waiting.

"Castalia, Your Highness," the first lady-in-waiting answered. Audrianna's eyes then glanced to the second lady-in-waiting.

"Ethlyn, Your Highness," she said, "before the princess could ask."

"Okay," the princess remarked, mentally rehearsing their names in her head.

"Rozelle… Castalia… and…"

"Ethlyn, Your Highness," they chorused.

"I knew her name was Ethlyn," Audrianna said, tilting her head to one side and looking at the ladies out the corner of her eye. "I just wanted to hear you call me 'Your

Highness' once more." She beamed a smile and giggled again pulling the covers up to her chin.

"Good night, Your Highness," Castalia said straightening the bed covers over

Audrianna.

"Good night, Cassie," the princess nicknamed her first lady-in-waiting.

"Sweet dreams, Your Highness," Ethlyn wished the princess.

"Good night, Ethel," she nicknamed her second lady-in-waiting.

"May God watch over Her Royal Highness through the night, Your Highness,"

Rozelle half-prayed over Audrianna.

"Thank you, Rose," she nicknamed her third lady-in-waiting.

Rozelle extinguished the lamps in the bedroom. Castalia secured the bedroom door.

Ethlyn stood guard at the end of the bed while the other two finished their tasks and rolled out their sleeping mats. Once everything in the room was still, and Ethlyn was convinced the princess was safe and resting, she rolled out her mat in between the other two ladies-in-waiting, and promptly fell asleep.

The sound of singing and celebration could still be heard echoing from the streets.

As the princess drifted off to sleep, the last sound Audrianna heard coming from the streets was the faint sound of a man far away, shouting at the top of his lungs, "God save the queen, Her Royal Highness, Princess Audrianna of Nadeau!"

Chapter 4

The next morning, Rozelle was the first one awake. As she sat up on her mat, she noticed the revelries outside had finally quieted down. It was hard to get good rest while the celebration was blaring in their window. Still tired from the night, she stood to her feet and walked to the princess's bed to see if she was still sleeping. To her horror, the bed was empty. Panic gripped her heart! Her first inclination was to assume the princess had been kidnapped while they slept. Oh! They were in trouble! Rozelle quickly ran to the other side of the bed to see if she might be on the floor using the chamber pot. No princess! She turned to wake the other two ladies-in-waiting, Castalia and Ethlyn, and alert them of their dilemma. As Rozelle looked at the floor, where the other two ladies slept, she found little Audrianna, curled up between Castalia and Ethlyn. She took a deep breath of relief, then knelt next to the princess to wake her.

"Your Highness?" Rozelle gently called. No response. "Your Highness!" she called again, this time louder and more determined. Audrianna wrinkled her nose, then, without opening her eyes, pulled herself closer to Ethlyn. "Your Royal Highness,

Princess Audrianna!" Rozelle half shouted. The other two ladies shot up from the mats to a seated position, causing the princess to be flung from a spooning position to flat on her back.

This time her eyes were fully open.

"Oh, Your Highness!" Ethlyn cried. "Is Your Highness okay?"

"Why was Your Highness sleeping on the floor?" Rozelle demanded. "I woke up last night having to pee. I jumped out of bed, used the chamber pot, but I couldn't get back up in bed."

"Why didn't Your Highness wake us?" Castalia asked, still trying to wake up. "We told Your Highness we'd help get her back in bed."

"I know," Audrianna admitted. "But, when I went to ask for help, I saw the three of you laying there, and I wanted to snuggle." The three ladies-in-waiting wanted to respond with an emotional, Ahhh! But protocol and propriety dictated that they respond in their usual fashion.

"Your Highness!" the three chorused.

"Let's get Your Highness dressed," Rozelle insisted. "Breakfast will be served in the royal banquet hall before we know it." The three ladies jumped into action, even more systematic than when they dressed Audrianna for bed after the coronation ball. Castalia opened the princess's clothes armoire. Ethlyn then opened one of the drawers inside the cabinet. Rozelle reached beside Ethlyn and pulled out a clean pair of underwear and a fresh pair of undergarments. As Rozelle stepped back, Castalia then reached into another drawer and pulled out a fresh bustier. Lastly, after Castalia slid her drawer closed and stood next to Rozelle, Ethlyn pulled out one of the princess's morning dresses, hanging on a hook just inside the main armoire door. She closed the door, then stood next to the other two ladies-in-waiting. The three of them stood in a line, each holding their own respective articles of clothing to dress the princess.

Impressed with their quick efficiency, Audrianna took one step forward and lifted her arms. Castalia stooped down and grabbed the hem of the princess's nightgown, then lifted it over her head. As she folded it and placed it back in the armoire,

Rozelle stepped forward and helped Audrianna slip on her undergarment over her fresh underwear.

Finishing that task, she walked to the dressing table to pick up a brush while Castalia began fitting Audrianna with her bustier.

"I hate this thing!" Audrianna remarked regarding the tight corset that the ladies-in waiting insisted she wear. "Why do I have to wear this?"

"It is a bustier," Castalia answered, "and Your Highness is expected to wear it. It is only proper."

"What's the point of a bustier, anyways?" Audrianna asked sharply. "It is to give proper support to Your Royal Highness's feminine figure." "I'm a little girl," Audrianna responded. "My feminine figure hasn't grown out—yet. I don't have anything to support." The three ladies smiled at the princess, but were undaunted at their task.

"That might be true, Your Highness," Rozelle answered. "But it is important for Your Highness to become familiar with how she is expected to dress." Audrianna loudly signed in resignation to how her ladies-in-waiting were dressing her.

As Rozelle began tightening the bustier she instructed Audrianna, "Take a deep breath, Your Highness." Audrianna inhaled deeply and held it as Rozelle pulled the laces as taut as she could without putting her knee into the little girl's back.

"How am I supposed to eat when I can barely breathe in this crazy bustier?" the princess wheezed.

"You will learn to adjust to the pressure," Rozelle reassured her. Next, Audrianna's everyday dress was slipped over the top of her head. She pushed her arms through her sleeves. This time, instead of her sleeves going all the way down to her wrists, her sleeves stopped just past the elbow.

"The sleeves on this dress are too short," she reported attempting to tug the sleeves further down her arm.

"No, Your Highness," Rozelle informed her. "This is Your Highness's morning dress. The sleeves are intended to be short so that Your Highness can eat her breakfast without the fear of soiling the sleeves."

"Oh," Audrianna answered, feeling a bit foolish that she knew very little about being a princess. "Does that mean I have to change again after breakfast?"

"Indeed," Rozelle answered, brushing out the princess's hair that had frizzed during the night. Audrianna sighed loudly again.

"What shoes does Your Highness want to wear?" Castalia asked, spying the long line of choices at the bottom of the armoire.

"I don't know," the princess answered. "What do you think would go with breakfast?" Castalia and Rozelle chuckled.

"Perhaps the brown sandals with the long straps and wooden soles?" "Yes," Audrianna answered, not knowing one pair from another. She sat in the chair in front of her dressing table under that large mirror. Trying to hide her feelings of nervous inadequacy, she raised her right foot and pretended to be a snooty dignitary. "You may proceed with the fitting, Cassie," she ordered.

"Yes, Your Highness," Castalia shot back, behaving somewhat with propriety, and somewhat playful. As Rozelle finished brushing her hair out, she quickly twisted the long strands of Audrianna's hair into a bun and began pinning it into place.

"There," Rozelle remarked. "Your Highness is ready to be escorted to breakfast." "What about my crown?" Audrianna asked. "Aren't I supposed to wear a crown?" "Only when Your Highness is in the presence of the court," Rozelle answered. "That will happen later today. Your Highness must hurry. She has a full schedule to keep. If Your Highness misses one appointment, she is not able to make it up later. That includes breakfast."

"A full schedule?" Audrianna echoed in disbelief. Castalia quickly finished tying the sandal straps around the princess's ankles. She dropped Audrianna's foot and helped her to her feet.

"Quickly, Your Highness," the three ladies chorused. They opened the door to her chambers that led out to the hallway. They pointed her in the direction she was to walk, but they were careful not to walk beside or in front of her. Their place was two steps behind her. They also were careful not to push her from behind, pull her by the hand, or handle the princess in anyway. The best they could do was quietly whisper, "This way, Your Highness."

As Audrianna and her three ladies-in-waiting marched out the door and down the grand staircase, the wooden soles of Audrianna's new sandals clicked on the granite steps. Through the marble hallway, her sandals clattered on the polished surface. Pastthe sliding mahogany doors, and on into the royal dining room, her sandals clopped on the wooden floors.

The four of them walked into the dining room that rested just inside a balcony overlooking the atrium. There, the king and the prince sat waiting for breakfast to be served. The king sat tall at the head of the table, his hands resting on the arms of his chair and his shoulders against its back. The prince sat to the one side of the table, slouched awkwardly in his chair, with his left elbow on the table and his head resting on the back of his hand.

"There you are, Your Royal Highness," the king greeted Audrianna, standing to his feet, and bowing to the crowned princess. Audrianna half-smiled as she looked up at the king. She felt she should genuflect in some way, but she had no idea if she should bow like the king, or what the protocol was.

"How big are your ugly feet?" Henry sharply demanded not moving from his chair. "Everyone in the castle can hear Your Highness trotting like a horse down the hallway." Audrianna was startled. Her smile dropped as did her head.

What a horrible man to be married to, she thought. "I'm sorry, Your… Majesty," Audrianna apologised, talking more to the king rather than the prince. "These are new shoes. I've never wore them before, and we were in a hurry."

"We?" the prince asked, intentionally excluding the ladies-in-waiting. "The three ladies behind me," she said, turning and pointing to them. The three women stood still, their hands folded in front of them and their heads bowed. "There is no one behind you," Henry reprimanded the young princess. "Begging Your Majesty's pardon," Audrianna replied, rather annoyed with his ugly tone and lazy posture. "Aren't you… I mean, isn't Your Majesty supposed to refer to me as 'Your Highness' when you speak to me?" Henry shot straight up in his chair, angered by the audacity of this little girl. He turned to look at his father hoping to see some type of disapproval in his face. Instead, Malcolm was impressed with her tenacious spunk. "You have not been properly educated in royal deportment," Henry countered. "Maybe not," Audrianna continued. "But I am still aware of many proper protocols. I expect Your Majesty to uphold your knowledge of such social proprieties." The king chuckled. The prince sat frozen, glaring at Audrianna. He attempted to stare her down and make her feel insecure and self-conscious. Instead, Audrianna looked straight in his face, opened her eyes wide, tilted her head, and wrinkled her nose— mocking his cold stare. The prince closed his eyes and sat back in his chair. "By the way, these 'nobodies,'" the princess declared, referring to her ladies-in waiting, "are Rose, Ethel, and Cassie." She pointed at each one respectively. "Oh, my!" the prince huffed. "She's gone to naming the rodents."

"They are not animals. They are my ladies-in-waiting, and my friends!" "They are servants—that's all!"

"They might do well at serving me, but they are not slaves! We have no slaves in Nadeau. You must go past the Andjety mountains to find slaves. Isn't that right?" The prince frowned at the princess. He felt uncomfortable with her affirming such information. He leaned forward in his chair towards Audrianna.

"Do not lecture me, the future king of Nadeau, on affairs of state. You are too young to understand such matters."

"Am I?" Audrianna challenged the prince.

"Yes!" Henry answered. "Too young!"

"Really?"

"YES!" Henry said emphatically, raising the level of his voice.

"You're a fool!" She yelled at the prince.

"And you're an infant!" Henry roared. At that moment, the king slammed his hand on the table, startling both of them.

"Enough of this foolish bickering," Malcolm scolded. "As of

last night, you both are crowned royals. You must behave accordingly." Both sat quietly at the table across from one another. Audrianna crossed her arms in a huff, and Henry clutched his satin napkin with both hands on the table. Soon after, the food was delivered.

One large silver platter was placed in the middle of the table. The platter contained portions of cooked veal in the centre, surrounded by small loaves of bread. The bread was surrounded by fresh fruit; melons, apricots, quince, cherries and pomegranates. At the edge of the platter were assorted sliced cheeses. The king grabbed a piece of veal with his one hand and a small loaf of bread with the other. The prince then followed in like fashion. Both took a bite of veal, then while chewing, took a bite from their small loaf of bread. Back and forth they ate until their portion was devoured. The king licked the remaining juice from the veal off his fingers. Audrianna chose to start with the fresh fruit. Cutting a pomegranate in half, she sucked the juice from around its seeds and discretely discarded the seeds into her napkin. After a few bites of pomegranate, she placed the remainder on her plate and grabbed a small loaf of bread. Cutting the bread into slices, she grabbed a piece of cheese and laid it over the heel of the loaf. She started eating her bread and cheese, and occasionally sucking juice from her pomegranate, when Henry started to mock her.

"Bread and fruit? You're gonna starve before you get halfway through sword practice."

"Sword practice, Your Majesty?" Audrianna asked, looking at the king. "Yes, Your Highness," the king declared. "It is imperative that every king and queen know how to use a sword and learn how to defend themselves. That goes for princes and princesses, too."

"Not like Your Highness should ever need to defend herself," the prince replied sarcastically. "What assassin could ever look into Your Highness's big green eyes and see you as a threat?"

"You know, Your Excellency," Audrianna replied to the king, "the way His Majesty behaves, I feel like we are more brother and sister than anything else." Henry was outraged by such a statement. He was going to be king. He should have already been king. And Audrianna was reducing his authority over her down to a common brother and sister relationship.

"I am not your brother!" he exclaimed, glaring at the princess. "I am your HUSBAND!"

"And I'm your WIFE!" Audrianna shot back, mimicking his voice. Henry sat back, shaking his head. Audrianna reached out and grabbed a piece of the cooked veal, placed it on a slice of her bread. She gracefully ate it, ignoring her betrothed and looking out the full-length windows in front of the balcony. The king watched the two of them ignore each other for a few seconds, then leaned forward and whispered to Audrianna. "Your Highness is going to love sword practice."

CHAPTER 5

The three ladies-in-waiting walked Audrianna back to her chambers and stripped her of her sandals, her dress, and bustier, and began dressing her in leather pants and a light blue cotton top, tucked into her pants, and the cuffs tied around her wrists. "Wait," Audrianna announced, "we forgot to put on my bustier."

"Your Highness is going to sword practice," Rozelle answered. "She does not wear a bustier to sword practice." A smile shot across Adrianna's face as she beamed with relief.

"His Majesty was right! I'm going to love sword practice."

"Your Highness does wear a vest over her blouse, though," Ethlyn clarified. "It's not as tight, but it is intended to preserve Your Highness's integrity."

"Well," Audrianna chuckled, "maybe in a few years when my integrity shows up." Within a few minutes, the three ladies had completely changed Audrianna's wardrobe, complete with her brown leather vest, laced in the front, and her boots that rose up to her knees. Once again, the princess and her entourage were out the door, with Rozelle giving whispered instructions on how to find the training courtyard. As they approached the courtyard, Henry could be seen in the distance, practicing his advanced sword fighting techniques with Pitt. Their swords sang with a harmonious TWANG as the full-sized swords beat against each other. Both men were sweating profusely as they seemed to be giving their absolute all without actually killing one another.

Rozelle directed Audrianna to the left of the courtyard where a kind-looking man stood with two wooden sticks in his hands.

"Your Highness," he greeted the princess with a bow. Audrianna smiled at him cautiously with her head turned to one side and looking up at him through the corner of her eyes. "My name is Rupp. I am the captain of the guards. I am here to teach you how to defend yourself and fight with a sword."

"Like that?" Audrianna asked, pointing to Henry and Pitt clanking their swords vigorously.

"Well," Rupp answered, watching their display over his shoulder. "That's a result of twenty years' practice. Let's start a little more basic, shall we?" At that, Rupp handed Audrianna a short wooden sword, with a handle just like a conventional sword. "This, Your Highness, is a training dagger, called a baton. It is much smaller than what I use, because you are much smaller and weaker." Audrianna frowned at Rupp.

"Weak? I'm no weakling, Mr Rupp!" she protested adamantly.

"Your Highness!" Ethlyn scolded. Audrianna turned to her three ladies-in-waiting and grinned.

"Okay, Your Highness." Rupp replied. "Let's see what you're made of." Rupp handed the princess her baton. "Alright, feet apart. knees bent slightly. Shoulders back. Now, look me straight in the eyes." Audrianna poised herself just as Rupp instructed. "Now, show me the meanest face you can give me." Audrianna grimaced a toothy snarl.

"Lovely, Your Highness," Castalia praised.

"Take no prisoners, Your Highness," Rozelle shouted. Rupp glanced at the three ladies-in-waiting standing under a shade tree just off to the side of the courtyard. As he glanced at the ladies, he pretended to not pay any attention to the princess. She took the opportunity to poke Rupp with the point of her baton. Without looking, Rupp deflected her assault with his larger baton, then with a swift stroke, knocked the training dagger out of her hand.

"Ooh, hey!" the princess shrieked in surprise. "It's my first day," she reminded Rupp. He smiled, then bowed.

"And tomorrow will be your second day, Your Highness."

"That wasn't fair, you know," Audrianna complained. "Your stick is longer than mine."

"It's not a stick, Your Highness," Rupp replied holding the baton straight up. "It is a baton, a training sword. In your case, a training dagger. It is much smaller than mine because, as I said, you are much smaller and weaker. As you get older and taller, I will give you a longer and heavier baton to practice with. This way, your training will be tailored to your personal size, strength, and ability."

"Okay," Audrianna agreed, feeling better that she wasn't going to be thrust into the ring with Henry who was obviously far above her skill level. Rupp led her to a pole that stood in the middle of the courtyard.

"This, Your Highness, is what I call the training tree," Rupp said. Audrianna wrinkled her nose at Rupp.

"Not much of a tree," she teased. "It has no limbs like a tree."

"Never the less, this pole has several important marks painted on it. Can you identify them?" Audrianna studied the pole for a few seconds.

"There is a blue line across the pole here," she said pointing at a line just below her shoulder level.

"Okay. Anywhere else?"

"There is a red circle on the side of the pole here," the princess identified at the same height, but on the left side of the pole. "And a green circle on the other side of the pole, here."

"Excellent. Do you have any idea what these marks are used for?" Rupp asked Audrianna. The young princess thought for a moment.

"Umm… target practice?" She asked, stabbing in the dark for an answer.

"Yes!" Rupp applauded Audrianna. "In many ways, those marks are used as targets. But not for arrows, but rather targets for swinging your baton."

"Okay," Audrianna answered trying to figure out what she was supposed to do. "Why do I swing my stick at the targets?"

"You're not just swinging your… baton… at a random target. This is an exercise for you to develop strength in your hands, and in your arms and in your shoulders. Every day I want you to take this… baton… grip it somewhat tight in your palm, and swing it at the green circle, then the red circle, then the blue line." Audrianna took the stance that Rupp showed her, then swung with all her might at the green circle, but missed the target by a few inches. The impact from the baton hitting the pole hurt her hand and she dropped the baton screeching.

"No, Your Highness. Higher on the pole. You must hit the target dead centre." "It hurt my hand," the princess complained. "I don't like that."

"It will hurt if Your Highness doesn't strike the target correctly. Now, take your stance again. Look at the target. Don't take your eyes off your target. Raise your baton where your hand is about level with your shoulder. Now… strike!" Audrianna swung her baton and hit the target dead centre.

"Ow!" she cried again.

"It will still tingle a bit," Rupp reminded, "because Your Highness is not used to sword drills. But it must have hurt less once you hit the target, right?" "Yes," the princess admitted. "And I didn't drop the… the… baton," she mimicked Rupp's tone when he stressed that the stick was called a baton.

"That's right! Your body will adjust rather quickly the more you practice." "So, every day I'm supposed to come here and swing at this pole?" Audrianna asked. "For now," Rupp assured her. "Every day, at this time, I want you to come and beat

on this pole. Red, green, blue! Red, green, blue! As fast and as accurate as you can. Hold the handle firm in your hand, keep your eyes on the target, think of three people you would like to hit, and swing with one fluid stroke—red, green, blue! Red, green, blue!" Audrianna regained her stance. She adjusted the baton in her hand, extended her hand to where it was at shoulder level, and swung.

"Red—green—blue!" Audrianna shouted as she hit the targets. "Henry—Henry— Henry! Red—green—blue! Henry—Henry—Henry!"

"Very good, Your Highness! Although I think we should work on your anger and resentment issues."

"Sorry! I really don't like him," Audrianna said, nodding towards Henry and Pitt practicing hard at the far end of the courtyard. "He's mean to me, and he's mean to my ladies-in-waiting."

"Don't worry about him," Rupp remarked, "It took His Majesty twenty years of practice to get to the level he and Pitt are at." He bent down to Audrianna's level, placed his hand gently on her shoulder and looked in her eyes. "But you could advance to his same skill level in five years, if your worked hard enough."

"Really?" the princess's eyes widened with surprise.

"Four years if you dedicated extra time each day."

"Really?" Audrianna wasn't sure it was possible.

"Absolutely, Your Highness," Rupp declared. "You have two major advantages that your husband doesn't have."

"What advantages?" she asked.

"First of all," Rupp answered, "you have the right physical gifts that lend to being a great sword fighter. It has been my experience that those with brown hair, green eyes, and left-handed. are the smartest, most creative, and imaginative people on the face of the earth. Do you have brown hair?"

"Yes," she said, pointing to her braided bun wrapped and pinned to the top of her head.

"Do you have green eyes?"

"Yes," she answered.

"And," Rupp pointed to her baton, which she held in her left hand, "you are using your left hand as opposed to your right. So, you have all the skills necessary in becoming a better swordsman than your betrothed." Audrianna cocked her head to one side and looked at Rupp through the corner of her eyes.

"And what's the second advantage I have over His Majesty?" she asked. "Rupp stood up straight and put his hands on his hips."

"You have a much better teacher," he winked.

"You?" Audrianna asked, not challenging Rupp's proficiency, but rather clarifying that he was talking about himself.

"Of course me," he answered. My hair is brown, my eyes are green, and…" He brushed away his jacket, revealing a scabbard with a large dagger strapped to his right side. Reaching with his left hand, he grabbed hold of the hilt of his dagger and with one fluid motion, flung the dagger from its scabbard, into the practice pole several meters

away. As the impaled dagger swung back and forth in place, Rupp looked down at Audrianna. "I'm left-handed." Audrianna, still looking at him from the corner of her eyes, beamed a smile.

After spending more than twenty minutes practicing her baton on the large wooden pole, Rupp dismissed her. It was coming close for both Audrianna and Henry to report to court. As Rozelle, Castalia, and Ethlyn led the princess back to her room to change into her court formals, Henry and Pitt caught up with the four ladies. Sweat trickled off Henry's chin as they walked.

"I saw you swinging your toy stick at the training pole," Henry teased, huffing from his workout. "I don't think the pole felt a thing."

"It's not a toy stick," Audrianna corrected. "It's a baton."

"Oooh," Henry mocked Audrianna, pretending to be surprised that she had learned something from her training. "And did you teach that pole to giggle when you tickled it?" The smell of body odour coming from Henry overwhelmed the princess. Audrianna felt incensed that she had to put up with such abuse from a man who was going to be her husband in just six short years. She was being treated like it was her fault he wasn't the king, when she wasn't even given a choice in the matter of being betrothed.

The only thing that gave her ten-year-old heart courage was the idea of Rupp training her to one day beat Henry at sword fighting before they were officially wed. In her mind, if she could defeat him once, she would gain his respect as someone not to be tangled with, and maybe think twice before insulting her as often as he did.

"You know today was my first day," Audrianna reminded Henry. "You went through the same training that I am. You know how hard it is until you get strong enough… and tall enough."

"Oh, I hadn't any problems being strong or tall enough," Henry prided himself. "I had a much better trainer than you do."

"You didn't have Rupp as your teacher?" Audrianna asked.

"Nope. I was taught by the captain of the guards that preceded Rupp. And now, Pitt here trains me to do all the special skills that my first trainer failed to teach me." "Oh," Audrianna answered. "Well, maybe once Rupp is finished teaching me, Pitt can teach me what he knows about his special skills." Both the men laughed at Audrianna's request.

"That is most unlikely," Henry replied.

"Why not?" Audrianna demanded to know.

"Your Highness, there is no way that I could teach my skill level to women or children," Pitt bragged, sneering at Audrianna. Audrianna tilted her head and looked at Pitt's haughty expression through the corner of her eyes.

"Well," Audrianna answered, "maybe if you practice hard enough, one day you might be able to." The two men immediately stopped walking and looked at each other. Audrianna and her companions continued walking briskly.

"That's not what he meant, Your Highness," Henry yelled out at Audrianna.

Chapter 6

The princess and her ladies-in-waiting climbed the steps of the grand staircase, turned the corner, and entered her bed-chambers. Almost immediately after the door shut, the three ladies-in-waiting began the task of stripping and redressing the princess. Audrianna took a deep breath and sighed from the arduous task of having to change outfits every couple of hours. Every new event for the day required a different outfit.

Audrianna was stripped down to her full-length undergarment, and before she realised, Ethlyn rapped a bustier around her front.

"Oh, please no!" Audrianna pleaded. "I was so enjoying the outfit I had on for the sword training. I could breathe without adjusting my clothing every few seconds." "I'm sorry, Your Highness," Ethlyn regretfully answered. "But Your Highness is going to court next, and she has to dress in her formals."

"Maybe we won't tighten the bustier as tight this time on Your Highness," Rozelle offered. Audrianna's eyes widened as she smiled at Rozelle.

"Really? Oh please! That would be so nice if you did that."

"Just be sure not to move around a lot, Your Highness," Rozelle suggested. "If the court notices that your clothes are not on right, we will be in a lot of trouble and we will never again be able to loosen your clothes."

"Okay," Audrianna promised. "I will walk into court, find a seat, and not move during all of court."

"Oh, Your Highness has a seat waiting for her already," Castalia announced. "What seat?" the princess asked.

"Your Highness is going to court," Castalia answered. "She will be sitting on her throne, next to His Majesty."

"His Majesty the king, or His Majesty the prince?" Audrianna asked for clarification. "I believe Your Highness will be sitting on one side of His Majesty the king," Rozelle answered. "With three thrones, the king must always be in the centre." The ladies-in-waiting took much of their time loosely tying Audrianna's bustier. It had to be tight enough so it wouldn't slide up and down under her dress, nor could it be loose enough to gap in the front when she sat. When they finally succeeded in securing her undergarments, they quickly slid her dress on, fastened its straps, and tied its sleeves. Then they brushed her long hair out again, braided it in three segments, and wrapped them in a decorative bun. After that, they set her royal tiara around the braids and pinned it in place. Ethlyn took a coarse cloth and vigorously washed Audrianna's face to give the princess a bright pink complexion to her cheeks. Rozelle and Castalia worked at lacing up and tying her formal boots. Next, they applied their own version of mascara, consisting of charcoal and goat bile, to highlight Audrianna's eyes. Finally, they smeared a thin glaze of pig fat over her lips to give an evanescent shine to them. With a spritz of perfume, the princess's companions lifted her to her feet, and guided her to the royal court.

As Audrianna and her ladies-in-waiting approached the royal courtroom, their shoes tapped loudly on the marble floor of the hallway leading to the large double doors of the court. Two large men stood guard in front of the doors, equipped with swords, daggers and various instruments of restraint. As they approached, without anyone saying a word, the two guards snapped to attention, grabbed hold of the giant door handles, and pulled to double doors open.

Inside, several tables lined the entrance to the room. Scribes sat with paper, ink wells and quills ready to take notes and write reports. Several other mean-looking guards circled the room. Just past the line of tables, stood Rupp. This time Rupp was dressed in a fancy coat, dress pants, and frilly shirt, with a large bow tie. He was still armed with a sword at his side. Audrianna took note that it was strapped to his right side.

"Rupp!" the princess excitedly declared.

"Your Highness," he answered, snapping to attention and giving a proper bow as she walked by. Knowing he was in the room made her feel safe. It was like she had a close relative or kinsman in the room with her—a brown-haired, green-eyed, left-handed kinsman. She stopped in front of Rupp, wanting to talk to him, but unable to think of anything to say in such a proper and official setting.

"This way, Your Highness," Rozelle whispered, directing the princess to her seat, on the left side of the king. Audrianna walked up the three large steps to her throne. Her ladies-in-waiting stopped at the bottom of the steps and waited for the princess to be seated. Audrianna stood in front of her throne and noticed a wooden box sitting in her seat. She quickly turned to look at the king, which was improper for her to do until she was seated. The king, looking straight ahead, leaned slightly in her direction and whispered.

"It's to help you sit at the proper height on your throne."

"Oh," she declared out loud, not realising how well her voice carried from the thrones in the court room. Sensing that she was doing everything improper, she spun around and sat on the box.

"No, Your Highness," Malcolm reprimanded. "You must first curtsy to the court, then sit down."

"Curtsy?" Audrianna asked. "I've never curtsied!"

"Do you even know what a curtsy is?" Henry sarcastically

inquired, slouched in his seat.

"Yes," Audrianna softly answered. "I've just never done it."

"You're the crowned princess," the king reminded her. "Do your best. No one will laugh."

"I will," Henry declared. "I can't wait to see what you've got." He sat smirking at the princess. Audrianna looked at the king.

"And he's nobody," he informed her. She smiled at the king then stood to her feet. Stepping to the edge of the landing, she put her right foot behind her, lifted up the sides of her dress slightly, and began to bend her knees. Malcolm was impressed that she was doing so well and was sure she would perform a curtsy perfectly. But, just as she bent her knees to a certain level, her right foot slid out from under her causing her to fall forward towards the stairs. Everyone in the room gasped as she tumbled down the stairs, landing at the bottom, on her rump, with both legs out in front of her. Her ladies-in

waiting started to come to her rescue, but it was inappropriate for anyone to run in the royal courtroom. Audrianna looked down at her dress and feet to assess any damage done to her clothes as well as her body. The next thing she knew, a gloved hand was being extended down to her. She looked up to see Rupp.

"Your Highness," he said, as if nothing was wrong nor out of the ordinary. Audrianna reached her hand up, which Rupp took and pulled her to her feet. By then, her ladies-in-waiting appeared at her side to help readjust any movement in her clothing. "How's your bustier?" Ethlyn whispered.

"It's fine," the princess assured her. "I believe it's fine." They straightened the rest of her clothes, as well as her tiara which tilted slightly on her head, then they walked back to their place to the side of the room. Audrianna faced the steps again and climbed back to the platform where her throne sat. She turned to the audience and grabbed the corners of her dress indicating she was going to try and curtsy again.

"Let's not..." the king stopped her. "Let's try it another time. We'll work on curtsying, maybe tomorrow."

"Thank you, Your Excellency," Audrianna answered the king. She sat on the box that still awaited her.

As she sat in her chair, she spread out her dress across her lap, and crossed her ankles, her feet dangling several inches from the floor. She looked all around the court room. Several people had been brought in just inside the doors. There was murmuring in the back as the subjects discussed their reason for being in the court, and signing their names to the court records.

Next to Audrianna sat the king, and on the other side of the king, sat her betrothed. She looked up at the king, then over to the prince. She then looked back at the king, then over to the prince again. The king, noticing that she seemed puzzled looked down at the princess.

"What's wrong, Your Highness?" he asked.

"Oh," she realised she might be doing something out of proper deportment. "I just noticed that each of our thrones are different heights."

"Yes, that's right," the king acknowledged. "No one is higher in authority than the king, so I sit the highest. The prince is second in authority, so he sits a little lower than me, then you are next in authority."

"Papa Bear, Junior Bear, and little tiny Baby Bear," Henry pestered. "But I thought the three of us sit in court together so we can make decisions together." Audrianna commented. "Henry scoffed at the princess's thought." "Well," the king explained, "while it is true that both you and your husband add valuable insight to the decision that must be made, I still am the supreme authority and must make the final decision."

"But wouldn't that mean that, after you, Prince Henry and I are equal in power?" Audrianna asked.

"No!" Henry protested. "When I become king, you'll be lucky to even be allowed in the royal court at all." Audrianna bowed her head in fear.

"Prince Henry," the king reprimanded. "the king still must uphold Nadeau law. The law states that the queen sits next to the king as his most trusted advisor. That's why the queen has always been chosen from among the people, and by the future king's father."

"The law also states," Henry reminded his father, "that the crowned prince must take the throne on his twenty-fifth birthday."

"Provided the prince is married on said birthday," the king countered. "The said prince would have been married on said birthday had the said king given him a woman to marry instead of this worthless child!" Henry screamed. "I'm not worthless!" Audrianna yelled at the prince.

"Excuse me?" the prince answered.

"Her Royal Highness is not worthless," she repeated.

"Really?" the prince challenged. "What value could you possibly have that would indicate you have the least amount of worth as a crowned princess and betrothed to the future king?"

"I'm left-handed," she proudly declared, sitting straight up in her chair, on the wooden box, and squaring her shoulders.

"You're what?" the prince asked.

"I'm left-handed," she repeated. Henry shrugged his shoulders and shook his head at her. "Left-handed people are the smartest and most creative and imaginative people on the face of the earth." She leaned forward to look past the king and glared at Henry. "That is why I should have a throne that is the same height as you." She then sat back in her seat, looked forward, uncrossed her ankles, and placed her hands on the arms of her throne. Her eyes met Rupp's, who gave her a discreet wink, then turned to face the court's subjects. Henry looked at his father, who returned the glance beaming from how much strain little Audrianna was placing on his unruly son.

"Well," Henry finally professed, "Suffice it to say, whomever sits in the highest chair, has the highest authority." At that, Audrianna immediately turned to the king.

"Your Excellency?" she implored. "May I trade seats with you?" Malcolm looked down at the princess who had cocked her head to one side and was looking up at him through the corner of her eyes.

"As you wish," he said, standing up from his throne. Audrianna jumped down, grabbed her booster box, and placed it in the king's seat, then sat down on the king's throne. Malcolm then took his seat on Audrianna's throne. Henry protested, but not with coherent words. He made guttural noises of protest. Now Audrianna sat as the highest point in the room. She sat as tall as she could.

"What are you doing, Your Majesty?" Henry objected.

"What can I do?" Malcolm answered. "She's left-handed!" Henry looked up at Audrianna. The princess squared her shoulders and pointed her finger at random to the back of the room.

"Off with his head!" she shouted. The entire royal court became still and silent, and all eyes turned to the princess. A man who stood nearest to Rupp, looked at Rupp, then at the princess, then back at Rupp again.

"Anyone in particular, Your Highness?" Rupp answered.

"Pick someone," Audrianna declared. Rupp smiled at her.

"This is the worst day of my life," Henry muttered to himself.

"Well, little princess," the king decided, "I think we need to take our usual seats. Court is about to officially begin." As the two of them exchanged thrones again, the court magistrate walked in the court room carrying a large velvet bag. The bag was long to where the magistrate held one end in his palm, and the bag extended up his arm and over his shoulder. As the magistrate walked up the steps, he stopped on the last step before the main platform, set the end of the bag that he was palming onto the floor. He then opened the top of the bag and pulled it down to the floor, revealing a tall brass sceptre. The king took hold of the middle and slightly lifted it in the air to allow the magistrate to discard the bag from the sceptre. Folding up the bag and neatly placing it on the far end table, the magistrate then called the royal court to attention.

"People of Nadeau," he called out, "our royal court of law is now in session. His Royal Majesty, King Malcolm the Merciful, His Royal Majesty Prince Henry, and Her Royal Highness

Princess Audrianna now presiding." At that, the king tapped the end of his large sceptre on the floor, making an echoing banging noise to draw attention to the king.

"May the court note that today is the eighteenth day of the fourth month of the thirtieth year of the reign of King Malcolm the Merciful," the king stated with a loud, strong voice. Audrianna tried to sit up straight, with her shoulders back and her head looking forward. But watching the king preside over the matters of state from the throne fascinated the princess to the extent that she had difficulty remembering her manners.

"Bring the first matter to the court's attention."

Several matters were brought up to the court, most of which were land disputes, official contracts that needed the royal court to notarise or approve, and a few cases of civil law, which was usually handled by lower courts. Audrianna sat as still in her chair as she could. There was a lot of words being used that she did not understand. There were laws of precedent that were being quoted that she had no frame of reference to follow.

Still she remained motionless. Her eyes glazed over and her eyelids drooped. After several hours, though, a case was brought to the royal court that suddenly grabbed Audrianna's attention. An old dusty man was dragged to the royal court with chains around his wrists. He looked up at the royal court and immediately removed his dirty hat. The expression of his face was sad and tired. He looked to be a strong man, like that of a farmer, but he was hunched over, like one who had recently seen horrific tragedy.

"State your name to the royal court," the magistrate commanded.

"Mason, sir." The old man stated, his head bowed, his eyes looking at the floor. Audrianna could see his hands were discreetly trembling.

"What brings this man to the royal court today?" the king asked.

"Your Excellency," the magistrate began, "Mason is a farmer that has about a hundred acres south of the Andjety mountains.

He claims that he has run into a recent misfortune that prevents him from paying his due taxes."

"How much do you owe," Henry asked.

"Three hun-hun-hundred. Three hundred coppers, Your Excellency," Mason stuttered, still looking at the floor.

"Three hundred?" Henry responded. "Is that all? Surely you can come up with three hundred copper coins for a man who owns a hundred acres of farm land." "Your Majesty, it-it-it's not farm land, sir."

"What do you raise on your land?" the king asked.

"I raise goats, Your Excellency," the old man replied.

"And you're telling me," Henry scoffed, "that out of all your goats, you can't sell enough to raise three hundred copper coins?"

"Beg-beg-beg-begging your pardon, Your Majesty," the man attempted to explain. "Pay your taxes, or be thrown into prison," Henry snapped, feeling the whole argument was a waste of time.

"But-but-but Your Majesties," the man began to tremble more noticeably. Henry motioned for Rupp.

"Take him away!" Henry demanded. Two of the large guards grabbed Mason by his arms. For the first time, the man looked up. His eyes met the eyes of Audrianna. She saw tears well up in his pain-stricken face.

"WAIT!" Audrianna shouted, jumping to her feet. The court stopped. Everyone was silent. Since the time that the king called the royal court in session, the princess had said nothing. Now, the first words from her mouth was loud and forceful.

"What is the matter, Your Highness?" the king asked her. Without saying a word, the princess hopped down each step to the main floor. She then walked briskly to the old man, who by now was wide-eyed, with his hat crumpled in his hands for fear. As she neared the old man, Rupp stood close by. He could not stop the princess from approaching the man, but he made sure she was safe in his presence.

Audrianna tenderly took the old man's hand. Since the first

time their eyes met, the old man wouldn't take his eyes off her. Audrianna held his hand with her right hand, and placed her left hand over the back of his hand.

"What happened to your goats, Mr Mason?" she kindly asked.

"They-they-they… they was taken, Your Highness." Mason said.

"Taken?" the princess asked.

"Stolen, Your Highness," he answered, tears running down his cheeks. "When did this happen?" Audrianna asked.

"About three months ago, Your Highness. I fed them that night, and during the night I woke up to a group of men stealing my goats. Every one of them." He then looked up at the prince. "It's true, Your Majesty! I reported it to the townspeople, but there was no trace of them goats, like I'd never had any. Fact is, they all knew I had them, just had no clue to go on." Audrianna motioned for him to stoop down closer to her. As he bent over, the princess whispered in his ear.

"I believe you, Mr Mason," she assured him. She looked up at Rupp who nodded at her, indicating she needed to return to the throne. She squeezed the old man's hand, then turned around and walked back to take her seat.

"Who do you think stole your goats?" the king inquired.

"Your Excellency, I saw them," the man answered. "I saw who they were. I promise you I know!"

"Who, then? Tell us, old man?" Henry demanded.

"I saw by the light of the moon. And I heard them. It was the Andjety people. They looked like them. They dressed like them. They sounded like them. It was the Andjety alright!"

The king and the prince leaned close to one another and began whispering to each other. Rupp approached the steps in front of the thrones.

"There have been many reports of Andjety activity in that region, sire," Rupp testified. "Thefts, murders, and many more." The two royals sat back in their seats. "Very well," the king announced, banging his sceptre on the floor. "Let the court note, the tax debt of three hundred gold coins are forgiven for the farmer, Mason. Moreover, I decree that one male and five female goats be granted Mason who has been dealt a devastating loss, for the eventual renewal of his livelihood." At that, the king banged his sceptre on the floor again, making his decree official.

"Thank you, Your Majesties," Mason gratefully replied. "Thank-thank-thank you all! Long live King Malcolm the Merciful! And long live Princess Audrianna—the Tenderhearted!" He then turned, and exited the courtroom.

"What about me?" Henry demanded, upset that the old man praised his father and Audrianna, but not him. He was even more incensed that he gave Audrianna the name, Tenderhearted. Audrianna leaned forward to look at Henry, past the king.

"You're Horrible," Audrianna replied. "Prince Henry the Horrible!" She let out a giggle as the little ten-year-old sat back and wobbled on her booster box.

CHAPTER 7

After several hours of sitting in court, Malcolm finally tapped his bass sceptre on the floor, declaring the end of the day's court. Both Henry and Audrianna let out a deep sigh of relief. Audrianna was tired and starving! She had nothing to eat since six o'clock that morning. Normally the royal court was brought fruits and breads to freely eat during proceedings to tide the royals over until supper time. However, not every day did this happen, and that particular day was one which a snack was excluded.

The Rozelle, Castalia, and Ethlyn led the tired and hungry princess to her chambers and quickly stripped her of her royal court formals, then redressed her in supper attire. Audrianna wanted to lie down on her bed and sleep until morning, but her ladies-in waiting recognised that much of her fatigue was due to malnourishment.

Audrianna's supper attire was somewhat like her breakfast attire regarding her shorter sleeves. However, the fabric was studier and thicker, and the colour was darker. Audrianna almost cried when they refused to remove her bustier. So, the three ladies decided to try an experiment and see if the fabric of her supper dress was sturdy enough to mimic her wearing a bustier. So, they removed her constricting undergarment, and put her supper dress on the princess. It almost seemed to work, except when she sat down for her hair to be brushed out, it sagged in the front, exposing the lack of her usual accessory.

"Sorry, Your Highness!" Rozelle admitted. "Your Highness is going to have to wear her bustier this time." Audrianna let out a loud exasperated sigh. "But we'll try something else tomorrow when you're… when Your Highness is not so sleepy and hungry."

"Thank you, Rose," Audrianna answered. "I know the three of you tried. Thank you for taking care of me." Her grateful answer made the three ladies want to strip her again and put her bed gown on her and bring her supper in bed. They wanted to pick her up in their arms and hold her all night while she slept. But, alas! It wasn't proper!

Audrianna was brought to the dining room for supper. This was a different room than where she ate breakfast. The dining table was long, and the room was huge. The walls were decorated with hung paintings, frescos and lavish drapes. The meal was not as extravagant as breakfast was. Mostly soups and breads. Four different soups were served, including a potato soup, a type of seasoned tomato soup, a beet soup, and a lentil soup—which was more of a beef stew, than a soup. There were flat breads, white breads, sweet breads, and several different types of pastries. The breads and pastries were on platters, sat in the middle of the long table.

The soups were brought one at a time, each in a small bowl to each of the three at the table. Audrianna liked the potato soup, of which she ate rather quickly. She thought the tomato soup was too spicy, but still ate every drop of soup. She noticed that the king and Henry both enjoyed the tomato soup with flat bread. She tried the two together and discovered the flavour was not as strong or overpowering when ate with the bread.

When the red, beet soup came out, she took two sips, and discovered she didn't much care for it. She shut her eyes and wrinkled her nose. She tried a third sip, but couldn't stomach any more. The lentil and beef stew was most to her liking. It reminded her so much of the food her birth parents served and ate on a regular basis. She dipped some of the white bread in it, which was like sourdough, but cut in long strips.

No one seemed obliged to talk during the meal. Henry was still angry over the fact that his orders to imprison the old goat farmer were countermanded by his ten-year-old wife. On top of that, the court began calling the princess, "Audrianna the Tenderhearted", initiated by the old man she had helped. Now, his father having a nickname, "The Merciful", and his betrothed nicknamed, "The Tenderhearted", and Audrianna calling him, "The Horrible" made him out to seem a cruel and heartless person. He didn't see things like that. He saw himself a victim of his father's insidious joke to betroth him to an adolescent, rather than an eligible maiden.

As the four soups had been delivered, and taken up, and most of the bread eaten, including the sweetbreads, Audrianna began to yawn uncontrollably. "Your Highness," the king called to Audrianna, who sat several feet to his left, "maybe you should have your ladies escort you to bed." The princess looked at Rozelle who had been fetching breads along the table for her at her requests. Rozelle nodded at Audrianna that it was past her bedtime.

"Thank you, Your Majesty," Audrianna answered, and excused herself from the table. The three ladies followed the princess, who by now had started to learn her way around the castle. As she left, Henry turned to his father.

"How long are you and I going to keep up this ruse, Your Majesty?" "Ruse, my son?" the king replied.

"Yes. This idea that I am going to have to wait six long years before I can take the throne simply because you chose a child to betroth me to rather than an adult maiden." "Six long years, my son?" the king answered. "Those six years are not expected to be any longer than three hundred sixty-five days, just as the others have been." "Father!" Henry scolded. "Do not mock me. I have every right to take the throne! I am old enough, and skilled enough. Why do you hold it back from me?" "Because, my son," Malcolm answered, "You are still not mature enough." Henry folded his arms and slouched in his chair. "You see?" the king continued, pointing to his son's posture. "You behave like a pouty ten-year-old. It is only natural that you be given a bride who matches your age."

"I am twenty-five!"

"Only on the outside," the king countered. "The law states that a maiden be chosen from among his people to help the king be able to fairly judge his subjects. But, what I saw today with the goat farmer, Audrianna would be more suited to be king before you." Henry sat up straight in his chair.

"How dare you!" he screamed at his father. "She is a child, and a girl! I am a man and an adult!"

"Who needs to stop behaving like a naughty little girl when he is in court." The king answered. "Henry jumped from his seat, knocking the chair to the floor." Without another word, he stormed from the dining room, down the hall, up the grand staircase, and around the corner to where his bedchamber was. The room was dark, so he closed the door behind him and entered very carefully. He hadn't walked more than a few steps into the room when an arm reached out of the shadows and grabbed him from behind while a dagger was placed alongside his neck. A voice forcefully whispered in the Andjety tongue in his ear. The prince raised his hands in a gesture of surrender. "What news have you brought?" the prince asked. The arm and the dagger lowered. The dark figure drifted through the room and stopped at the table nearest the window. A match was struck, and the table lamp was lit. The light from the lamp filled the room with a dim light. Standing next to the lamp was Pitt, Henry's sword instructor. "It seems that several bands of marauders have been raiding small farms nearest the mountain range of the kingdom. They steal as much livestock as they can lay their hands on and drag them back up and over the mountains."

"Andjety?" the prince inquired.

"Yes. And they are under direct command of the Witch."

"The war empress?" Henry asked.

"None other, Your Majesty," Pitt affirmed.

"How many bands, and about how many in each band?" Henry asked. "Hard to say, Your Majesty," Pitt admitted. "But it would be my estimate—based upon what we witnessed—that there could be thousands under the Witch's command." "We don't have an army big enough to defend nor attack such a foe. My father is short-sighted, determined to make Nadeau a peace-loving nation. He has no vision for building a strong military to protect our lands from the Andjety threat." "They are strong, Your Majesty. And getting bigger and stronger day after day." "We have got to do something," Henry decided. "Tonight! We cannot wait until my father decides to act. We need to gather sufficient intelligence to make plans to build up an opposing military force."

"We, Your Majesty?" Pitt asked. "Just how many are you considering making up your group of 'we'?"

"You and me. We leave immediately. I need to see with my own eyes just what we're up against."

"But, Your Majesty," Pitt suggested, "wouldn't it be wise to bring several of our most valiant men to ride along side of us to make sure you are safe. After all, you are the future king."

"Afraid of our odds, Pitt?" the prince accused.

"Not in the least, Your Majesty. A hundred men is not enough to defeat the skills that you and I possess. This is what I have trained you for. I just think a few extra men will ensure your safety."

"Don't worry about me. I'm ready. Let's go and see what the Andjety are made of." The prince quickly changed into a casual attire so that he would appear as a wandering traveller. Pitt chose to wear a disguise that made him appear to be a merchant, but one decked out with weapons to defend himself from thieves and robbers. Within the hour, the two men whisked through the darkness unnoticed.

Meanwhile, as Audrianna was properly dressed for bed, her ladies-in-waiting finished brushing or her hair. Both the ladies as well as Audrianna admired her long silky hair. The three ladies began straightening her room a bit while the princess had the first opportunity of the day to brush her own hair. She loved grabbing a handful of her hair and brushing out the very ends that tended to get tangled the worst.

She was so tired, but the regular bedroom ritual had to be followed before Rozelle, Castalia, and Ethlyn would allow the princess to climb into bed. Not to mention, she wasn't able to get into bed with out their assistance. The three ladies laughed about the happenings of the day. How the princess reminded Prince Henry that not only was he her husband, she was his wife. They giggled how the king and princess traded thrones to prove a point to Prince Henry, and how Audrianna playfully cried out, "Off with his head," to a random stranger. But the biggest joy the court seemed to have was when the princess gave the prince the nickname, "Henry the Horrible."

"Everybody's talking about it," Ethlyn told Audrianna. "By tomorrow's court, I'll bet they will announce His Majesty as, 'His Majesty, Prince Henry the Horrible'!" Again, they all laughed in unison.

"I loved the expression on the prince's face when Your Highness called him that," Castalia recalled.

"It was like someone stepped His Majesty's toes," Rozelle remarked with Ethlyn mimicking what his face must have looked like. They all laughed.

"Poor Henry," Audrianna responded. "He is going to be in a foul mood tomorrow." "Yes," the ladies chorused, then all laughed again. Audrianna walked over to the bed and flung her arms up on the mattress and rested her chin on the bed in a passive way of saying she wanted help to get into bed. Rozelle came up behind her and lifted the princess under her shoulders until she could put her knees on the bed. She then flopped herself on her back and laid there for a moment with her arms and legs stretched in every direction. Rozelle and Castalia pulled the blanket and sheet out from under her and covered her up for the night. Audrianna poked her hands out from under the fluffy blanket and held it by the hem. Ethlyn extinguished the light from the lamps around the room. Only the moonlight through the window lit the room. The ladies-in-waiting retreated to their mats. Within minutes, everybody was fast asleep.

Meanwhile, several hours later, in the wee hours of morning, before light broke past the peaks of the mountains, two disguised figures, riding horses, rode up a trail that led from the palace city, over the Andjety mountains. Staying as much as possible to the shadows, the two lone riders eventually rode to the peak of the western mountain and stopped under an olive tree to rest. The two men dismounted, tied their horses to a branch of the tree, and pulled provisions from a knapsack and began to eat. The horses also feasted on what few patches of grass they could find and reach.

"How much further to the nearest Andjety village?" Henry asked his companion. "Another two hundred kilometres over this ridge, down the trail, to the bottom of the valley," Pitt answered. "Very soon we should come upon a patrol. They will ask us who we are, where we are going, and what our business is."

"What should we say?"

"I'll do the talking, Your Majesty," Pitt said. "I know the language, and have mastered their dialect. If you speak, you will give away the fact that you are from Nadeau, as well as royalty. Just keep your head covered, your face down, and pretend you are a mute."

"A mute?" Henry protested. "Do you expect me to remain silent the entire time we are in Andjety?"

"Your Majesty," Pitt quickly reminded the prince, "we are here as spies. If they get wind to our true intentions, they will not hesitate to execute the both of us." "I understand," Henry conceded. Not another word did Henry speak while they rested and ate. They soon were refreshed from their break, mounted the horses, and travelled another two hours. They were very careful to watch out for patrols and hoped they wouldn't encounter any—however unlikely that might have been. Every sound of the wind, every tumbling rock, every sound of a bird or various animal, the two of them quickly jumped in anticipation of trouble.

Nothing.

They made their way down to the village and slipped into the local pub. The pub served as a place of residence for travellers. Pitt walked boldly up to the bar and asked the man behind the counter for a room in the Andjety language. The man looked Pitt over for a second, then answered him. He then turned around and pulled a key from the drawer and handed it to Pitt. Henry eagerly wondered what Pitt and the man were saying to one another, but he stayed calm and intentionally wore an expression on his face that made it out to seem he knew everything that was happening.

Soon, the two of them walked up the creaky staircase to second floor, and the third room on the right. The door whined as it opened, Pitt pulled a match from his pocket and lit the lamp on the centre table of the room. Vermin scattered in all directions as the light exposed their locations. Henry closed his eyes and slightly turned his head in disgust. "What did you and the man say to one another," Henry quietly whispered as the door was shut and the two of them surveyed the accommodations.

"I basically asked him for a room. He told me it would cost eight silver knuckles." "Knuckles?" Henry asked. Pitt made a fist and showed Henry his knuckles. "Eight silver nuggets the size of these," he answered.

"I didn't see you pay the man," Henry replied.

"In Andjety, you pay after the services are provided. That way, if the services are not satisfactory, you insult them by not paying. The innkeepers are much more motivated in providing excellent service."

"I wouldn't pay for this room if I were you," Henry answered.

"Believe me," Pitt replied, "I've spent a lot of time learning about the people of Andjety. This is one of the better rooms. Bugs and mice do not seem to bother them." The two of them rested for a few hours. Their horses were taken to the stable and bedded down with fresh straw.

By morning light, Henry and Pitt made their way down the stairs to the pub area and ordered breakfast. The food that Henry was used to in the castle was different than the food that they served in the pub. He was used to fruit, breads, and freshly butchered and cooked meats. The meats that were offered to them were days from being freshly butchered. The smell of the aging food churned Henry's stomach. Pitt ignored the stench and lapped up the meat and some kind of sour soup that Henry could not imagine what it once was in its former life.

After devouring his breakfast, Pitt went to work mingling with the people in the pub. This was what their mission was from the beginning—to establish some intelligence regarding the attacking marauders that continued to attack the villages of Nadeau. However, even though Henry could not understand the language or dialect of the Andjety, he became increasingly concerned that Pitt might have embellished his ability to do as such. In every person Pitt encountered, it took a few seconds for the people to listen and understand what he was saying. The way Pitt pronounced his sentenced sounded awkward and unnatural in flow and tempo. Henry noticed how people that Pitt talked to would later congregate in the back of the room. Henry believed they needed to get out of the village immediately.

The two problems that hindered Henry from pulling Pitt aside and insisting they leave was, first—Henry could only speak Nadeau, which would be picked up on and give them away as spies. Secondly—it was daylight outside. They intended to gather intel all day indoors, and then leave by cover of night. If they left right away, they would be recognised by the first patrol coming down the road.

Before Henry could decide what he should do, four armed men burst into the pub. The entire room fell silent. One of the men yelled a command at the crowd. Not a person moved. Henry glanced at Pitt who by now had stepped back against the far wall. The man yelled again. Everyone turned their heads to look at Henry, who was sitting at a table in the middle of the room. Henry wore a cloak with a hood, which partially covered his head. As the crowd looked in his direction, Henry's head slowly dropped to hide his face. He never felt more conspicuous.

The four men strutted over to Henry. He knew the man was

going to yell at him in Andjety. He would have no way of reply-ing, which, he felt, didn't seem to matter anymore. They were caught. It was over.

"Are you the man pretending to be a travelling merchant," the soldier asked in the Nadeauan language, "asking questions about Andjety hoards crossing the mountains and attacking Nadeau?" Henry sat silent. He knew they had him. There was no way to escape these four large men. The only thing he could do was keep any attention from going to Pitt. At least his father would hear and either rescue him, or avenge his blood.

"Are you from Nadeau?" the large man asked. Henry remained silent. He looked up at the man to see if any kind of bluff would be in order. Pitt had once said a thousand Andjety men could not compare to the skill that they possessed. Sounded good in the castle. It felt different in an Andjety pub surrounded by armed soldiers.

"I am," the prince replied.

"Stand to your feet," the soldier commanded, which by now Henry had guessed he was the captain of their unit, or an equiv-alent. Henry stood to his feet. The captain snapped a few orders and two of the men frisked Henry for any weapons. Henry's sword was laid on the table. As well as, two daggers, his money purse, and a jagged rock.

"Are you alone?" the captain asked.

"Yes."

"Reports said that two of you had come to this inn last night. Where is the other man?"

"He left late last night or early this morning. He's no longer here." Henry hoped that no one understood what he and the captain were talking about and give Pitt away. Suddenly, the door that the four soldiers secured burst open. Two men, more valiant than the other four entered the room, followed by a woman. Henry turned his head slightly to see who came in the pub. When he saw the woman, he winced, closed his eyes, and lowered his head even more.

The woman was beautiful at first glance, but she wore a sword strapped to both hips. Her hair was pulled back, and she wore a red military coat that dated back to the Andjety Liberation War, of which her father served in, fought, and died. She was a rogue war empress, and she had influence over much of the Andjety military, even though she was close to the same age as Henry. Her name was Zymjai, but the Nadeau referred to her as, the War Witch, or simply, the Witch.

"This is the spy, Madam," the captain called out to the Witch. She walked up to Henry's table and lifted his head with her index finder and its long sharp nail.

"Hello, Henry," she greeted him with her throaty coarse voice.

"Zymjai," he answered trying to not look her in the eyes.

"Should I call you, Prince Henry? I heard about your coronation, and its profound disappointment." Henry realised that the Witch knew about the events of the previous two days, about Audrianna, and quite possibly that they were planning to cross the mountain range and spy out Andjety.

"Your intel is obviously better than mine," he stated.

"It is. Well enough to know that you are not here alone. Where is your friend—Pitt, is it?" Henry was ready to deny any recognition of his friend, Pitt. The thought did enter his mind that Pitt could be the informant sharing intelligence with the Witch. There was a part of him that wanted to see how the Witch and his friend interacted so he would know if his suspicions were true. However, he wasn't about to betray his friend over a hunch or a lie that the Witch was using to manipulate him.

"I'm here alone," he replied.

"No, Henry. You're not," she emphatically stated as she looked about the room. Her eyes gazed past the obvious Andjety peasants. She knew Pitt would be in disguise, but someone who lived in the castle would not know how to look poor like a peasant. After examining the people seated around the tables, she spotted Pitt standing in the shadows.

"There you are, my pet," she said proudly. Pitt stepped into the lit area of the pub. "Why would the honoured armour-bearer to the future king of Nadeau need to hide in the shadows like a scared doe?"

"I wasn't hiding," Pitt declared. "I was waiting for an opportunity to defend the prince."

"Oh," the Witch replied. "You were waiting on an opportunity. Maybe an opportunity to prove yourself to be the heroic and courageous personal advisor to the future king?" Pitt said nothing. The Witch drew one of her swords. "This would be your opportunity to show the prince just how heroic and courageous you really are."

"That will not be necessary, Zymjai" Henry assured her.

"Oh, yes." The Witch responded. "Every warrior needs the opportunity to show their leader just how fearless they can be. The two of you have trained together, but have you seen him fight in battle?"

"Not necessary—Zymjai!" Henry argued. The Witch walked over to Pitt and lifted her sword to his neck. Pitt's eyes glazed over as he stared at the Witch. "If you can disarm me, then you will have a chance to kill me, and the two of you will go free. If you can't take the sword from me, then both your lives are forfeit to me. This is your opportunity, Pitt, to defend your king." Pitt knew his life was over. There was no way to win. There was no way the Witch would permit him to win. "If I win, what about your soldiers?" Pitt asked.

"If I die, there will be no one in authority over them," the Witch pointed out.

"That is a good point," Pitt agreed. He raised his hands somewhat out to his sides. Henry knew that Pitt expected him to make his way to the side of the room so he could escape if possible. He stood and walked to the side of the room with the other villagers in the pub. Pitt and the Witch walked in a circle a few times with the Witch still holding the sword under his chin. Pitt stood staring down the Witch, not an expression of fear or of confidence was on his face. Inside his mind, Pitt began psyching himself up, looking for the opportunity to wrestle the sword from the Witch's grip.

After what seemed to be an eternity, the Witch seemed to

relax her guard. Pitt sprang into action to grab the sword. But as he lifted his hand, reaching for the sword, the Witch quickly flicked the end of the sword's hilt, causing the sword to jump in the air. Startled, Pitt reached high in the air to catch the sword as it landed. At the same time, the Witch pulled a knife from a tiny scabbard belted around her chest. Before Pitt knew what happened, she plunged the knife into his chest. His arms and hands froze. He looked towards the door as he saw the prince dash out the door. Pitt fell to his knees.

"My opportunity," he uttered to the Witch, as he fell limp to the floor. He let out a loud exhale, clutching the dagger with his right hand.

Pitt was dead.

CHAPTER 8

That previous night, Audrianna slept very soundly due to the vigorous schedule of activities that occurred the day before. She was alarmed when Ethlyn shook her to wake her up. She turned to see all three of her ladies-in-waiting standing at the end of her bed, each holding an article of clothing. Audrianna rolled her eyes and rolled out of bed.

"How many outfits do I have to wear today?" she asked.

"Actually," Rozelle answered, "we were going through Your Highness's wardrobe and have figured out a way to limit how many times Your Highness has to change, and how many pieces of clothing she has to use."

"Really?" the princess asked excitedly.

"Well," Castalia explained, "we decided to help Your Highness by dressing her in her undergarments, then dressing Your Highness in her training pants and blouse." "Then," Rozelle added, "We will put Your Highness's breakfast over the top, so it seems like Your Highness is wearing a bustier, but she isn't." Audrianna's eyes grew big with excitement.

"So, I don't have to wear that horrid thing at all today?" she asked. "We can't promise Your Highness that we won't have to put one on her for court," Ethlyn replied. "There's a lot Your Highness can get away with at breakfast and sword training. The Royal Court is much harder because of the formal expectations." "I understand," Audrianna answered. She then jumped to her feet on the bed, walked to the edge and threw her arms around all three of her ladies. "Thank you Rose, and Ethel, and Cassie for taking good care of me. I love you all!" Such sentiment meant so much to the three of them, but it was improper for them to exchange such pleasantries. How they would've loved to say they loved her back. But that would display a level of familiarity that the ladies-in-waiting were not permitted.

Audrianna jumped from the bed with Rozelle holding her hand to make sure she didn't tumble and hurt herself. Immediately the three ladies set to work at dressing the princess for the day, just as they had proposed. In half the time as the day before, Audrianna was dressed and out the door. She scampered down the hall, and down the staircase, through the castle, and to the breakfast room where the king sat alone.

"Where is Prince Henry?" she asked Malcolm.

"Most likely still in bed, Your Highness," the king replied. "He does that sort of thing—a lot!"

"How long till he comes down for breakfast."

"Oh, he probably won't make it for breakfast. No. And we won't wait, either," the king assured the princess. At that, he rang a bell that say next to the king on the table. Servants came rushing in with platters of food, much like the breakfast that was served the day before. Both the king and the princess picked their choice of foods from the platters and hurriedly ate their portions.

Before she knew it, the ladies-in-waiting came walking up to her chair to silently indicate that it was time to return to the room to prepare for training. Without a word she jumped from her chair, and gave a clumsy curtsy to the king, then spun around to walk with the ladies to her bedroom chamber.

"Make sure Lord Rupp teaches you a bit on how to curtsy," the king called after her, still food in his mouth. "You will be expected to try again in court today." The four of them hurried to the room, upon which Rozelle and Ethlyn quickly pulled Audrianna's dress up and over her head. Castalia held the leather vest out for the princess to push her arms through. Within minutes, Audrianna was ready, out the door of her bedroom, and hastily making her way to the courtyard where she found Lord Rupp waiting for her. Rozelle stayed behind to clean up the chamber while Audrianna, Ethlyn, and Castalia were at sword practice.

Rupp stood by the practice pole with one hand on his hip, and Audrianna's baton in the other. She walked up to Rupp and tried to take the practice baton from him to begin practicing right away. Rupp held the baton up in the air, just out of her reach.

"And what do we call this today, Your Highness?" Rupp asked. Audrianna stopped to think. She wasn't sure she could remember. It started with a "b", she thought. Bantern—benton—borton… She struggled to remember.

"Baton!" she finally blurted out.

"Very good, Your Highness," Rupp replied as he handed it to her. She took it in her left hand, as she and Rupp exchanged glances. Then, she walked over to the practice pole and began swinging wildly at the practice marks. Her arms were so sore from the thirty minutes she practiced striking those marks the day before.

"Faster!" Rupp called out to Audrianna. "Faster, Your Highness!" She gave every ounce of reserve that she had, and within five minutes, she was completely spent. Sweat dripping from her forehead, she stopped to pant.

"I can't do it," she resigned. "I can't go on! I don't have the strength." "Your Highness has no more strength?" Rupp asked. "All of her energy is depleted?" "Depleted?" Audrianna asked.

"I mean," Rupp explained, "if you were to fall, you wouldn't be able to get back up again?"

"I don't even have enough strength to fall down," she answered.

"Then you completed your first exercise for today."

"I did?" Audrianna asked. "What did I do?"

"It is important, Your Highness, that when you are building up your body and your muscles, that you push as hard as you can, and then on the second day you push even harder to reclaim the ground that you already covered."

"And… I did that?" the princess remarked.

"Yes, Your Highness. Imagine that your muscles are like horses that have never been ridden. Do you know what horses do when someone tries to ride a horse for the first time?"

"They are kicked off," Audrianna answered.

"Exactly. An unbroken horse will fight you and fight you until it gets used to being ridden, and then it calms down. Your muscles right now are unbroken. You have to push yourself to use your muscles more and more until they are used to swinging a baton, and then a sword."

"And did I break my horse today?" Audrianna asked.

"Well, you're not broken yet, but you had a good day of work. Now…" Rupp changed the subject. "I have a personal request sent to me by the king. The king has told me he wanted me to work with you on a special lesson."

"No, no," Audrianna responded, remembering what the king had said as they were leaving breakfast.

"Oh. Your Highness knows about this lesson, do you?"

"Please," Audrianna pleaded, "I'm too tired to work on curtsying." "It's very simple, Your Highness. You simply grab the hem of your dress on both sides," Rupp explained, pretending to be wearing a dress and grabbing his hem. "Lift your dress about half an inch, like this." Audrianna rolled her eyes at him with the thought that she could see Rupp wearing a dress. "Then place your right foot behind your left, bending your toes, with your heal pointing up, then bend your knees and bow." Rupp placed his index finger under his chin as he bowed, and his pinkie finger sticking out. Audrianna shook her head with a fearful expression. "That is the most complicated bow I have ever seen. Why can't I bend at the waist when I bow like the men do?" "Because it isn't lady-like, Your Highness."

"I'm the lady," Audrianna angrily replied. "Don't you think I can decide how a lady will bow?" Her voice grew louder.

"Well," Rupp answered, "A lady must preserve her integrity at all times. A man has nothing to hide when he bows. But a lady must bow straight down and back up so her bosom isn't exposed."

"What's the deal with everybody afraid of seeing my bosom, or knowing that one day I might get a bosom?" Audrianna shouted. At that point, Castalia and Ethlyn stepped in to stop the princess from continuing her inappropriate conversation.

"Your Highness," the two softly chorused. By now the princess was starting to lose control of herself.

"I'm so tired of my stupid long underwear, and my stupid bustier, and my stupid vest…" she screamed with tears welling up in her eyes.

"YOUR HIGHNESS!" Castalia yelled, holding a handkerchief in front of the princess's mouth. Audrianna violently pushed the handkerchief away from her face, her tears started streaming down her red cheeks. "Let's not forget our propriety, Your High- ness," Castalia said calmly, smiling nervously at Rupp. Audrianna looked up at Rupp who smiled patiently at her, maintaining a cool disposition. Now she felt completely humiliated for having a meltdown. She pushed Castalia away and ran as fast as she could for her bedchamber.

"A thousand pardons, Lord Rupp," Ethlyn said as they turned to follow the princess. Rupp gave a forgiving bow as he held out his arm pointing the way to the castle. As Audrianna made her way up the stairs and around the corner to her bedchamber, she pushed the door, but it would not open. It was locked. She turned her back to the door and leaned against it as she slouched to the floor crying uncontrollably. Her tears mixed with fluid from her nose that trickled off her chin and into her lap. Suddenly, she heard the door unlock from the inside. She scrambled to her feet to see who was inside her room. As the door opened she was met by Rozelle. The Lady in Waiting looked down at little

Audrianna, her face hot and flushed and wet from tears. "Your Highness?" Rozelle remarked. "What has happened? Is Your Highness well?" Audrianna pushed her way past Rozelle and into her room. She made her way to the trunk that sat in front of the window, covered with a large soft fur. The princess jumped up on the trunk and sat there with her face pressed against her knees. She had no more strength to cry. She just wanted to rest.

"What's the matter, Your Highness? Did you get hurt?" No response. Rozelle walked over to her and examined the princess as best she could and as much as Audrianna would let her. There were no obvious injuries. She must have been frightened or upset about something, Rozelle determined. The Lady in Waiting was young, but so much older than the princess. Audrianna was a crowned royal, but still a little girl.

"Does Your Highness need to lie down and rest for a bit?" Audrianna raised her head from between her knees, and without saying a word, ever so slightly nodded her head. Rozelle walked over to the water basin and rinsed out a cool soft cloth and brought it to the princess and began washing her face from the tears, mixed with dirt, and sweat, and mucus. She then swooped the princess up in her arms and carried her the few steps to her bed and gently laid her on her back in the middle of the bed. Audrianna was still upset, but managed to pull the corners of her mouth up to a discreet smile.

Rozelle walked over to the open door and looked out into the hallway to see if there were the other two ladies coming to the room. She saw no one. She closed and locked the door again. She then walked over to the bed and climbed into the bed with Audrianna. Audrianna looked at her with surprise.

"Is this proper?" she asked Rozelle.

"Sometimes what we need, outweighs social propriety," she whispered in the princess's ear. Rozelle then gathered Audrianna into her arms and cuddled her tight against her body. Audrianna softly cried a little more. She needed—craved—the touch of a mother, or a close companion, to hold her. After all, she was only ten years old.

Rozelle gently stroked Audrianna's hair as she felt the tense princess relax. Within a few moments, the worried remaining ladies-in-waiting tried to enter the room. The door was locked. Castalia knocked.

"Rozelle? Are you in there?" Castalia asked.

"Yes," Rozelle answered.

"Did Her Highness, Princess Audrianna, come to the room?"

"Yes," she answered. "She is in here with me."

"Then can you open the door for us?" Ethlyn demanded.

"No," Rozelle answered. "She is resting. Come back later." The two ladies stared at each other. Later? Their responsibility was in the room with the princess. What was happening in there? The two ladies walked circles around the hallway for several minutes, arms folded, with impatience.

"We don't even have a stool," Ethlyn replied. Castalia shook her head in agreement. Soon enough, Audrianna regained her composure. She sat up in bed, as did Rozelle. She gave her Lady in Waiting a firm hug.

"Thank you, Rose," she said. "I needed that for a long time. But I think I need to go back to Rupp." Rozelle smiled and watched as the princess hopped out of the bed and walked to the door. She pushed the big iron bolt to one side and opened the door where Castalia and Ethlyn stood with worried looks on their faces.

"Who wants to walk me back to the courtyard?" Audrianna asked, as if nothing was wrong, nor did anything happen. The two ladies glanced at each other as the princess walked past, in between them, and down the hallway. They both turned to peek in the bedroom and saw Rozelle sitting up in the princess's bed, her dress draped over the bed as a fan, like one who had been laying down. Rozelle looked back at both of the ladies who wore expressions of confusion.

"What?" Rozelle asked, pretending nothing was out of the ordinary. Audrianna bounded down the staircase, down the hallways and out the door to the courtyard where she met Rupp, sitting on a bench, polishing one of his broadswords. "Your Highness," he greeted her excitedly. Audrianna was embarrassed by her meltdown, as she lowered her head to the ground and folded her hands. "Lord Rupp, I am sorry for how…" Rupp stopped her when he realised she was trying to apologise.

"No, Your Highness!" he scolded her as he stood to his feet. His scolding alarmed her as she stopped and looked up at the imposing man. "Do not ever apologise to the likes of me, or anyone else."

"What—" Audrianna began to ask. She had been raised to always apologise for any wrong doing. An emotional meltdown seemed to fit into that category. Rupp cut her off again.

"You are the crowned princess, Princess Audrianna the Tenderhearted. You don't need to tell anybody you're sorry for having a bad day—save the king! If what we're doing is too much, and you need to stop and clear your mind, do so! Your Highness is going to be the queen someday. You have the right. I don't have the right, nor a need of an explanation."

Audrianna looked up at Rupp. His face displayed a firm resolution, but his words were compassionate and gentle. Audrianna's heart began to strengthen. Rupp looked around the courtyard, then bent down on one knee to look eye to eye with the princess.

"The next time you leave and come back, don't say, 'I'm sorry.' Just look at me, or whoever else and say, 'Lord Rupp, I am ready to continue my lesson.' Can you say that to me?" Audrianna straightened her shoulders and tugged at the bottom of her vest.

"Lord Rupp," she repeated with an air of authority. "I am ready to continue my lesson." Rupp quickly stood to his feet and snapped to attention.

"Yes, Your Highness," he replied. Audrianna beamed a wide grin. "Shall we try to curtsy, or shall we practice with the baton?" he asked the princess. By this time Castalia and Ethlyn had caught up with Audrianna.

"Don't you think that ladies are best equipped at teaching the curtsy?" Castalia asked, volunteering their services.

"Perhaps. If you want her to curtsy like a lady," Rupp teased. "But the king wants her to curtsy like a queen." Castalia scowled at Rupp, completely aware that he was teasing. "Please," Rupp offered. "Show her how a lady curtsies."

Both Castalia and Ethlyn stepped forward like a rehearsed presentation of synchronised curtsies. They pulled back the one side of their dresses, placed their foot behind them, and bowed gracefully at the knees, without bending forward. "Wow!" Audrianna exclaimed, wide-eyed at their talented agility.

"Almost, ladies," Rupp criticised. "That was a superb effort. But there was an important detail that you two missed."

"What did we miss?" the two chorused.

"Watch me and see if you pick up on it," Rupp answered as he pretended to pull up his dress, he wasn't wearing, placed his foot behind him, bent his knees, rested his finger on his chin, and bowed his head. Audrianna applauded as he stood straight again. "Nicely done, Lord Rupp," Ethlyn commended.

"Very nice, indeed," Castalia agreed. "However, I find it necessary to bow the head only in the presence of the king or queen. Princess Audrianna will one day be the queen. What need does she have to bow the head?"

"That's a good point, Your Highness," Rupp replied, looking at little Audrianna. "Disregard the head bow. Let us see Your Highness do a curtsy."

Audrianna rolled her eyes and took a deep breath. She really embarrassed herself the day before in front of the entire royal court—including Henry. But, not wearing a dress at that moment, she pretended to pull her dress up slightly, then slid her left foot behind her.

"Right foot, Your Highness," Rupp coached. "Always place your right foot behind you." Audrianna tried to quickly switch feet, but stumbled over her own feet and fell forward on her stomach. The two ladies rushed to help her up and brush her off.

"Try again, Your Highness," Rupp encouraged. Audrianna placed her right foot behind her left, but was very unsteady. She was left-side dominant, and rather awkward getting her right foot to place itself in the right location. Her arms shot out to her side to keep her balance.

"No, no, Your Highness," Rupp corrected. "Keep your hands down at your side. Remember, you are only slightly raising the hem of your dress, not over your head!" "I can't keep my balance with my right foot behind me." Audrianna complained, beginning to get frustrated again. Rupp knew she needed some help to remain balanced while she was learning the mechanics of the curtsy. He walked over to her and took her by both of her wrists.

"Okay, Your Highness," he calmly and softly encouraged. "I have a hold of you. You won't fall."

"Okay," Audrianna sighed with relief.

"Now," Rupp instructed. "Let's go down together. Right foot behind…" Both Rupp and Audrianna slid their right foot behind their left. Audrianna took a little extra time rightly placing her foot so her toes bent with her heal straight up.

"Good," Rupp replied. "Now, bend the knees and go down…" They both lowered at the same time. "Good. Now, up again." The two of them returned to their original position. When they ended, Audrianna let out a forced exhale of relief. From behind, the two of them heard someone clapping. They turned to see the king standing to the side of the courtyard.

"Good," he said. "You both did very well. Rupp, you will make a fine Contessa someday."

"No need, Your Majesty," Rupp replied. "I already married one. That's where I learned to curtsy."

"Your wife taught you how to curtsy?" the king asked rather puzzled. "Amongst other things, Your Majesty," he answered. "She also taught me how to use a knife and fork."

"Ha!" the king laughed. "I wondered how you were so well trained." "Well, Her Highness will need much more practice before she can curtsy without assistance. But might I suggest for today, Your Majesty, that you hold her by the hand to keep her steady as she curtsies?" Audrianna's face lit up.

"Oh, yes! I would very much love for Your Majesty to hold

my hand while I bow, so I don't fall." The king thought for a moment.

"Very well. Today in Royal court, I will take your hand to help you curtsy to the court. I just hope both of us don't fall."

There was no sign of Henry at the royal court. Although Audrianna didn't like him as a person, or a husband, she was concerned that nobody had seen him. "Don't worry, Your Highness," the king assured her as they stood in the hallway, waiting for the royal court to be called into session. "He does this all the time. He'll either sleep the whole day away, or he and his companion, Pitt, will go off hunting and exploring. Prince Henry doesn't have much of a sense of responsibility." "How's he going to be king, then?" Audrianna sincerely asked. The king turned to look her in the eyes.

"There will be many a day that you will have to sit on the big throne and make decisions as the queen that will benefit your people, because either your king won't be around to act, or he will never care enough to do so either." Fear washed over Audrianna's face.

"I... I... I don't know if I'll know what to do," Audrianna stammered. "Yes," the king quickly answered without hesitation. "Yes, you will. I know you will, because you saved a poor man yesterday that had no hope but prison. Yet, you jumped in, saved his life, and now—people call you 'Tenderhearted'!" "Only that poor farmer called me that yesterday," Audrianna pointed out. "Oh, no," the king replied. "Everyone in court today has been calling you that as they enter the court room. That title is spreading through the whole kingdom like wildfire."

"How is that possible?" the princess asked. "Who's been telling everybody to call me that?"

"I have, for one," Rupp said as he casually passed in the hallway. "Your Highness," he added over his shoulder. The princess slouched just a bit in embarrassment. "Don't feel uncomfortable, Your Highness," the king responded. "Such a name as 'Tenderhearted' is evidence that the people have the utmost confidence in you as their future queen. This is a good thing."

"Yes, Your Majesty," Rupp added, walking back in the opposite direction. "Your Highness could have been stuck with a title like, 'the Horrible," Rupp said, relating the title that Audrianna gave to Henry.

"Oh, poor Henry," Audrianna confessed. "Don't tell me that has been spreading too."

"No," Rupp admitted. "And it's not legal for me to encourage such behaviour towards a future king. But, I love the title just the same." Rupp continued walking. "Your Highness," he again added over his shoulder.

A few moments later, the magistrate came walking down the hallway, carrying the brass sceptre in its velvet bag, preparing to enter the court room. Audrianna's stomach started to become knotted. She knew in just a few minutes she would have to climb the steps to her throne, then curtsy in front of the entire royal court. Her knees began to tremble and wanted to knock together.

"Are we ready, Your Majesty," the magistrate asked the king. Malcolm turned to look at Audrianna.

"Are you ready, my dear," he whispered. Audrianna didn't say a word, but slightly nodded. As they entered the court room, Audrianna leaned over and whispered to the king.

"Will Your Majesty hold my hand while I try to curtsy?" she asked. "I wouldn't have it any other way," he replied. As they approached the steps leading to the thrones, Malcolm reached towards Audrianna and offered his hand. She raised her hand and placed it in his. They walked up the steps hand in hand until they came to the thrones. Then, they separated so as to turn around, and joined their other hands. The king bowed to the people, then straightened up. He then lifted Audrianna's hand up, and pulled it closer to him, to give her more stability. She raised the front of her dress up with her free hand, and slid her right foot behind her left. Her formal shoes were much more slippery that her training shoes, and she struggled to keep her toes bent and her heal up.

After a couple failed attempts at securing her foot, she simply hooked her toes against the heal of her left foot and bent her knees. It was rather awkward, but it looked perfect to the court, since it had been over two decades since they had female royalty doing a curtsy. She bent her knees and went down, the king keeping her from falling, then he gave her the right amount of resistance to pull herself back up. Under the circumstances of her falling the day before, the spectators applauded Audrianna's success.

The magistrate called the court into session. The king and princess were seated. "His excellency King Malcolm the Merciful, and Her Highness Princess Audrianna presiding, with His Majesty Prince Henry in abstencia." At that, the king tapped the large brass sceptre on the floor.

"Abstencia?" Audrianna asked.

"He's not here," the king explained. The princess nodded with understanding. For over an hour both the king and princess listened to a multitude of cases. Much of time Audrianna had no idea what the people were talking about, but she sat and attentively listened to every case trying to make sense of what she heard. She started to learn certain words and phrases, as well as things like, "lower court" which people would try and work out their issues before having to come to a "higher court", meaning the royal court.

She also began to witness how often people would try and twist the details of their cases to make them seem different than what was happening. Some would use flowery statements to make them seem innocent, or a victim of circumstance. Audrianna was impressed how the king could see through a lot of the rhetoric that was being presented.

Audrianna was starting to feel rundown and tired of sitting straight on her throne with the pillowed booster box under her. She looked at the shadows on the wall and knew that it was going to be a while until the shadows pointed at the ceiling.

The next case that was brought forth was for a woman by the name of Lady Bellamy. The magistrate announced that she was in a dispute with her sister over who owned their house after their father died. Lady Bellamy was brought forward and she stated her case, but rather than speaking to the king, she began to appeal to the princess.

"Thank you, Your Majesty and Your Highness. Your Highness is so beautiful and I'm so happy to finally meet Her Highness. I have heard many people tell me the story of happened yesterday and how you are so smart and they call you Audrianna the Tenderhearted. I think that is so wonderful. I know for sure you will help the king in making the best decision for my case and I absolutely trust you in every way. I know you are so loving and compassionate to do what you know is right."

"State your case, Lady Bellamy," the king commanded.

"Yes, Your Majesty," she answered with a bow. "My father who I loved and adored and had the closest connection with, died last year rather suddenly, leaving me broken hearted. My sister and I continued to live in the house until my sister recently got married and wanted to move her husband into the house rather than finding a place of their own. I told her that this was my house from our father and I felt her husband should provide a house of their own to show that he is a fit man. So, I'm bringing this case to the royal court to help us decide this case, because I know the king is merciful, and of course the beautiful princess is tender-hearted and will one day be a wise and wonderful queen someday."

Audrianna began to smile. She wanted to look up at the king, but she knew that wasn't permitted. Each throne sat as an individual judge, and for her to look to the king while deciding a case would diminish the authority of that throne. So, she considered what Lady Bellamy had said.

"You flatter me, Lady Bellamy," Audrianna answered.

"Your Highness?" Lady Bellamy asked, a little surprised with the little princess's response.

"I like all that you have said. It makes me feel good to know that people like me. But—from the time I was five years old, my father would play a game with me that he called the 'flattering game'. He flattered me about all sorts of things—being pretty, being smart, and how good I was at doing things, and on and on. Then, he would ask me to do something he knew I didn't like or want to do, just to see if he could flatter me enough to do what he wanted me to do. He had me shine his boots, sweep the house, weed the garden, and even clean out the chamber pot. It wasn't until I was seven that I fully realised what he was doing, and why he flattered me."

"Lady Bellamy, I like you. And I want to continue liking you. Please don't change that by throwing a bunch of flattery at me hoping I'll take your side of this dispute between you and your sister. Your sister is not here to share her side of the story. So, please go, try and fix this issue between you two in the lower court, and if that doesn't work, the two of you can return together and let us help fix the matter. Is that fair, Lady Bellamy?"

Lady Bellamy was shocked to hear the princess speak with such wisdom for being so young and inexperienced.

"Yes, Your Highness," she answered while giving a bow. "That seems fair." The king tapped his sceptre on the floor.

"Let the records show that this issue between Lady Bellamy and her sister be tabled until such time that a lower court can hear the case and rule a provisional decision." Lady Bellamy walked out of the courtroom backwards, half bowing as she left. The court room erupted in a multitude of conversations regarding the princess's response to Lady Bellamy.

CHAPTER 9

By the end of the day for the royal court, Audrianna was emotionally and physically spent. So much so, that Rozelle and Castalia locked arms with the princess so as to hold her up while walking back to the room. Once in the room, the three ladies-in-waiting stripped her and dressed her for bed. Audrianna didn't even realise much of what they did to her until she came to her senses and found herself lying in bed. She felt her arms, stomach and head and realised that she was wearing her nightgown, her corset was gone, and her hair was unbraided and brushed out.

How did I miss all that? She thought to herself. She smiled at her silliness, then rolled over on her side, pulled a big fluffy pillow into her arms and drifted to sleep within a few minutes. As she slept the ladies-in-waiting were now able to dress for bed themselves. Over the next hour, while Audrianna was asleep, they brushed each other's hair, laughed about the day, admired each other's dresses, and told stories from home.

Soon enough, they all rolled out their mats and blankets, and fell asleep, lined up in front of the door.

Audrianna had slept peacefully for a few hours but was suddenly awakened by a strange noise. The princess sat up in bed. She looked towards the door and saw her three ladies sleeping on their mats.

"Pssst…" she whispered to wake them, but not draw attention to herself. "Pssst!" The ladies remained asleep. She didn't know what the sound was, but it kind of sounded like a moaning, or a howling. Someone being tortured, maybe?

Audrianna slid off the high bed and hit the floor with a loud thud. She rolled under the bed and looked at the other three, still peacefully sleeping. The noise wasn't coming from them. It sounded far away, perhaps down the hall, or in one of the towers. It wasn't a constant moan, just ever so often. It stopped for a while, so Audrianna pulled the large blanket off her bed and covered herself with it. She then crawled on her belly, like a bizarre-shaped turtle, towards Ethlyn. She grabbed Ethlyn by the foot and pulled on her big toe to wake her. Ethlyn stirred and looked down to see who or what was pulling at her feet.

"Your Highness? It that you under the blanket?" Ethlyn asked still rather groggy. Audrianna poked her face out from under the blanket, while keeping her head covered. "Quick!" she exclaimed. "Come under the blanket." Ethlyn sat up and shook her head to clear her tired mind.

"Your Highness wants me under the blanket with her?" Ethlyn asked.

"Yes! Come quick!" Audrianna answered, then hid herself under the blanket once more. Ethlyn scratched her head, wondering what was the matter. She lifted one side of the blanket to reveal a frightened princess coaxing her under the blanket. She crawled towards the little girl, and they both sat with the blanket shrouded over the two of them in the middle of the room.

"What's wrong, Your Highness?" Ethlyn asked.

"Listen!" Audrianna commanded. They both sat silent for a few seconds. Nothing.

"What am I listening for?"

"Shhhh!" the princess whispered.

Nothing.

"What did Your Highness hear?"

"Listen!" she told Ethlyn. "It sounded like someone moaning." They both sat quietly for a few more seconds.

"I don't hear anything, Your Highness. It might have been the wind." "It didn't sound like wind to me. It sounded like someone in pain." "In pain, Your Highness?" Ethlyn asked, uncovering the two of them of the blanket. Audrianna thought for a moment.

"Is there someone locked up in the dungeon, maybe?" she asked.

"Dungeon?" Ethlyn answered, half chuckling. "This castle doesn't have a dungeon. All the prisoners are sent to the prison on the other side of the city." Audrianna folded her arms in frustration.

"Well, I definitely heard someone moan in pain. It sounded far away, but not across town, but somewhere in this castle." She stared at Ethlyn with a scowl. "Maybe if I help Your Highness back in bed. Your Highness can listen for the moan from the mattress, and I'll listen for the moan from the floor." Ethlyn stood to her feet, picked up the blanket and laid it out over the bed. She then reached her hand out to help the princess into bed. Audrianna grabbed both her hands with hers, put her foot up against Ethlyn's thigh, and hoisted herself up into bed. Ethlyn was surprised at what Audrianna did, and Audrianna giggled over her ingenuity as she bounced onto the mattress. Ethlyn tucked the princess back into bed, then laid down on her own mat nearest the door. Everything went still again, and was quiet for close to twenty minutes. Audrianna was almost asleep when the sounds wisped through the room again. Immediately Audrianna rolled onto the floor again and crawled as fast as she could towards the door. "Ethel! Ethel! Ethel!" she cried. All three ladies-in-waiting woke up! "What!"

"What is it?"

"What's the matter?"

Audrianna climbed in between Rozelle and Ethlyn and balled up into the foetal position.

"I heard it again!" Audrianna said, her face buried in her arms. "Just a moment ago!" "Heard what?" Rozelle asked.

"Her Highness has been hearing moaning coming from somewhere in the castle," Ethlyn informed everybody.

Rozelle and Castalia looked down at Audrianna, then up at Ethlyn. "Did you hear the moaning, Ethlyn?" Rozelle asked.

"No," Ethlyn admitted. "I listened for a long time while Her Highness and I were hiding under the blanket." The two ladies disregarded the comment about the blanket. "And you heard nothing?" Rozelle clarified.

"No."

"Your Highness," Castalia counselled, "You have been under a lot of stress, this is only Your Highness's third night in this room, and only about a week since she arrived. Your Highness will hear many strange noises that she is not used to, but I'm sure it is okay."

Audrianna was not certain right away. The three of them coaxed her back into bed. For the rest of the night it seemed to the ladies that the princess had calmed down and was able to sleep. However, by morning, when they all awoke, they didn't find the princess in her bed. She had rolled out of bed again, pulled the blanket down to the floor, and was sleeping under her bed, completely covered with the blanket again.

Rozelle reached under the blanket and grabbed Audrianna by the hand and slid her out from under the bed, and the other two helped raise her to her feet. She was still somewhat asleep.

"Your Highness," Rozelle called to her. "Your Highness, wake up!" Audrianna groggily opened her eyes.

"Your Highness! It's morning," Ethlyn stated.

"We need to get Your Highness dressed for breakfast," Castalia said in a hurried tone. Audrianna slowly opened her eyes.

"I'm so tired," she answered. "Why can't we just skip breakfast… and training… and court…"

"No, Your Highness!" Ethlyn replied. "You kept me up most of the night, now it's my turn to keep Your Highness going most of the day." Audrianna groaned. The ladies began the long process of dressing her, which included waking her every few minutes. Castalia started braiding her hair, and had to hold her braids as if they were reins with a wandering horse at the end of them. She had to pull on the braids to get Audrianna to straighten her head, or lift her head, or turn her head back to where it was. Finally, the ladies finished the princess's preparation. They pulled her by the hands and lifted her to a standing position. Ethlyn poked her in the back towards her side, which caused her to jump and move forward.

The four of them made their way to the breakfast room, taking much, much longer than usual, but found that no one was there.

"Did we miss breakfast?" Rozelle asked one of the kitchen servants. "No, Ma'am," the servant replied. The king has ordered for Your Highness to eat as soon as she shows up. The king and the prince are in private council. "Private council?" the princess asked. "They are having a meeting without me? Is it about me?"

"I'm not privy to any of that," the servant answered.

"I wonder what could be going on," Ethlyn replied.

"Don't know," Castalia responded.

"It must be something very important," Rozelle pondered. "Like, an emergency." Audrianna sat down at the breakfast table, mainly to slouch and rest, but she was still interested in eating. A large platter of breads, fruits, and cheeses already sat in the middle of the table. She reached out and pulled a piece of sweetbread from the middle and placed it on her plate. She then helped herself to some rye bread, and oat bread, and a slice of sour dough bread. She took a slice of cheese of every colour she could find, not knowing one cheese from another. She would take a bite from this bread, then that cheese, then some of those fruits. She leaned her head against her palm, propping herself up, and doing what she could to not fall to the floor in exhaustion.

About that time, Lord Rupp passed by in quite a hurry, almost running into Castalia who had half-sat near the door. None of the ladies were permitted to sit at the table, even if it was only the princess who was eating.

"Pardon me, ladies," he said as he passed by. He realised almost after the fact that they were the attendants for Audrianna. He quickly whirled around on his heels and re entered the room, holding his sword at his side.

"Forgive me, Your Highness," Rupp exclaimed. "An important matter has come up that needs my immediate attention... There will be no sword exercise today." "No sword practice?" Audrianna sat up straight with a beaming smile. "No, Your Highness! You will be free the rest of the day until royal court." "Free? Free to do what?" Audrianna asked, slouching back in her chair. She couldn't think of anything outside of her daily schedule. Rupp walked up to her chair and looked straight down at her. She felt a bit unsettled by his height. But, he spoke softly to her. "Just, go and play, Your Highness. Be a child. Be a little girl. Take your ladies-in waiting with you and go have fun together." He abruptly turned and quickly left the breakfast room and hurried down the long marble hallway.

Audrianna slouched in her chair again and leaned her head against her hand. She grabbed a piece of melon from the closest end of the platter and lazily plopped it in her mouth and chewed laboriously.

"Hmm," she grunted. "I wonder what a little girl does for fun."

After breakfast, Audrianna and the ladies went back to the room and all changed into outside dresses. Not her usual exercise clothing. That was inappropriate for any place outside the training courtyard. Rather a long dress that went down past her ankles, but was made of lighter fabric so that the princess could walk, or run, or sit, or lay down in the grass and not get overheated.

Audrianna and her three companions decided together that it would be fun to leave the castle for a change, and walk around the marketplace. No one had seen the princess since her coronation as the crowned princess and betrothed to the prince, except for the few that had visited the royal court. Besides, the ladies were dying to visit the local marketplace.

Escorting them were four men, two of which were palace guards, and two of them were the royal envoys who had originally brought the princess to the palace, Rolf and Rodrick. Audrianna was very shy and reserved towards the royal envoys. Her experience of being found, nabbed, and told that she was being brought to the palace to be married to the prince, and discovering how horrible the prince was, gave her every reason to be a bit stand-offish with the two men. Rodrick was the older envoy and seemed to be a bit more understanding and flexible. But while in transit from the east side of the kingdom to the palace city, Rolf was a by-the-book kind of rookie that would not stop for supper or the bathroom unless it was expressly on the daily schedule.

However, for their adventure outside the castle walls, their main purpose and agenda was to play, have fun, and kill time until they needed to get back in time for royal court. So, they started at the marketplace. Ethlyn was so excited to get to browse the different market booths, she started to pull the princess down one aisle of booths and up another. Rozelle, who played the mother hen, had to remind Ethlyn several times that this was Audrianna's day out—not hers. Castalia wasn't interested very much in the marketplace as she was into Rolf, who was good-looking and seemed to be the same age as her. Rolf tried to shrug her off by reminding her that he was on official duty— which caused her to be even more attracted to him.

After an hour or so, Rozelle asked Audrianna if she wanted to go and see the ships, and perhaps pick some flowers for their room. Audrianna wasn't interested in the ships as she was about decorating their room with fresh flowers. So, off they went towards the coastline, the two palace guards leading the way, Rozelle and Ethlyn each holding one of the princess's hands, and Rodrick and Rolf following behind, with Castalia walking as close to Rolf without making physical contact—except the occasional "accidental bumps".

Near the coastline, there was an overlook that greeted the path leading down to the shipyards. From that overlook, one could see just about every ship in the king's armada. About a hundred yards to the left stood a cliff where the lighthouse sat, warning ships as they came close to the coastline during the night or morning fog. It was nearest the lighthouse that had a nice fertile patch of land where wildflowers grew.

Audrianna began to pick a multitude of flowers and group them into arrangements for certain areas of her bedchamber. Rozelle had brought some twine with her in a knapsack and bound the arrangements together, then gently laid them in the same knapsack. The princess enjoyed picking flowers for about thirty minutes, then she sat down with the ladies and watched the seagulls fly overhead. Rodrick, Rolf, and the two palace guards stood a far off, watching the shipyards, and talking about issues stemming from their responsibilities.

"What do you think they are talking about back at the castle?" Audrianna asked. "Who, Your Highness?" Castalia asked. "Rolf and the others?" Audrianna rolled her eyes at Castalia.

"No, not Rolf! Prince Henry, Lord Rupp and the king back at the castle, silly." "Sorry, Your Highness," Castalia replied sheepishly.

"Rolf has somehow preoccupied Castalia's mind, today," Ethlyn teased. "No, he hasn't," Castalia replied.

"Not much," Rozelle responded. "Just followed him through the marketplace, up the road, across the meadow… She was walking so close to him, I thought for sure the two of them would have to be wed before the day was over."

"Oh, she would want nothing less than that," Ethlyn retorted. By now, Audrianna stood up and pretended to be Castalia. She put one hand on her hip and held out the other in a dainty-like fashion. She cocked her head to one side and looked at the ladies through the corner of her eyes.

"Oh Rolf!" Audrianna teased. "You are so strong and handsome! Your uniform makes me so excited! What's a Lady to do? Let's run away together!" Castalia was worried that Audrianna's voice would carry over to where the men were standing. She didn't mind the teasing so much, but she would be mortified if Rolf heard what the princess was saying about her.

"Hush, Your Highness!" Castalia scolded. "The menfolk will hear you." "Don't forget about the royal insignia on his shoulder," Rozelle said, getting into the teasing.

"Oh, Rolf," Audrianna continued, "your insignia, with its red and blue all swirled together. I love it so much! It just makes me all so sweaty!" The other two ladies burst out in laughter. Castalia lifted her dress just enough so she could sit up on her knees. "Please, call me Cassie!" Audrianna concluded her teasing. Castalia reached out and grabbed the princess and pulled her into her lap. She began avenging herself by tickling the princess. Audrianna squealed and giggled with delight.

By now, the two palace guards and the two envoys returned.

"We should return to the castle," Rodrick informed the group. "It will be time for royal court in a couple hours. You ladies will need time to change and prepare the princess."

"Yes. Thank you, Rodrick," Rozelle answered. "Ladies, let us be going." Audrianna jumped from Castalia's lap and skipped ahead towards the castle. As she skipped along, she saw a long stick to the side of the road. It reminded her of a baton that she used for sword practice. She picked it up and began pretending she was learning to fight Prince Henry.

"Prepare to be defeated, Prince Henry! What's that you say? You've never lost a fight against a girl? Well, then! Today is a new day, isn't it?" Audrianna began swinging the stick wildly, making clanging sounds like she heard when Henry and Pitt would spar.

"CLANG! CLANG! Wait! Wait!" Audrianna screamed, mimicking Henry's voice. "I didn't know a girl could know so much about sword fighting."

"Yes, we can!" she exclaimed in her own voice. "And now I will defeat you so bad, even looking at your own sword will cause you to cry and wet yourself. CLANG! CLANG!"

"You're so much better than I am," she mimicked. "Please don't hurt me!" "You're lucky then that I am so—tenderhearted!" she exclaimed, still swinging the stick.

She ran along the path leading up to the bridge that crossed the river next to the castle. The palace guards, the two envoys and the three ladies followed close behind her. "CLANG! CLANG! Ha! Ha! I have you on the run, Henry!" she shouted. "Don't hurt me," she mimicked. "I'm going to run away before the crowned princess hurts my boyish soft skin!" At that, Audrianna picked up a rock to throw it at her pretend adversary.

"You can't run fast enough, you cowardly prince!" She reached back to throw the rock, when something freakish caught her eye next to the bridge. She dropped the rock and ran towards the sight. As she ran, she had trouble adjusting her eyes to what she saw. It was like her mind didn't want her to see what was right in front of her. As she came close, she realised what it was.

She jumped back from fear and fell to the ground. She opened her mouth to call for the others, but her lungs wouldn't let her exhale to make a sound. She scrambled to her feet and ran towards the first person she could get to. One of the palace guards was in front of the others. Audrianna ran into him so hard that it knocked her back on the ground.

"Your Highness," he replied, stooping down to help her up off the ground. He reached his arm out, and Audrianna grabbed it, stood to her feet, and without saying a word, pulled him with all her might towards the bridge.

"What's the matter, Your Highness," Rozelle asked. She could see that the princess was fearfully excited and pale. Before the princess could gain her composure to be able to speak, the palace guard saw what Audrianna originally saw. He called to the other guard, as well as the envoys. When Rolf saw it, he turned around to face the ladies and ordered them to stand back. Audrianna grabbed a hold of Rozelle's arm and wouldn't release her.

What a horrible sight it was!

CHAPTER 10

Audrianna and her three attendants were ordered back to their room while King Malcolm, Prince Henry, and Lord Rupp conferred with the two guards and the two envoys.

"This is an outrage," the king shouted. "Not only do the Andjety have the audacity to invade our territory, and approach the castle, but to do such atrocity to one of our own." The king turned to Henry. "What exactly were you and Pitt doing in the Andjety village?"

"We were collecting intelligence. It had come to our attention that Nadeau has spies here in the city, perhaps even here in the castle. Pitt and I wanted to covertly infiltrate the nearest village to see if we could uncover any information that would give us a clue as to who they are."

"And how did you propose that would happen?" the king demanded. "Were you just supposed to show up and they were going to spill their guts?"

"It was my understanding that Pitt could speak Andjety fluently," Henry answered. "However, while in the pub, it became clear that while Pitt may have known a great deal of their language, he was not as proficient in their dialect. While attempting to pump people for information, he must have given away our identities."

"I have noticed for some time," Rupp interjected, "that Pitt had a high opinion of himself, but not a realistic one. It would be safe to assume that Your Majesty's assessment of the situation could very well be accurate."

"Well, that's all fine in regard to how the two of you were discovered," the king retorted. "Meanwhile, we have a disembodied head on a pike, found by Princess Audrianna, which was set up in front of the castle bridge, in broad daylight, and a war empress that has spies within the city, and perhaps within the castle." The king looked at the prince, then at Lord Rupp, and back at the prince. "Did I miss any detail that I should still address?"

"That would be the summation of the predicament, Your Excellency," Rupp answered. The king rung his hands and paced back and forth on the lower floor of the royal court room.

"What a terrible, terrible pigswill we must deal with," the king replied.

"We have no option but to go to war, Your Majesty," Prince Henry responded. "War?" the king bellowed. "Is war your answer to everything? Is violence your

standard solution?"

"Father," Henry pleaded, "You must see that a diplomatic solution is not possible. Zymjai, the Witch, knew everything about me, and Audrianna, and the fact I couldn't take the throne. She sees our kingdom as weak. We must attack to demonstrate to her that we are indeed strong, and her act of aggression against Pitt will not go unpunished." "I hear what you are saying, Henry, my son," the king answered, attempting to soothe

the anger that was pent up in Henry's heart over the desecration of Pitt. "But even though we have a respectable size army, they are still no match for the marauders from the mountains."

"True your majesty," Rupp added. "However, if we plan no contingency against an onslaught, we will stand here vulnerable."

"Exactly," Henry replied. "All I'm saying is, we need to establish a plan of defence first, but also a plan of attack, keeping our eyes open for the opportunity."

"I guess it would be smart to do so," the king yielded. "Notify the magistrates. We will not have regular court today. I need all of our strategists to report here in one hour."

"Yes, Your Majesty," Rupp answered, then spun around and dashed out the door. "Thank you, father," Henry said.

"All I can say is, this will be a way that you can win some valuable trust from me. Handle this situation with leadership skills, the skills of a king, and I will know you have what it takes to be a king someday—soon."

Audrianna and her ladies-in-waiting were soon notified that there would be no royal court that afternoon.

"Amazing!" Audrianna exclaimed, her eyes wide with excitement. "No sword drills. No royal court. The better part of the morning picking flowers. And now, the afternoon decorating the room. What a great day! I feel like a child again."

"Your Highness is a child," Rozelle replied. "And since she doesn't have to dress up in her fancy clothes, I think it would be good for Your Highness to go into the wash room, and take her bath."

"A BATH?" Audrianna shrieked. "You want me to take a bath so far away from the weekend? Will you make me take another one in two days?"

"There is nothing wrong with taking two baths in one week," Rozelle answered. "Yes, there is!" the princess snapped. "Getting wet this far in the season can cause me to get the coughs."

"Not if the water is hot enough," Castalia argued. Audrianna's head shot up in Rozelle's direction, and she began to beam.

"I get to take a hot bath?" she asked?

"Of course, Your Highness" Rozelle replied.

"I've never taken a hot bath before," the princess chimed.

"What about your coronation as the crowned princess? Didn't they give you a hot bath then?" Ethlyn inquired.

"They didn't give me a bath so much," Audrianna recounted. "They made me stand against the wall while old women came and scrubbed me, threw water over me, then dried me off. I felt humiliated. I hated every minute of it."

"Well," Rozelle said. "You were just a little girl then. Now you're the crowned princess. And princesses get to take hot baths." Audrianna smiled again.

"And don't forget about the bubbles," Ethlyn added. "Bubbles?" Audrianna asked, a bit unsure what that meant.

"We'll give Your Highness the full treatment," Rozelle stated. "Today is your day, Your Highness. No swords, no court, no bustiers. You got to pick flowers, play outside the castle, and now a bubble bath."

"Don't forget I also got to see a dead man's head!" Audrianna remembered, making a wincing face.

"All the more reason to relax in a hot bath," Castalia said.

Audrianna went into the bathing chamber and removed all her clothes. She then wrapped herself in a large towel that went around her thin frame more than twice, and covered her from her shoulders, almost down to her ankles. She watched as five hefty chamber maids came one by one, each carrying two wooden buckets a piece of steaming hot water brought from down stairs in the kitchen.

After all ten buckets were poured into the tub, the tub barely looked like it had any water in it. Back down into the kitchen the five maids returned, then up to the bath chamber they came again and poured their buckets into the tub. Three times they did this, and by then the tub looked like it had enough water for Audrianna to be able to soak up to her waist. The princess shed her towel and slowly slid into the warm water.

Rozelle, Castalia, and Ethlyn sat in the bath chamber with her, talking mostly to each other, but occasionally including the princess. Donning their nightgowns, they brushed each other's hair, and experimented with various styles of braiding.

"Oh," Ethlyn remembered. "Don't forget about the bubbles," she said as she pulled out a pouch and poured a stream of powder into the water.

"What's it supposed to do?" Audrianna asked. "Just wait and see," the three ladies chorused.

Audrianna laid back in the tub until the water rose up around her ears. She bent her legs so her knobby knees were sticking up in the air. Before she knew it, the chamber maids brought fresh hot water up from the kitchen and poured the buckets into the tub.

Oooh! A surge of soothing hot water rushed through the tub and caused Audrianna to shiver with delight. Goosebumps formed on her arms. She watched as bubbles rose from the pouring water.

"Bubbles!" she exclaimed. The ladies smiled at the little princess's elation. As the fifth maid poured her final bucket into the tub, the tub was more than two thirds of the way full. The maids left their buckets laying on the floor around the tub. They would need them later to bail the water out once the princess was finished bathing.

Audrianna loved the feel of the hot water on her body. She felt so relaxed. The muscles in her arms and hands had been sore for the past three days with all the training she was receiving from Rupp. But now, the bubble bath seemed to be washing all that into the past.

The princess played with the bubbles, trying to make a bubble castle, or a bubble mountain, or a bubble boat. She would take the bubbles and place them on her face, then look at the ladies and say, "I'm King Malcolm." Then she would giggle, lay back, and kick her legs in the air and see what they looked like with bubbles surrounding them.

After about twenty minutes of bubble jubilation, all the bubbles died down, and Audrianna's fingers and toes were pruned. Rozelle came and placed a hand on Audrianna's back, and one on her head and told her to submerge her head. Under the water she went, then up again. With her hair completely wet, Rozelle began washing her hair with a bar of lye soap. The soap seemed to burn uncomfortably on Audrianna's scalp, and she couldn't wait until Rozelle made her submerge again to wash all the lye out of her hair.

When she was done, Castalia held the towel out while Rozelle took the princess by the hands and helped her out of the tub. Castalia wrapped her in the towel, then sat her on a stool next to the tub. Ethlyn took another towel and vigorously dried her hair. Rozelle then brushed out all the tangles from her long brown hair. When she was done, Castalia stood Audrianna up, threw the towel to the side, then she and Ethlyn helped dress the princess in her nightgown.

It was still very early, but all four of them knew there was nothing left for them to do but have supper. Under the circumstances, they could insist that supper be brought to their room. Rozelle poked her head out of the room and called for the chamber maids to come and bail out the tub. When they came it, she asked one of the maids to run down to the kitchen and ask for a platter to be sent up to their room.

The other two chamber maids bailed water from the tub by scooping water with their wooden buckets, then carrying the buckets to the window of the bed chamber, and tossing the water to the ground. However, the water barely reached the ground, because right outside the open window was a large tall magnolia tree. It was a rather healthy-looking tree. Castalia commented that it must have had a lot of bath water tossed on it over the years to have grown so fertile.

Audrianna looked out the window as the maids poured water out the window, and down over the tree. She noticed a large branch that jetted from the trunk, and up near the ledge of the window.

"I'm sure if I wanted to, I could jump from the window and land on that branch, then slide down the trunk and onto the ground." the princess commented.

"Oh, no, Your Highness," Rozelle reprimanded Audrianna. "That is too dangerous. Your Highness might miss the branch and fall all the way to the ground! You could get badly hurt, or even killed!"

"Well," the princess confessed, "I really wouldn't want to try unless it was an emergency. Like if we were being attacked and I needed to jump out the window to save my life."

"If we are under attack," Rozelle replied, "I promise I will let you jump out the window, but only to save your life." Audrianna smiled and looked back out the window. "Besides," she added. "There are so many branches. If I miss one, I'm bound to land on another."

About the time the chamber maids had finished bailing the water, one of the servants from the kitchen knocked on the door and presented a large covered platter with a variety of meats, breads and cheeses. As they lifted the lid off the platter, both the ladies as well as the princess became excited that they had the privilege of eating in their room. They all sat cross-legged in a circle on the floor around the platter, like a house full of sisters. Audrianna began brushing her long hair. This was the first time that they all had the privilege to eat together. Audrianna was expected to always eat separate from the "servants", even though the ladies-in-waiting were assigned to be companions to the princess above anything else.

As the rations on the platter began to diminish, another knock was heard at the door. Castalia slowly opened the door just a crack, since all four of them were modestly dressed for bed. On the other side of the door stood a palace messenger.

"Madam," the messenger spoke rather officially, "the king has requested that Her Highness, Princess Audrianna, be present in the royal court room immediately."

"The royal court?" Castalia replied. "The royal court is not in session this time of day."

"No, madam," the messenger responded. "This is a special meeting of the royal family. Princess Audrianna has been coronated the crowned princess. Therefore, her presence is requested."

"Did you hear that?" Ethlyn asked Audrianna. "They want you to attend a special secret meeting of the royal body."

"Very well," Castalia replied. "We will bring her down as soon as we can appropriately dress her." Castalia went to close the door, but the messenger stopped the door with his hand and foot.

"A thousand pardons, madam," the messenger said, still holding the door. "But the king instructed that I personally escort the princess to the meeting—alone."

"Alone?" Castalia answered.

"Those were the king's instructions."

"Very well. Give us a few moments, and we shall have the princess ready for you to escort." At that, Castalia pushed the door all the way closed. She then turned around to face a shocked little princess.

"Why do they need me?" Audrianna asked. "I'm only ten years old."

"While that is true," Rozelle replied. "You must stop thinking of yourself as a little helpless ten-year-old girl."

"Since the coronation, you are the crowned princess, and the future queen of Nadeau," Ethlyn pipped up. "That counts for something."

"Evidently," Rozelle added, "when the king wants his trusted advisors and his heads of state to meet, he thinks highly enough of you to call you to the royal court." Audrianna took a deep breath and gave out a loud sigh.

"What am I expected to wear? My formals?"

"I would assume that would be expecting too much this time of day," Castalia answered. "Probably your dinner wear should suffice. What do you ladies think?"

"Yes," Rozelle replied. "I think her dinner dress will work."

"No reason to do anything more than her dinner wear," Ethlyn responded.

Therefore, with the verdict in, and the consensus agreeing on an outfit, off came the nightgown, on went the undergarment, the bustier—loosely fitted—and on went the evening dress that was reserved for the dining room. Audrianna quickly brushed her hair a bit more, but she still looked a bit dishevelled. But this was an emergency meeting.

The messenger, however, was getting impatient as he expected the king to become increasingly impatient with him waiting on the princess. He knocked on the door a few times and was pacified by being told she was almost ready. Finally, the princess was shoved out the bed chamber door, and the messenger led the way to the royal court room for the special council meeting.

Meanwhile, the king, the prince, Lord Rupp, and several magistrates sat in chairs in a circle on the main floor of the royal court room.

"I don't understand why we need to wait for the princess to arrive before we proceed," Henry said.

"She is part of the royal crown," the king replied. "She is ten years old," Henry adamantly said.

"True," Rupp responded. "However, she is wise beyond her years. It would be prudent to at least get her involvement in the matter."

"Fine," Henry conceded, folding his arms as they waited. "But I believe we should take her advice with a grain of salt. Just because she might suggest something does not mean we are obliged to act on it."

"Of course not," Rupp replied. "We will only give it the same consideration that I give all of your suggestions." Henry looked at Rupp, tossed his head, then slouched in his chair.

"I know that's right," Henry replied.

Soon enough the messenger arrived with Audrianna in tote. The king and Rupp stood to welcome the young crowned princess, while Henry—her betrothed—remained slouched in his seat.

"Welcome, Your Highness," King Malcolm said, standing and taking her by the hand, then leading her to a chair. Audrianna was obviously nervous and self-conscious of sitting with such prestigious men in the royal court. Much more nervous than sitting on the throne in the royal court.

"Thank you for inviting me, Your Excellency," the princess answered. "What is this secret meeting all about?"

"Oh, it's not a secret meeting. Just a private meeting of the royal crown and my personal advisors," the king assured her.

"Your Highness," Rupp began explaining, "We came together because of the terrible event that you stumbled upon this morning."

"The head that was cut off?" Audrianna asked.

"Yes," Rupp replied. "Do you know whose it was?" The princess silently shook her head. "It was the head of Lord Pitt, the prince's armour-bearer."

"Pitt?" Audrianna exclaimed. "Oh, poor Pitt." She turned to look at Henry. "I'm so sorry to hear about your friend," she said.

"He was not my friend," Henry assured her, rolling his eyes, and sitting up in his chair. "He was my armour-bearer. That was all."

"Oh," Audrianna answered.

"At any rate," Rupp continued, "it happened because Prince Henry and Pitt infiltrated the Andjety region to acquire intelligence regarding the marauders who have been attacking our farms."

"And killing my family," Audrianna responded.

"True," the king affirmed. "And that was orchestrated by an Andjety war empress by the name of Zymjai."

"Zymjai?" Audrianna asked.

"They call her, 'The Witch of Andjety'," Rupp replied. "She's a witch?" the princess asked wide-eyed.

"She's not really a witch, like one that casts spells," Henry interjected. "She is just called that because she is a very evil woman."

"Oh."

"Now, the reason we are having this private discussion is because we need to decide whether we will gather our troops and attack the Andjety, or if we should double our defences and prepare for an inevitable onslaught form the Witch's forces."

"I say we attack!" Henry angrily announced. "Hit them hard and fast before the day is over."

"I am not sure that we could muster enough troops before the end of the day," Rupp responded with grave concern. "We haven't been to war in so long, our men are not prepared."

"Exactly why I have pushed that we have an active military," Henry retorted, "training daily for such a contingency. Our men are nothing but soft."

"Our men are farmers," the king responded. "Training for battle is not what they want to do on a daily basis."

"Perhaps," Henry responded. "But I am sure they don't want to continue being robbed, murdered, and otherwise at the mercy of these marauders from the mountains." "Well," the king replied, "the questioned remains. Do we attack the Andjety on their soil, or do we strengthen our borders and equip our people to defend themselves?" Everybody sat silent for a few seconds.

"Your Highness," Rupp asked. "What are your thoughts?" Everyone turned to Audrianna to hear what she might say. The princess sat in her chair looking from one face to another. She looked down at her feet for a couple seconds then looked up at Rupp, who she saw as a safe person.

"Well," she finally said. "How does our army compare to the enemy army?"

"They outnumber us ten to one," Rupp answered her. Audrianna looked back at her feet, then up again.

"So," she said methodically, "In order to win against the Andjety, every one of our soldiers would have to kill eleven men."

"No," Henry answered. "They outnumber us TEN to one, not eleven to one." "Right," Audrianna answered. "But if we want to win, each man will have to kill eleven. Am I right?"

"That is correct, Your Highness," Rupp said, smiling at the princess.

"What does ten or eleven have to do with anything?" Henry demanded, scowling at Audrianna.

"Well, my question is," Audrianna clarified, "Are our soldiers capable of killing eleven Andjety soldiers a piece?" Rupp and the king exchanged glances, then looked at Henry as if expecting him to answer, who sat in his chair flabbergasted at the princess's question.

"No," Henry finally answered. "I don't believe they are equipped."

"Then I think it would be smarter to build up our defences, since we don't have a chance to win at attacking. Don't you think?" The princess looked dead into Henry's eyes at her question. The prince felt very uncomfortable being shown up by a tiny ten- year-old.

"I guess so," he answered, slouching in his chair and putting his arm over his face. "It is settled then," the king responded. "Lord Rupp?"

"Yes, Your Majesty?"

"You know what you must do! Prepare the castle and the city for an impending attack."

"Very good, Your Excellency," Rupp replied. "May I recommend watchmen posted at every corner of the city, with hourly reports?"

"You are captain of my guards, and lord of national defence. You see to it."

"Yes, Your Majesty." Rupp answered, standing from his chair, and rushing out the door. The king then motioned for Audrianna to come close to him. She stood and slowly walked over to the king. He held out both of his hands, and she did the same. He grabbed a hold of her wrists rather firmly, which at first startled her, but she knew he meant no harm.

"Bless you, dear child," the king replied. "You are so wise. You may have just saved our kingdom from disaster."

Henry sat up in his chair and placed both hands, palms down, on his knees. He showed no expression on his face, good or bad. But inside, he was livid! His father never once praised a decision he had made, never once told him he was proud of his son, never once called him to him even to hold his own son's hand.

Now, the betrothed bride that he didn't want, the little girl who prevented him from taking the throne, had even taken his place in his father's heart.

Henry abruptly stood and stormed out of the room towards the grand staircase. He hurried towards his room, which was where he went each time his father made him upset. He would always go and complain to Pitt, using him as a sounding board, and he and Pitt would usually go and spar to relieve his anger and hostility.

As he quickly climbed the stairs, his thoughts suddenly caught up with him. There was no one waiting for him in his room to go spar and joke with. Pitt was dead! His emotions started to get the best of him. He was angry that his father once again disregarded his feelings and needs. He was angry with how a little girl showed him up. He was incensed that he was going to have to marry that girl he despised in six years. And he was upset that he had to wait those six years before he could be king.

But now, all that anger suddenly turned to overwhelming grief over his best friend being killed, beheaded, and desecrated on a pike in front of his own castle. He wanted the king's approval to attack the Andjety and avenge his friend's death, but Audrianna had inadvertently put a stop to it. Tears welled up in his eyes as he stood on the middle step and gripped the brass rail for all he was worth. He was desperate for release! He was desperate to do something to honour the memory of Pitt—his friend.

"Are you okay?" a voice echoed behind Henry. It was Audrianna.

"I'm fine," Henry adamantly answered, wiping away the tears in his eyes with his thumb and forefinger.

"I'm sorry about your friend Pitt," Audrianna attempted to comfort her grieving betrothed. Maybe this could be a turning point for them, she thought.

"Are you?" Henry snapped. "Are you really sorry, or are you just trying to prove that you might matter more to the king?" The princess immediately felt hurt from Henry's accusation. She wanted to express sympathy, but now she began to feel hostility.

"I'm not trying to prove anything," Audrianna answered. "I was asked a question, and I answered it the best I could." By then she folded her arms in defiance towards Henry.

"Maybe so," Henry countered, "But you have no idea what damage you have done." "Tell me," she said, arms folded and eyes glaring. Henry wanted to yell profanities at her, grab her by the throat and stick his sword through her.

"You have no idea how you have dishonoured me and sabotaged my very existence?" he screamed.

"I have dishonoured you?" Audrianna asked boldly. "I've sabotaged you? Your very existence?" She couldn't believe that there was possibly anything in his life that she was personally responsible for. And yet, it was for him that she had been drug from her home, that she was forced to endure countless hours of sword drills and sitting in royal court in an uncomfortable formal dress. It was for him that she was forced to change complicated outfits three to four times a day. She never asked to be a princess, and she certainly never asked to be a queen, married to a monster like Henry.

"Yes," Henry quickly answered. "You and your stupid answers and solutions to things going on in royal court, and your stupid answers to affairs of state that you truly don't understand. How my father dotes on you because of your pretty hair and your emerald-green eyes. He is infatuated with you, all the while looking at his own son with contempt. I hate you! I hate every ounce and every inch of you! You—YOU—LITTLE NAUGHTY GIRL!" The prince's eyes blazed with fury, while Audrianna maintained her composure. She unfolded her arms, cocked her head to one side and looked at Henry through the corner of her eyes.

"Well, then," she challenged Henry. "Why don't you spank me?"

Audrianna truly believed that such an ultimatum would cause Henry to see how foolish he was being. But instead, in a blind fury, Henry grabbed Audrianna by the arm. His grip was so tight, she thought he was going to break her arm. He began dragging her up the stairs to the door of her bedchamber. He loosened the belt to the scabbard of his dagger. Once the belt was free, he flung the dagger out of the scabbard, which bounced on its handle against the stone floor with an echoing CLICKITTY CLANG CLANG! He then wrapped the leather belt around the long scabbard and knelt to one knee. He forced the princess over his other knee. He then held the scabbard over his head, and swung the leather sheath against Audrianna's rump.

Three times he slapped her posterior with the scabbard, all the while the princess remained silent. Her mind spun with confusion. As the swats stung her backside, she was shaken back to her painful reality. She couldn't believe that her betrothed was actually spanking her. After the third strike, she came to her senses, reached up, grabbed his coat, and pulled herself off his lap.

"STOP IT!" she shouted. "How dare you, you dirty maggot! I'm supposed to be your wife, not your child. You don't have the right!" Tears ran down her face. "You don't have the right to beat me! ME! You're supposed to be the king someday. You should be merciful, not hateful!" Her face started to glow bright red. The commotion was overheard by her ladies-in-waiting, who by now had opened the door, and started to witness their verbal exchange.

"I'm not Malcolm the Merciful," the prince shouted back. "I'm Henry—the Horrible!" His face shone with such hatred, that the defiant little Audrianna trembled with fear. She began to break down and weep uncontrollably. The three ladies immediately rushed out of the bedchamber to rescue the princess. However, they dared not step in between the prince and the princess. Henry was the second most powerful man in the kingdom.

"Your Majesty," Rozelle softly replied, not accusingly, but firmly. At last, Henry grabbed Audrianna by the arm again and hauled her into her room. The three ladies followed. Henry threw her against her bed, walked out of the room, and slammed the door behind him. He then pulled a key from around his neck, placed it in the door and locked it. He then walked down the hall to his own room and slammed that door also. After the sounds of the slamming doors finished echoing throughout the hallways, the castle was quiet again.

"What a worm!" Castalia voiced. "Doesn't he know that these doors lock from the inside. All we have to do is this… and the door is no longer locked." At that, she slid the bolt to the left, and with a loud CLANK, the door popped open.

All three turned to look at the princess. Audrianna leaned over the bed with both her hands covering her backside. They could hear her weeping with her face buried in the mattress.

"What happened?" Rozelle asked, foregoing the normal protocol of addressing the crowned princess as Your Highness. The princess answered with her head still buried and her words deeply muffled.

"Pwenff Henfwee poof me offaw hiff nee ann bee mee!"

"Could you repeat that," Ethlyn asked. Audrianna lifted her head from the mattress. "Prince Henry put me over his knee and beat me!"

"He beat you?" the ladies chorused.

"He told me I was a naughty little girl, and I told him then to spank me." Audrianna answered.

"You told him to spank you?" Rozelle asked incredulously.

"We were angry with each other. I really didn't think he would do it."

"Let's see what damage he did to you," Castalia offered. Audrianna lifted the hem of her dress above her rump, while the ladies examined her. There were no lacerations, but her skin was beet red. The marks were sensitive to the touch, which Rozelle voiced she thought might end up bruised by morning.

Audrianna was infuriated! She quickly stripped off her dress without any help. She then proceeded to put on her training clothes, including her pants, button up shirt, and vest. She then painfully sat on the floor and saddled her feet with the shoes she wore for sword drill.

"Where are you going?" Ethlyn asked. "You can't go practice your baton this time of night."

"Oh, I'm not going to practice anything!" Audrianna dogmatically replied. "What are you planning to do?" Rozelle asked.

"Remember your promise, Rose?" Audrianna asked. "What promise?" Rozelle asked.

"You promised me that if we were under attack, you would let me jump out the window." Audrianna stepped up on the ledge of the small window of her room. A light wind coming into the window wisped her long hair to one side.

"I meant, if an enemy army was storming the castle, you could jump out the window, onto the tree limb, to save your life," Rozelle clarified.

"Well," Audrianna replied, "I was just under attack, and I am NOT staying here any longer. I will NOT be the wife of that monster!"

"But Your Highness," Ethlyn began to plead. Before they could say another word, Audrianna jumped out the window, and onto the limb under the ledge. However, the princess did not realise the limb was not as sturdy as it seemed.

As her feet landed on the limb, the limb shifted to one side, causing her to tumble headfirst towards the ground. She spun head over heels through the thick foliage of the tree. Audrianna's long hair whipped around her head and quickly became caught in the thicket of branches. The ladies-in-waiting watched helplessly as the princess dangled eight feet off the ground by her hair. Audrianna reached up and tried to yank her hair free, but eventually caused it to be more tightly knit within the twigs, leaves and limbs of the tree. She feebly kicked her feet to free herself, and lost one of her shoes.

Castalia began to panic at the sight of Audrianna hanging in a tree, fearful that the princess's life was in peril. Castalia ran out the door, down the hall, and down the stairs, yelling for help as she ran. Several of the guards came running to her rescue.

"What is it?" a guard inquired. "What's the matter?" another asked.

"The princess jumped out of her bedroom window, and is now hanging from the tree by her hair!"

"The princess?" "Yes!"

"Which tree?"

"Come," Rozelle calmly replied. "We'll show you." She quietly led the guards out the side door that opened to the castle garden. Hanging from the foliage of the tree were two skinny legs, one foot with a shoe and the other without. The legs appeared to be lifeless, but as they approached, the princess heard them running to her rescue, and began kicking her feet.

"How did she get up there?" one of the guards asked.

"She didn't go up from here," Ethlyn exclaimed. "She went down from up there." She pointed up to their bedroom window, which they could barely see through the thicket of branches and leaves.

One of the guards walked under the princess and put her feet on his shoulders. "Okay, Your Highness," he called to her. "I've got you down here. Can you free yourself from up there?" Audrianna twisted herself, squirmed, and bent her knees a few times.

"No," she answered. "My hair is all tangled in the limbs of the tree. I need someone to come and cut the branches free from my hair."

Before long, the whole castle was buzzing over Audrianna's predicament. The news finally made its way to the king, who came walking out to the terrace to see how the rescue was progressing. He kept hearing the frustration mount as to how the princess's hair was getting more and more tangled within the tree the more they tried to free her. Upon hearing their concern, the king left the terrace, walked up the stairs to Henry's room, and banged on the door. Henry answered and was surprised to see his father.

"Your wife is stuck in a tree outside her window. I recommend you do your duty as her husband, and as her king, and rescue her." The king abruptly turned around and walked back to his room. Henry stood at his door, watching his father walk off, wondering how Audrianna could have possibly gotten stuck in a tree. He quickly dressed, belted his sword to his side, and ran outside where much of the servants were gathered.

Henry walked under Audrianna and grabbed a hold of her

legs. He tugged on them a couple of times until she let out a high-pitched squeal.

"Ouch! My hair is caught in the branches. You're pulling my hair. It hurts!"

Henry had such an unpleasant evening, including his altercation with Audrianna. Now, seeing her stuck in the tree made him chuckle to himself. This definitely was an amusing sight to behold. However, he knew what he had to do to free the princess.

"Alright," he said to all the servants watching. "Every one of you need to go back to your rooms or your responsibilities. We don't need to embarrass Her Highness any further."

The crowd quickly dispersed as Henry assessed whether he should climb up the tree, or jump down to her level. Although it was risky, he felt jumping down to the princess was easier than climbing up to her. So, Henry made his way up to the second level, and into the princess's room. He climbed up on the ledge inside her bedroom window and looked down at the limb in question.

"That large limb is not stable," Rozelle warned, shouting at the prince from the ground. "The moment you try and stand on it, it will bow and shift."

"And you'll hang from your hair," Audrianna interjected.

Henry looked straight out and saw the tree trunk. It was a good two meters away. However, if he jumped towards the trunk and landed where the large branch met the trunk, he should do just fine. Henry straightened himself on the ledge, rubbed his hands together, took a couple of deep breaths, and lunged towards the trunk. Just as he planned, he landed squarely where the trunk and the branch met, and grabbed hold of the trunk to keep from falling.

Henry then climbed down several branches until he was level with the chaotic thicket of twisted hair, leaves, branches and twigs. There was no inkling as to where the ends to Audrianna's hair was in that jumbled mess.

"Maybe if you get an axe and chop several of the limbs off the tree," Audrianna suggested. "Once I'm free, Cassie, Ethel and

Rose can untangle the branches and help me comb the leaves and twigs out of my hair."

"You would have me chop up the king's prized magnolia?" Henry asked.

"It'll be okay," the princess assured him. "The branches will eventually grow back." "True," the prince declared. "But that's not all that grows back." At that, the prince drew his sword and began hacking away at Audrianna's long, brown hair.

CHAPTER 11

"NO!" the princess screamed, hanging from the thicket of the tree by her hair.

WHACK! Henry swung his razor-sharp sword, chopping a section of Audrianna's hair off.

"Please, no! Please, no! PLEASE—NO!" the princess begged, raising her hands in defence.

"Move your hands!" the prince demanded. "Move your hands or I'll cut off your hands as well." The princess lowered her hands and clenched her fists.

WHACK!

"Not my hair! PLEASE—not my hair!" WHACK!

With the third stroke of his sword, the princess broke free of the magnolia and dropped to the flower bed beneath her. Falling on her swollen rump, she sat stunned for a few seconds, then looked up at her ladies standing around her, and saw their bewildered faces. She reached her hands up and felt her hair—her jagged short hair! Frantic, she scurried to her feet, covered her head with her arms, and ran screaming through the castle to her bed chamber. Palace guards, servants, and magistrates moved to one side to avoid blocking the princess in her state of hysterics.

Audrianna ran into her room and straight to her vanity. She peered into the large mirror on the wall, and through tear-filled eyes, studied the condition of her hair. It was a dreadful sight! Her bangs were long in the middle and short on one side, cut at an odd angle. The part of her hair directly atop her head was so short, it stood up on end. None of her hair dropped past the bottom end of her ears, and both ears seemed to stick straight out from among the oddly cut strands of hair. Her hair was so horrifying! What was she going to do? What could she do? Years of carefully grooming her hair, daily brushing out every tangle, and now—THIS! She looked around the room and saw her large fluffy bath towel folded neatly at the end of her vanity table. As she heard the ladies walking up to her chamber door, she quickly grabbed the towel, wrapped it around her head, and laid her face on the table.

The ladies entered and saw the princess with her head covered and her face to the table. They could barely see the complete condition of her hair out in the garden due to how quickly Audrianna scampered away with her arms covering her head. Now, in the privacy of their bedchamber, Rozelle, Castalia, and Ethlyn were determined to ascertain the gravity of the situation.

Not knowing what to say to the weeping princess, Rozelle quietly reached out and laid hold of the towel and began to uncover Audrianna's hair.

"No!" she protested. Castalia and Ethlyn jumped back.

"Let's see how bad it really is, Your Highness," Rozelle recommended.

"I've seen it," Audrianna replied, wrapping the towel more firmly around her head. "It's bad. It's horrible!"

"Your Highness," Rozelle softly but firmly responded. Audrianna dropped her hands to her side. Rozelle slowly lifted the towel off the princess's head to reveal the carnage her betrothed had inflicted with his sword. No one said a word, but they all three made sympathetic guttural noises after fully investigating Audrianna's hair. One by one Audrianna's ladies-in-waiting wagged their heads with total resolve that nothing could be done other than wait for it to grow back out.

"Maybe we should cut the rest of it off," Ethlyn recommended. "You know, finish the job and let it all grow back evenly."

"I'm not walking around the castle looking like a flea-bitten farm girl. That's what they do to little girls who get bugs in their hair. I don't want to look like them."

"Well," Castalia replied, "As it stands, you look like a stray dog with scabies." Audrianna dropped her forehead against the table in disgust. Rozelle gave Castalia a haughty look of contempt. Castalia quietly mouthed an apology at her.

"I'm ugly! I'm hideous! I can never again show my face outside these walls ever again, until my hair completely grows back out. I just have no idea how long that will be. It will literally take years! I mean—YEARS!"

Suddenly, there was a firm knock on their chamber door. Everybody looked at each other as if to ask the same question, Who could that be? Audrianna quickly covered her head again with the towel. Ethlyn was the only one brave enough (or foolish enough) to walk to the door and open it just a crack to see who was knocking.

It was the king!

Ethlyn swung the door wide open and curtsied. "Your Majesty!" Ethlyn responded.

"Your Majesty," the two other ladies chorused, also curtsying. Audrianna remained seated, with her head covered, and her face prostrate on the vanity table.

"Good evening, ladies," the king greeted. "If I may be forward, I would like to speak to Her Highness privately, please."

The ladies all nodded and quietly excused themselves to the hallway. The king walked over to the vanity and placed his hand on the young princess's shoulder. Audrianna, still holding the towel over her head, looked up at the king.

"Your Majesty," has her soft reply.

"Audrianna," the king said, calling her by name, breaking social propriety. The young princess was startled by the king's familiarity of her. She turned her body from facing the mirror, to facing the king.

"I wanted to come talk to you," the king said nervously, as if something important was on his heart. "I know this week has been… probably the worst week in your entire life. I blame myself for that."

The king turned to see if there was a chair he could perch himself on, so his knees would not knock together from his nervousness. The closest thing to the vanity was a chest that the ladies stored their sleeping mats and night gowns. The king scooted it closer to Audrianna and sat down, closer to her level.

"I know you didn't ask to become Henry's wife, nor did you ask to become the crowned princess, not even to come to the castle to live. Your parents died. That was traumatic enough. Then my two envoys came and grabbed you and brought you here against your will. And the next thing you know—you're betrothed to the next king of Nadeau."

Audrianna dropped her hands into her lap, the towel still wrapped around her head, covering her hair. The last month and a half had indeed been one nightmare after another. The little princess remained silent. Her facial expression was a flat affect, with the exception of her eyes that had a look of bewilderment, like she was trying to make sense of all the king was saying.

"I wrongfully used you as a tool to prevent my son from taking the throne for another six years. I was afraid of what he might do with the kingdom. I didn't stop and realise what he might do to a precious little girl like you. I had no idea how special you are! You are intelligent, beautiful, witty. I am honoured to have you as the crowned princess, as if you were my own daughter. I am only sorry that you have to endure the abuse of my lousy son."

Audrianna's eyes dropped to the floor. She thought carefully about the words that Henry had spoken previously to her, just before he took her over his knee. He accused the king of favouritism, and how he would dote over Audrianna and return nothing to Henry but criticism and disapproval. Audrianna wanted to tell the king how he was treating his own son was wrong, and he shouldn't show such preference to the princess at the exclusion of the prince.

"Your Majesty," Audrianna replied, intending to share what Henry had told her on the steps of the grand staircase.

"Please," the king stopped her. "Let's not be so formal. Just call me, 'Papa.'"

When Malcolm asked her to call him "papa", she couldn't hold her emotions back anymore. It was a trigger that suddenly took her all the way back to her own father, holding her tightly in his arms and calling her his princess. She wanted to tell Malcolm about Henry, about the hurt and the betrayal he felt from the king. But her own feelings of betrayal and hurt over her hair being chopped off by Henry got the best of her. She couldn't bring herself to defend that monster!

"Oh, Papa," she cried, pulling the towel from around her head. "Look what he did!

Look at what happened to my beautiful hair!"

King Malcolm was aghast at the sight of Audrianna's hair. He knew that his son had cut some of the princess's hair to free her from the tree. How much exactly, the king hadn't known until the towel came off her head. He thought that Henry might have had to cut a small section that wouldn't come free, but now he realised the full extent of Henry's behaviour, and how far his resentment towards the princess led him.

Without another word to Audrianna, the king stood up and walked to the door. As he opened it, the three ladies-in-waiting stood waiting, leaning on the far side of the hallway wall, with their hands behind them as a barrier to keep their clothes from becoming soiled.

"Guards!" the king cried aloud. Three palace guards instantly snapped to attention in front of the king.

"Quickly, call for the royal hair cutter and have him sent to Her Royal Highness's chambers to do whatever necessary to repair her hair damage."

"At once, Your Majesty!" the guards answered. All three turned and dashed down the hall, down the staircase, and through the castle to the lower quarters to find the royal haircutter. Within half an hour, the same man that was responsible for braiding and fixing Audrianna's hair for her coronation, came to repair the savage chopping of her hair.

"What the heck happened to your beautiful hair?" the haircutter shouted aloud the moment he saw the princess.

"His Majesty the Prince cut it with a sword," she replied.

"Your hair was the most perfect in all of Nadeau! Such a terrible crime to do such a horrible thing. If he wasn't the crowned prince, I would say he should be flogged." The man went straight to work at trimming this bang, cutting to match one side of her head with the other side. He tilted her head to one side, then the other. He had her look up, trimmed a little bit of hair, then he made her tilt her head down, and trimmed a little bit. "I am so sorry, Your Highness," the man would say each time he had to trim a section of her hair. Audrianna half-smiled at his responses, knowing the sight of her hair hurt the haircutter more than it seemed to hurt her. She looked up periodically at her ladies who stood silently in a line behind the haircutter, their hands folded in front of them. Each time the man tilted Audrianna's head to the left, the ladies would tilt their heads to her right. Then he would tilt her head to the right, and all three would tilt their heads, in unison, to the left. When she was asked to tilt her head up, they tilted their heads down, and likewise. The princess realised that the three were doing it for no other reason than to entertain Her Highness while suffering through such a debilitating experience.

After what seemed to Audrianna as an eternity, the haircutter finished what work he could do in restoring a reasonable look to the princess's hair. Audrianna was turned to face the large mirror over her vanity. She peered into the glass and took a deep breath and sighed. There was little that could be done on the very top of her head. The haircutter did his best to even it out, but her hair wanted to stand straight up. It was so short. Her bangs were almost completely gone on one side, but the rest were cut at an angle to give the appearance that her hair was combed to one side. As far as her hair over her ears, they still had some length to them, but now were cut just above her jawline to make them even all the way around. Audrianna tilted her head from one side and then to the other. She shook her head. She looked like a boy. Not even closed enough to resemble a pageboy. She looked up at the haircutter, who raised his hands in resignation.

"At least it will one day grow back," he replied. "That's the wonderful thing about hair. Just please come to me the next time you need your hair trimmed. Not your husband!" Audrianna rolled her eyes.

"I will never let him touch my hair again, if I can help it," she answered.

The haircutter left and the princess was left alone with Rozelle, Castalia, and Ethlyn. Audrianna stood in the middle of the room as the three of them circled and inspected the end result of her hair repair. Ethlyn ran her fingers through the sides of Audrianna's head, and suggested if curling her hair might give the princess more of a feminine appearance. Castalia brushed the top of her head, recommending they tease her hair to see if it might cause it to lay down on top. All the while, Rozelle simply stood facing the princess with her hands on her hips.

"What do you think, Rozelle?" the other two ladies asked her. Audrianna looked up at her to see if she had any sage ideas. Rozelle slowly shook her head.

"I think," Rozelle finally commented. "I think the princess needs to refrain from jumping out any more windows."

Audrianna dropped her head with a sheepish grin. She was rather ashamed of the fuss and problems that the day seemed to have issued. But now it was late, and way past their normal schedule of bedtime. The three ladies helped to dress the princess for bed, except for the routine of brushing out her beautiful long hair. That part was deeply missed and bereaved.

"Don't worry," Ethlyn chimed, "In another four to six weeks your hair will have grown out enough that we can curl or braid it. You just wait and see." Audrianna didn't care about what her hair would look like in four to six weeks. She just hoped that her hair would be fully grown out again within the next six years.

The princess was helped into bed, while Rozelle, Castalia, and Ethlyn laid down on their sleeping mats, and the room grew quiet again. Audrianna quickly fell into a sound sleep. It had been quite an eventful day. More than just a full daily schedule. She had enjoyed the countryside outside the walls of the castle, discovered a severed head, been privy to an executive meeting in the royal court, spanked by the prince, jumped out the bedroom window, hung from a tree by her hair, and had her hair chopped off. Yes, it had been quite an eventful day.

However, a little over an hour into the night, the princess was again startled by familiar sounds. It was that creepy sound of a person moaning somewhere in the castle. Audrianna was frightened all over again. She rolled onto the floor with a THUD, and slid underneath the bed. Rather than wake one of the ladies, she decided to listen carefully to the sounds.

It didn't come at regular intervals, which meant there was no way to predict when the moaning would happen. But each time the sound appeared, she listened intently to figure out if it was a person, or an animal, or perhaps a bird. Each time Audrianna heard the noise, she couldn't imagine anything else but a person moaning in pain. There had to be someone in the castle either being tortured, or hurting from an ailment. She considered investigating to see where the moaning was originating. But she was so tired from her long day, and frightened of what—or who—she might discover. She decided to go back to sleep, but not in her bed. She once again pulled her comforter off the bed, and wrapped herself in it—under her bed, and fell asleep.

The next morning, Audrianna informed the ladies that she had heard the noises again. The ladies were weary from the drama the day before so they paid her no mind. They hoped that this day would be more of a regular schedule. The first week watching over the newly crowned princess was quite an extraordinary experience. Nothing like what they were expecting.

This time, the princess was dressed for breakfast thirty minutes early, even before the king and prince had arrived. This was an amazing feat, since the three ladies had to spend extra time grooming Audrianna's hair to make it presentable.

There, the princess sat, hands in her lap, shoulders straight against the back of her chair, and dress neatly draped over her lap and chair. The sides of her head were braided tightly against her scalp, and the top of her head was combed over and began to slightly rise from its place. But the princess chose to sit as proper as she knew how, and pretend that nothing was out of the ordinary regarding her appearance. And if anyone mentioned her hair, such as the prince, she would simply ignore the comment as if it was never said. She was the crowned princess. That meant something.

The king joined Audrianna for breakfast, but the prince was nowhere to be found. They both started eating without him. The king told her that he probably would be a bit sparse in appearance. There were already whisperings in the castle about how the prince had chopped off the princess's beautiful hair and how upset many of the women were. To many a man, short hair is not a big deal. But to a woman, her hair is her glory! To hack off a woman's hair was equal to cutting off her nose. And, to hear how wretched the princess's hair looked, made many of the men angry as well. It was as if the prince desecrated a portrait of his own mother, Queen Luella—the Beloved.

"Well," Audrianna responded, "I can't say that I feel any pity for the prince, under the circumstances."

"If you would like," the king offered, "I can commission one of my wig makers to fashion a wig that looks exactly like your hair before the tree incident."

Audrianna thought to herself, It wasn't an "incident", it was a brutal attack!

"No thank you," she kindly replied. "I don't wish to cover up what happened to my hair. I expect most everyone who sees me, and has not heard the story, will take one look at me and say, 'What happened to your hair?' And I will tell them, the crowned prince chopped it off with his sword."

"Do you feel that to be wise?" the king asked, thinking of how that might incite a lot of hostility towards the crown.

"If I must live with my shame, he should live with his!"

Prince Henry never made it to breakfast. The ladies escorted the young princess back to the room, and helped her change into her exercise clothes. What was odd on this day was the fact that the ladies themselves also changed into similar attire.

"Why are you three changing clothes," Audrianna asked. "Today, we all will be participating," Rozelle answered.

"Really?" Audrianna asked excitedly. "You mean, all four of us are going to practice with the baton today?"

"No," Ethlyn answered. "We all have our specific disciplines that we have learned over the years."

"Disciplines?" the princess asked, not knowing what she meant. "You'll see," Rozelle assured her.

Audrianna and her three escorts walked together to the courtyard where Rupp was waiting to do more training. At the exact moment that Rupp laid eyes on the princess, he blurted out in surprise.

"What on earth happened to your hair, Your Highness?"

"His Majesty, the prince, cut my hair with a sword last night," she answered Rupp, as promised.

"His Majesty did what?" Rupp exclaimed. "Why would he cut your hair with his sword?"

"Her Highness was hanging from a tree by her hair," Rozelle answered.

"Why was Your Highness hanging from a tree by her hair?" Rupp asked the princess. "I was wanting to run away," Audrianna answered.

"Why did Your Highness wish to run away?" Rupp continued to question. "Because His Majesty, Prince Henry, took me over his knee and spanked me

yesterday," she answered. Rupp looked at Audrianna for a few seconds, wanting to ask another question, but didn't like the direction the answers were taking him.

"Let's begin with our training," Rupp responded, deciding to change the subject to the agenda at hand. "As most of you know, the royal council met yesterday to decide what should be done about the impending Andjety threat. Our friend and comrade, Pitt, was brutally murdered, and his head was impaled on a post just outside the castle walls. It was discovered by Her Highness."

"It was horrible!" the princess confirmed.

"Yes," Rupp affirmed. "Now, everyone of us have been trained with special skills," Rupp pointed to Audrianna, "or are being trained with special skills. So, during this time of exercise, we will continue to sharpen our tools of defence to fend off any threat of attack."

Everybody stood motionless looking at Rupp as he paced back and forth in front of them.

"Any questions?" Rupp asked. Silence.

"Her Royal Highness is learning sword fighting. Lady Castalia, what is your special fighting skill?"

"The crossbow," Castalia answered.

"Oooh!" Audrianna and the other two ladies chorused. "Very good," Rupp responded. "Let's see a demonstration."

Castalia walked across the courtyard to a crossbow sitting on a table. Picking it up, she loaded an arrow into its slot, and pulled the bow back until it clicked without any effort. She then proceeded to the target area, lifted her arm with the crossbow straight out in front of her, and pulled the trigger. The arrow sliced through the air and hit the target, just above and to the right of the bullseye. Everyone applauded such a nice shot for a cold beginning.

"Not bad," Rupp responded. "That was a fine display of your skills." Turning to Ethlyn, Rupp asked her, "Lady Ethlyn? Your special skills—if you please."

Ethlyn walked to the other side of the courtyard and opened a large wooden box with screened windows on all four sides of the box.

"What is she doing?" Audrianna whispered to Rozelle.

"Shhh! Wait and see," Rozelle answered. Audrianna twisted her mouth and wrinkled her nose in impatience. Before long, Ethlyn turned around to display a large leather glove on her hand that extended almost to her elbow. On that glove sat a large brown and white falcon.

"It's a bird," Audrianna exclaimed. "Shhh!" Rozelle scolded. "It's a falcon." "Looks like a bird," she replied.

"So, your special skill is falconry," Rupp said. "Yes, Lord Rupp," she answered.

"A demonstration, if you please."

Ethlyn walked to the middle of the courtyard with the falcon latched to her glove by its talons. Upon the bird's head sat a leather cover to shield the falcon's eyes so it would not be distracted before the trainer could give the bird direction. As Ethlyn lifted the cover off the falcon's head and held the bird up, over her own head, the well-trained falcon spread its wings out, waiting for the signal to be given. Ethlyn made a loud and distinct clicking noise with her tongue, upon which the falcon soared from her hand and zipped straight up into the air. Before the falcon flew too far away, Ethlyn gave a different clicking noise upon which the bird whipped around, and zoomed back through the courtyard like an arrow, then circled the castle. As Ethlyn clicked another command to the falcon, the feathered comrade came to an accurate, soft landing on Ethlyn's glove. Everyone applauded.

"Amazing, Lady Ethlyn," Rupp commended.

"What good does a stupid bird do in the heat of battle," Henry shouted as he walked into the courtyard from inside the castle. Ethlyn grinned as she placed the covering back over the falcon's head.

"A falcon can be a valuable asset in time of battle. They can report how large an army is that is approaching the castle."

"How do they do that?" Audrianna asked.

"Well," Ethlyn explained, "Lu is trained to circle an enemy army in a special pattern to tell me from what direction they are approaching, and about how large the area of the army covers. If there are enemy soldiers hidden in the crevices of a mountain, Lu will swoop down to point them out."

"You named your stupid rooster, Lu?" Henry asked.

"Begging your pardon, Your Majesty," Ethlyn replied. "Lu is a female. I call her Lu, which is short for Luella—in honour of your mother." Henry rolled his eyes.

"Why did you pick a female falcon instead of a male falcon?" Audrianna asked. "Is it because you want to breed more falcons?"

"Not really," Ethlyn answered. She bent down as if she planned to whisper a secret to Audrianna, but never lowered her voice. "I chose a female, because they are smarter than males." She winked at the princess, who grinned in return.

"And you, Lady Rozelle," Rupp pointed to. "Your special skill, if you please." "Well, my special skill is similar to His Majesty's," Rozelle answered.

"My skill?" Henry asked.

"Yes," Rozelle said. "My special skill is swordsmanship."

"Well," Henry countered. "That is one of many special skills that I possess." "Excellent," Rupp responded. "Let's have the two of you give us a demonstration at the same time."

"What?" Henry asked. "You don't expect me to fight a woman, do you?"

"Yes," Rupp answered, his face expressionless. "The Witch is a woman. You most likely will have to fight her someday, and I expect you to win."

The prince and Rozelle walked together to the table to select their choice of swords that they intended to fight each other with. Henry picked up a handsome looking sword with a beautiful handle. Rozelle chose a similar sword, but one whose handle seemed a bit more worn.

"What say?" Henry snapped at Rozelle. "First blood?" "Sounds acceptable. I hope you don't bleed easily."

"I am way out of your league, little chamber maid," Henry slighted Rozelle. Rozelle, who had already taken her stance, straightened up.

"Hold on, please. I wish to shed some excess baggage." Rozelle walked over to Castalia and Audrianna. With her back to Henry and Rupp, she discreetly began unbuttoning the front of her dress.

"What does first blood mean," Audrianna asked.

"The prince wished to sword fight with me until one of us is able to cut and draw from the other. That is called, 'First Blood.'"

With Castalia's help, Rozelle shed the first layer of clothing, then picked up her sword again, and walked over to Henry. Henry stood speechless at the sight of Rozelle wearing only her undergarments.

Now, in reality, Rozelle had just as much material covering her body as the other ladies. Her arms were not bare. Her legs were not bare. Neither was there any skin showing between her neck and her ankles, save her hands and fingers. It was the thought that Rozelle was standing in the middle of the courtyard revealing her undergarments to the prince. It was quite scandalous!

To the prince, it was a distraction. To Rupp, is was humorous. To Castalia and Ethlyn, is was bold and audacious. To Audrianna, it was courageous on one hand, but unsettling on another. The princess wasn't sure how she felt about her Lady in Waiting exposing herself to her betrothed. He was a monster in her estimation, but that didn't excuse him looking at other women.

Henry took his stance opposite Rozelle. Rozelle took her stance. She waited for the prince to make his move so she could deflect it. He didn't move.

"What's taking so long, Your Majesty?" Rozelle asked. "Make your move, sire."

"I can't," he answered. "I don't feel I can look at you in good conscience to find a respectable spot of attack."

"You can't look at me?" Rozelle asked. "Am I so hideous?"

"Um," the prince tried to respond. "I am just not used to seeing maidens in their undergarments."

"Is Your Majesty saying," Rupp remarked. "that of all the

young maidens you have kissed, you never once saw one of them in their undergarments?"

Henry stood speechless and motionless in front of the partly clad Lady in Waiting. "That's right," he answered partly blushing.

"How many maidens has Your Majesty kissed?" Audrianna demanded to know.

Henry glanced her way. The princess wore a scowl of disapproval on her face. "A few," was his pacifying answer.

"A few dozen," Rupp remarked. Audrianna frowned all the more.

"I've never kissed anyone," the princess remarked, making a statement of her displeasure of his antics.

"I'm twenty-five, Your Highness," he defended himself, circling the courtyard in a mirrored stance against Rozelle. "I'm more than twice your age."

Audrianna wrinkled her nose at Henry while continuing to glare at him. Henry obviously was having difficulty maintaining his composure against the Lady in her undergarments.

"Just don't forget who you're betrothed to," Audrianna replied. Henry shot a look back at Audrianna with a raised eyebrow as if to say, I know who my betrothed is— unfortunately!

Finally, as Henry was distracted with the princess, Rozelle swung her sword towards the prince, who deflected the strike with a CLANG! He immediately counter-swung towards Rozelle's torso who deflected his strike with a TWANG! Back and forth, back and forth the two evenly matched opponents banged their swords against each other's. For a good ten minutes they fought, neither one of them shedding blood.

Finally, Rozelle took an evasive stance by extending her right leg out in front of her. She grabbed the legging of her undergarment, pulled it up slightly, exposing the lower part of her lower leg. Henry froze with embarrassment and looked away out of royal courtesy. At that moment, Rozelle struck the prince in his upper arm with her razor-sharp sword, leaving a small gash in his shirt and causing blood to spurt out, wetting his shirt.

"Ouch!" the prince exclaimed. "You cut my arm!"

"As I said," Rozelle declared, "I hope you don't bleed easily."
"Very good, Lady Rozelle," Rupp commended.

"It's not fair to fight against a woman who uses her feminine qualities to distract her opponent and then to strike," Henry protested.

"As I said," Rupp reminded, "The Witch is a beautiful woman that will use whatever means she can to distract, cheat, tempt, or whatever to get her way and to kill the opposition. Your Majesty must harden his heart against any type of sinister distractions that would take your mind off the present here and now."

Rozelle returned to the other two ladies-in-waiting who helped her put her outer dress back on and button it up. She then returned her sword back to the table and walked over to Audrianna who by now had her arms folded and wore an ugly scowl. Rozelle affectionately put her arm around the disapproving princess. Audrianna looked at Henry as he walked by. Even though he lost the sparring match, his partial grin showed that he obviously enjoyed the sultry encounter.

"You know," Audrianna commented to Henry, "I'm going to look like that in six years."

Rozelle squeezed Audrianna close to her and cupped the princess's chin with her other hand. "One can hope, Your Highness," Rozelle replied. Audrianna rolled her eyes and smirked at Rozelle.

Chapter 12

The prince and the princess continued to train along with the three ladies-in-waiting up until it was time to change and get ready for royal court. They had no court the day before, so everybody was expecting a large crowd to appear, hoping to have their case heard by the royal family. As Henry began walking back to his room to change for court and bandage his arm, Audrianna ran up to join him. The princess's three ladies-in-waiting lagged behind to help feed and pet Ethlyn's falcon.

"How do you like my new hair cut?" Audrianna asked the prince. Henry took one look at his handiwork, then looked away.

"How do you enjoy walking on the ground again?" he retorted.

"Much better than sitting, thanks," she answered, referring to how painful her buttocks felt after the prince spanked her. Henry didn't respond.

They continued to walk together in silence until they came to the grand staircase. The staircase represented the spot where the altercation between the two of them started. They both paused as if paying their own due respects to the event the day before.

As they walked up the steps in tandem, Audrianna asked Henry a question that was burning in the back of her mind.

"Henry," Audrianna asked. "Do we have any prisoners that are being held captive somewhere in the castle?" Henry looked down at the princess and read the sincere expression on her face.

"Prisoner?" he asked. "We have no prisoners in the castle. All criminals are taken to the jail the other side of the city."

"That's what I've been told," Audrianna replied. "Do we have anybody in the castle that is sick or injured that you know of?"

Henry began to worry where this line of questioning was leading.

"What are you wanting to know exactly?" he inquired, stopping near the top of the staircase, and turning to look down at his betrothed. Audrianna took a deep breath. None of the ladies believed that she had been hearing moaning throughout the night, and she certainly didn't want Henry to have more opportunity to make fun of her.

"Well," she said. "I have been hearing some strange noises almost every night since I began staying in my royal bedchamber. They sound like someone moaning, or an animal howling. But I can't figure out what it is."

Immediately, when Audrianna said 'howling', Henry knew exactly what she was talking about. He was familiar with the noise. He straightened up, put his hands on his hips, and turned his head to see if the ladies had caught up with them, or if anyone else were within earshot. He then looked into the princess's face and solemnly answered her. "Your Highness," he said with a serious tone. "The sounds you hear are the moanings

of the castle ghost."

"A ghost?" Audrianna repeated, turning her head and wrinkling her nose at Henry.

She studied Henry's face to see any evidence that he was putting one over on her. "That's right."

"A ghost is haunting the castle?" she asked sceptically.

"Oh, this ghost has been walking the halls of the castle for decades," Henry replied. "Not everybody hears the moanings. They are the cries of the spirit of King Horatio the Aged."

Audrianna's eyes grew wide as she listened to Henry convincingly spin his yarn concerning the nightly noises echoing through the castle.

"He was my grandfather who built this castle more than sixty years ago. Rumour has it that the same year the castle was completed, King Horatio was killed by a large stone falling on him from the northwest tower."

"Oh," Audrianna responded. "Poor Horatio!"

"Yes," Henry replied. "So now, the ghost of old Horatio wanders the hallways night after night, seeking the man, woman, or child responsible for dropping the tower stone on top of him."

"Is he dangerous?" Audrianna asked.

"Only if he believes you might be the one who killed him. And since you can hear him moan, it means—he is after you!"

Audrianna's face gave a fearful look.

"What can I do to convince him I didn't do it?"

"Who knows?" Henry replied, lowering his voice to a deeper, more sinister octave. "Who can argue with a spirit? You can't see them. You can't touch them. And spirits don't talk to us. Horatio just wanders the halls, looking for justice."

Audrianna turned to look down the hall where their bedchambers were. She then turned to Henry with an expression of desperation on her face.

"I don't want Horatio to come after me," she said. "I'm afraid he'll hurt me because he thinks I dropped a stone on top of him. What should I do?"

"Well," Henry began to reply, but the three ladies finally caught up with Audrianna. "I'll tell you later—at royal court," he promised. Audrianna nodded, then turned to face her ladies coming up the stairs. Henry walked into his room and shut the door behind him. Audrianna and her ladies walked back to their room.

All the while the ladies dressed the princess, and while Audrianna sat through royal court, she could think of nothing else but what Henry had told her. If the moanings she heard at night were the cries of dead King Horatio, then Henry had answers she needed to hear. However, the thought that he might be preying on her gullibility also continued to race through her mind. Audrianna was indeed wise beyond her years, but, coming from a simple peasant family, she was exceptionally superstitious.

Finally, after painfully waiting through several hours of court proceedings, the king pounded his sceptre on the floor and announced that court was dismissed. All three royals stood to their feet. Henry and king Malcolm exited out the side door, opposite from the door of the main entrance to the courtroom. Audrianna quickly made chase to stop Henry and talk to him.

As the princess quickly made her way through the side corridor to find the prince, her three ladies called after her.

"Your Highness," Castalia shouted. "Your Highness, wait!"

Audrianna stopped, not seeing any sign of the prince in the back corridors leading to the grand staircase. The ladies approached her.

"Why did Your Highness run off without us?" Rozelle asked. Audrianna loved her ladies-in-waiting, but so far, they hadn't believed a word she shared concerning the nightly moaning and howling noises. She was afraid that her companions would discourage her from talking to or listening to Henry, taken his recent treatment of the princess. But she needed answers.

"I don't need babysitters, Rose," she snapped. All three ladies stopped cold. What hurtful words came dripping out of the princess's mouth to the very three that had done nothing but encourage and support her.

"We aren't your babysitters," Castalia replied. "But we are responsible in making sure Your Highness is safe." Audrianna suddenly realised how hurtful she was being.

"I'm sorry, Cassie," she said. "I need to talk to Henry, and I need to speak to him privately."

"As you wish, Your Highness," Rozelle softly responded. "We will be in your chambers preparing to help change your attire for supper." Rozelle gracefully turned towards the staircase and step-by-step, walked up the stairs to the hallway leading to the princess's room. The other two ladies followed behind her.

Audrianna walked up the stairs to the hallway, walked past her door, and up to the prince's. As she knocked on the door, Henry opened it just a crack.

"Your Highness," Henry greeted.

"I am eager for you to finish telling me about King Horatio," the princess replied. "Especially how to keep him from coming into my room at night."

"Yes, Your Highness," Henry acknowledged, swinging the door wide open and stepping out into the hallway. The prince looked down both directions to the hallway, then stared down at the princess.

"Well?" Audrianna asked expectantly.

"The answer to your question," Henry answered, "is turnips."
"Pardon?" the princess responded.

"Turnips, Your Highness. As many as you can eat."

"I have to eat turnips to keep the ghost of King Horatio away from me?" Audrianna asked.

"Yes, Your Highness. It is a well-known fact that grandpa Horatio detested turnips.

He wouldn't go near them."

"I don't like them either," Audrianna protested.

"Well," Henry replied, "suffice it to say, if you want the ghost to stay away from you, you might consider taking up eating turnips."

"Do I have to swallow them?" the princess asked. "Or can I just chew them up and spit them out?"

"You have to ingest enough turnips that the ghost can smell it on you at all times. Smell them on your breath, smell them coming out your pores, and smell them on your clothes. After a while, the moanings will fade away, and the ghost will stay away from you."

Audrianna grimaced. Turnips. How could she possibly stomach a plate full of turnips? The princess returned and walked back to the room where her ladies-in-waiting were ready to change the princess's formals to dinner wear.

At supper, Audrianna and Henry sat opposite each other, as usual, with the king at the head of the table. The princess's ladies-in-waiting sat in the kitchen, eating their own supper. The servers brought platters full of cheeses, breads, and fruits like they always did. Only this time, when one of the servers asked the royal family if there was anything they would like brought to them, Audrianna quickly responded.

"Yes," she quickly answered. "Are there any turnips in the kitchen?" "Turnips?" the server asked.

"Turnips?" the king asked. "Turnips," Audrianna confirmed.

"Your Highness wishes us to prepare you a cooked turnip?" the server asked. "Several," Audrianna answered. "Maybe, four. No—three."

"Why on earth would you want to eat turnips?" The king asked. Henry held his napkin to his face and chuckled under his breath. "They are peasant food. Pig food, even."

"Well," Audrianna commented, "I once was a common peasant girl. I'm not used to all this rich food that's served here at the royal palace. Not that I really like turnips, but I feel I need some variety in my diet."

"Variety is one thing," the king responded. "Turnips are another. I'm sure the kitchen can find a vegetable that is more agreeable than a turnip."

Within ten minutes the server returned to the dining room with three steaming turnips. The aroma from the cooked turnip caused the king to gag. He did not find the idea of someone eating cooked turnips, in the royal dining hall, at all appealing.

Audrianna poked the turnip with her fork to see how tender the vegetable was. Aside from being hot, the turnip seemed just as firm after being cooked as she imagined it to be straight from the garden. She questioned why she was putting herself through this ordeal, and then her mind raced back to the frightening noises that continued to echo through the castle at night. Henry told her that the ghost of king Horatio was offended by turnips, and she was determined to make these turnips offend him to the best of her ability.

With great effort, the princess sliced a section off the first turnip with her knife and fork, then stuck the slice in her mouth. The earthy taste of the vegetable made Audrianna want to immediately spit it out. She sat in her chair for a few seconds, letting the piece of turnip rest in her mouth without chewing. What was she doing, she thought? Slowly she began to gnaw the hard piece of turnip in her mouth.

She chewed… and chewed… and chewed… and chewed.

The piece of food was not getting softer, and she didn't seem to be effectively grinding it up, either. Finally, after what seemed to take the entire dinner hour, the princess was able to choke down the first slice of turnip. Tears welled up in her eyes from the effort of choking down what seemed to be indigestible food. She gave out a deep sigh of relief that the first bite had been swallowed. Looking at her plate she wondered how on earth she could get through just her first turnip.

"Are you really going to eat all three of those turnips?" the prince asked with a subtle smirk on his face. Audrianna cut another slice off the turnip and stuck it in her mouth.

"Yeth," the princess replied with the slice of turnip partially sticking out of her mouth. "I'm twying. Did you want thum?"

"Why are you doing this?" the king asked shaking his head. "Vegetables have no nourishing benefits," as was the common sentiment among the royalty back in the days of Nadeau.

"I know," Audrianna grimly replied, a tear streaking down her cheek as she swallowed. "But I miss them so much."

As the princess bit into the third slice, she imagined the turnip to be food that was more to her liking. She chewed the rigid portion of turnip, all the while pretending she was eating one of her favourite sweetbreads. Her fourth bite of turnip, she pretended the vegetable was a well-done steak. Before long, she was able to arduously swallow the entire vegetable.

As Audrianna looked at the remaining two turnips on her

plate, she decided that she needed to think less about what she was eating or whether she liked it, and focus her mind on other things instead. As she took one bite after another, the princess studied the frescos and paintings on the walls. She imagined interacting with the people in the paintings. Whatever she could do to distract herself from what she was eating.

By the time she choked down the second turnip, her untrained stomach began protesting. She felt her stomach rumble and grumble. Maybe she had eaten enough. Two turnips were not enough food to sustain her until morning, but she no longer had any appetite to eat anything else.

Horatio better appreciate how much I did for him, she thought.

By this time Audrianna's ladies joined her in the dining room and followed her back to their bedchamber. Every step that the princess took seemed to churn the unwanted food in her stomach. As she climbed the steps of the grand staircase, she thought for sure she was going to vomit up both turnips on the top step. She weighed in her mind if leaving turnip vomit on the stairs would chase the spirit of Horatio away, or if she should try to keep it down so he might smell it on her. She agonised at keeping her supper down as she kept walking until she made it to her room.

"Is Her Highness alright," Rozelle asked Audrianna.

"I'm fine," she answered. "I just ate some food that didn't agree with me." "What did Your Highness eat for supper?" Ethlyn asked.

"Mainly, two turnips," Audrianna replied.

"Turnips?" Castalia responded. "Why would Your Highness eat turnips?" "Because," Audrianna began to explain, then looked at the incredulous looks on her

ladies' faces. "Never mind," she said. "I don't wish to talk about it right now."

The ladies helped undress the little princess, then helped slip her nightgown over the top of her head. As Castalia untied all her small braids on the side of her head, Audrianna was reminded once again of how Henry had sliced off her hair with his sword. *Why on earth did I listen to him about eating turnips?* she thought. *What are those nasty vegetables going to do to me?*

As they helped the princess into bed, Audrianna's stomach hurt as well as her chest. She could still feel the food rumbling in her stomach. As firm as the turnip seemed in her mouth, she wondered how long it would take to fully digest in her stomach. Rozelle covered her up with the large comforter, and Ethlyn and Castalia tucked her in on both sides. Audrianna then wound herself up in her blanket by balling up into the foetal position to help alleviate her stomach and chest cramps.

Within minutes of the lamps being lowered in the room, Audrianna began burping wildly one after the other. Each burp seemed louder than the last. Yet, with every burp, the tightness in her chest and the discomfort in her stomach grew less and less. The taste of the turnips came back in her mouth.

However, as the princess's discomfort lessened, the more she tried to burb, to completely alleviate her cramps. As the cramps lessened, the more she drifted off to sleep. Just as she was about to fall asleep, a sudden surge of discomfort moved through the lower half of her stomach. Her eyes popped open and she realised she was going to need to jump out of bed rather urgently and find her chamber pot. As her feet hit the floor, the muscles in her abdomen tightened, causing her to involuntarily expel a surplus of gas with a loud flapping rumble. The three ladies, who were fast asleep, shot up from their mats, alarmed by the unexpected noise.

"What was that?" "What happened?" "What's going on?"

Audrianna walked from the far side of her bed, over to where the startled ladies were sitting up.

"It's okay," the princess declared. "I was just chasing the ghost of King Horatio from the room."

"You were what?" Rozelle asked, still half asleep.

"Don't worry," Audrianna said. "I don't think Horatio will come near this room for some time."

By now, the aroma of the princess's expulsion had drifted to where the ladies sat. "Oh, my heavens!" Castalia declared. "That chamber pot needs to be emptied right

away!"

"There's nothing in the pot," Audrianna said to Castalia. "It was a bad case of flatulence."

"Whew!" Ethlyn remarked. "That smells ten times worse than the original aroma of cooked turnips." All three ladies' eyes began watering. They covered their faces with their blankets attempting to filter out the horrid smell. After several minutes of tossing, turning, and gasping for fresh air, the gaseous scent dissipated. Although everyone was awake, the room was quiet again.

As everyone lay awake, eyes wide open, a voice could be heard from the castle watchtower, piercing the quietness of the evening.

"It is the third hour of the night, and all is well!" Silence.

"Who the heck is Horatio?" Ethlyn finally asked, breaking the stillness of the room.

CHAPTER 13

The next morning, Audrianna felt rather foolish with herself for allowing Henry to beguile her the way he did. It dawned on her throughout the night that had the ghost of Horatio been a true story, more people would be talking about it. Moreover, neither the king, nor the prince seemed inclined to eat turnips—ever—and the king didn't see any value in them. If anybody had a reason to be afraid of a vengeful ghost, Audrianna reasoned, it would most likely be Henry.

Now, having eaten only two turnips the night before, the princess was ravenous. As breakfast was served, Audrianna dove into the food like she had just walked out of a desert after being lost for the past two weeks. She ate so aggressively that the king dared not interrupt her, lest she might turn on him and bite his hand.

"Feeling better, my dear?" the king asked little Audrianna as her rapid consumption began to taper off to a subtle nibbling.

"Yes, Papa," Audrianna answered. "I was rather hungry after last night's meal. It was difficult to last through the night having eaten only two turnips."

"Tell me again why you chose to eat turnips rather than the meal that was already prepared," the king inquired. Audrianna decided to lay everything out on the table, even if it meant looking foolish in front of the king.

"I'm afraid of the ghost of grandpa Horatio," the princess answered.

"Grandpa who?" the king responded. With the king's response, Audrianna knew immediately that Henry had again manipulated her.

"Grr!" she grunted. "Henry told me there was a ghost haunting the castle, and that it was the departed spirit of his grandfather, king Horatio, who built this castle sixty years ago and was tragically killed by a falling stone which causes him to haunt the castle looking for the person responsible for his death." Audrianna took a deep breath and sighed. Malcolm sat back, taking in everything that the princess told him. A smile shot across his face, and he let out a chuckle.

"Well, now," the king answered. "Let me help clear up this tangled mess by saying you should have known better than to trust Henry to give you a straight answer." Audrianna turned up the corner of her mouth and rolled her eyes.

"My father's name was Albert, not Horatio. He was not a castle-builder as much as he was a womaniser."

"A what?" Audrianna asked.

"Also," Malcolm continued, ignoring the princess's question, "King Albert did not build this castle, it was given to him as a wedding gift from the Andjety king, Xandju, who was grateful for Nadeau's assistance in supplying aid during their first liberation war. And Albert was not killed by a falling stone, he was killed by a flung dagger."

"Who threw the dagger at poor grandfather Albert?"

"Poor grandmother Agnus, my mother, in a jealous rage," Malcolm explained. "What!" Audrianna asked surprised.

"Yep," Malcolm replied. "Caught him with a couple of chamber maids, doing extra chamber activities. I was already the king by then."

"So, who is Horatio?" Audrianna asked.

"Don't know," Malcolm admitted. "I don't have anyone in my family by that name. Best ask your husband." Audrianna shook her head in disbelief that she allowed herself to be taken in by such trickery and superstition.

As the princess and her ladies began walking back to the room to change for sword practice, Henry came bounding down the grand staircase in the opposite direction. As he locked eyes on the princess, he realised by the look on Audrianna's face that she had figured out his elaborate scheme regarding the spirit of Horatio. His first inclination was to turn around and bound back up the stairs to his room. As he turned, the princess called after him.

"Hold, there, young man!" the princess cried out.

"Young man?" Henry responded. "I am two and a half times your age, little girl." "Who you took advantage of last night. I ate turnips because of you. I had stomach

cramps all night because of you. And I had horrible flatulence last night because of you." Henry cupped his hand over his mouth, attempting to cover his laughter.

"Don't laugh at me, Henry the Horrible!" the princess exclaimed, smiling and chuckling also. With the princess starting to chuckle, Henry laughed even more.

"It's not funny!" the princess scolded. Before long, both the prince and the princess were laughing so loud, tears began welling up in their eyes. The three ladies-in-waiting looked at each other in disbelief at this unusual mutual exchange between the prince and princess.

"Okay," the prince coughed out, regaining his composure. "I'll come clean regarding the spirit of Horatio." He wiped the tears from his eyes with his thumb and forefinger. "Follow me, please."

Henry led the princess and her three ladies up the grand staircase, around the corner, and down the hall to their room. Passing the princess's chamber, and before they made it to Henry's door, the prince led them to an open tower window with a suit of armour standing next to the window.

"This is Horatio," Henry said with a half-cocked smile. Audrianna looked at the suit of armour, then at Henry, then back at the armour.

"Don't try and fool me again, Henry," the princess responded.

"No," Henry answered. "It's true. This is the howling that you hear on most nights."

"Really!" the princess replied sceptically. "How does a pile of metal make a howling sound?"

"Ho-ho! Little girl!" the prince answered. "Watch and be educated. You're about to feel very, very foolish."

"Hmmph," the princess scoffed. "You should have been with me last night. I don't think I felt any more foolish."

The prince grinned, grabbed a hold of the middle of the suit of armour, and pushed the armour towards the window. The feet of the suit stood on a platform that had eight tiny wheels close to the ground. As the prince pushed the armour, it rotated to the side and rested in front of the window, facing out. Henry straightened up and raised his arms with a gesture of presenting his find to the ladies.

"So?" the princess challenged. "What are you trying to prove?"

"Well," the prince explained, "some twenty-eight years ago the king needed more men to guard the castle to prevent the Andjety from attacking. He didn't have enough, so the king commissioned suits of armour to be placed at strategic locations around the castle to give the appearance we were heavily fortified. But these suits are completely hollow. When the wind blows through the window, it causes the armour to make a sinister howling noise."

Audrianna wrinkled her nose at the prince in disbelief. Henry, realising he was losing what little faith the princess still had in him, leaned out the window and put his mouth against the point of the face plate, then blew into the armour as hard as he could. A menacing howling noise came bellowing out of the armour.

"Holy maggots!" Audrianna exclaimed. "That is the very noise I keep hearing at night!" She then began to chuckle. "You ladies were right from the start. It was the wind I was hearing!"

"Every evening," Henry explained, "the castle guards place suits of armour in front of every window, while they stand guard within the hallways. It gives the impression that we have twice the amount of guards than what we really have. It is very windy at night, with the wind blowing in from the sea. The wind causes the armour to howl, which most of us who have lived here for the past twenty-five years, are used to hearing."

Audrianna felt relieved to finally know where the sound of the howling was coming from. She could now sleep much easier at night, not only knowing that the sound was nothing more than armour, but the idea of the sound meant the castle guards were also on duty just outside their chamber doors.

Over the course of the following several weeks, Audrianna, Henry, and the three ladies-in-waiting, continued their physical training, preparing for the threat of an Andjety attack. However, with the death of Pitt, the need for Prince Henry having an armour- bearer became obvious. Several men were considered, yet repeatedly, the young envoy, Rolf, continued to rise to the surface of eligible candidates.

When Rolf was brought in for official training with the prince, princess, and Audrianna's three ladies, no one was more excited than Castalia. She would stand and gawk at the two men spar with their swords clanging and twanging, back and forth, until both men were glowing with shimmering sweat. Several times Rozelle would take Castalia by the hand and lead her away from the two men and set her in front of Rupp for more intense training.

For Ethlyn, Rupp had brought in a specialist in falconry. The specialist taugght Ethlyn how to give the falcon a special command that would tell her to attack an adversary that might pose a threat to Ethlyn. Ethlyn trained Lu to recognise the special command, of which the falcon would come swooping down and attack anyone who was within a few feet of her handler.

Part of Rolf's initiation into their circle of the royal court involved a hazing by which he was forced to put on protective clothing and stand next to Ethlyn when she gave her falcon, Lu, the command. Lu immediately came swooping down at Rolf, clawing and pecking, to try and chase him away from her handler. The new armour-bearer was taken by surprise and mistakenly defended himself by swinging at the falcon and striking her over the head with his padded arms. The falcon let out a loud throated squawk to let Rolf know that the terms of their relationship had suddenly changed.

Lu swooped down again, attacking Rolf so belligerently that he ran screaming from the courtyard and into the castle. The castle might have proven to be adequate safety for Rolf had it not been for the fact that Ethlyn taught Lu to give chase through open windows. Lu circled the castle until she came upon a window, swooped in, and hunted down the unsuspecting Rolf. Within a couple minutes of the falcon entering the castle, Rolf could be heard screaming from inside the castle.

"I think you should go inside and deliver poor Rolf from his feathered adversary," Rupp told Ethlyn. Ethlyn shrugged as she slowly walked towards the castle doors.

"He's got plenty of padding," Ethlyn replied, obviously upset with Rolf striking her falcon. "He just needs to learn to hold his arms up to cover his head, and he'll be fine."

"Ethel, please!" Castalia impatiently demanded. "Call off your devilled bird!" Once inside the castle, the sound of Ethlyn clicking her command to Lu could be heard all the way out in the courtyard.

The squawking ceased, and the screaming stopped. All was quiet.

A few moments later, Ethlyn returned with Lu perched on her arm, with the leather cap over the falcon's head. A piece of padding and twine could be seen dangling from the falcon's beak.

"Not a very brave armour-bearer," Rozelle commented to Castalia. "He's just sensitive," Castalia remarked. "That's all."

"Oh," Ethlyn replied. "He's going to feel a bit sensitive around his ears for a few days, at least." Castalia gave Ethlyn a scowl of disapproval.

"Okay, ladies," Rupp called out, "Let's come together once again. Lady Castalia, you and I have worked on a special skill with regards to your crossbow. Would you please give a demonstration?"

Castalia walked over to the weaponry table and picked up her favourite crossbow. She then picked up a large square napkin, which she promptly folded in half, corner to corner, and tied around her face. With her eyes covered, she felt around her quiver for a dart, loaded her crossbow and pulled the bow back until it clicked.

"Prince Henry," Rupp called out. "Walk over to the target, if you please." Henry hesitated, staring at Rupp for a few seconds. "Don't worry, Your Majesty," Rupp replied. "Lady Castalia has been well trained at shooting the crossbow blindfolded. She just needs someone to tap the target to help her know where it is."

"Has she shot anyone by mistake?" Henry asked, approaching the target.

"Why do you think I need a new volunteer, Your Majesty," Castalia teased. Henry shook his head.

"How good of a shot are you, anyways," he asked.

"I'm actually a better shot blindfolded than I am sighted," Castalia replied, holding her crossbow out in front of her, pointing up. "My ears are sharper than my eyes." Henry stood next to the target and picked up a bamboo pole leaning against the easel of the target.

"Just tap the centre of the target," Rupp called out, "and Lady Castalia will know where to aim."

Henry reached out with the wooden pole and tapped the centre of the target. The moment Castalia heard the target tapped, she instantly dropped the front of the crossbow towards the sound and pulled the trigger. The dart zipped through the air and struck both the target as well as the tip of the pole that tapped the target. Henry jumped back, rather startled how automatic

Castalia's reflexes were. He half expected her to give him enough time to step away from the target before she fired. Castalia pulled the blindfold off her face.

"Why didn't Your Majesty lower the pole once you struck the target?" she asked. "Why didn't you tell me you would shoot the dart right away?"

"Once I hear the tapping, I have to shoot. For each second I hesitate, my accuracy drops rapidly."

"Well," Henry responded, still a bit shaken, "Shooting blind-folded might be entertaining for a market festival, but I see no value such a skill could have in the heat of battle." Castalia could see several applications of being able the shoot the crossbow blindfolded. However, it was not her place to disagree with the prince.

Audrianna continued to practice her baton training all the while Ethlyn and Castalia gave their demonstrations. She was determined to advance past her first level of training. The muscles in her hands and arms already began to tone up and hurt less. She was now ready for her second level of training which involved sparring with a partner.

Rupp led Audrianna to a tiered platform with a drop-off at one end. He instructed the princess to stand at the edge of the drop-off, and Rupp stood facing her. With Audrianna standing on the platform, both the princess and the captain of the guards were the same height. Rup then slipped on a leather jacket with patches on each sleeve, and a patch in the front. One patch was red, the other green, and the third one was blue. Rupp held a wooden baton in his hand.

"Okay, Your Highness," Rupp said, bringing the training to an official start. "You have practiced on the training tree, striking in the pattern of red, green, blue. Correct?"

"Yes," Audrianna responded.

"Now, I am your new training tree. I have the same coloured patterns on me as the tree. Correct?"

"Yes," Audrianna answered.

"Good. Now slowly, I want you to tap the patches on my jacket in the same fashion.

Red, green, blue. Red, green, blue."

Audrianna extended her baton out in front of her and gently tapped Rupp's jacket. Red, green, blue. Red, green, blue. Out loud they both chorused the pattern every time Audrianna tapped a patch.

"Red, Green, Blue. Red, Green, Blue."

"Good," Rupp commended the princess. "Now, I want you to tap those same colours, in the same order, but as fast as you can. And, when you get to blue, thrust with the point of your baton as hard as you can at my blue target. Can you do that, Your Highness?"

"Yes," Audrianna answered, taking her trained stance.

"I will be okay," Rupp commented. "Not that Your Highness asked or seemed concerned." Audrianna smiled, but maintained her focus. "Ready, Your Highness?"

"Ready!" Audrianna answered.

"Begin," Rupp instructed. Audrianna swung with all her might and as fast as she could towards the red patch on Rupp's left sleeve. Before she could strike his arm, Rup deflected her baton with his, just as the princess half-expected. She then countered towards his right side as fast as she could at the green target. Again, Rupp deflected her strike. She then thrust as fast and as hard as she could towards the blue target located on Rupp's chest. With a single motion, Rupp again deflected the princess's advance.

"Very good," Rupp responded. "You are becoming stronger and faster." Audrianna smiled. It meant a lot to her to have his approval, and Rupp always made her feel empowered. "Let's continue this drill for the rest of our time together. I want you to push yourself as hard as you can, and as fast as you can. But remember, accuracy is a must."

Audrianna swung with every ounce of energy she had. Sparring with Rupp was much easier than swinging at the training tree in the sense that Rupp's deflections did not hurt like hitting the tree did. At any rate, Audrianna's arms and hands were much more toned, and her endurance was higher. However, after fifteen minutes of intense training, Rupp

commanded the princess to stop. With sweat dripping from her forehead, around her face, and off her chin, Audrianna felt every muscle in her body begin to tighten up.

"Drop your baton!" Rupp instructed. Audrianna released her baton and let it fall to the ground next to her. "Now, bend at your waist and grab your ankles with both hands." Audrianna bent down, wondering why Rupp commanded her to do such a strange act. She could feel the muscles in her legs stretch and pull. Rupp walked up the steps of the platform, positioned himself behind the princess, and put his knee up against her rump.

"Give me your hands," he instructed. Audrianna reached back and grabbed his hands which he held out to her. While leaning slightly against her rump, and gently pulling her arms in the opposite direction, Rupp stretched the muscles in Audrianna's arms and back.

"Stand up straight," Rupp commanded. Audrianna obeyed.

"Feet apart. Fold your arms."

Audrianna did as she was instructed. Rupp firmly grabbed a hold of her shoulders from behind, and with a swift jerk, popped several joints in the princess's back.

"Oh," the princess yelped from the sudden release of tension. "Thank you, Lord Rupp."

"You worked hard today," Rupp replied. "I'm proud of your progress. Every day we will work hard, like you did today. I will stretch your muscles, and you will become stronger. Very soon, I will give you an iron sword to work with."

"Really?" the princess beamed. "My own sword? I can't wait to get a real sword." "Hold on, now," Rupp quickly corrected the princess. "A wooden baton is just as

real of a sword as an iron one. Your wooden baton successfully helped you develop past the first few levels of training. Don't discount the effectiveness of what it has already accomplished."

"I am sorry, Lord Rupp," the princess apologised. "I'm sorry, Mr Baton," the princess said to her training sword, holding it up to her face and giving it a kiss.

"I must warn you, though," Rupp continued, "an iron sword means your training will become harder, more intense, and more dangerous."

"I understand, Lord Rupp," Audrianna replied, standing as straight as she could and looking directly into Rupp's eyes. A look of serious resolve washed over her face. "I am ready to accept the next level of training."

"Soon," Rupp answered. "Soon, but not yet."

Just inside the castle door, opposite the courtyard where the royal family trained, stood a slender figure watching from the window, hidden within the shadows. As the prince and his armour-bearer, the princess and her ladies all trained, the ominous figure floated among the shadows of the castle hallway on the lower level, within the servants' quarters. Very few servants were in that part of the castle that time of day. Many were either dealing with laundry, or cooking, or sweeping and mopping, or preparing for the royal court beginning in a couple hours. No one was around to witness this lone figure walking through the dark corridors of the lower castle.

Soon enough, the figure approached a doorway that was usually left locked, to where no one could enter from the door's exterior. The figure pulled a key out from a side pocket, placed it in the keyhole and turned the key until the lock shifted with a CLANK. Turning around and looking in all directions to see if someone might be observing the figure's movements, the shadowed figure entered through the door and locked it behind them with another CLANK.

A small candle sat lit on a table near the far wall, opposite the doorway. The strange figure walked halfway into the dark room, approaching the flickering candle.

"How many of you have come?" the figure asked.

"Not many," a throaty coarse voice echoed back from the darkness. "Three, and me." "I was able to negotiate with the royal family not to send an army to attack your

people. They are convinced we are outnumbered ten to one."

"Very good," the voiced responded. "And how did you accomplish this?"

"The little princess is young, naïve, and very impressionable. She convinced the royal court to build up our defences instead. It is easy to put thoughts in her head that she has no idea are being put there."

"Yes," the voice from the darkness answered. "However, a bit of caution. Do not underestimate a little girl with a strong sense of empowerment."

"Empowerment?" the figure asked. "She is being trained to fight, but I wouldn't call that empowerment." A gloved hand picked up a knife from the table and waved it over the flame of the candle.

"Empowerment goes deeper than knowing how to wield a dagger," the voice echoed, waving the knife back and forth over the candle. "The more she is allowed to believe in herself, the stronger she will become."

"Are you afraid of a ten-year-old girl?" the figure asked.

"I am not afraid of who she is," the voice announced. "I am afraid of who she might become."

"You mean, the next queen of Nadeau?"

"Yes," the voice answered. "The day she becomes queen, all will be lost for the Andjety."

CHAPTER 14

As Audrianna's skills grew, it became obvious that her stature did as well. Rozelle had measured the princess on the doorway of the bathing chamber the first night Audrianna was given a hot bath. Now, as her stature became noticeably taller, Rozelle measured her again and found that she had grown from four-feet three-inches, to four-feet seven-inches tall.

The sudden growth spurt of the princess caused the castle to be in a frenzy. This meant a new wardrobe to ensure that her dresses reached the floor, so that her ankles were not inappropriately exposed. She also needed new shoes, as her feet began to grow as well. The princess's ladies-in-waiting also requested the princess be given a new bustier. Not that the princess had grown into the necessity of one, but that her frame was longer and wider, and it was becoming more difficult to loosely fit the corset on the princess without it becoming obvious.

"Someday soon," Castalia remarked, "Your Highness is going to have to wear her bustier in the manner it was intended to be worn. There won't be any way to avoid the functionality of your accessories."

"I understand," Audrianna replied. "Maybe by then I'll be used to having my body squished together by my tight garments."

"No," Ethlyn commented. "One never does. One just puts up with it."

It also became apparent to the royal court that Audrianna would soon no longer need a booster box for her throne. Soon, she would be tall enough that the booster seat would put her at the same height as Henry on his throne, which made him rather unhappy as he witnessed her statue catch up with him.

After several weeks of Rupp sparring with the princess using wooden batons, the ladies and Audrianna appeared for exercise drills to find Rupp waiting with a special gift.

"It is your battle gear," Rupp declared.

"Battle gear?" the princess asked. Rupp held up what looked like a mask.

"This is a face shield to protect you from being harmed if you are struck in the face with a sword."

Audrianna looked over the face shield that Rupp placed in her hands. It looked like an iron bowl with what reminded the princess of a small metal gate wielded onto the side. Audrianna looked up at Rupp bewildered, who took the helmet from the princess and placed it over her head. The princess's eyes had difficulty looking through the metal bars without crossing her eyes.

"I also have a breastplate for Your Highness to wear over her torso," Rupp announced, lifting what appeared to Audrianna to be a flattened turtle shell with straps. Rupp helped the gangly adolescent strap the protective gear around her lanky thin frame. "Very good, Your Highness," Rupp remarked, looking at the young princess wearing an oversized helmet and an oversized breastplate along with her long, out-of-proportion arms and legs. "One more thing you need to complete your ensemble," Rupp announced, turning around and pulling an iron sword from his belt. "Your new sword."

Audrianna's eyes grew big with excitement. She pushed the helmet backwards to see through her faceplate until the tip of her nose stuck out between two of the metal slats. She then reached out to take hold of her first iron weapon. She giggled with glee.

"Remember, Your Highness," Rupp responded, "your training is going to be more intense. You are stronger now, so I expect Your Highness to train at her new level of strength. I will expect nothing less than your all."

"Yes, Lord Rupp," Audrianna answered. "I am ready for the challenge." "Good. Shall we begin?"

"Yes," Audrianna replied standing up tall, pushing her helmet forward, and holding her new sword up in front of her. She took her usual stance that Rupp had trained her to take.

"Okay," Rupp coaxed the princess. "I want you to slowly tap the colours on my training jacket. Red, green, blue. Understand?"

"I understand," Audrianna answered.

"Red, green, blue," the duo chorused as the princess slowly tapped Rupp's left sleeve, then his right sleeve, then the circle on his chest with her iron sword. "Red, green, blue."

"Excellent," the captain responded. "Notice how the sword is heavier and harder to hold straight out like Your Highness was able to do with the baton?"

"Yes, sir," the princess answered.

"It will take a few weeks for your hands, wrists and arms to compensate, but Your Highness will soon be able to handle the sword like how you wielded the baton. Are you ready to do a bit of sparring?"

"Yes," she answered.

"Very good," Rupp replied. "For the next couple of minutes, I want you to give me every ounce of energy you have by swinging with all your might, and as accurate as you can, at my colour patches. Red, green, blue. Ready?"

"Ready," the armour-clad little girl answered. She took her trained stance and swung for all she was worth at the centre of Rupp's red patch. Before her iron sword could hit the target, Rupp deflected it with a dull CLUNK, causing the tip of the princess's sword to strike the ground.

"Ow!" the princess shrieked. "I almost dropped my sword!"

"Hold on to the scabbard a bit more tightly. Hold the handle closer to the hilt. That should give you better control of the sword." Audrianna choked the handle a bit higher with her hands. "Let's try green," Rupp commanded.

The princess swung in the other direction, to the green patch, which Rupp deflected again, causing the princess to bounce the tip of her sword off the ground again. Audrianna shook her hands, one after the other, indicating that the strain of swinging such a heavy sword, and having it deflected, was taxing to her hands.

"Can Your Highness thrust her sword towards my chest?" Rupp asked. At that command, the princess gave her instructor her last bit of energy with a final push. Rupp swung his sword at Audrianna's, knocking it out of her hand, and slapping it to the ground. Looking down at her defeated sword, Audrianna shook both her hands at once, then looked up at Rupp. Sweat dripped off the tired student's face.

"Not a bad first day, Your Highness," Rupp commended the princess. Audrianna looked back down at her silent, still sword. Every muscle in her arms and legs ached, although she didn't feel she had nearly the workout she had the day before.

"Pick up your sword, Your Highness," Rupp ordered. Audrianna picked it up from the ground and dusted it off.

"Now squat down on your ankles as if you were sitting in a chair. Try and squat as close to the ground as possible, without truly touching it." The princess obeyed, feeling the muscles in her legs stretch.

"Now," Rupp directed, "hold your sword out in front of you, one hand by the handle, one hand by the blade." The princess obeyed, holding her sword, with both hands out in front of her. This time she could feel the muscles in her back stretch, and a few in her arms.

"Hold your posture. Don't move, Your Highness." Rupp counted in his head, slightly moving his lips, and after a few minutes, Rupp announced the end of the exercise.

"You may now relax." The princess crumbled to the floor. Rupp walked over to the princess and held out his hand. She reached her hand up to her instructor and took his hand, as he raised her to her feet.

"After a few weeks of training," Rupp declared, "you will be strong enough to learn how to deflect my advances." A look of worry swept over the princess's face. Was he really going to swing his sword at her, expecting her to defend herself in just a few short weeks? She realised she was going to have to work hard at advancing through this new level of sword drill.

Later that day, as Audrianna sat through Royal Court, she discovered that it had become increasingly difficult to sit straight up in her throne due to several muscle cramps in her arms and back. She wondered if that was why Henry had become accustomed to slouching in his chairs all the time. She didn't feel it appropriate during court to slouch and see if she might gain some relief to her aches, and she certainly didn't want to turn into Henry. So, she did her best to endure the pain until court was concluded.

However, as she sat fidgeting on her throne, trying to maintain her composure, while at the same time attempting to find a comfortable position, a luxurious thought suddenly came racing to her mind.

A bath! A hot bath, to be exact! That was what she needed. Oh! Soaking in a hot bath was precisely what would soothe her aches and pains. She could instruct the kitchen to bring supper up to her chamber—enough for both her and her ladies—then she could eat at her leisure and soak in the tub. Now she squirmed in her seat with a completely different motivation for Royal Court to be over.

When Malcolm pounded his sceptre on the floor and declared Royal Court to be over, Audrianna squealed out loud with delight. She jumped from her throne, hopped down the steps, bounded out the side door, and waited for her ladies to catch up with her in the corridor leading to the grand staircase.

As the three ladies approached her, they were concerned something might have been wrong, seeing the princess could not seem to stand still.

"What's wrong, Your Highness?" "Is Your Highness alright?"

"Does Your Highness need a chamber pot?" "No," Audrianna answered. "But I want a bath."

The ladies, realising the princess's request was not urgent, all gave a loud sigh of relief, and each placed a hand on their hips. They looked down at the princess with laboured expectation.

"Your Highness wants a bath?" Rozelle asked.

"Yes, please," the princess pleaded, a smile beaming across her face. "A hot bath, with bubbles!"

"Why does Your Highness want a bath?" Castalia asked surprised, since all three usually had to coax the princess into the tub at planned bath times.

"I also want to ask the kitchen to bring supper up to our room, just like we did the night I jumped out the window. Remember?"

"Oh," Ethlyn chimed in, "we remember that night quite well, Your Highness."

"I mean, remember us eating on the floor, in a circle, and then me taking a hot bath. I loved every minute of that night—until Henry took me over his knee, and… well… you know."

"Actually, Your Highness had her bath before we ate our meal," Rozelle responded. "I will go and find the chamber maids and tell them to heat the water in the kitchen. You three go ahead to the room, and you ladies help undress Her Highness for her bath. I will also speak to the kitchen about bringing our supper to the room."

As Audrianna prepared for her bath, Henry and the king sat at the dinner table waiting for the princess to appear. Besides the evening of the emergency council meeting, Audrianna was always present for every meal. It was not like the princess to decide to stay in her room and not join the royal family. Malcolm asked one of the kitchen servants if they had heard from Her Highness, and they informed the king and prince that she had decided to stay in her room and take a bath that evening.

An hour later, as Audrianna lay soaking in her bath chamber, a knock was heard at her bedroom chamber door. Rozelle opened the door to find Henry standing out in the hallway.

"Is Her Highness well?" Henry inquired. "She did not come down for supper, I was concerned."

All three ladies-in-waiting were astonished to hear the sincerity in the prince's voice and look of worry on his face. Neither one of them had ever seen him behave in such a manner towards the princess.

"Her Highness is well, Your Majesty," Rozelle answered. "She has worked hard at her training, and needed a hot bath to soothe her aching muscles." Henry nodded in recognition of Rozelle's words.

"I understand," he replied. "Please tell Her Highness I wish her well this evening." "We will, Your Majesty," all three ladies chorused, with Ethlyn and Castalia

standing behind Rozelle. Henry turned and walked towards the grand staircase, and Rozelle gently closed the door behind him.

"That was a unique occurrence," Castalia remarked.

"I don't believe I have ever before seen His Majesty display any concern for another person the entire time I've lived in the castle," Rozelle added.

By this time, Audrianna had poked her head out of the bath chamber, wondering what the commotion was in the main bed chamber. The princess was completely naked, and still dripping wet.

"Your Highness," Rozelle squealed. "Please return to the bath chamber and let us help dry you off and dressed before you catch the coughs!" The naked princess spun around and ran back into the bath chamber, slipping, sliding, and yelping, due to the puddles of water she had trailed between the doorway and the tub. Her attendants followed close behind.

Meanwhile, Henry decided to stroll outside in the main courtyard of the castle. As he inspected the castle grounds, he was met by Rupp. Rupp had recently finished assisting in the changing of the guards for the fourth shift of the day.

"How goes the night, Lord Rupp," Henry inquired. "Strangely quiet," he replied. "Where are you off to?"

"Well," Henry said. "I have just checked on the princess. She didn't show for supper, and I was concerned she might have taken ill."

"You, Your Majesty?" Rupp quickly countered. "You were concerned regarding Her Highness's well-being? I had the impression you despised the little girl."

"I do," Henry responded. "I despise the fact that my father betrothed me to her for the sole purpose of depriving me of the throne. I despise the fact that she has caused several of my ideas and instructions to be circumvented."

"How much of that really is her fault?" Rupp asked.

"Whether intentionally or unintentionally, she aggravates me beyond measure," Henry barked.

"Her simple innocence leaves a lasting impression on you, though, doesn't it?" Rupp remarked.

"Oh," Henry responded, "There is nothing innocent about that little mouse. But she indeed leaves an impression."

"Well, Your Majesty," Rupp began, then Henry suddenly noticed an alarming oddity.

"Hold on!" Henry urgently declared. "How long has it been since the tower watchmen have given an hourly report?"

"Hmm! It has been some time," Rupp replied. "Watchman of the north tower," the captain bellowed. "Report!"

Silence.

"Report, north tower watchman!" Silence.

"Watchman of the east tower," Rupp cried out. "Report!"

Silence. Rupp and Henry looked at each other in horror. Together they ran to the far side of the courtyard and approached the opposite wall.

"West tower watchman," Rupp desperately called out. "Report!" Silence.

"South tower watchman," Henry called out, his voice cracking with fear. "Report, please!"

Nothing.

"We had better climb the tower and see what is going on," Rupp suggested. The two men ran towards the tower door. Rupp pulled a ring of keys from a satchel hanging over his shoulder. He quickly thumbed through the keys until he found the correct key to unlock the tower door. Thrusting the key into the door and turning the lock with a CLANK, the captain of the guards swung the tower door wide open, and both he and the prince pushed their way up the spiral staircase, one after another.

Within minutes, the winded pair reached the platform of the tower. In the corner of the tower lay a body, face down. Rupp rushed over and turned the body over. The watchman was dead. His throat was cut, and a puddle of blood lay around the unfortunate soldier. Rupp looked up at the prince with grave resolve.

"We've been invaded!" he said. Henry took a step back, looking wide-eyed down at the dead watchman.

"Are they all dead?" Henry asked. "All four watchmen?"

"I would assume," Rupp answered. "For how long, would be anybody's guess." "What should we do?" Henry asked Rupp, beginning to panic.

"Follow me down to the castle. The first thing the Andjety will try and do is secure the king, yourself, and the princess. Once they have you three under their control, they'll have control of the kingdom. It is imperative that you stay by my side."

The two men ran for all they were worth down the spiral staircase. Once in the courtyard again, Rupp and the prince made their way to the king's bed chamber. As they approached the door, the two men drew their swords expecting the worst.

Henry turned the latch of the door, and slowly opened it all the way to the wall. The room was dark, except for the moonlight that splashed against the floor from the open window.

"Father?" Henry called. "Father, are you in here?" From the faint light of the moon, Henry could see a dark silhouette of his father, sitting up in bed.

"Father," Henry called again. "Father, are you awake?"

"Your Majesty," Rupp cautioned. "Stay here with me. Don't go into that room without a lamp." As Henry stepped through the doorway, he opened his eyes as wide as he could to adjust them to the sheer darkness of the room. Stumbling halfway into the royal chamber of the king, a match was suddenly struck in the proximity of the king's bed. The burning matchstick was led to an open lamp, and lit the oil. Light licked away the darkness, revealing the king sitting straight up in bed, dressed in his bed clothes. His feet were buried under the covers and straight out in front of him. The king's eyes were closed, his mouth partially open, and the colour of his skin was ashen.

"Father?" Henry asked one last time. At that moment, the king fell forward—from the waist—his head falling limp in between his legs. Behind the king, sat the Witch, Zymjai.

"Long live the king," the Witch said in her throaty coarse voice. Her right hand still clung to the dagger that she had thrust into the king's side and held there. Henry, being startled, took a few steps backwards towards the door.

"Hello, Henry," the Witch greeted.

"What have you done, Zymjai?" Henry exclaimed.

"I have made you the new king. Isn't that what you always wanted?" "You killed my father! I did not want this!"

The Witch stood from the bed, from the side of the dead king. "Such ingratitude for such a generous gift."

Rupp pulled the prince from the room and pushed him down the corridor leading to the princess's chamber. The two of them ran for all they were worth. As they turned the corner of the hallway, the two were suddenly met by Andjety militants. Rupp pushed the frightened and panic-stricken prince to one side as he engaged the invaders. Their swords sang and loudly echoed throughout the castle corridors as the captain of the guards fought valiantly to protect what was left of the royal family. Rupp thrust his sword into the heart of the first assailant, then kicked the second Andjety backwards so he could work his way towards Audrianna's bed chamber.

Shouts of fighting and screams of dying vigilantes alerted the princess and her ladies to the invasion forces. Rozelle poked her head out the door and saw Rupp and Henry engaged in fighting off assailants. She quickly shut the door and bolted the lock.

"We're under attack, ladies!" Rozelle announced. "Quickly! Hide the princess!"

Castalia and Ethlyn latched on to the princess, picked her up, and carried her to the bed. Rozelle pulled the blanket up on one side, revealing the reason Audrianna's bed was so high. Rozelle opened a hidden compartment in the lower half of the bed, large enough to hide the princess during such an attack. The two ladies stuffed her inside the hiding place, head first.

"Now, be quiet, Your Highness," Rozelle ordered. "No matter what happens, do not give yourself away!"

The shouting in the corridor grew louder as the fighting between Rupp and the Andjety came near the chamber. The sound of clanging metal, swearing, and dying exhales could be heard just the other side of the door. The three ladies armed themselves with swords and daggers that had hung on the walls posing as decorations. They waited for the enemy to chop their way through the door. They waited their turn to engage the attackers. They waited their turn to give their lives for the princess.

Almost in an instant the sounds of fighting abruptly stopped. Then, the sound of a key being slid into the lock of the door, and the door unlocked, then popped open. The three ladies lifted their swords, ready to fend off whomever entered the room.

Through the door, Rupp pushed his way in, followed close by Henry. They closed the door again and latched it.

"Where is Her Highness?" Rupp asked. "In her hiding place," Rozelle answered.

"Get her out," Rupp commanded. "She and Prince Henry must leave right away." "The courtyard is swarming with enemies," Ethlyn declared, looking out the window. "They are killing the castle guards one after another!"

Rozelle opened the compartment of Audrianna's hiding place. She and Castalia pulled the princess by the feet until she slid all the way out.

"Where are we going?" Audrianna asked. "I'm only in my night gown."

Rozelle stooped down and grabbed the hem of the princess's night gown and lifted it above her head and off her body. Both Rupp and Henry instinctively turned their backs to the princess while the ladies-in-waiting changed her into travel attire. As Ethlyn and Castalia finished tying the sleeves to Audrianna's blouse, the sound of banging erupted on the other side of the door. The voice of an Andjety mercenary could be heard screaming right on the other side of the door. Rupp peeked back at the women to see if Audrianna was modestly dressed. He spun around to face the princess, then nudged Henry who also turned to face the princess.

"You must go now, Your Highness," Rupp impatiently remarked. "Where are we going?" she asked, looking up at Rozelle.

"We are not going anywhere," Rozelle clarified. "You and Henry are fleeing the castle together."

Audrianna looked up at Henry who wore a painful scowl. "Henry and I?" Audrianna asked. "Together? Alone?"

"Yes, Your Highness," Rupp responded. "There's no time to lose. The enemy is just outside the door, and they will do whatever is necessary to take control of our kingdom."

"And that means kill you and me," Henry asserted.

"But what about you, Lord Rupp?" the princess asked. "And Cassie? And Rose? And Ethel? What will happen to all of you?" Ethel jumped in front of Audrianna, put her arms around her, and gave her a tight squeeze.

"Don't worry, Your Highness," Ethlyn assured her. "We will be okay. We gotta make sure you have enough time to get free of the castle."

"Just go!" Rozelle commanded. "Go! You don't have time for foolish sentiment!"

Henry climbed up on the ledge of the window, turned to the princess and held out his hand. Audrianna looked up at Henry, then turned around to face the others. A look of uncertainty shown on her face.

"But…" the princess wanted to plead for the others to come with her. Everyone that she considered to be safe in her life was staying in the room. Henry had recently shown a touch of compassion towards her, but for the most part, she did not truly feel safe with him.

As she tried to work out the matter in her head, Henry jumped from the window, onto the branch closest to where the branch and the truck met. Rupp picked up the princess and stood her up on the window ledge. Henry motioned for her to jump towards him. The thought of her jumping out the window again required more courage than what she had in reserve. Rupp stood on the ledge with the princess. For a second, Audrianna thought that Rupp has decided to join them in their escape. But as the two of them stood next to each other, the door of Audrianna's chamber burst open. The Witch entered the room with a sword in both hands.

Without hesitation, Rupp picked up the ten-year-old, and tossed her towards her betrothed. Audrianna took a deep breath as she sailed through the air towards the tree. In an instant, the princess collided against the prince, knocking him off the limb, then tumbling through the foliage together, down to the castle garden. Both landed on their rumps opposite each other.

None of the invaders on ground level witnessed the two fall through the magnolia tree. Everyone was busy fighting their way into the castle, and dispatching Nadeau guards. The sound of the Witch screaming incomprehensible orders to her warriors could be heard from inside the castle. Both Henry and Audrianna scrambled to their feet and ran towards the stable. Acquiring a horse was the only guarantee of their safe passage away from the city under siege. As Henry pushed the stable doors open, both their hearts sank.

No horses. They had all been stolen or scattered by the Andjety.

"What do we do?" the princess asked her betrothed. Henry scanned the courtyard. Two Andjety officers came trotting through the gates of the castle. They wore heavy armour, and each one carried a shield in front of them.

"We'll take their horses," Henry responded, guiding the little girl to the side of the building and coaxing her to squat in the shadows. Audrianna could feel her sore muscles stretch as she squatted.

"How, Henry?"

"Not sure, yet," Henry confided. "We'll wait for an opportunity."

The two of them sat in silence. Soon the two officers dismounted and tied their horses to the training tree in the middle of the courtyard. They laughed as they strolled towards the doors leading into the castle.

"Do you know how to ride a horse?" Henry asked the princess.

"I can ride a horse just as good as you can," she bragged. Henry raised an eyebrow and glared at her.

"No, you can't," he replied. The princess shrugged. "Do you even know how to mount a horse?"

"Not really. You asked me if I knew how to ride. How hard is it to ride?" "In that case, we will ride out together on the same horse, understand?" "I understand," Audrianna answered.

"Okay. When I give the word, we'll run as fast as we can for that first horse closest to us. I'll mount it first, then I'll reach down and pull you up. Got it?"

"Got it!" Audrianna answered. They waited for Henry to spy the right opportunity to steal one of the horses.

They waited. And waited.

Several minutes they waited. Every time the princess thought the moment had arrived for them to break for the horse, Henry hesitated.

"Now?" she asked. "No," he answered. They waited. "Now?" "No. Not now."

"Henry," the princess whispered. "When are we going to run

for the horse?" "I can't find the right moment," he told her.

They waited. Audrianna saw a perfect moment. Both officers had entered the castle. The enemy mercenaries could be heard inside jeering and sneering at the prisoners they had taken. No one was paying attention to the horses.

"Follow me," Audrianna whispered to Henry. She bolted towards the horses, stooping low, and staying within the shadows as best she could.

"Wait," Henry quietly called after her. "What are you doing?"

The little princess reached the first horse, turned to look at the prince, and motioned for him to follow. Looking to the left and to the right, Henry ran towards the horse, keeping to the same shadows as Audrianna, and stooped close to the ground as she had. By the time he reached the horse, Audrianna had put her foot in the horse's stirrup and pulled herself up into a standing position on one foot. She was too short, though, to hike her leg over the saddle and sit up top of the horse. Henry grabbed her about the waist with both hands and lowered her to the ground. He quickly mounted the horse, grabbed the reins, then reached his arm down to the princess. Audrianna took his arm as he raised her into the saddle with him.

"Were you going to lift me into the saddle with you once you mounted the horse," Henry asked Audrianna.

"If I had to," she answered. Henry kicked the sides of the horse to give the signal for the beast to take the two of them out the gate and into the darkness.

CHAPTER 15

Henry and Audrianna raced down the moon lit trail as fast as the horse could carry them. For more than an hour, the pair bounced around on top of the saddle, heading east, towards the far side of the kingdom. The princess's sore muscles ached from the fierce demands of riding a horse galloping down the stony path.

"Please, Henry," the princess cried out. "Please stop! I can't… I can't go on much farther. I hurt so much!"

Henry didn't say a word. He continued to push the endurance of the horse for another couple miles.

"Please, Henry! Please stop and let me rest!" Tears began to roll across the side of her face due to her achy fatigue as well as the fact that she was again being whisked away from her home.

As the horse bounded up the side of a hill, the stamina of the beast began to wane, and slowed to a sluggish trot as it reached the peak of the knoll. Audrianna continued to softly cry, with her head down and her hands gripped to the front of the saddle. Henry guided the horse down a side trail and came across a clearing that obviously was once used as a camp site. A small pile of half burnt wood lay in the middle of the clearing.

Henry brought the horse to a stop. Without a word, he picked the princess up from the saddle, and slid her softly onto the ground. Audrianna fell to her hands and knees, and crawled from the horse, over to the side of the cold, dark, fire pit. Henry slid off the horse and tied the horse to a nearby olive tree. He then unstrapped the saddle, and pulled it off the back of the horse. Laying the saddle to the side, he removed the horse blanket. Walking over to where the weeping princess lay on the ground, Henry laid out the blanket next to her, then walked back to the horse and began brushing him down.

Audrianna rolled over onto the blanket, and balled up on her side, with her knees up to her chest and her arms wrapped around her legs. When Henry had settled the horse, he walked over to the cold princess and folded the blanket in half, covering the princess to keep her warm. He then set to work at gathering kindling and starting a fire. Using a flint in one of the horse's pouches, the prince had a fire going within a few minutes.

As the fire began to light up the camp area, and warm the traveling fugitives, Audrianna peeked out from under her blanket to where Henry was. He sat on the other side of the fire, his back towards the fire and the princess. She sat up to look more clearly at Henry. His back was hunched and he looked straight at the ground. She stood on her knees to see over the flames of fire. Something seemed odd to how he was behaving. She noticed that he was shaking, or shivering, as if he was cold.

The princess stood to her feet and picked up the blanket. She walked around the fire to face the prince. Henry looked up at her, not saying a word. Tears on his face sparkled from the light of the fire pit. The expression on his face displayed painful fear. He was crying, and he was afraid.

Audrianna held the blanket out to her betrothed and placed it in his lap.

"You seem a little cold," she said. "Go ahead and cover up with it. You need to stay warm." The prince slowly shook his head at the princess.

"I don't know what to do," he cried. "I lost the kingdom, and I don't know what to do."

"You haven't lost the kingdom, Henry," Audrianna replied. "We're just running away for a bit to get our bearing. It'll be alright."

"No," the prince exclaimed. "It won't be alright. We have nothing. Nothing! No armies. No weapons. No allies. Nothing but you and me." Henry paused to chuckle. "Ha! And we don't even like each other."

Audrianna reached out to touch Henry's face. A tear was dripping from his right eye and streaking down his cheek. She touched it with her finger and wiped it off his face.

"Rupp and the others will come looking for us," she said. "They will help us restore the kingdom back to the rightful king." Henry began shaking his head violently.

"No! No! No, Audrianna!" he shouted, becoming angry. The princess stepped back not sure if he was going to reach out and grab her, or start punching her. The tone of his voice was aggressive and hostile.

"Don't you get it?" he screamed. "The king is dead!" "The king?" Audrianna asked. "The king is dead?"

"I saw the Witch sitting behind my father, and my father collapse onto the bed with a dagger sticking in his back. The Witch sneered at me and said that she made me the new king of Nadeau. From there, Rupp and I made our way to your room."

"Well, then," Audrianna assured Henry, "Rupp is a great warrior. He and my ladies will come and find us."

"No, Audrianna! Rupp is dead! Rozelle is dead! Castalia is dead! Ethlyn is dead!"

Audrianna shook her head. There was no way in her mind that all four of her friends could have died that night. Not all four! They trained together. She saw what her ladies- in-waiting were capable of. And yet, aside from Rozelle having access to a sword, the other two did not have the resources pertaining to their special disciplines. But Rupp? Was it possible for the Witch to kill such a skilled swordsman?

"No," she answered Henry. "They are not dead! Do not say that!"

"They are, Audrianna," Henry persisted. "They are all dead! They fought the Witch so we could escape. They did what they were trained to do. Protect us at all costs."

The princess refused to believe Henry's conclusion.

"How?" she asked. "How could the Witch defeat all four of them?" "Did you hear them fighting in your room after we fell from the tree?"

"No," the princess answered.

"Do you think the Witch would allow Rupp to leave the room alive?" "Probably not," she answered.

"Do you think that if Rupp survived, it would mean he killed the Witch?" Henry asked.

"Yes," she answered.

"If he had killed the Witch, don't you think the Andjety would have surrendered?" Audrianna pondered what Henry told her. Tears began welling up in her eyes as all hope began to get choked from her heart.

"But—But, Henry?" she pleaded. "What's going to happen to us, then?"

"We will be hunted down and killed," he answered starting to weep again. "As long as we are alive, we are a threat to the Witch."

Audrianna sat down next to her betrothed. She laid her head against his knee and began to weep also. Even though the fire that Henry built was hot enough to keep them both warm, the shock of being hunted fugitives caused them both to shiver and shake. Before long, Henry unfolded the horse blanket and draped it across the two of them. Without thought of how he once despised little Audrianna, or how much resentment once filled his thoughts daily, he put his arm around her and pulled her close to him. She, in turn wrapped her arms around his knee. For the past four months, they hated each other. But none of that seemed to matter anymore. They needed to stay alive. They needed to trust one another to survive.

For more than an hour, the two of them clung to each other, their backs to the fire, the blanket draped over their shoulders. They watched the silhouettes of their shadows dance in the light of the fire. They said nothing to each other, though their minds were absorbed with the same thoughts.

But by now, they were exhausted. They had to get some sleep to prepare for their flight at first light. Henry gently pushed Audrianna to one side as he stood up, then spread the horse blanket on the ground. He then walked over to the horse and picked up one of the saddlebags. He tucked the saddlebag under the end of the blanket to use as a pillow. "Get some sleep," he ordered, pointing at the blanket. Audrianna looked down at the

makeshift bed, then up at Henry.

"What about you?" she asked. "Where will you sleep?"

"I won't," he answered. "Someone needs to stay awake and keep watch. I don't know how far away the Witch's army is, and they are for certain searching for us."

"So," Audrianna replied, "when will you sleep?"

"When we're safe," he answered. He walked past the fire, and sat opposite the princess, giving her any necessary privacy to sleep. Audrianna propped herself up on one arm and watched Henry act as sentry. After a few minutes, she laid her head on the saddle bag. Her mind continued to race over the past day, the past week, and through the past several months. It seemed almost impossible for her to relax. But soon enough, her fatigue caught up with her, and within minutes, she was fast asleep.

After a few hours of restful sleep, Audrianna woke up. Her eyes popped open and she realised she needed a chamber pot somewhat urgently. She raised her head to see that the fire had died down to a pile of glowing hot coals. Henry sat on a large rock opposite the fire, still with his back to the princess.

Audrianna sat up, then slowly walked over to Henry and sat next to him on the rock. She was not sure how she was going to broach the subject of a chamber pot with Henry, nor how he would react. It was not appropriate for a lady to speak of such things in the presence of a man, or to a man for that matter. However, Henry was her betrothed. Sooner or later they would have to discuss such matters with each other once they were married. "Henry," the princess began, "I need to talk to you about something." Henry turned his head to look at the princess. "Alright," he said.

"I normally get out of bed this time of night to… uh… use the chamber pot." She bashfully looked down at her feet, then slowly raised her head and looked at Henry. Henry shot her an understanding grin.

"The best I can offer you is a bit of privacy over behind that tree," he answered, pointing at a dark shadow just outside the light of the glowing coals. "You should be able to do what is necessary out there rather effectively."

Audrianna sat in silence, staring up at Henry. Henry, who had looked away, looked back down at the princess.

"What's wrong?" he asked.

"Henry," she softly attempted to explain, "I can't just simply pee."

"Okay," he responded. "Whatever you need to do, just do it on that side of the tree." The princess still sat in silence, staring at Henry.

"Henry," she replied, trying a third time to explain without coming out and saying it, "I need some… assistance."

"I am not going to hold your hand while you pee," Henry adamantly remarked. "No," Audrianna calmly replied. "I need to take something with me, that I don't

have, to help with what I need to do."

"Oh," Henry responded, suddenly realising what the princess was talking about. "You mean, you need a cleaning rag."

"Yes," she answered.

"Well, hmm," Henry thought for a moment. "I always carry extra rags in the saddle of my horse. But since this is not my horse, I really couldn't tell you if there is one or not. But, let's go check."

The two of them walked together to inspect the saddle of the horse and see if there was anything that resembled or could be used as a cleaning rag. Nothing seemed to work.

"Maybe there is something in the saddlebag that you are using for a pillow," Henry offered. The two returned to the camp fire and searched inside the saddlebag. From inside the bag, Henry pulled out a folded white rag.

"Here we go, Your Highness," he proudly presented the rag to Audrianna. The princess held the rag in her hand and carefully examined it in what little light the glowing coals permitted.

"Has this been used?" she asked Henry.

"It could be anybody's guess," he answered.

The princess pursed her lips and turned up the corner of her mouth.

"I think I will improvise," she said, handing the rag back to Henry. "Maybe the 'chamber tree' has some ideas that neither of us have thought of." Audrianna walked towards the large shadowy silhouette of the tree. After several minutes, she walked back to the camp site, laid down on the blanket next to the hot coals, and propped herself up on one elbow. She stared at Henry for several minutes who had turned to face the glowing fire pit.

"I think," Audrianna broke the silence, "the first village that we come across, we need to buy certain necessities for our journey." Henry looked up at the princess.

"That's all well and good," Henry replied. "But, with what money do you plan for us to buy our necessities?"

"Not sure yet," she replied. "But I'll have it all figured out by morning." At that, the little girl laid her head back down on the saddlebag and closed her eyes to finish sleeping. Henry watched her laying down with her eyes closed, then back to the smouldering fire. He contemplated going and searching for more wood to throw on the fire. Suddenly, a giggling sound was heard coming from Audrianna. Henry looked up at her.

"Horatio," she said continuing to chuckle. "Horatio, the castle ghost? What a silly name for a king!" Henry smiled as the princess continued to giggle.

"You believed it," Henry commented.

"Of course," Audrianna said. "I'm a ten-year-old little girl. And I was tired. And, I was starving!"

Henry began to laugh. "For a starving little girl, you sure didn't eat very much that evening." Audrianna sat straight up on the blanket.

"Oh, let me tell you, Henry, turnips are an awful vegetable! Not only did I go to bed hungry that night, but I didn't get much sleep either! Do you know that as bad as turnips smell when they're cooked, the flatulence they cause is much, much worse!"

They both continued to laugh.

"Why would you do such a thing like that to me, Henry?" the princess asked. "Actually," the prince explained, "when you asked me about the howling in the

castle, I saw an opportunity to play with your gullibility. I invented King Horatio on the spot, but I wasn't sure what I wanted you to do until I fully thought it through during Royal Court. Getting you to eat disgusting vegetables I thought would be mean, but for the most part harmless."

"It was mean alright," Audrianna confirmed, laying her head back down on the saddlebag. "And loud…" She looked over at Henry and smirked. Henry smiled back at her. Within a few minutes, the little princess was fast asleep again.

As the sun peaked over the Andjety mountains, and the sky turned from a pitch black to a pale blue, Henry and Audrianna packed up their camp site and were ready to mount their stolen horse.

As before, Henry mounted the horse first, then reached down and pulled the princess in the saddle in front of him. Audrianna grabbed a hold of the reins as Henry turned the horse away from the camp site.

"Which way should we go?" Audrianna asked, as if she was the one steering the horse.

"We came from the valley back that way," Henry explained,

pointing west, "so, I believe we should continue east, and see what village we might stumble upon."

Grabbing the reins from the princess, Henry placed his arms under her armpits and slightly squeezed her sides to ensure she wouldn't get tossed off the saddle. He then kicked the sides of the horse to coax it into a steady trot down the road leading westwards.

After several hours of bouncing on the saddle of the trotting horse, the riders rode to the peak of a hill, and spotted a village down in a valley. A nice flowing river rolled alongside the town. Henry led the horse through a thick grove of trees, and down to the riverside. The two dismounted, and Henry pulled a wooden cup from the saddlebag, drew some water, and offered it to the princess. Audrianna gulped down the water, and handed it back to Henry.

After refreshing themselves, the two travel-worn companions began to wade in the river to wash their faces and hands. Henry led the horse to wade in the water to also refresh itself with water. Audrianna bent at the waist and dunked her head. With her head submerged, she ran her fingers through her scalp in a makeshift attempt to wash the dirt out of her hair.

"Have you figured out a way for us to acquire some money?" Henry asked.

"Yes," the princess replied. "I think we should sell our clothes. Since we are being hunted by the Andjety, we need to dress like other people. Our clothes give us away as royalty. But we could probably sell them at a good price."

"Okay," Henry responded. "There's just one problem with that proposition. How will we sell our clothes, if they are the only clothes on our backs?" Audrianna stared at Henry, then to the left, then down at her feet.

"Well," she answered, "I would say we ask if the local tailor will buy the clothes off our back, and let us buy other clothes with the money to change into."

"I guess that would work," Henry agreed. "But we need to be sure the rest of the village doesn't spot us in our royal garments, otherwise the Andjety will be able to track us."

Henry and Audrianna mounted the horse and rode up the side of the river, staying close to the tree line, and in the shade. From the saddle, they scoped out the tiny town to see if they could determine which building was the local tailor.

As they passed by a grove of trees, they spotted a long chord that was tied to two trees, and several articles of clothing were hanging on them. Someone had recently washed their clothes in the river and hung them out to dry. There were pants, shirts, blouses, and skirts. There was an outfit for a man, one for a woman, two small boys' outfits, and a little girl's outfit that looked close to the size of Audrianna. Henry felt the clothes and discovered they had already dried.

"We can take these clothes, sell our own, and not worry about buying any new clothes," Henry whispered.

"No, Henry," Audrianna scolded. "We can't take these clothes."

"Why not? These are the perfect disguises. I'll look like a common peasant, and you can be my daughter."

"I mean," the princess clarified, "we can't steal these clothes. These are most likely the only outfits the family has. They might be sitting in their house, without any clothes, waiting for their clothes to be dry so they can wear them again. That was common in my home village."

"But we need these clothes. Our lives are at stake."

"True, but they have no way of replacing their clothes. They can't leave home naked.

The father can't go to work without clothes. And we have other options."

Henry looked at Audrianna's sincere gaze. He knew she could not, in good conscience, allow such an act. And yet, he felt it was the safest course of action to disguise themselves before interacting with the townsfolk.

"How about we borrow their clothes, sell our clothes, and with any money we can spare, leave them in their clothes as payment for their services?"

Audrianna pondered the prince's suggestion. "I guess that would work," Audrianna agreed.

The two fugitives snatched the clothes from the line and darted towards the thicket of trees. They quickly shed their own clothes, then pulled the borrowed clothes over their undergarments. Henry's outfit sagged rather loosely over his torso, while Audrianna's was too short above her ankles, and too snug around her waist.

"The father of the family must be a bit more muscular than I am," Henry commented. "And the daughter must only be nine years old," Audrianna remarked. "She needs another year of growing to be the same size as me." With their old clothes neatly folded

and tucked under their arm, they made their way to the village tailor to barter. "Have you ever sold clothes before?" Henry asked the princess.

"No," she answered. "I've only been to the marketplace once before."

"Well, you need to understand that merchants always try to cheat you. They will intentionally offer less money than what the clothes are worth. They will try and convince you that our clothes are inferior, or not worth very much. You have to demand more money than what they ask, and point out the quality of the material, and the meticulous handiwork in stitching the clothes together."

"Wait," Audrianna commented. "Where are you going to be? Aren't you coming in to barter with me?"

"No," Henry answered. "I am going to the stables and see if I can sell the horse." "The horse?" Audrianna asked. "What are we going to ride if you sell the horse?" "The horse is an Andjety officer's horse," Henry answered. "It would be spotted

almost immediately—perhaps even sooner than we would be recognised. Besides, most commoners are on foot, and I've seen farmers with horse and wagons pick up travellers alongside the road."

"I don't know if I can sell these clothes by myself. I've never bartered before. What will I tell the tailor if he asks where I got these expensive clothes?"

"You'll do fine," Henry assured her. "Tell him you bought them in the city of Nadeau, but now you have to sell them because you need the money." Henry turned to lead the horse in the opposite direction. "Just don't accept anything less than forty-five silver coins."

Audrianna pondered what Henry told her. She tucked the clothes under her arm, and walked towards the main road through town. She rehearsed her story in her head, and how she wasn't going to let the tailor cheat her of any money. Forty-five silver coins, she thought.

As the princess walked through the door of what seemed to be a tailor shop, she was startled by the beautiful display of various dresses. Although the dresses were a style typical of farm girls, there was a variety of different colours, designs, and sizes.

"Hello?" Audrianna called out in the empty shop.

"I'm coming," a woman cheerfully answered from a back room. Audrianna walked among the dresses, holding her stack of clothes against her chest. She bent over to closely examine some of the handiwork of the shop's dresses. She noticed how nice they were stitched together. After several minutes, a plumb older woman with a kind face entered the main shop. As she laid eyes on Audrianna, she jumped back almost as if the princess's appearance frightened her.

"Good heavens," the woman exclaimed. "What on earth happened to your hair, little miss!" Audrianna had completely forgotten how startling her haircut was to strangers. But she knew she couldn't give the standard answer that the prince cut it with his sword. "I was in a tree and got my hair tangled in its branches. My friend had no choice but to cut my hair to free me from the tree."

"Good heavens," the woman repeated. "I hope you don't climb any more trees in the future."

"No, madam," Audrianna adamantly answered. "May I talk to the tailor about some clothes I have with me?" The old woman chuckled.

"This is not a tailor shop," she answered. "This is a seamstress shop. Tailors are for men's clothing. Expensive men's clothes. All the men in this village are farmers. They never dress fancier than what is necessary to plough their fields."

"Oh," Audrianna replied, looking down at her feet.

"My shop makes clothes that are of a practical nature. I make ordinary men's clothes, women's clothes, little boys' clothes," the old woman bent down to look straight into Audrianna's face, "and even clothes for pretty little girls like yourself."

Audrianna beamed a smile.

"So, tell me about the clothes you brought into my shop to-day," the old woman asked, standing straight up and looking down at the princess. "What are you needing me to do for you? Alterations? Repair stitching? Are they clothes you bought in this shop?"

Audrianna, who was still clutching the clothes to her chest, lowered her arms to reveal the fine royal clothing.

"I bought these in Nadeau, but I need to sell them, because I need the money." The woman examined the clothes, holding the fabric close to her face. She then looked down at Audrianna and scowled.

"I'm sorry, little miss," she answered. "I cannot buy these clothes from you. You'll have to try someplace else." The seamstress folded the clothes and shoved them back into Audrianna's arms.

"Why?" the princess asked.

"Because you are lying to me," she replied. Audrianna was alarmed by her response. "What do you mean?" Audrianna asked.

"There is no way a little farm girl like yourself could possibly afford to buy such expensive clothes in Nadeau." The woman's countenance shifted from a kind old lady, to that of anger and resentment. "You most likely have stolen these clothes from a nobleman and his daughter. If I was to buy them, not only will

I be encouraging your thieving habits, but I would be in trouble for selling stolen property. They might even think I stole them in Nadeau."

"I didn't steal them, madam," Audrianna replied. "I acquired them honestly, but I need to sell them because I have no money."

"And what does a little girl like yourself need with money?" the woman asked accusingly. "Where are your parents? Who are they?"

"I don't have any parents," the princess answered, forcing her eyes to well up with tears, "I'm an orphan!" Audrianna cocked her head to one side and looked up at the woman through the corner of her eye as tears began streaking down her cheek. "I have no family," she sobbed. "No home. No food. Nothing but the clothes on my back. I'm all alone!"

The weeping princess caused the seamstress's countenance to change from suspicion to sympathy. She cupped her hand over her mouth and placed the other on Audrianna's shoulder.

"Good heavens," the seamstress replied, comforting the devious little girl. "You poor dear! I had no idea of the circumstances. Of course, I'll buy your clothes from you. I'll give you a fair price, too."

Audrianna continued to wail as the woman studied the condition and quality of the clothes. As Audrianna sobbed, the woman pulled a handful of coins from the drawer and placed them in a leather pouch. She then held the bag out in front of the princess.

"I'll give you thirty silver coins for both outfits," the woman announced. Immediately Audrianna quit her caterwauling, snatched the pouch and gave the woman a serious gaze.

"Give me forty-five, and you've got yourself a deal!"

CHAPTER 16

Audrianna and Henry returned the borrowed clothes to the laundry chord from whence they found them. At Audrianna's request, Henry tied the leather pouch she had acquired to the line, with fifteen silver coins inside. Now, with the money from the seamstress, after acquiring new clothes for the two of them, and the money from selling the horse, the two royals walked down the dusty path with one hundred and eighty silver coins.

The pair walked for hours, hoping a farmer would come down the path in a horse and wagon to give them a ride. Nothing came. Several people drove by on their way to the city of Nadeau as Henry and Audrianna walked in the opposite direction. But no one drove in the direction they wanted to go.

Soon, the pair became increasingly hungry. They dared not buy too many provisions in the previous village, due to the fact they had sold an Andjety officer's horse, as well as royal garments. Too many questions could be asked if they stayed too long. But now, they were feeling the pangs of their former choices. And they weren't sure how much longer they had to walk before they stumbled upon the next village.

Now the sun was beginning to set, and they had gone all day without eating. Henry tried to pretend that he wasn't all that hungry and that he could wait until morning if necessary. Audrianna, however, could not mask her displeasure in having nothing to eat. The longer they went without food, the grumpier she became. After a while, her attitude had become so intolerable to Henry that he wanted to take her over his knee as before. But he restrained himself.

Finally, as dusk settled in, the two weary travellers spotted the next village. With renewed vigour, they hurried down the trail hoping they might find a place to buy food. As they entered the centre of small town, Henry spotted the local pub.

"The pub will have food, provisions, and a room for us to sleep," the prince informed his companion. The two of them scurried through the door hoping to be able to eat whatever was readily available. Very few people were in the pub. This made it very easy for the two of them to remain, for the most part, unnoticed. Audrianna tied a scarf over her hair, to avoid any more people being shocked at her appearance, and drawing attention to the two of them.

Henry ordered the little princess to sit at a table in a dark corner of the room. Henry walked to the counter and paid for a meal, a room, and a few other provisions. He then returned to where Audrianna sat and waited for their food to be prepared.

Within minutes, a bar maid brought the two of them a platter with cooked meat, vegetables, and bread. Although Henry was not used to eating vegetables, since they were considered peasant food, they both quickly devoured whatever their hands could get hold of.

As Henry and Audrianna began to feel satisfied from their meal, the thoughts of their responsibilities as crowned royals started to take hold in their minds. Since the campfire the night before, Henry had done nothing but express a sense of hopelessness in regard to his kingdom. He was used to being surrounded by guards, armour-bearers, and royal advisors that protected him, and explained to him everything that needed to be accomplished. Now, having no sense of safely or security, or anyone to advise him above the age of ten, Henry felt tremendously vulnerable.

As they sat in silence, finishing their meal, Audrianna looked up at Henry. For the past several hours, her hunger had kept her in a less than cordial mood. Now with her hunger satisfied, she wanted to dialogue with Henry in hopes that he might have an idea as to what they should do about the overthrow of their kingdom.

"Henry," she called for his attention louder than she needed to in a sparsely populated pub. "Have you thought about what we need to do?"

Henry quickly glanced at the occupants of the pub to see if there was anyone that looked in their direction, and perhaps might recognise who they were.

"Shh!" he whispered, scolding the princess. "Don't call me 'Henry', Your Highness."

"Don't call me 'Your Highness', Henry," she quietly snapped.

"Listen, Audrianna," Henry continued to whisper, "While we on the run, it would be best if we have cover stories and false names that we go by. That way we have the same answers no matter who asks us, or which one of us they question."

"Ok," the princess agreed, excitedly happy to create a different persona. For her it was a type of perpetual play-time.

"You and I will pretend that we are brother and sister," Henry asserted, "traveling from Nadeau to the east side of the kingdom in search of work."

"Yes," Audrianna agreed. "Because we lost our parents, in a tragic carnival accident…"

"Carnival accident?" Henry questioned.

"Yes," Audrianna answered, cocking her head to one side and looking up at Henry through the corner of her eye. "We told mama and papa that those bears looked hungry," she continued starting to sob. "But papa just wanted to know what wild bear fur felt like." Tears began rolling down her cheeks as Henry sat back in his chair, folding his arms and slowly shaking his head. "And before we knew it, papa was petting the bear from inside its belly."

"Really?" Henry asked incredulously.

"Uh-huh" the princess continued, still pretending to weep. "Mama grabbed hold of his foot, just as he was going down, but the bear ended up sucking her down as well!"

"Okay," Henry interrupted, rolling his eyes. "That doesn't make any sense. That's not how bear attacks happen. You make a bear eating a person sound like a frog eating a cricket." Audrianna began to giggle. "Let's be serious now," Henry demanded. "Telling people that we are brother and sister is probably the most realistic. We can say our parents died, and that's probably all we need to tell them. There is enough sickness and death going on these days, that no one feels obliged to request an explanation."

"Yes, sir," Audrianna replied. "I just thought if we were going to make up a story, it might as well be an entertaining one."

"Entertaining is not the same as believable," Henry commented. "As fugitives, we need to remain as incognito as possible."

"What's incognito?" Audrianna asked.

"That means we need to blend in with the people and the environment, so those who are looking for us, can't find us."

"Why don't we tell the villages who we are?" Audrianna asked. "Aren't we their rulers? Don't they feel a sense of loyalty to us? We protected them from the Andjety and the Witch."

"Yes," Henry answered. "But most of the villages are loyal to whomever controls their land. It's not that they are loyal or disloyal to the royal family. It is a matter of survival. Like you said earlier today, all that these people have are the one pair of clothes and what little food their farms provide. The Witch can easily take what little they have away from them."

"I can't imagine anyone becoming loyal to the Witch," Audrianna replied. "She has hurt so many people."

"True," Henry responded. "but it's important to know that the Witch will do whatever she can to manipulate you."

"Me?" the princess asked. "How is she going to manipulate me?"

"Listen, Audrianna," the prince looked sincerely into the little girl's face. "The Witch is a master manipulator. She will make you think she is your friend, or sympathises with your fears, or wanting to help you in some way. All the while, she is grooming you to do what she has wanted all along. She might convince you that she cares about you, then kill you! Or she might make you think she is trying to help, then betray you. However she tries to manipulate you, she always does it almost flawlessly." Audrianna listened to every word her betrothed told her. She took his stern warning very serious.

"Okay," the princess said. "Now let's discuss names. We can't go around calling each other 'Henry' and 'Audrianna', or 'Your Majesty' and 'Your Highness.'"

"You're right," Henry replied. "What name should I call you by?" The princess thought for a while. She loved the name Audrianna, and nothing else seemed to fit her personality. "How about 'Gertrude'," Henry suggested.

"Call me that again, and I'll stab you with this fork," she protested, holding up a wooden fork that she used with their meal.

"How about, Audrey?" Henry recommended. Audrianna wrinkled her nosed and squinted her eyes in objection.

"Too fancy for a common peasant girl," she commented. "Most farm girls have one syllable names like, 'Sal', or 'Jean', or 'Kam'. How about calling me 'Ree', which is short for Aud-REE-anna? What do you think?"

"Ree?" Henry asked. "Yes," Audrianna replied.

"And by what name should you call me?" Henry asked. "Albert?"

"No!" Audrianna exclaimed. "That is not a fitting peasant name. However, I think you might be on the right track. I'll name you after the castle ghost."

"Horatio?" Henry asked. "Do you honestly think I look like a Horatio?"

"Not Horatio," Audrianna replied. "But I do think you look like a Horace." Henry grimaced at the sound of the new name Audrianna gave him.

"Horace?" he asked. "You're seriously going to call me Horace?"

"Yes," she replied. "As a farm boy, you look like the spitting image of someone named, Horace."

"Horace sounds like a guy who's more brawn than brains," Henry stated.

Audrianna raised her eyebrows, cocked her head, and stared at Henry for several seconds.

"You are NOT calling me Horace!" he reaffirmed. Audrianna beamed a smile. After paying for their meal, Henry inquired about a room from the owner of the pub.

The owner looked down at the little girl, then back up at Henry. He gave Henry an uncomfortable stare.

"She is my sister," Henry retorted. "Isn't that right?" he asked Audrianna to back up his story.

"That's right, Horace," she answered. "He's my brother." The pub owner, seemingly satisfied, pulled a key from a drawer and pointed to the stairs. "We're related," the princess added as they walked up the steps to the room.

Upon entering the room, Henry cautioned the princess from walking too far into the dark room without first letting him light the lamp. He lit the lamp, then together, they inspected the amenities of the simple, little room. There was a small rope-tied bed that laid close to the floor. Several old rags were stuffed within what resembled a lumpy, thin mattress. There was also a table with a large rusty metal basin that was used for washing and refreshing oneself. There was no pitcher to go with the basin. An empty bucket sat on the floor next to the table.

"Is that bucket supposed to be for water, or is that a chamber pot?" Audrianna wanted clarified.

"I believe it is for drawing water, either drinking or washing," Henry answered. "But, I'm not sure those before us understood that distinction." Audrianna stuck out her tongue in disgust.

The room for the most part had been swept clean, and there was no evidence of a rodent problem. The main comforter over the bed had been beaten out recently. There were no windows in the room, due to it being a contained room within the second floor. There were no paintings or decorative décor to speak of, though the princess thought a crack scaling up one wall looked like a flowery tree.

"So how are we going to sleep," Audrianna wanted to know. She was quite aware that the two of them sharing a room was taboo, and certainly the two of them sleeping in the same bed was out of the question. Not that either one of them were inclined to share the same space.

"I think that I should have the bed this time," Henry demanded. "I made you a nice bed last night with the horse blanket and saddlebag, and stayed up all night keeping watch, while you slept."

"I wasn't going to argue with you, Horace," Audrianna defended herself. "I was even going to suggest you sleep in the bed this time."

"Thank you, Audrey," Henry responded. "I appreciate…"

"Ree!" the princess interrupted. "Not 'Audrey'! 'Ree'! I'm a poor farm girl with only a one-syllable name. Call me 'Ree'!"

"I'm sorry," Henry replied, laying back on the small bed. "Ree, Ree, Ree!" He put his arms behind his head and closed his eyes. For several minutes he lay there, squirming only enough to test the tightness of the ropes of the mattress. Soon, he laid still, feeling his body relax. He had been awake for the past thirty-six hours, and he hoped the next eight hours would make up for the deficit his body was feeling. The sound of drunken revelries could be heard downstairs, but Henry was able to put it out of his mind and begin to rest. All was quiet in the room.

"Horace," a soft voice spoke next to his bed. Henry opened his eyes to see that Audrianna was still standing next to him, in the same place when he closed his eyes.

"Yes, Ree," he answered.

"Where am I supposed to sleep?" she patiently asked, trying not to disturb her companion's rest.

"Go stand in the corner," he sighed. "Make sure you face the wall."

Audrianna slapped Henry's chest in protest. Henry rolled out of bed and lifted the comforter from the rope mattress. From between the ropes nearest the corners, he pulled out several wadded-up rags. Two of them he stuffed inside each other and tied the ends to make a small pillow. The other two rags, which were larger, he tied together at the corners to make a thin blanket, a little shorter than the princess. Laying the crudely improvised blanket down, with the pillow on top, he ordered the princess to lay down by pointing at the mangy rags.

"Get some sleep, Ree. Tomorrow is a longer day than today."

"How is tomorrow longer than today?" she asked as she placed her head on the makeshift pillow.

"Because," Henry answered, laying back on his bed and closing his eyes once more. "Today is almost over, and tomorrow hasn't even started yet."

Audrianna chuckled, and Henry smiled as they both drifted off to sleep.

By morning, the two refreshed travellers made their way down the dusty trail leading them further east. Neither one had any idea where they were going, or what they should do, but to keep moving to avoid the Witch from catching up with them and killing them. "It's been a day and a half since the castle was invaded and the king was killed,"

Audrianna remarked. "Why hasn't anybody heard about it? I mean, wouldn't everybody be talking about it and grieving the death of Malcolm the Merciful?"

"Well," Henry stated, "I guess it takes a long time for news to travel this far east.

The witch could also have the city under siege, with no one being allowed in or out." "Strange that we haven't seen a hunting party or anything come by, looking for us,"

Audrianna commented.

"You want a hunting party to catch up with us?" Henry asked.

"No," the princess replied. "I just think it strange that in such a long period of time, there has been no sign of the Andjety trying to hunt us down."

"Oh, they are out there," Henry responded. "They are most likely turning over every stone to make sure we don't slip through their fingers. But they will be making their way east, in our direction. If we don't keep moving, they will definitely overrun us for sure." The pair continued walking down the road in silence for several minutes. Although Audrianna had slept on the hard, wooden floor, she was refreshed and full of energy.

Henry also was rested, but sore from the uncomfortable bed.

As Audrianna walked down the road, she took high steps, kicking her knees in the air and bouncing her head to the left and to the right. Her scarf was stuffed in a small satchel tied to her waist, and her ungroomed hair stuck straight out on both sides of her head. As she bounced, her hair would flutter and wave from the movement of her head. Henry walked behind her and watched the spectacle of her high energy.

"Must you bob your head when you walk?" he asked. Audrianna stopped bouncing her head, turned to look at Henry as she kept walking, and beamed a mischievous grin.

They walked a little further in silence. As they walked, they came to a bridge crossing a clear water stream. They both decided it was a good time to refresh themselves with cool water. As Audrianna waded in the water to drink and wash herself, she could see her reflection. Most importantly, she could see the condition of her hair. She quickly pulled her scarf out and tied it over her head. How she missed the royal hairdresser!

Within a few minutes, the two continued to walk down the path. The day had not been far spent, so they hadn't any need to rest very long. As they journeyed along, Audrianna, feeling full of energy, became rather talkative.

"So, Horace," Audrianna pondered, "if King Malcolm is dead, does that make you the new king?"

"Not quite," Henry answered. "I can take the throne as the crowned prince, but I still will not be considered the 'king' until I have a 'queen' sitting by my side."

"But, you do have a queen," Audrianna responded. "Me!"

"You are no more the queen than I am the king," Henry replied.

"So, what keeps us from becoming the next king and queen of Nadeau?" "We have to get married," Henry reminded the princess.

"Well, let's get married, go back to Nadeau, and take over the throne," Audrianna simply answered.

"It's not that simple, Ree," Henry remarked. "According to Nadeau law, you have to be at least sixteen years old to marry."

"That's stupid," Audrianna replied. "I can rule just as well as you can, even at ten." "That is probably true," Henry answered. "However, the law is in place to protect you, not deprive you."

"Protect me from what?" she demanded.

"Well—" Henry squirmed, searching for the right words. "There are many nations and cultures that practice child marriages. We find that detestable, so the law states that you must be old enough to be able to make your own conscientious choice."

Audrianna stopped dead in her tracks and stared at Henry. Henry, in turn, stopped to hear what Audrianna seemed upset about.

"At what point, when I was taken from my home without warning, sent to Nadeau without asking, betrothed to you without my consent, and coronated as the crowned princess against my will, was I making a conscientious choice?"

Henry looked solemnly at the little princess. Her eyes shown a gravely sad expression. Choices? He realised that neither one of them had been offered any kind of choice in the matter of their betrothal.

"King Malcolm may have been a merciful king in Royal Court," Henry interjected, "but he was an unloving tyrant all the years I grew up. 'Malcolm the Merciless' was the father I knew. A man that always got what he wanted. When he took over from his father, Nadeau was a much smaller, impoverished kingdom. Most of this land to the east belonged to the Andjety. But, through ravenous war and bloodshed, my father expanded his kingdom to twice the size that it was. This is why the Andjety constantly raid our land and villages. In their minds, it's still their land, crops, and farm animals."

"So, what makes us any better than the Andjety?" the princess asked. Henry thought for a moment as they continued to walk.

"I don't know, Ree," he shamefully answered.

"Well, make sure you figure that question out before you and I become the next king and queen. You have six years, after all."

They continued walking in silence.

"What's the big deal of having to be sixteen, anyways?" the princess asked. "How is sixteen old enough to make a conscious choice?"

"Conscientious," Henry corrected.

"Conscientious," she mocked. "What difference does that make?"

"Getting married requires a little more maturity than a ten-year-old can handle," Henry remarked.

"Why?" Audrianna asked. "All you have to do is stand in front of the groom and say, 'I do'. I think I've mastered the dialogue."

"Well, if you stick to those two words our entire marriage, you'll be a prized wife," Henry chuckled. Audrianna stopped walking, thought for a minute, then grinned.

"Okay," she replied. She then mimicked an adult's voice. "Your Highness? Do you beat your husband every day?" "I do," she answered in her own passive voice.

"Do you sprinkle his food with poison?" "I do."

"Do you feel being married to King Henry is the worst thing that could have ever happened to you?"

"I do."

"Alright," Henry broke in. "You proved your point. Besides,

you and I cannot be considered officially married until we consummate our marriage bond. And you're too young for that. That is the main reason why you have to be sixteen."

"What is 'consummate'?" she asked.

"Well…" Henry suddenly realised he broached a subject with a ten-year-old that he was not prepared to explain. "It's… It's what happens… after the ceremony… to—to seal the deal…"

"Oh," Audrianna nodded, thinking she understood what Henry was talking about. "That's when the priest tells the man and woman to kiss."

"Well," Henry stammered, "That's… the beginning of it," he said, nervously looking in all directions for an escape from the conversation.

"Well," Audrianna casually responded as she started to walk again, "I don't mind consummating our marriage at the beginning. But don't think I'll do it very often."

As they continued walking, the sound of horse hooves came trotting up behind them. The two turned to greet whoever seemed to be passing, in hopes of acquiring a ride to the next village. The horse pulled a simple wagon, and in the wagon sat an old man dressed as a land-owning farmer. As the wagon approached, the old man pulled back the reins and gave the command for the horse to stop.

"Blessings upon the two of you," the old man kindly remarked. "To what village are you two travelling?"

"As far east as the road will lead," Henry answered. "How far are you going?"

"I'm on my way to Pachenthou, the very centre of this fine kingdom," the old man announced. Henry was taken aback by the refinement with which the farmer spoke. Most farmers that came to Royal Court could barely speak the Nadeau language correctly, even as their native tongue.

"Pachenthou sounds like a pleasant village to visit on our journey," Henry replied, "if you could stand some company to ride along with you."

"I would be happy to have you and your daughter join me," the man responded. Henry stopped short and looked up at the man with the intention of correcting him with their brother and sister cover story. Audrianna, however, decided to roll with the misunderstanding.

"Goody, papa," she giggled. "Up, papa! Up!" she shouted holding out her arms for Henry to pick her up.

"Stop that," Henry whispered, lifting her in the wagon. "You are ten years old, not three. And close enough to five feet that you should start climbing in on your own."

The three rode in the wagon, with the old man sharing intricate details of landmarks they passed, stories relating to the rivers and streams, and anecdotes about people and their houses. After sharing almost everything he could think of, the old man turned to Henry.

"Tell me about you two," he asked. "I don't even think I caught your names." "My name is Ree," Audrianna pipped up. "And my papa's name is Horace." "Thank you, Ree," Henry admonished. "But I think I can speak for myself."

"Just wanted to make sure you got your name right, papa," she offered. "I know my name," Henry shot back.

"Careful, my friend," the old man warned Henry. "It is an unmistakable fact that when your daughter grows up, she will one day be looking for a husband. And do you know what kind of man she will be most attracted to?"

"Probably one that is deaf and dumb," Henry replied, "so she can talk all she wants and not be interrupted." He turned to look at Audrianna who was seated behind the two men in the wagon. Audrianna crossed her eyes and wrinkled her nose at Henry.

"No," the farmer corrected, pointing his finger at Henry, "your daughter will look for a man that is just like her father. That is who she will marry. If you have a temper, she will seek a man with a temper. If you shout a lot, she will look for a man that shouts a lot at her. If you are loving or tenderhearted, that is the kind of man she will look for. She will marry what she is accustomed to living with."

"Did you hear that, papa?" Audrianna responded over Henry's shoulder. "I'm going to marry someone just—like—you!" Henry looked away and the princess sat back and snickered to herself.

"How far did you say you two were going?" the old man asked smiling at Henry. "To the far east end of the kingdom," Henry answered.

"Why on earth would you go all the way out there?" the old man asked. "Business?

Family?"

"No," Henry replied, "Just wanting to get as far away from the City of Nadeau as possible."

"Horace," the man leaned towards Henry and lowered his voice, "are you in some kind of legal trouble with the king? Or maybe the prince?"

"No," Henry tried to assure the stranger.

"Because," the old man looked into Henry's eyes, "I know that the prince can be a heartless, gutless, absolute pain in the backside kind of a man." Henry felt sweat bead on his forehead. He swallowed hard to think of how he could answer the man.

"Wow," Audrianna spoke out, "he sure is! You described that lousy prince quite well."

"Be quiet, Ree," Henry yelled.

"Do you want to know something else I know about the prince," the old man asked, pulling on the reins and bringing the horse and wagon to a stop. Henry suddenly realised that they had been found out. Whoever this man was, he had Henry and Audrianna pegged from the start. He wanted to jump from the wagon and run, but he wasn't about to leave the princess alone with what could be a bounty hunter or a mercenary.

"What do you know?" Henry nervously asked.

"I know that the city of Nadeau has been for the past day and a half under siege from the Andjety. I know that the prince and the princess have been on the run since the city was invaded."

Henry tightened his fists ready to lunge at the stranger. He had no weapons, but he wasn't about to be captured without a fight. Maybe at least little Audrianna could run away and find refuge somewhere.

"I also know," the old man continued, "that the former Captain of the King's Guards gave the prince a scar across his right shoulder while training him for sword fighting." Henry felt a chill go down his back, as well as a sense of relief that he might be in company of an ally. But he wasn't sure which.

"And how would you know such a thing?" Henry cautiously asked.

"Because," the old man explained, "you may not recognise me, but I am Balen, your former instructor, and former Captain of the Royal Guard."

CHAPTER 17

Henry examined the old man's face. In his mind, he looked past the grey scraggily beard and smoothed out the wrinkles under his eyes. Yes, it was Balen after all.

"Balen," Henry began to smile. "I haven't seen you…" "In ten years," Balen finished the prince's statement.

"Yes," Henry lowered his head, "I guess it has been ten years since…"

"Since you were fifteen," Balen interrupted, staring down his passenger. Henry hung his head even lower.

"Yes," Henry replied. "I was fifteen."

"No matter," Balen replied. "In spite of our history together, you need to understand that above all, I am a loyalist."

"What do you mean, a loyalist," Audrianna asked.

"I mean, Your Highness," Balen answered, "no matter what the crown has done to me, or how I've been treated, I am—and forever will be—loyal to the kingdom of Nadeau and to the crown." Audrianna smiled, and slapped her hand on the stocky shoulder of Balen.

"You're my kind of fellow," the princess remarked. Balen turned and looked at the beaming princess. He then looked back at Henry and announced, "Let me take you to my house in Pachenthou. There's someone there I want you to meet." Henry's eyes grew wide.

"You don't mean…" Henry stammered. "She's not going to be there, is she?" he asked looking fearful. Now Balen smiled a mischievous grin and without a word, whipped the reins to tell the horse to continue trotting.

"Who's she?" Audrianna asked. No one answered.

As the wagon rolled down the road, through groves of trees, and past several villages, Audrianna watched intently at the changing scenery. The further east the wagon drove, the less green everything became. As they passed by farms and villages, Audrianna began to see a recurring image painted on the sides of barns and houses. It was a triangle with a line centred over the top. After seeing the same symbol three times on three different buildings, the princess leaned forward and placed her hand on Balen's shoulder.

"Mr Balen, sir? What does that mean?" she asked, pointing to one of the images. "That, Your Highness, is the symbol for balance. It is a peaceful protest of the

Nadeau people to request a queen that would help temper the roguish behaviour of the prince. The people desire the kingdom to be like it was in the days of Luella the Beloved."

"So, it's a symbol representing me?" the princess asked.

"That depends. Do you temper the behaviour of your be-trothed?" Balen asked in reply. Audrianna's head dropped as she thought. She then lifted her head in response.

"I don't know," she answered. "But he always has a nasty tem-per when I try." Balen roared with a jolly laugh.

"You might be the one the people have been hoping for," Balen said, laughing as he spoke. Henry folded his arms and slouched on the bench of the wagon as they continued to ride down the road leading to Pachenthou.

After a couple hours of the wagon rattling and shaking as the horse pulled it down the path, Balen pulled back the reins bringing the horse to a stop.

"Are we here?" Audrianna excitedly asked. "Where were you hoping to be?" Balen asked.

"Pachenthou. Are we in Pachenthou? I've never been to Pachenthou!" The princess began to wildly bounce in the back of the wagon.

"Actually," Balen commented, "you have been to Pachenthou. Many months ago, on your way to Nadeau from your home out east." Audrianna stopped bouncing and stared at Balen wide-eyed. "But we are not in Pachenthou. This is my home. We are close to town, though."

Henry helped the princess down from the wagon and Balen unhitched the horse and led it to the stable. A light shone from inside the simple house. Henry gripped both sides of the princess's shoulders as if he was using her as a human shield.

"Horace?" Audrianna quietly whispered. "Yes, Ree," he answered.

"Why are you hurting me?" she asked. Henry immediately released his anxious grip on her shoulders.

"Sorry," he apologised. "I'm a bit nervous of being here." "Why? What's here?" she asked.

Balen returned from the stable and re-joined the two royal travellers. From inside the house stepped a beautiful older woman. She had long dark hair, and wore a simple, yet graceful, farm dress. She had stunning steel-blue eyes that immediately caught one's attention. Henry slowly began to squeeze the princess's shoulders again.

"Ah, there you are my dear," Balen called out to the woman. He walked towards her and greeted her with a soft kiss. He then turned to face Henry and Audrianna. "My friends," Balen announced, "this is my wife, Olivia."

"Hello, Olivia," Audrianna replied, giving a clumsy curtsy.

"Lady Olivia," Henry greeted, remaining frozen next to Audrianna. Olivia walked straight to Henry and stood a few inches from the prince.

"Henry," she responded in a kind, soft voice. Henry gave a relaxed sigh, and nodded to the woman.

"It's nice to see you…" Henry began to reply. Olivia suddenly reared back and struck Henry in the face with a THWACK! The unsuspecting impact with Olivia's fist caused

the prince to tumble to the ground. Audrianna burst out laughing with an unruly and unbridled laugh.

"I've repressed that for ten years, Your Majesty," Olivia remarked to Henry shaking her hand in the air. Audrianna continued to belly laugh, and chuckle, and snort, and giggle. She laughed so hard, she found it hard to breathe.

"Olivia," Balen reprimanded. "He is the crowned prince." Audrianna began to squeak from lack of oxygen, as she pointed at Henry who picked himself up from the ground.

"I don't care if he is the king," Olivia touted. "He had it coming." Audrianna clapped her hands trying to respond to Olivia but had no breath to talk.

"He is the king, now," Balen replied. "Prince Henry witnessed the Witch stab King Malcolm in the back just before the two of them fled the castle."

"Really?" Olivia replied shaking her head. "The death of Malcolm the Merciful is the end of an era." By now, Audrianna had grabbed her sides and began breathing normally.

"And what is your name, my dear," Olivia greeted the princess.

"Ree," she answered with laboured breath. "I'm his daughter," she said, pointing at Henry. Olivia shot a look at Henry. "But not really his daughter. I'm also his sister." Olivia looked back at Audrianna. "But not really his sister. I'm also his wife." Olivia put her hands on her hips as the princess continued to list all their aliases. "But, I'm not really his wife, yet. I am his betrothed, though. And that's the truth."

"You seem a little young to be betrothed to a prince of twenty-five." Olivia observed. "That's what I've been saying for the past four months," Henry interjected.

"Oh," Audrianna added, turning to the lady of the house. "And my name isn't really Ree. It's Audrianna. I'm the crowned princess of Nadeau."

"Well," Olivia responded, "in that case…" She grabbed the sides of her farm dress and gave a perfect and graceful curtsy.

"Wow!" Audrianna replied. "I wish I could curtsy as flawless as you." "I've been curtsying longer than you've been alive, Your Highness."

"Enough chattering out here," Balen admonished. "Let's go inside where we all can get comfortable. These two refugees have walked many hours, and probably are hungry. Am I right?"

"Yes—Yes—Yes!" Audrianna exclaimed at the sudden thought of food.

"Well, let's go inside," Olivia directed. "I have supper prepared. I wasn't expecting anyone else but Balen, but we have plenty of food to eat."

The two royals and the two farmers entered the house upon which Olivia began to assign each person a different responsibility. Henry was asked to fetch two more chairs stored out by the barn and dust them off. Balen was send to the garden to get another basket of vegetables, wash them, and then cut them up per his wife's instructions.

Audrianna was handed a bucket and sent to the well to draw water. Everyone obeyed without complaint, except the princess.

"I don't know if I'm strong enough to pull the rope out of the well with a full bucket at the end," she whined.

"Do your best, Audrianna," Olivia remarked. "If you have trouble, I will have you draw water all day tomorrow until your arms get strong enough to do it without effort." Audrianna frowned and wrinkled her nose at Olivia at what she thought was an unreasonable proposal.

"Oh, little girl," Olivia snapped at the princess. "You did not give me a dirty scowl, did you?" Audrianna froze and looked wide-eyed at Olivia. "Do you know what happens to little ten-year-old girls that give me a dirty scowl?" Everyone in the house froze along with Audrianna.

"No," was the princess's soft reply.

"They get switched!" Olivia exclaimed looking dead into the princess's face. Audrianna held the water bucket tightly in her arms. She looked to the left and to the right, then at Olivia.

"Switched with who?" the princess sincerely asked. Olivia didn't say another word, but pointed towards the door. Audrianna did not fully understand Olivia's threat, but she did understand she had best draw water without another complaint.

The princess did all she could to wrestle the bucket from the well, and carry it back into the house. She was not about to be forced to carry a water bucket all day the next day, if she could help it. Once inside, Olivia remarked to Audrianna that she had only brought half of the bucket's water into the house. Audrianna disagreed by telling her the other half she carried in on her clothes.

With the water Audrianna had carried into the house, Olivia ordered everyone to wash themselves before sitting at the table for the ready meal. After inspecting everyone's hands, she directed each person to the exact chair she desired them to sit at. Balen sat at the head of the table, with Olivia at his side. The table was arranged in such a way as to depict the host and hostess as the king and queen of their home.

As the four sat around the table, Henry and Audrianna eyed the spread of food waiting for them with distain. Most of the food was garden vegetables. There were parsnips, and carrots, and potatoes, and radishes, and broccoli, and rutabagas, and cucumbers, and peppers, and zucchini, and most favourite of all, turnips. None of the food was cooked, but rather chopped, and served raw.

"Look, Horace," Audrianna called, "turnips!"

"Yes, Ree," Henry responded. "I see the lovely looking turnips."

"Audrianna, dear," Olivia asked the princess in a calm, tender voice, "would you please remove your scarf. Scarves are for outdoors, not at dinner tables." Audrianna shot a look of foreboding at Henry. Henry also looked a bit worried. She knew there was no sense in arguing with the lady of the house. She slowly untied the knot under her chin and slid the scarf off her head.

"What on earth!" Olivia shrieked, standing to her feet. "What hairdresser cut your hair in such an ungodly fashion?"

"It wasn't a hairdresser," Audrianna announced, pointing. "It was Henry." "Your Majesty," Olivia scolded with a condemning tone.

"She was stuck in a tree, hanging by her hair," Henry defended.

"And, I assume," Olivia replied, "you tried to cut the branches free before you took such a drastic measure?"

"No," Henry sheepishly answered. "I was upset with her at the time."

"I see," Olivia remarked. "Do you understand how serious it is to cut off a woman's hair?"

"She's not a woman," Henry retorted. "She's a child." "She is your wife," Olivia reminded him.

"She's not my wife, either," Henry countered. "She is only my betrothed." "Betrothal is an official declaration. In all respects, she is your wife, waiting for the

day that she is old enough to be bound by law in matrimony."

"Yeah," Audrianna added, "we were already talking this afternoon about consummating it."

"No, we weren't!" Henry shot back, his voice nervously crackling. "She doesn't know what she's talking about. She thinks that means something else." Both Balen and Olivia stared Henry down with a scowl.

"What does it mean, then?" Audrianna asked, looking back and forth between Balen and Olivia.

"You're a barbarian," Balen accused Henry.

"Everyone," Olivia called the table to order. "Let us eat the food set before us. Balen?" Balen closed his eyes and looked upwards. Audrianna and Henry started to reach for food when Balen began praying.

"Merciful God," Balen prayed. The two royals froze, with their arms stretched over the table. "We have worked hard for the food set before us. You gave us land. You gave us food. For that, we are eternally thankful. Amen."

As the four began scooping small portions of different vegetables onto their plates from the centre of the small table, Audrianna noticed that the meal was void of any type of meat. She herself was accustomed to eating at least three kinds of meats throughout the day, but the only food on the table was raw vegetables. Raw vegetables. None of it was even cooked to a tender texture.

"Madam Olivia," Audrianna questioned, "do we have any meat to eat tonight?"

"I'm sorry," Olivia scolded. "Is my food, that I've worked hard in my garden, and in my kitchen, to prepare and serve to you, at no expense, not good enough for you to eat?"

"No, ma'am," Audrianna softly responded. "I'm just used to seeing meat on the table."

"How many cows did you see outside when you went to draw water?" Olivia asked the princess.

"One," Audrianna softly answered.

"That's right," Olivia replied. "We can't be killing our only source of milk just because we want some meat on the table."

"Now, Olivia," Balen reprimanded, "You shouldn't be too hard on Her Highness. She and the prince are used to a different type of food. I'm sure after a few days, they will get used to a farmer's meal."

"You mean a peasant's meal," Olivia snapped, folding her arms. Audrianna quickly scooped up a pile of chopped vegetables with her fork, and shoved them in her mouth and began chewing. She smiled a laboured smile as she chewed. The last thing she wanted to do was offend Olivia.

The princess wasn't sure if she was afraid of offending the lady of the house because of her stern countenance, her open generosity, or the fact that even though Olivia was treating her harshly, there was a dim reminiscence of her own mother in Olivia.

After Henry and Audrianna had choked down a good portion of vegetables, Olivia stood from the table and walked silently out of the room. Audrianna sat wide-eyed, not sure where Olivia went, or what she was going to do. After a few minutes, Olivia returned with a small baked pie.

"I think you two have suffered enough peasant food for the evening. I baked this for Balen yesterday, but I'm sure he doesn't mind the two of you having a piece."

"My dear!" Balen exclaimed. "What kind of pie did you bake me?" "Your favourite," Olivia announced.

"Blackberry pie?" Balen asked.

"No," Olivia replied. "Your other favourite." "Gooseberry pie?" he asked.

"No, dear," Olivia replied. "Your other favourite." "Rhubarb!" Balen teased.

"No," Olivia sighed. "Your other favourite."

"This is going to go on all night," Henry whispered to Audrianna, who snickered in response.

"Well," Balen replied with a half-chuckle, "if it's not blackberry, or gooseberry, or rhubarb, then there is only one other pie it could be."

"I swear to you, Balen," Olivia warned, "if you dare say plum, I'm going to push this pie into your face." Balen let out a hearty laugh. Olivia sat the round pie onto the table and whirred around to hunt for a knife.

"What kind is it?" Audrianna whispered to Balen. "Raspberry fig," he answered with a wink. "My favourite."

Olivia returned to the table with a large knife and cut the pie in half, then into slices. From the slices, she served the eager royals a hardy helping of the delicious looking raspberry fig pie. Audrianna dove into the sweet flavoured pie for all she was worth. Henry also consumed his portion rather quickly. When they cleaned their plates, the two sat back with a sense of finality to the meal.

As evening came, Balen set up a crude bed for Henry in the hay barn. Olivia supplied a heavy quilt to keep him warm, and Balen made a mattress of hay, with a pillowcase stuffed with straw for the prince to sleep on.

For Audrianna, Olivia made up a bed that was kept in a spare room. The bed had fluffy sheets, a fluffy pillow, and a thick, warm comforter over the top. The princess commented that it was the nicest bed she'd ever slept in. Olivia tucked the little girl into bed, and kissed her on the forehead.

"Hmm," the young princess hummed out loud. "What's wrong?" Olivia asked.

"Nothing," Audrianna answered. "I just haven't been kissed since the night before my parents were killed."

"How long ago did they die," Olivia asked.

"Almost six months ago," the princess answered, "and I dream about them every night."

"And that makes you sad?"

"Not really," Audrianna replied. "I look forward to seeing them in my dreams.

Almost like they've come to visit me."

"Do you think they are?" Olivia asked. "Are what?" Audrianna questioned.

"Do you think when you dream of them, it's your parents coming to visit you?" Olivia asked.

"Of course not, silly," Audrianna answered. "They're dead. But I do miss them. And I enjoy thinking about them." The princess smiled at Olivia. "You remind me of my mama."

"Well," Olivia remarked, "I will take that as a precious compliment. But, for tonight, you go to sleep, and in the morning I will cook you a special breakfast like you've never seen before."

Olivia kissed Audrianna on the forehead again, then lowered the light from the lamp on the nearby table. Leaving the princess in darkness, Olivia closed the door to the room. Her heart was moved with the thought that Audrianna saw her as a mother. She had always hoped to have a child.

The next morning, Olivia woke everyone, just before the sun peeked its light above the Andjety mountains. Again, she assigned each member in the house a chore to fulfil as she prepared the morning meal. Since Henry was already outside in the barn, Balen went out and showed him how to milk the cow. Audrianna was fearful she would be assigned the task of fetching water again. Instead, Olivia handed her a broom and instructed her to sweep out the house. This she did rather excitedly, since it was a task that seemed to fit her age, height, and strength.

After every task was completed, Olivia presented a simple, yet appetising meal. The meal included, sour dough bread, fruit breads, croissant bread, and rye bread. There also was a spread of various cheeses including Brie, Gloucester, and Parmesan. Both Henry and Audrianna looked enthusiastically at the food, as it was more to their eating choices. As they sat around the table, Balen gave the usual blessing over the food. "Merciful God, we have worked hard for the food set before us. You gave us land. You gave us food. For that, we are eternally thankful. Amen."

Henry and Audrianna helped themselves to a portion of every bread and every cheese. The two ate and ate until they couldn't possibly take another crumb of food into their stomachs. Olivia also sat warm milk on the table in a metal pitcher, of which everyone poured a hearty amount into their respective wooden cups. Whatever room remained in their bellies from breakfast was topped off with the milk.

As Olivia began the task of cleaning the kitchen from breakfast, Balen led the two guests outside behind the barn, where a large clearing sat. On the backside of the barn, a large rack was nailed to the wooden exterior, upon which a multitude of weapons hung. Swords of different sizes, battle axes, spears, daggers, crossbows, all hung in an organised fashion along the rack. Henry and Audrianna stood in the middle of the clearing as Balen stood facing the two of them.

"How far have you advanced since I last worked with you?" Balen asked Henry.

"I have mastered the double broadsword advance, dagger

throw, mace, bludgeon, quarterstaff, and crossbow."

"Nice progress." Balen remarked. "I look forward to testing the level of your boasting." Balen then turned to the princess. "Tell me about your training," he requested. "How far have you advanced in the last four months?"

"Well," Audrianna looked down at her feet. "I have only progressed past the wooden baton. My instructor had given me my first iron sword, but the only thing I was able to do so far was get it knocked out of my hands."

"I see," Balen answered, walking towards the weapon rack and picking up a short iron practice sword. "Show me what you can do with an iron sword."

Audrianna took her trained stance opposite Balen. She held up the sword in the attack position.

"Nice form, thus far," Balen commented. He, too, took his defence stance. "Begin," he ordered. Audrianna swung for all she was worth, and began shouting as she swung.

"Red, green, blue." Each time she swung, Balen blocked her advance with his sword. "Red, green, blue?" Balen asked. "What significance do the colours make to your

swinging?"

"Sorry," the princess answered. "That was part of my training. Lord Rupp used colours to show me where he wanted me to swing."

"Well," Balen commented, "every instructor has their own way of teaching. The method is not as imperative as the results. I can see that your instructor built up a good measure of strength in your arms. That is important. However, I intend to continue your training. And now, I want you to focus more on how you swing, rather than where or with what force. Okay?"

"Yes, sir!" Audrianna answered with the same serious tone that she had given to Rupp.

"Now take your stance just as you did before," Balen commanded, and the princess immediately obeyed. Balen came around to her backside and grabbed her wrist and hand that held the sword. "Are you truly left-handed?" he asked.

"Yes sir," she answered.

"Very well," he said as he guided her hand and arm to make a level stroke with her sword. "I want you to keep the edge of your sword flat like this. Imagine the blade being the surface of water. Water always finds its own level. The blade must have a fluid stroke as it cuts through the air. Now, practice swinging your sword through the air, back and forth, keep it level to the ground, and make your strokes fluid, not choppy."

"Like this?" Audrianna began swinging her sword with greater precision, keeping its movements steady and smooth, and staying level with the ground as best she could.

"Just like that," Balen replied. "Now keep practicing swinging your blade as accurately as possible for the next hour."

"An hour?" Audrianna asked. "I have to swing the sword in the air for an hour? What are you going to do?"

"I'm going to show your betrothed what defeat looks like," he said with an arrogant smile. Balen walked over to Henry and called him to attention. The princess continued to swing, not as hard or wildly, but slowly and methodically. She looked in the direction of where Balen and Henry stood.

As Audrianna blindly swung her iron sword, it made contact with another sword, making a loud CLANG sound. Startled, Audrianna turned to see what her sword must have struck. To her surprise, Olivia stood before her, wearing leather pants, a leather vest, gloves, and metal shoulder guards. A spirited grin shown on her face.

"Madam Olivia," Audrianna replied. "Have you come to practice with me?"

"The first thing you need to know about me," Olivia answered, "is that my title is Lady, not Madam."

"Lady Olivia?" the princess asked.

"That's right," she said. "I am the former Lady in Waiting for Her Highness, Queen Luella, the Beloved." Audrianna looked at Olivia and beamed a broad smile. "The second thing you need to know is, posture is everything."

"Posture?" Audrianna asked.

"Yes. The way you stand, how you hold your head up, how you push your shoulders back, with your sword out in front of you. The way you were standing while practicing your sword drill, was much like a wounded gazelle beating off vultures."

Audrianna hung her head. "Would you help me, Lady Olivia," the princess gently asked.

"Are you begging me?" Olivia asked in response. "That is not becoming of a princess." Audrianna immediately squared her shoulders back, remembering what Rupp once told her.

"Lady Olivia," the princess replied, taking her training stance, "I am ready for my lesson. You may begin." Olivia smiled and slightly bowed to acknowledge the princess's command.

"Now, you are becoming a princess," Olivia commended, holding up her sword to touch the princess's. "Now, swing your sword just like Balen taught you. Smooth and level. One fluid stroke." Audrianna swung her iron training sword slowly and as accurately as she could. Each time she touched Olivia's sword, she turned it over, and swung in the opposite direction, making sure it was level to the ground. After a while, Olivia would swing her sword to meet Audrianna's. Back and forth the two swung their swords, a little harder at certain intervals. Olivia would also command Audrianna to swing her sword faster, but to maintain control and accuracy. Soon enough, the two ladies were banging their swords together hard and fast to where they began singing with a CLING—CLANG—TWANG.

Before long, Audrianna felt her arms begin to ache. She wanted to stop, but she did not want to disappoint Olivia. She decided to push herself and see if Olivia would bring the lesson to an end on her own, or if she might start to tire out as well. Back and forth the two sparred. The princess's arms began to burn with fatigue. She didn't know if Olivia was having too much fun to end the lesson, or if the Lady in Waiting to the Queen wanted to test the little girl's endurance.

"I'm done," Audrianna finally said, dropping the tip of her

sword to the ground.

Sweat poured around her beet-red face. "I'm sorry. I can't go on."

"You did well, Your Highness," Olivia announced. "However, when you finish with your sword, do not drop the blade to the ground. Hold the sword against your shoulder like this." While still holding the hilt with both hands, Olivia brought her sword against her shoulder with the end of her sword pointing upwards. Audrianna mimicked her actions. "Good. Now let's move on to another skill. One that might come in handy."

"What skill is that?"

"Hurling daggers," Olivia responded.

"You mean throwing a dagger?" Audrianna asked. "At people?"

"Well, let's start with a target," Olivia suggested. "If it becomes necessary, we will designate a person." Audrianna nodded in agreement.

Olivia led the princess to the far side of the barn where a large wooden panel was leaning against the wall. On the panel was painted the silhouette of a man. In every respect, it appeared to Audrianna to be the outline of Balen. From a small sheath on her belt, Olivia drew a dagger and held it by its blade. She stood sideways facing the target. She adjusted her footing, putting her right foot forward, then squared her shoulders, and held up the dagger, ready to throw.

"Why did you punch Henry?" Audrianna wanted to know. Olivia lowered the dagger, stood up straight and looked down at the princess.

"You mean to tell me, that Your Highness has never wanted to punch His Majesty before?"

"Oh," Audrianna replied, "I want to punch him every day. But I want to know the reason that you punched him yesterday right after we arrived. There must some sort of grudge that you've held onto since you last saw him." Olivia half-chuckled.

"Not so much a grudge, as it was—unfinished business."

"Okay," Audrianna replied, "So what was the unfinished business?" Olivia stared into the princess's face, studying it, and thinking over her options.

"I'll tell you what," she answered, "If you can throw the dagger from the same distance as me, and get the blade to penetrate anywhere on the target, I will tell you the reason I struck your husband." At that, she turned to face the target, set her footing, raised the dagger by the blade, and hurled it at the wooden panel. The dagger whizzed through the air and stuck into the wood at the very centre of the silhouette's chest, close to where the heart would have been.

"Wow!" Audrianna exclaimed in amazement. "That was a great throw." Olivia walked over to the target and wiggled it out of its landing spot. She then returned to where Audrianna stood waiting.

"The way to throw a dagger is to flick the blade, to cause it to spin, and giving enough strength to make it all the way to the barn. Now, you try it."

Audrianna took the same stance that Olivia had, lined up the dagger with the target, and hurled it with a twist. The dagger stuck into the ground just a few feet away from the princess. Audrianna looked down at the half-buried dagger, then back up at Olivia.

"I guess your secret is safe with me."

CHAPTER 18

After spending the better half of the day refining their sword skills, Balen and Olivia took Henry and Audrianna down to the nearby river to refresh themselves. Splitting off in different directions, the men walked upstream, while the ladies walked downstream to a secluded and overgrown bend in the river. The ladies disrobed and entered the rejuvenating water. Audrianna's arms and hands hurt from the morning workout, but the cool temperature of the river seemed to soothe her aches and pains. She waded in the water up to her neck.

Olivia and Audrianna both laughed and giggled as they swapped stories from their time spend in the castle. The princess told Olivia about Horatio, the castle ghost, and the practical joke that Henry had pulled on her. Olivia told her that she and Luella called the noise, the 'Wolf of Nadeau Castle', because they thought it sounded like a howling wolf. Audrianna was amazed to see such a loving side to Olivia, since her first interactions with her seemed cold and harsh.

Upstream, the menfolk waded in the water up to their waist. They splashed water over their own torsos, but for the most part stood motionless facing each other with their arms folded. They talked briefly about different options regarding taking the castle back from the Andjety overthrow. Neither one laughed. Neither one smiled, nor looked up at the other.

After an hour, the four met again at the farmhouse. Olivia and Audrianna worked together to prepare food for the afternoon meal. Balen and Henry baled hay, fed the cow, and scattered feed for the chickens. Upon entering the house, Henry was handed a bucket to fetch water, and Balen swept the table off with a short broom. The house had a constant breeze blowing through to moderate the temperature, but it caused the house to be per-petually dusty.

Soon enough, Audrianna and Olivia presented a lovely meal of fruits and breads, as well as an assortment of vegetables. Everyone sat in their designated spot. Balen gave his usual prayer of thanksgiving.

"Merciful Lord," he prayed, "We have worked hard for the food set before us. You gave us land. You gave us food. For that, we are eternally thankful. Amen."

As they ate, Balen asked Henry questions regarding his experience with the Andjety. Henry told the host and hostess about how he and his friend Pitt infiltrated an Andjety village, and how the Witch seemed to have inside knowledge of their plans and actions. Balen suggested a spy within the castle was tipping the Witch off to their actions and defences.

"It's the only thing that makes sense," Balen remarked. "They knew when you and your armour-bearer left, and where you were going, as well as an intimate layout of the castle's defences."

"Well," Henry added, "it wasn't Pitt. The Witch killed him right in front of me." "Perhaps," Olivia interjected. "But appearances can be deceiving. And the Witch is a master manipulator. Could it have merely appeared that the Witch killed him?"

"She chopped his head off," Audrianna replied. "That's pretty hard to pretend." Olivia and Balen looked at the princess in astonishment.

"She's telling the truth," Henry remarked. "Audrianna was the one who found his head, impaled on a pike, at the entrance to the castle bridge."

"That bastard Witch!" Olivia exclaimed. "What a horrible thing to do! Even beyond the killing of a friend."

"Well," Balen continued, "if Pitt is not the Andjety spy, who else has intimate knowledge of the castle?"

"There were only six others, but all are now dead," Henry solemnly answered. "Name them," Balen requested. Henry began listing members of the Royal Court. "My father, King Malcolm," Henry answered looking up as he thought. "Lord Rupp, the captain of the royal guards. Ree's three ladies-in-waiting. And Rolf, the royal envoy who became my armour-bearer after Pitt." All four sat thinking over Henry's list.

"Well," Audrianna responded, "I don't think Rose, Cassie, or Ethel were spies. They took good care of me."

"Don't confuse hospitality with loyalty," Olivia remarked. "We're talking about the Andjety people. They are ruthless!"

"True," Henry said. "But Her Highness's ladies pretty much stayed with her every hour, except for when they ate."

"No," Balen replied, holding a fork in his hand with a speared slice of zucchini. "But we should seriously consider Rupp."

"Not Lord Rupp," Audrianna argued. "No way! There is no way that he could be on the Witch's side!"

"We need to realistically look at all the facts and options, Ree," Henry replied. "As much as you care about your ladies and Rupp, we can't be swayed by our own opinions."

"Don't let your feelings rule your heart, my dear," Olivia replied to Audrianna. "Besides," Henry added, "it is reasonable to assume that Rupp and the ladies were killed by the Witch. If so, then that would leave us empty on all suspects." "Except your armour-bearer," Balen replied.

"Rolf?" Henry asked. "It could be a possibility, but Rolf was not part of the Royal Court until very recent. Our mystery spy had to have infiltrated us much sooner than Rolf."

"He's kind of timid for an armour-bearer anyways," Audrianna stated. "Timid?" Olivia asked.

"Lady Cassie said he was sensitive," the princess answered. "But I thought him to be easily startled and scared." Balen sat back in his chair and stroked his beard.

"Easily startled and scared," he repeated. "That is an Andjety trait." "It is?" both Henry and Audrianna chorused.

"I thought Lady Olivia said they were ruthless," the princess replied.

"Oh, they act all fearless and tough at first, but they are highly superstitious and easily intimidated," Balen informed the group.

"You seem to know a lot more about the Andjety than I do," Henry commented. "Oh yes," Balen responded. "I helped to lead the king's special forces against the

Andjety back when they first began attacking Nadeau. It's amazing how quickly you pick up on…"

"That's it!" Audrianna shouted, startling the other three. "That's how we can get the castle back!"

"What's that, Ree?" Henry asked as all eyes turned to the princess. "The king's special forces," she remarked.

"What about them?" Henry asked.

"Remember when you and I were crowned as royals?" "Coronated? Yes."

"The king gave a speech beforehand talking about all that he did to preserve the kingdom. He talked about the famine that struck twenty-eight years ago, and the Andjety raids some twenty-one years ago. He said that he had special swordsmen and archers defeat the attacking murderers."

"Marauders," Henry corrected.

"Right," Audrianna said enthusiastically. "Why can't we get them together and use them to fight off the Andjety again?"

"Your Highness," Olivia responded, "That was more than twenty years ago. The king's special forces are long since retired, and many have already died. They are of no use to us."

"Hang on, Olivia," Balen argued. "You and I were part of the king's special forces.

We still have plenty of fight in us."

"Well, once you have it in your blood," Olivia admitted, "it's hard to let it go to waste."

"Besides," Balen replied, "they are the only allies that we have. There might be a chance that several have kept up their skills as we have."

"Where can we find the king's special forces?" Audrianna asked.

"It's hard to know," Balen answered. "They scattered to various farms here in the east region of the kingdom. But I might know someone in the village that stays in contact with a good number of them."

"And where can we find him?" Henry asked.

"Hmm," Olivia replied. "That dirty dog stays close to the pub every evening. He stays drunk most of the time."

"Dirty dog?" Henry asked. "You'll see," Olivia warned.

"If we hurry," Balen said, "we might get to the pub early enough before he drinks himself into another stupor."

As the four finished gobbling up their food, they quickly cleared the dinner table and cleaned the kitchen from the preparation of dinner. Olivia voiced a disinterest in going to the pub, while Audrianna begged to tag along. As the menfolk hitched the horse to the wagon, Olivia brushed the princess's hair to make her look more presentable and not so alarming.

The former Lady in Waiting decided to quickly braid Audrianna's hair, with tiny braids, to make it appear as if her hair was supposed to be tight to her head. She tied white ribbons to the braids to give the princess a more child-like feminine look. Audrianna relished the motherly treatment from Olivia that her own ladies used to give her before the invasion. Audrianna had a sizable length of hair hanging in the back, so Olivia decided to put it in a bun and slid a white ivory hair slide through the bun to hold it in place.

As soon as Henry announced they were ready to leave, Audrianna jumped into the back of the wagon, behind Henry and Balen. Henry turned and stared at Audrianna's freshly groomed hair.

"What's wrong?" the princess asked.

"Your hair looks nice, for once," Henry almost complimented. Balen looked over to admire his wife's handiwork.

"Nice to have a Lady in Waiting attending you again, eh?" Balen asked. Audrianna shrugged.

"It's nice to have someone being a mother again," she responded. Balen grinned out the corner of his mouth as he and Henry exchanged glances. Balen whipped the reins to give the horse the command to trot.

The horse pulled the wagon down the winding trail. The trail was overgrown with thick tree cover. The princess watched the scenery pass by on their trip to the village, ever so often spotting a deer or a rabbit. Before she noticed, the tree cover opened, revealing their arrival to the small village of Pachenthou.

Balen stopped the horse and wagon in front of the village stable. While the village itself was nothing to boast, it had every kind of convenience and service one could imagine. The three climbed out and walked down the road to the local pub, which sat at the very centre of the village. There were many men and women scurrying in and out of the pub. To the village, the pub was more than a bar. It was a hotel. It was the village meeting hall. It was the place where official announcements were made for the village. But, on that day, it seemed the centre of a festival.

The three pushed their way into the overcrowded pub and searched for a place to sit. Audrianna kept getting pushed backwards and forwards by the sea of enthusiastic patrons. She was much shorter than the crowd and not very visible. Henry picked her up by her waist, and lifted her to the same head level as everyone else, then pushed her through the crowd. The crowd thinned further past the entrance of the pub.

"A lot of people in the pub tonight," Henry commented.

"Yes," Balen agreed. "It's the annual village festival. The pub is normally packed for days in celebration."

"It is going to be difficult to find who we're looking for."

"Not at all," Balen remarked. "He's right over there." Balen pointed to an old man, sitting by himself in the corner, with his back to the crowd. Henry and Audrianna looked at each other and nodded.

As the three walked to the table, the man turned his head slightly to get a glimpse at who was approaching.

"Jaako," Balen greeted.

"Balen," the man stoically answered. The two men extended their arms and tapped the back of each other's wrists as a secret greeting.

"I have brought two people for you to meet," Balen announced.

"Not interested," Jaako replied. The old man glanced at the prince and princess with a sneer. However, when his eye caught Audrianna, his attention perked up. "Who is she?" he asked, pointing in the princess's direction.

"Ree," the princess answered.

"Ree?" Jaako asked. "Such an odd, but useful name." "Useful?" Audrianna asked.

"Ree can be useful in such words as, ree-ligion, or ree-bellion, or ree-deem. You can also use your name to remove, reveal, and repeat. How do you use your name best little one?" Audrianna wasn't sure what the scruffy old man was suggesting, but she began to feel extremely uncomfortable.

"Revolted," she answered. Jaako smiled and laughed, exposing his dark rotting teeth. The smell of ale wafted over the princess, causing her to turn her head and silently gag. "Jaako," Balen reprimanded, "we are here to talk to you concerning a serious matter."

"If you wanted me to be serious, and pay close attention, you should have brought that fetching wife of yours. She always could hold my attention. Unlike this little maid you brought with you, who hasn't even started to bud yet." All three scowled at Jaako.

"You're a maggot!" Audrianna exclaimed. Jaako looked directly in her face and pointed his finger.

"I am a dog," he stated. "A dirty dog! Don't forget that."

"And I am Her Royal Highness, Princess Audrianna," the princess emphatically responded. "Don't forget, that!"

"Really?" Jaako asked incredulously. Both men nodded in agreement.

"And I am His Majesty, Prince Henry of Nadeau," Henry interjected. Jaako gave a pained look at Balen.

"What have you done, Balen?" he asked. "You can't bring crowned royals into this pub. On this particular day!"

"Why not?" Audrianna asked. Jaako leaned towards the princess, resting his elbow on the table and pointing his finger at her again.

"You come to speak to me, little girl, regarding some important matter, as if you can order me about. I am not a loyalist! I care nothing for the crown. What have you done for me, huh? After I fought for my life on the other side of the mountain, watching my friends die one by one? What have you done for me…"

"The king is dead," Henry interrupted. Jaako stopped scolding the princess and turned to look at the prince.

"What?" he asked, looking back and forth at the two men and smiling. "You… You actually think the king is dead?"

"Horace saw it happen with his own eyes," Audrianna remarked. Jaako rested his hands on the table and sat up, studying the princess's face for a moment.

"Who the hell is Horace," he shrugged. Audrianna pointed her thumb at Henry.

Jaako looked at Henry and squinted.

"She calls me Horace," Henry explained. "It's her little nickname for me. It's a long story."

Jaako chuckled once again.

"She calls you Horace," he replied. "As an endearing term?" Jaako continued to laugh.

"Perhaps if you take Her Highness to the bar and find her some refreshment," Balen suggested to Henry, then looked down at Audrianna. "Stay there while the three of us talk."

Audrianna wanted to argue with Balen. Coming to find information regarding the king's special forces was her idea, and her plan. She was offended that she was being sent away, like a child sent to bed while the grown-ups talked. At the same time, she was even more offended by the crude behaviour of their informant. She decided not to argue with Balen, but followed Henry to the front of the pub. Henry picked her up and sat her on a stool on the corner of the bar where several patrons were enjoying their rum and ale beverages.

"What kind of refreshment do you have for a little girl?" Henry asked the man serving drinks.

"Our special sassafras drink," the server recommended. Henry pulled out a copper coin from his money pouch and laid it on the counter.

"Give her a tall glass, please," Henry requested, indicating he wanted her to be given a large amount to occupy her. The server behind the counter winked at Henry and poured the princess a drink in a tall metal mug, then slid it in front of her.

"Stay here," Henry commanded the princess. "And take small slow sips." He then turned and walked back to the spot where Balen and Jaako were sitting. Audrianna leaned on one elbow and rested her chin on the back of her hand as she watched the crowd of patrons walk back and forth in the pub.

"Don't worry," Balen remarked to Jaako as Henry returned to their table, "the two royals are traveling incognito."

"Yes," Jaako replied, "but for what purpose?"

"Because we are being hunted," Henry answered as he sat down at the table again. "Yes," Jaako replied again, "But by whom?"

"The War Witch, Zymjai," Henry answered. "She invaded the castle, killed my father, along with Rupp…"

"No she didn't!" Jaako exclaimed. "Pardon?" Henry asked.

"The king isn't dead," Jaako replied.

"Yes," Henry responded, "I saw the Witch stab the king and

he fell forward on his bed—dead!"

"Really," Jaako questioned Henry with a tone of scepticism. "I saw with my own eyes," Henry answered.

Audrianna sat at the bar, staring at her tall drink of sassafras. She never had sassafras before, and wasn't sure whether she would like it. She tipped the full mug towards her, and took a small sip. To her surprise, she found she liked the sweet root-like flavour. She quickly took a bigger sip. The drink had a subtle bite to it, but overall, very pleasant. The scent of the drink reminded her of a field of flowers that she loved to walk in as a small child.

"Explain to me, then," Jaako spoke accusingly at Henry, "how the king gave a Royal Proclamation yesterday from his balcony if he was dead?"

"What? Impossible," Henry declared. "I saw him die! That man is an imposter!" "Or you are," Jaako replied.

"He is not an imposter, Jaako," Balen reprimanded. "I know Henry, better than I wish to know Henry. He is definitely the crowned prince."

"Then we have a serious situation in Nadeau," Jaako replied.

"That is exactly what I've been saying," Henry said. "The king is dead, we're on the run, and we want to know who of the king's special forces are still alive."

Audrianna by now had finished half of her sassafras drink. She began to feel warm and relaxed. Her eyelids began to droop. Every time she took a sip, she thought to herself that sassafras was the best drink she had ever had. It was officially her favourite drink of all time. She loved it! She continued to repeat the name of the drink in her head. Sassafras! Sassafras! Saffasass! What a great name, she thought as she took another gulp.

"Why do you want to know about the king's special forces?" Jaako asked. "Because they are the only allies we can trust," Henry answered, beginning to raise his voice.

"Ah," Jaako responded, "but can the king's men trust you?" "It's not me they are trusting."

"Then who?"

"Her Highness, Princess Audrianna," Henry answered. "It was her plan to regain the castle by entrusting the services of the king's retired special forces. It will take an act of aggression that the witch will not see coming. Especially if there is an imposter king acting as if nothing has happened."

"What about the prince?" Jaako asked. "What about me?" Henry asked.

"Not you," Jaako answered. "The 'king' had a 'prince' standing next to him at his public address. My question would be, who is this prince?"

"Was there a little princess too?" Henry asked. Jaako thought for a moment.

"I didn't hear of one being spotted," Jaako replied. "But you might assume she was too short to be seen."

Audrianna began looking across the long counter of the bar. Some of the patrons would look at her, to which she would smile and wave. Many would stare at their drinks and never look up. As the princess watched the people at the bar, one of the men closer to her, snapped his fingers at the server. When the server turned to see who was snapping their fingers, the man at the bar gave a circular motion around the rim of his mug. The server refilled the patron's mug with ale. The man placed a copper coin on the counter and the server slid the coin off the counter and into his hand.

Audrianna thought the gesture was the funniest thing she had ever seen. She quickly reached inside her own money pouch and pulled out a copper coin and laid it next to her mug. She then gulped down the rest of her drink, and snapped her fingers at the server. The server turned to look at her. She slowly repeated the same circular motion the other patron did, then grinned at the server. The man slid the copper coin towards him, then picked up her mug and refilled it with sassafras.

As the princess began to sip her freshly filled mug, music began to play inside the pub. She swung her feet around to see what was going on. Both Balen and Henry turned around in their seats to see what was about to happen.

From the middle of the room, a young man, about twenty, stood up on the table. People began to crowd into the pub as the man announced that it was time to sing a song in honour of the festivities.

"Who is that?" Henry asked.

"That's Bow-legged Jenkins," Jaako remarked. "He's a local minstrel that writes songs for special festivals such as the one today."

"What festival is the town celebrating?" Henry asked. Both Balen and Jaako shot a look at each other, then back at Henry.

"Maybe you should turn and face us, and listen to the songs," Balen suggested. "They will explain themselves."

"Yes," Jaako agreed. "And whatever you hear—don't turn around." Henry began to cringe at the thought of what might be coming.

Jenkins, the minstrel, stood on the table and began to play a hand-held accordion. As he played the lively music, he began to jump and dance about while the crowd clapped their hands and bobbed their heads back and forth with the music. Audrianna took a giant gulp of her drink, then laid it on the counter and began clapping and bobbing as well.

"Sing!" a person shouted at Jenkins. "Let's hear it!"

"We want to sing with you!"

The friendly musician began to sing a song that seemed very familiar to the waiting crowd. It went like this:

"Lords and ladies, friends and folk, listen to my tale. Listen close, to the story, as you drink your ale.

Many years, on this fine day, a maiden fair was born.

A peasant girl, with but one dress, and no jewellery to adorn. She married herself, to the king, no longer was she poor.

She stole his heart, reformed his ways, and changed us evermore!"

As the minstrel finished the first stanza of his song, Henry looked up at Balen. He realised that the young man was singing about his mother. It was the day of his mother's birthday. The entire crowd joined in the chorus:

Now raise your drinks up high, To the beloved queen who died. We'll make a boast,

Then drink a toast,

To Luella—the Nadeau kingdom's pride!

Jenkins went on to sing the second stanza:

Queen Luella was the image, Of kindness and rare beauty. She helped us poor to face the king, she always did her duty! She saved us from the famine, she saved us from the war.

But she died too soon, to ever save us, from the crummy prince she bore.

Henry glared at Balen and Jaako.

"Yeah," Jaako remarked, "they really don't like you here in Pachenthou." Jaako smiled. "But, that's not even my favourite stanza."

Audrianna leaned back to laugh at the second stanza. She rocked in her chair, then twirled around and took another gulp from her drink.

The whole pub began to enthusiastically sing the chorus together, lifting up their mugs and spilling their drinks all over each other.

Now raise your drinks up high, To the beloved queen who died. We'll make a boast,

Then drink a toast,

To Luella—the Nadeau kingdom's pride!

As the chorus to the song was finishing, and the third stanza was ready to be sung, the singing bard spotted Audrianna sitting at the corner of the bar, just a few feet from the table he was standing on. Ceasing from playing the music on his accordion, Jenkins jumped off the table and landed directly in front of the princess.

"Come with me, little lass," the minstrel said, "I need someone to play the princess." He held his hand out to Audrianna. Audrianna, having discarded all her inhibitions, took his hand, and Jenkins pulled her up to the top of the table. He wanted to use the princess to illustrate the final stanza. Unbeknownst to Jenkins, the very person he chose to illustrate the final stanza was indeed the very person he was going to sing about. He stood the princess at the centre of the table, played his accordion, and sang:

Now when the princess, whom the king betrothed, finishes her waiting term. she'll be given to the shoddy prince, and their marriage will be confirmed. Upon the night, of their union, while in the bridal room,

She'll discover the prince's hidden truth—he's packing a tiny worm!

Again, Henry glared at Balen and Jaako.

"THAT, is my favourite stanza," Jaako replied, holding his sides and laughing loudly. Audrianna danced atop the table, spinning in a circle, as the pub all sang the chorus together:

Now raise your drinks up high, To the beloved queen who died. We'll make a boast, then drink a toast,

To Luella—the Nadeau kingdom's pride!

As the song concluded, everyone applauded. Audrianna, caught up in the revelries, stopped spinning, and tugged on Jenkin's arm.

"Let me sing another curse," Audrianna begged.

"Sing another chorus?" Jenkins asked. The princess nodded. Jenkins called the patrons of the pub to attention.

"Lords and ladies," he announced. "The young maid would like to sing the chorus again for us. Let's listen to the fair 'princess.'"

Jenkins started to play his accordion to accompany the princess. Audrianna began to dance and sing the chorus again, but with an impromptu change in the lyrics. All the occupants of the pub listened with great interest:

Now raise your drinks up high, For your new queen has arrived! Bake a roast, and burn the toast!

I'm Audrianna! Your new Nadeau kingdom's pride!

As the princess was singing, Balen leaned over to Henry.

"She's drunk!" he exclaimed. "You'd better get her off that table!"

"How could she have gotten drunk?" Henry asked. "I told the server behind the counter to give her a drink appropriate for a little girl."

"Oh, no!" Jaako replied. "He didn't give her the sassafras drink, did he?" "Yes," Henry answered.

"They mix the sassafras with a shot of rum," Jaako informed the prince. "What?" Balen and Henry both chorused.

"They gave my ten-year-old a shot of rum?" Henry asked.

As Audrianna finished her improved lyrics to the song, she grabbed the corners of her dress and curtsied. It was a perfect curtsy! The only time the princess could do a perfect and flawless curtsy, and she was befuddled. The entire crowd of patrons in the pub stopped their applause and merrymaking. The room fell dead silent. All eyes were fixed on the princess. They had never seen anyone do a curtsy before. Could this little girl be the actual princess?

Before Audrianna realised what was happening, she bowed, lowering for all to see the top of her head. As she bowed, the three men sitting in the corner all let out a gasp. The ribbons that Olivia tied to Audrianna's hair made a clumsy triangle when her head was lowered. What's worse, and the finishing revelation, was the hair slide. The slide was a perfect white line over the top of the triangle. Besides her drunken song, Audrianna inadvertently declared herself to be the long sought-after princess.

From the back of the room, a large man with a booming voice shouted out with enthusiasm, "Behold! Her Royal Highness—Princess Audrianna of Nadeau!"

Immediately, the entire pub became electrified with excitement. Drinks were spilling everywhere as people applauded while still holding their mugs. People beat on the tables and walls. Everyone in the room became elated. Henry quickly ran towards the table and pulled the princess down. Audrianna giggled as she fell into his cradled arms.

"There's my husband!" Audrianna declared. Another voice shouted from the back of the room.

"His Royal Majesty—Prince Henry. The future queen's betrothed!" Everyone applauded again. Henry was irate, and shook his head. How humiliating to be reduced to nothing more than the future husband of the crowned princess.

As Henry carried the inebriated little girl towards the door, the server behind the counter called out to them.

"Is she really truly Princess Audrianna?" he asked. "Yes," Henry called back over his shoulder.

"Congratulations," Balen remarked to the server. "You intoxicated the future queen of Nadeau."

As they exited the loud, celebrating pub, Audrianna began to drift off to sleep. Henry looked down at what now had morphed into an angelic looking face. The two men made their way to Balen's horse and wagon, to where Henry laid the princess in the back of the wagon, and covered her with a blanket. Before climbing into the wagon, Henry turned to Audrianna and said, "You, little girl, are a kettle full of trouble just waiting to boil over."

"I know," the princess softly replied with a smile, her eyes still closed. She then fell sound asleep.

CHAPTER 19

Audrianna awoke the next morning. As she slowly sat up, her head began to ache mercilessly. At first, her head hurt so bad, she could barely focus her eyes. She didn't remember how she got back to Balen and Olivia's farmhouse, nor how she got into bed. She held out her arms to discover that she was wearing the nightgown Olivia had given her the previous night. But she was certain neither she, nor Olivia, had put the nightgown on her. For one thing, the nightgown was on her backwards. For another, she was still wearing her full-length undergarments. Most likely either Balen or Henry, or perhaps a collaboration of efforts, dressed the princess for bed, but were unwilling to venture past the first layer of clothing.

As she rolled out of bed, she suddenly felt lightheaded and nauseous. Before she could think about what she should do, she felt a surge of vomit race up from her stomach and out of her throat. Almost instinctively she fell to her knees and pulled the empty chamber pot underneath her. Three times she retched and spewed.

The sound of Audrianna spewing caught the attention of

Henry who was in the kitchen doing morning chores Olivia had assigned him. Both Balen and Olivia were outside pulling vegetables from the garden. Henry ran to the bedroom to see the princess on the floor grasping hold of the chamber pot.

"I'm sick," the poor little girl declared. "And I have a horrible pain in my head!" "Of course you do," Henry scolded. "Little girls that get drunk are going to have a bad headache come morning."

"I was drunk?" Audrianna asked, pushing the chamber pot back under the bed. "How did I get drunk? I didn't drink any of the bad drinks. I only had Sassafras."

"Well," Henry confided, "do you remember, I asked the server to give you a drink suitable for little girls?"

"That's right," Audrianna affirmed, grabbing hold of the bed post and pulling herself to her feet.

"As it turns out," Henry explained, "the server has an understanding worked out with several of the towns people. If they are forced to tote one of their children with them, the server gives the child a sassafras drink with a shot of rum."

"A shot of rum?" Audrianna asked, holding her head with both hands, and slowly sitting herself back on the bed. "Why would they do that?"

"Well," Henry continued, "the child gets sleepy, and the parent plops them in a bed in the first room upstairs to sleep off the rum. The parent is then free to drink, dance, and celebrate, without being encumbered by their children."

"That it a dirty trick," Audrianna said, frowning and holding her stomach.

"I am surprised you got this sick from one drink, though," Henry remarked. "Granted, it was a tall drink."

"I had two tall drinks of sassafras and rum," the princess declared. "Two?"

"I paid for a second drink. I didn't know it was hobnailed."

"Well…" Henry replied, putting his hands on his hips, mimicking a responsible parent, "You definitely will be sick the rest of the morning. That is the result of being drunk the night before."

"Drunk people are sick the next morning?" Audrianna asked. "Every time."

"Why would you get drunk if you have to suffer being sick the next morning? That's stupid."

"It is indeed," Henry assured her, placing his hand on her shoulder and giving it a gentle squeeze.

By this time, Balen and Olivia entered the house, bearing a basket full of various vegetables.

"We have some good news and some bad news for you two," Balen announced. "Really?" Henry asked, sitting next to the princess on the bed.

"Yes," Balen answered. "A fox attacked two of our chickens last night, and they died. That's the bad news. However, the good news is that we will be able to have baked chicken for dinner tonight."

"That is good news," Henry commented, putting his arm gently around Audrianna in a manner to encourage the ill-felt princess. "When will we be able to eat them," he asked.

"Well," Balen answered rolling his eyes towards Olivia, "that's where we circle back around to the bad news. You two will have the task of plucking and cleaning the chickens in preparation of them being cooked."

"I don't know if I'll be able to clean chickens," Audrianna replied, holding her stomach with both hands.

"Why not?" Olivia demanded, not knowing the goings on the night before.

Audrianna looked up at Olivia with a pained expression.

"I have morning sickness," the princess answered. Olivia shot a look at Henry who quickly retrieved his arm from around Audrianna.

"No she doesn't," he quickly asserted, standing up from the bed. "It's morning, and she feels sick. But it's not morning sickness."

"What were you three up to last night?" Olivia asked.

"We went to speak to Jaako, just like we intended," Henry explained. "But he made a couple of rude comments to Ree, to which I escorted her to the bar to get a refreshment…"

"Oh, no," Olivia remarked. "Not the sassafras drink."

"Does everyone know about sassafras but me?" Henry adamantly asked.

"When it comes to the Pachenthou pub," Olivia replied, "a drink that is safe for a ten-year-old, comes from a fruit—not a root."

"Well, anyway," Henry responded, "I paid for one drink, and Audrianna bought herself a second. Before we knew it, she was dancing on the table, singing a drinking song, and telling the entire crowd in the pub that she was the new queen of Nadeau."

Audrianna, still sitting on the bed, buried her face in her lap in embarrassment. "What do you remember about last night," Olivia asked. Audrianna popped her head up, looked at Olivia, and tucked her hands under her legs.

"I remember the Luella song starting. I remember clapping by hands and bobbing my head. Then, I remember riding in a bumpy wagon. Then, I remember waking up without my dress on, and my nightgown on backwards, pulled over my undergarments."

Olivia crossed her arms and glared at the two men. Both Balen and Henry glanced at each other for moral support.

"Did you two enjoy playing dress up last night?" Olivia sarcastically remarked. "Not really," Henry replied. "I suggested she sleep in her clothes." Olivia looked at Balen.

"Well," Balen responded, clearing his throat, "I wanted her to sleep comfortably through the night. I didn't know there was a front or a back to her gown."

"Why did neither of you two come and wake me to help take care of the princess," Olivia asked.

"I was embarrassed with the fact that we came home with a drunk little girl," Balen answered.

"Like we weren't taking good care of her," Henry interjected.

"You weren't," Olivia shrieked. "That's why you came home with a drunk little girl!" Both men hung their heads in shame. Audrianna held both sides of her head with her hands from Olivia's shrieking. "Audrianna," Olivia commanded, "come with me. I have a few things I need to discuss with you now."

Audrianna stumbled to her feet and followed Olivia into a back room. Balen and Henry silently watched as the princess followed Olivia into the master bedroom and shut the door. The two men sat waiting quietly as they listened to the muffled scolding that Olivia began delivering. Both men could also hear the soft weeping of the princess.

"Wow," Henry replied. "Lady Olivia is really laying into Ree in there."

"Sounds like it to me," Balen remarked. "Olivia is setting a few things straight for Her Highness."

"Maybe I should intervene," Henry suggested. "It was my fault she got drunk." "Not if you value your head attached to your shoulders," Balen responded. Henry gave a pained expression to Balen. "Don't worry, my friend. My wife comes on a bit strong, especially for those she deeply cares about. But I guarantee, after she is done with the princess, Her Highness will be sitting in Olivia's lap, and they'll be hugging each other."

As the two men talked, and Olivia and Audrianna were having it out in the bedroom, a knock was heard at the door. Balen opened the door to find three old men, dressed as farmers, holding their hats in their hands.

"Can I help you gentlemen?" Balen asked.

"We were at the pub yesterday," the one man declared. "We wanted to know if Her Royal Highness is okay."

"She is fine," Balen reassured the men. "A little hungover, but fine nonetheless." "We would like to have an audience, if we may," the second man requested. "Please," Balen invited. "My house be your house," he said, an old Nadeau expression. He led the three old men to the table, and each man took a seat. "What is your business with us," Henry asked the three men.

"Begging your pardon," the first man replied, "but our business be with the princess."

"The princess?" Henry asked. "Yes, sire."

"Princess Audrianna?" "Yes, sire."

"What kind of business do you three have with a ten-year-old girl?"

"Begging your pardon," the third man spoke, "but we were told Her Highness was looking for the king's retired swordsmen."

"That is why we were in the pub last night," Balen shared. "Would you three men be sent by Jaako?"

"That dirty dog?" the second man asked. "Not on your life! But we did hear from him what you were there for. And we saw the affect that Her Highness had on the crowd last night. We wanted to come and offer our services to the princess."

"You three are the king's special forces?" Henry asked.

"Not all of us," the first man replied. "But the services we desired to offer was to take the princess to meet the leader of the alliance."

"Alliance?" Henry asked.

"An alliance of the king's special forces. Young and old. But, mostly old."

"What kind of an alliance is it," Henry pointedly asked, worried they represented a resistance faction within the kingdom.

"Well, we are more of a support group to satisfy our thirst for battle and weaponry," the third man revealed. "We supply each other with weapons, medicines, and the occasional mercenary job."

"I don't know if we should be talking to you men anymore," Balen remarked, starting to rise from his chair.

"Our leader is very anxious to have an audience with the princess again." The first man responded.

"Again?" Balen and Henry chorused. The three old men smiled.

"Yes," the second man stated. "He and the princess have met under an official circumstance."

"What do you mean?" Henry asked.

"That is all we are at liberty to say," the third man intervened to prevent the group from revealing more than what they were allowed. By that time, Audrianna slowly opened the door to the master bedroom. Her sleeping gown had been properly turned back around on her body. She determinedly walked over to Henry as if she had an important matter on her mind. Upon seeing Audrianna, the three men, seated at the table, stood to their feet to greet the princess. Henry looked at the princess, wanting to tell her of the three mystery men who waited patiently to be introduced to her. Before Henry could speak to Audrianna, the princess raised her hand and slapped Henry across the face.

"Ow!" Henry yelped. "Why did you slap me?"

"Lady Olivia just explained to me what 'morning sickness' is, and what 'consummate' means. Let me tell you, Horace the Horrible, you and I are NEVER going to 'consummate' any time soon!" Henry turned to look at Audrianna's angry expression. "It's Henry the Horrible," he said. "And that's plenty fine with me." Audrianna turned to storm out of the room, then whirled around again.

"I don't know why Lady Olivia punched you," she added, "but for whatever reason, part of that slap was for her as well."

"When you do find out," Henry inquired, "are you planning on slapping me again?" "No," she answered. "I'll probably punch you as Lady Olivia did." She turned to leave the room again, when her eye caught the three old men standing beside the table with their hats in their hands.

"Good morning, gentlemen," the princess greeted.

"Good morning, Your Highness," they responded. Audrianna was taken aback by their response. She didn't know who they were, but they obviously knew who she was. She turned to look at Henry for an explanation.

"These men came to the farm to seek an audience with Your Highness," Henry stated.

"You men want to talk to me?" the princess asked.

"Actually," the first man replied, "we came to escort you to the one that requested an audience with Your Highness."

"Who would that be?" the princess asked.

"We are not at liberty to say," the third man replied. "But the leader of our alliance is anxious to meet you."

"I'm anxious to meet him as well," Henry announced.

"Begging your pardon, Your Majesty," the first man clarified, "but our leader was very specific that we were not allowed to bring Your Majesty to meet him."

"What?" Henry asked. "Do you expect us to allow you to take the princess alone without an official escort?"

"The leader of the alliance definitely does not want you to come to his house, Your Majesty," the first man interjected. "He does not trust you."

"I can understand his reasoning," Henry answered. "I've not been the most judicious aristocrat in the kingdom. Not by far. But I am not comfortable for you, nor anyone, taking the princess to a secret location where I am not able to find her later. She is my betrothed. I have a responsibility to take care of her."

Audrianna looked at Henry. She had never heard the prince speak of her with such concern before. Up to that point he had been her greatest source of fear and despair. Now, he was doing all he could to assure her safety.

"I will go with her," Olivia announced as she entered the room. Everyone turned to look at her. "She will be safe with me."

"That I can be sure," Balen responded. He turned to look at Henry. Henry sighed in resignation.

"Very well," he said. "I still feel uneasy about this." Audrianna beamed a smile at Olivia.

Within an hour, the two ladies climbed into the wagon and headed off down the road with the three old men leading on horseback. For several hours, the men led them down twisting trails, through streams and creeks, up steep hills, and down into low valleys. Finally, after what seemed to take the entire day, the men led them to a large, flat, dirt valley at the end of a canyon. There didn't seem to be anything in that canyon, save one small dilapidated house. The men dismounted, and Olivia jumped out of the wagon.

"Stay in the wagon until I am certain we are safe," she told Audrianna. Olivia approached the men and began inquiring about the location of the canyon and house. The men smiled at her and coaxed Olivia and Audrianna to follow them into the house. Olivia helped the princess out of the wagon and told her to hold her hand and stay close.

As the two of them entered the house, they noticed the absence of any type of furniture, except a large table in the middle of the one room. Even the table was void of any chairs. Seven men, dressed in military regalia, circled the table looking at charts and maps. Leading Olivia and Audrianna towards the table, the three men stood in a line shielding the women from the goings on at the table.

"We have brought Her Royal Highness, Princess Audrianna, to meet with you, as requested," the first man announced. The three men then parted to either side to reveal the princess and her Lady in Waiting to the expectant men. When Audrianna looked at the table of men, she quickly recognised an old man, dressed as a farmer, standing dead centre of the room.

"Well—well—well—welcome Princess Audrianna, the 'Tenderhearted'," the man stuttered. Audrianna beamed with enthusiasm.

"Mason," she declared. "It's wonderful to see you again!"

"It's goo—it's goo—it's good to see you again," Mason greeted. "What happened to your hair," he asked. Audrianna gave a deep sigh.

"Mason," Olivia declared, "you old goat! I should have known you were behind this motley group of militant has-beens."

"Has-beens?" Mason questioned. "I've see—see—see—seen your weapons barn, too, you know."

"Keeping up with my skills is not the same as forming an alliance."

"And yet," Mason argued, "you and the princess are seeking our help, are you not?

Is—is—is that why you were in town last night?" "That is correct," Audrianna responded. "Your Highness!" Olivia scolded.

"Then I am offering my services, my men, and our weapons at your disposal." "How many men do you have at our disposal," the princess asked.

"Your Royal Highness!" Olivia scolded again.

"I-I-I-I have twenty-six men who are ready at a moment's notice," Mason announced. "But there are eighty-one who are within a day's journey."

"Good," the princess declared. "Bring them in and outfit them with weapons." "Audrianna!" Olivia protested.

"Yes, Lady Olivia?" Audrianna innocently asked.

"This is highly inappropriate! These men are mercenaries, not the king's special forces anymore."

"Maybe," the princess declared, "but we need them to help us re-take the castle from the Andjety."

"I don't know how well we can trust these men. They rely solely on profit, not patriotism," Olivia warned.

"Ah," Audrianna shrugged, "I think we can trust Mason. He's an old friend of mine. I helped him with his farm when the Andjety came and stole all his goats. The king awarded him six female goats and one male goat to replenish his flock."

"Really?" Olivia asked. "Yes."

"Then where are all his goats?" Olivia asked. The princess walked over to and peered out the small window. She saw no evidence outside that goats had even been in that general area.

"Mr Mason," Audrianna admonished, "where are all your goats? I don't see any goats out there."

"That's right," Mason replied. "You won't find any goats on this land." The princess spun around and faced Mason.

"Did you lie to me in Royal Court, Mason?" Audrianna responded. "Did you take advantage of me?"

"No-no-no. Not-not-not at all," Mason nervously answered. "I said that I have no goats on this land. But this land is not my goat farm. This place is our headquarters."

"You mean this place is your hideout," Olivia remarked. Mason bobbed his head back and forth.

"You could say that," he chuckled. "But my goat farm is about twenty miles from here. This canyon doesn't have any green foliage suitable for goats."

"Why do you hide out here, rather than on your goat farm?" Audrianna asked.

"My goat farm is full of trees, gullies, rolling hills, and of course, goats. It is hard to train for battle when you are already battling the terrain and livestock."

"The canyon also hides our goings on from spying eyes while we train," one of Mason's men added.

"What exactly are you training for?" Olivia demanded to know.

"We train for the sake of training," another old man declared. "You never know when the king might need to call on us again."

"The king is dead," Audrianna exclaimed. "The Witch killed him in his bed." The entire group of men hung their heads. Several removed their hats and held them in their hands.

"My husband, Prince Henry, is not fully decided as to what should be done," the princess announced. "But I am." Olivia and the princess looked at each other attempting to read each other's thoughts on the matter. Audrianna's mind raced back to Rupp's advice to apologise for nothing, but to command those under her authority. She also remembered her ladies-in-waiting telling her not to think of herself as a helpless ten- year-old girl, but as the crowned princess of Nadeau. Olivia gave a nod to the princess. Audrianna stood up tall and squared her shoulders.

"I believe I can trust you, Mason," Audrianna said. "I am prepared to employ your men to help in the attack on Nadeau castle."

"We are at your service, Your Highness," Mason excitedly

replied. The princess then turned to the men standing around Mason, listening and watching on.

"Are you men prepared to go to battle?" she asked.

"Yes, Your Highness," the men quickly replied without hesitation.

"Are you men prepared to die on behalf of the kingdom of Nadeau?" she asked. "We are prepared to die for Her Highness, the Tenderhearted," one of the men responded. Everyone shouted their approval.

"If you die for me," Audrianna replied, "then you die for the kingdom and the crown," she answered, taking a step towards the group of men. Everyone snapped to attention as she moved forward.

"Long live the future queen of Nadeau," one of Mason's envoys declared. "Long live the queen!" everyone chorused.

"Good," Audrianna responded, standing as tall as her four-foot seven-inches stature could stretch. "I expect to see all of you, your twenty others, and the eighty-one men, at the farm of Balen and Olivia—in two days. I expect to see you all dressed for battle and ready to fight. Understand?"

"At your command, Your Highness," Mason answered as he and his men again snapped to attention.

"Then pledge your loyalty," Olivia demanded Mason, and his men standing around the table. "Make your pledge to the queen." Audrianna looked up at Olivia. "Hold out your hand, Your Highness," Olivia commanded the princess. Audrianna held her hand out to Olivia, not sure if she was going to slap it or not. "Not to me," Olivia whispered. "To them."

Audrianna held out her hand to the Nadeau mercenaries. One by one, each man knelt before the princess, took her hand, kissed it, then touched their forehead to her hand. Everyone took their turn, with Mason being the last. As he finished kissing her and touching his forehead, he arose and stood before her, not letting go of her hand.

"We-we-we who were once the king's special forces, are now

Your Highness's special forces," Mason declared. "The special forces of Princess Audrianna of Nadeau." They all cheered in agreement.

"Very good," the princess remarked. "Lady Olivia, let us be going."

"Yes, Your Highness," Olivia responded, slightly curtsying. Olivia quickly rushed to the door and opened it for the princess. Audrianna began walking out the door, shoulders back, head held high.

"Your Hi-Hi-Hi-Highness," Mason called after the princess. Audrianna stopped and looked over her shoulder at Mason.

"Yes?" she asked.

"We have a gift for you," he replied. "Consider it another token of our sincere loyalty to the crown."

"A token of loyalty to the crown?" Audrianna asked.

"Well," Mason thought for a second, "at least your crown, Your Highness." Audrianna walked up to Mason as the old man pulled out a small glass jar. The entire jar fit in the palm of the old man's hand. "It is a jar of exquisite perfume. Worthy of a princess, and a queen." Audrianna eyed the jar excitedly.

"Thank you, Mason," she replied, opening the jar and giving the perfume a strong whiff. "Oh," the princess responded. "That is a wonderful aroma. What is it?"

"A lilac extract," Mason answered. "A very expensive perfume, mixed with special Egyptian oil." The princess quickly dipped her finger in the ointment and padded the oil on her neck.

"Very nice," Olivia commented. "Your husband will love it." Audrianna wrinkled her nose at Olivia.

"I'll let that frown go this time, Your Highness," Olivia warned. "Let us get underway, back to the farm."

It was late afternoon that Olivia and the princess returned to the farm. Henry and Balen had spent a significant amount of their time training with Balen's homemade weapons and tactical gear. As soon as Olivia and Audrianna arrived, Olivia put everyone to work at preparing a late lunch. She and Balen went to work in the garden, while Audrianna and Henry worked at plucking and cleaning the chickens that the foxes killed during the night. As they sat across from each other, Audrianna kept looking up at Henry, smiling, then back down at the chickens she was plucking.

"Why are you looking at me?" Henry asked. "Do I have feathers on my face?" "No," the princess replied. "I was just thinking about this morning, when the three men came to the house."

"What about them?" Henry asked.

"You called me your betrothed, and told them I was your responsibility, and you weren't going to let them take me away to where you wouldn't be able to find me later."

"That's right," Henry said.

"I've never heard you ever speak with genuine concern towards me before," Audrianna remarked.

"Well," Henry replied, "We've been through a lot together the past several months. I guess I've gotten so used to your weeping and slobbering, and your runny-nose, and your baby diaper smell, it wouldn't seem right without you."

"My baby diaper smell?" Audrianna asked irately.

"Although," Henry continued, "I must admit, you do smell rather pleasant since coming back from Mason's hideaway." Audrianna smiled.

"Lilac extract," she commented. "A gift from Mason."

The two of them continued in silence, plucking feathers off the dead chickens. "Does that mean that you love me?" Audrianna asked. Henry stopped plucking, not looking up at the princess.

"I wouldn't call it love," he responded. "You might call it 'familiar admiration'. I respect you, and I care about your welfare. But, I wouldn't call it 'love'." He continued plucking while Audrianna stopped and looked at him.

"In other words," she remarked, "you love me in your heart, but not in your head." Henry stopped plucking, while Audrianna continued.

"My heart and my head?" he asked.

"A few years ago," Audrianna explained, stopping her plucking while Henry continued, "I was angry with my father because he refused to take me with him and my mother to the village festival."

"They probably didn't have any sassafras," Henry interjected.

"When they returned, I stayed in my room and wouldn't speak to him, except to say I didn't love him anymore. So, my father told me he knew I still loved him in my heart.

It was just my head that stopped loving him. He told me that in a few days, the love in my heart would catch up with my head, and I would love him both heart and head once again."

"What are you saying, Ree," Henry asked, both stopping their plucking. Audrianna looked at Henry.

"You demonstrated to me today that you truly love me in your heart. You just have a lot of resentment and anger preventing you from loving me in your head."

"And what happens when my head catches up with my heart?" Henry asked.

"I'll probably die of old age," she answered, looking down and finishing the plucking on her chicken.

As Henry finished plucking his chicken, the two of them looked around the kitchen and noticed that feathers were scattered throughout the better half of the little farmhouse. Some were still floating in the air in the immediate kitchen, gliding on wind wisping in from the window. Audrianna quickly stood to her feet and looked out the window to see if Olivia was coming in the house anytime soon. Henry grabbed a broom and began sweeping up the excess of feathers covering the floor. As they worked, Henry changed the topic of their dialog.

"Why did Olivia scold you this morning in her bedroom?" he inquired. "I was about to barge in and rescue you, but Balen stopped me."

"Olivia was upset that I had put myself in a compromising situation, insisting on going to the pub with the two of you. She said the pub was no place for a princess, nor a lady, much less a little girl."

"That's true," Henry remarked.

"She told me that even though it wasn't my fault that I had gotten drunk," Audrianna reported, "doing so was completely unbecoming of a princess, and that I could have undermined all that you and Balen are trying to accomplish in restoring the kingdom."

"I can understand her point of view," Henry replied. "Although I feel the most responsible for what happened. I will be more careful concerning your welfare from now on." Audrianna blushed and looked down at her feet.

"She also said that I could have gotten hurt at the pub in ways that I did not even understand. That opened the discussion of what 'consummate' truly meant, as well as other topics. I was horrified, at which she told me never to go against her counsel again, and it is my duty to the crown to remain in her protective custody so she can ensure my safety."

"Then you came straight out and slapped me," Henry stated. "For three good reasons," Audrianna replied.

"What good reasons?"

"Well," Audrianna answered. "First, because I needed to slap someone. Second, because I realised how you had placed me in danger last night. And, third, because I've wanted to slap you in the face for over four months now."

As they finished cleaning up the feathers from the floor, Olivia and Balen came in from the garden, each carrying a basket full of fruits and vegetables. Olivia began to prepare the two naked chickens for baking while Balen showed the princess how to best cut and slice the vegetables. Each type of vegetable was cut and sliced in its own unique way. Henry was given the task of lighting the fire inside the small iron oven, which he found rather arduous.

While the chickens baked in the oven, Olivia and Audrianna changed into suitable clothing to do a bit of sword training. Olivia had Audrianna spar with her as before, swinging her heavy iron sword rather slow and precisely, then gradually swinging faster, maintaining her accuracy.

As the princess swung her heavy iron sword with all her strength, Olivia deflected the sword up in the air, or down to the ground. Again, Audrianna felt the muscles in her arms and wrists ache and burn. However, she began to realise that she could grip hold of the sword much more firmly than before. It also was becoming easier to swing the heavy iron sword with greater precision.

After half an hour of intense training, Audrianna lifted her sword to her shoulder, indicating she needed a break. Her face glowed bright red. Sweat poured down her face and drenched her blouse. Her hair matted on top of her head in all different directions. Olivia directed her to a bucket of water, sitting under a tree, to refresh herself. Audrianna took a drink, then plopped herself in the shade to rest.

While resting, Olivia presented Audrianna with another gift. She took the heavy iron sword from the princess, and in its place, gave her a sword of steel. The princess jumped up from the ground with giddy enthusiasm. Her new sword, much longer and boarder, was also much lighter and stronger than her iron sword. The only unfortunate part of her gift was that she could not sheath her new sword around her waist. The scabbard drug on the ground, making wearing the sword with her belt an impossibility.

Now the princess took to her swordsmanship with greater dedication than ever before. While her arms still ached from her fatigued and developing muscles, she found her new level of training much easier. The princess and Olivia once again began to beat against each other's swords for several minutes. At the end of their first round, it was not the princess's aching arms that caused her and Olivia to stop, but rather the aroma from the house, indicating that the two chickens were finished baking.

"You are progressing very rapidly, Your Highness," Olivia observed. "After supper, we will work on your dagger throws."

"Does that mean you will tell me why you punched Henry if I am able to land the dagger into the target?" Audrianna asked.

Olivia smiled.

"I will keep my promise, Anna," Olivia answered the princess. Audrianna beamed a smile back at Olivia. It was the first time Olivia had called her Anna. To Audrianna, being given a special nickname meant Olivia began to love her both in heart and head.

Before Olivia could stop her, Audrianna grabbed a dagger, took her stance, and hurled the dagger at the target against the barn. The dagger spun through the air with a low whistle, and slapped sideways against the wooden board, then fell helpless to the ground. Audrianna looked up at Olivia rather sheepishly, to which Olivia patted her on the shoulder.

"Retrieve the knife, then let's go eat," she told the princess. "A little bit of food might help you earn the right to learn secrets."

Upon entering the house, both Olivia and Audrianna sighed deeply at the tantalising aroma of fresh baked chicken. The princess began to dance excitedly as she quickly grabbed up wooden plates and set the table. She then circled the table a second time placing wooden forks in their designated spot. Soon enough, all four were seated at the table looking at Balen expectantly for him to say his prayer of thanksgiving before they ate.

"Merciful Lord," Balen prayed, "We have worked hard for the food set before us.

You gave us land. You gave us food."

"And you sent us foxes to kill two of the chickens," Audrianna abruptly added.

"For that, we are eternally thankful," both Balen and Audrianna finished the prayer together.

"Amen," everyone chorused together.

Balen stood from his seat and began carving up the two small chickens, placing meat on everyone's plate. Audrianna waited patiently for everyone to receive their fair portion. She swallowed hard several times due to the fact her mouth watered excessively. As Balen sat down, she looked Olivia's way. Olivia gave a subtle nod, to which Audrianna stabbed at her portion of chicken with the wooden fork and rapidly devoured it. Balen glanced over at Olivia, who shrugged in return to allow the princess the one uncontested liberty.

As soon as supper was finished, and everyone pitched in to clean up afterwards, Olivia led the princess to the outside table where they had previously left the daggers. Olivia handed one of the daggers to Audrianna, and slid the other in her belt.

Audrianna took her stance, sideways, facing the silhouette against the barn wall. She held out the dagger, holding it by the blade. She bent her arm towards herself, then with a firm, fluid throw, she flung the knife towards the target. As before, the dagger spun towards the target, but landed hilt first, then fell to the ground. Audrianna raised her hands in a gesture of resignation.

"My turn," Olivia remarked. She then took her stance, flung her dagger, which stuck into the wood, dead centre on the silhouette of the head.

"Maybe I should ask you to tell me one of your secrets," Olivia suggested. "I hit the target, and my dagger stuck in the wood. What secret have you withheld from everyone else?" Audrianna looked at Olivia wide-eyed, then down to her feet. She thought for a minute, then looked back up at Olivia.

"Well," Audrianna confided, "I've never told anyone this before, but I was once in love back in my younger years."

"Your younger years?" Olivia questioned.

"Yes," the princess answered, cocking her head to one side and looking at the Olivia through the corner of her eyes. "I was eight, and foolish. He was close to my same age, maybe a little older. But he was so cute and irresistible. His big brown eyes, and his long light-coloured hair."

"Are you serious?" Olivia asked Audrianna.

"Yes," she answered, nodding her cocked head. "Mama and papa didn't know about us. They wouldn't have understood the love we had for one another. He would kiss me goodnight every evening as I held him in my arms. He'd watch me through my window as I slept, as he would lay in the tall grass out in the field."

"Out in the field," Olivia remarked. "Are we talking about a dog?" she asked.

"The most beautiful stray sheep dog I'd ever known." Audrianna let out a vocal sigh. "Ah! My first love!"

"A stray sheep dog?" Olivia asked.

"Yes," Audrianna replied. "I called him Baxter."

"Enough of that foolishness," Olivia scolded, walking over to the target and wiggling out her embedded knife. "It is your turn to throw the dagger."

Audrianna picked up another dagger from the table. She took her stance, one foot out in front, standing sideways, her hand holding the dagger by the blade, her arm held out straight, bent at the elbow. Olivia walked up behind the princess and corrected her posture as well as how she held the dagger. She grabbed hold of the princess's wrist and demonstrated how she needed to fling the knife. Olivia stepped back and encouraged Audrianna to give it another try. Audrianna flung the dagger towards the silhouette target, which struck the right shoulder of the target. The dagger, though, fell to the ground rather than penetrating the wood.

"That was a good shot," Olivia announced. "It's too bad you did not give it enough speed to stick into the target."

"Does that count?" the princess pleaded.

"Sorry," Olivia replied. "My secret is worth at least sticking the dagger into the wood from twenty paces." Audrianna turned her back to Olivia and wrinkled her nose.

"Was that a frown?" Olivia asked. Audrianna whirled around with a shocked look on her face. "I know a frown when I see one, even if it's on the other side of your head." Audrianna quickly picked up another dagger and flung it at the target. That dagger also hit the lower left leg of the target, but fell to the ground without sticking into the wood.

"This isn't fair," the princess remarked. "My throwing is fine, but I'm not strong enough to make the knife stay on the board."

"Your throwing is fair," Olivia responded, "but you need to practice more. I know your arms and wrists are strong enough from all your sword training. You should be able to land your knife in the wood, if you throw it right." Audrianna turned the left corner of her mouth down and raised an eyebrow at Olivia.

"Little girl," Olivia scolded, "a half frown is a full frown to me." Audrianna squared her shoulders in defiance.

"I'm not a little girl," the princess angrily declared. "I am Her Royal Highness, the future queen of Nadeau!" Olivia folded her arms and scowled at Audrianna.

"I'll swat that little Highness of yours if you continue to speak to me that way." Audrianna looked at the ground, frowned, then grabbed the last dagger on the table, and threw it angrily at the target. The knife spiralled through the air, and stuck in the target, dead centre of the silhouette's belly. Audrianna spun around to face Olivia, and smiled with enthusiasm at her success.

"It would seem, Anna," Olivia announced, "that I owe you a secret. And a switching." The princess's smile dropped. "Which would you prefer to redeem first?"

CHAPTER 20

As the heat of the day began to cool, and the bright sky began to dim, Olivia led the princess down to the river to wash up before bed. Audrianna had expended a lot of energy practicing her swordsmanship, as well as throwing daggers. Olivia knew the princess had perspired liberally under her multiple layers of clothing. After assisting Audrianna in removing her clothes, Olivia dipped the clothes in the river, wrung them out, then hung them on a tree limb to dry. Olivia sat on the log of a fallen tree, while the princess submerged herself in the river, then waded towards the bank, till the water came to her shoulders.

"Okay, Lady Olivia," Audrianna announced from the river. "I'm ready to hear the story behind why you punched Henry in the face the other day." She beamed a smile of anticipation as Olivia leaned back on the log and began to explain.

"Well, Anna," She began to recount the story, "when Luella was wed to the king, I was given the honour to watch over the queen, as her Lady in Waiting, and to protect her at all costs. She and I took to each other right from the start. We ate together, slept next to each other, helped dress one another, and brushed each other's hair every day. We rode horses together, practiced swords together, and swam in the river together. We were the best of friends."

"Just like my ladies-in-waiting were to me," Audrianna replied.

"When Luella was with child, it became evident to everyone that baby Henry was taking a toll on her thin, fragile body as she attempted to carry him to term."

"To term?" Audrianna asked.

"Yes, Anna," Olivia answered. "It takes nine months from the time a woman is with child till the day when the baby is ready to come out of her."

"Argh," the princess grimaced. "We have to carry a baby inside us for nine months?

What does he do in there all that time?"

"A lot of moving, kicking, and stretching. Also, sword practice, horseback riding, and dagger tossing. At least, that's what it feels like," Olivia stated. Audrianna giggled. "Anyway, Luella had become so ill by the time Henry was ready to come out, it was evident that she might not make it past delivery. I was with her the whole time she was delivering. It was just Luella, me, and the midwife. She became so pale. I had never seen the queen so pale before. She could barely hold my hand without my assistance. I knew she was dying."

"How awful," Audrianna consoled, stepping out of the water and wrapping herself in the large towel they had brought from the house. The princess sat on the log next to Olivia, holding the towel around her, and looking up at her.

"Before she passed away, she faintly asked me to take care of Henry. I told her with God as my witness, I would watch after him."

"So, what happened?" Audrianna asked. "Why did you leave him?"

"I didn't leave him, Anna," Olivia answered, looking down at the princess. "I stayed with him day and night, nursing him with goat milk, poured into a napkin with a hole poked through the corner. I changed his diapers, I bathed him, and as he grew older, I mashed vegetables up to spoon feed him. Not once during that entire time did the king look in on Henry to see how he was doing. He would ask me at times, if passing me in the hallways or in the outer courtyard, but never intentionally come and check on the boy in his room."

"Henry told me," Audrianna added, "the king never once took any interest in him because of his grief over the queen's death."

"That is true," Olivia stated, "but not a reasonable excuse. Henry may not have ever met his mother, but, to my observation, a boy growing up without a mother, grieves the same as his father." Audrianna leaned against Olivia, while Olivia put her arm around the princess, stroking her wet, matted hair.

"So, when Henry reached the age of eight, I felt it was time to wean myself away from the prince, and in my place, he was given a Lord in Waiting to attend to his needs of dressing him and making sure he was bathed and put into bed at a reasonable time. Balen became his sword instructor, being the captain of the royal guards at the time, and I kept my distance."

"So, what happened?" Audrianna anxiously asked.

"To make this long story shorter, Balen and I spent a lot of time together in sword training, and dagger tossing, and archery, and every kind of discipline the captain felt inclined to teach me."

"And?" the princess prodded.

"And we fell in love," Olivia announced.

"What does this have to do with punching Henry?" Audrianna asked. "Get to the part where you lay the prince to the ground."

"I'm coming to it, Anna," Olivia reassured her. "I was in love with Balen, and he was in love with me. But Henry had an obvious infatuation for me as well."

"Infatuation?" the princess asked.

"He liked me," Olivia explained. "He liked me a lot! In fact, I would catch him staring at me in royal court, and at sword drills, and during meals. He seemed to think of nothing else but me and what I was doing. If I stooped down to pick up a fallen arrow, or bend over to retrieve a sword, he watched my every move with voracious longing. It was unnerving, and it was making Balen mad. Not only was Balen upset with how much the prince lusted over me, but also how little he would concentrate on the matters that required his attention. I was Balen's interest, and Henry was merely fifteen years old."

"Did Balen want to punch Henry too?" Audrianna asked.

"Yes, indeed," Olivia answered. "But Henry was the prince of Nadeau. He wasn't officially the 'crowned prince' until earlier this year when he was coronated along with you. However, to show any kind of aggression towards a royal could result in death."

"Oh, my," Audrianna replied. "What did Balen do?"

"There was nothing he could do," Olivia responded. "But there was something I felt inclined to do."

"What did you do," Audrianna asked, looking up at Olivia, who by now had placed both her arms around the princess and pulled her close.

"I marched up to Henr y out in the courtyard before he and Balen could begin their sword training. Balen was busy on the other side of the courtyard cleaning his equipment. I told him I knew about his infatuation, but that he needed to stop watching me. I was more than twice his age, and his mother was like a sister to be, making me a surrogate aunt to him."

"What did he say?" the princess asked.

"He told me I was beautiful, and how he would very much like to kiss me in exchange for leaving me alone."

"Did you kiss him?" Audrianna eagerly asked, leaning away from Olivia so she could look her in the eyes.

"I told him I had never kissed any man, and that I was saving my first kiss for my true love, meaning Balen."

"Oh," Audrianna remarked. "What a sweet thought. I've never kissed any man either. Should I wait until the right moment?"

"Well, you're betrothed," Olivia answered. "You won't have a choice. Sooner or later you'll have to kiss Henry, whether the two of you are in love or not." Audrianna hung her head.

"That's not fair," she replied, laying against Olivia again.

"Anyway, when I told Henry that I was saving my first kiss for my true love, he told me that he was my one true love. I told him he wasn't, but that Balen was the one I loved and hoped to marry him someday."

"What did Henry say to that?" Audrianna demanded to know.

"Nothing. He looked over to see if Balen was watching, then grabbed the back of my head, and forced me to kiss him."

"He force-kissed you?" Audrianna asked incredulously.

"He did indeed," Olivia recounted. "Before I could push him away, I heard Balen screaming behind Henry. Henry turned, and ran into the castle, while Balen ran to get his sword." Audrianna leaned back to look up at Olivia again.

"He was going to kill Henry?"

"Well," Olivia continued, "he wanted very much to do the prince bodily harm. But I ran up to Balen and grabbed his wrist that held his sword. I began to talk him down, but Balen began to tear up, stating that that kiss was meant for him, not the prince! He continued to yell that the prince stole his wife's first kiss."

"He called you his wife?" Audrianna asked.

"He did indeed. That was the first time I realised Balen's intentions for me." "What did you and Balen do?" the princess asked.

"We went straight to seek an audience with the king," Olivia answered. "We announced our engagement to the king, as well as our desire to surrender our titles, and to leave the city of Nadeau for good."

"What did the king do?" Audrianna asked.

"He refused to accept the surrender of our titles, but he granted us to leave, and gave us a gift of land that we are now living on. That is why we live all the way out here in Pachenthou, and why we still hold the titles of Lord Balen and Lady Olivia."

"Wow," Audrianna responded. "My husband sure is a maggot, isn't he?"

"That was ten years ago, Anna," Olivia replied, standing to her feet. "Your betrothed was only fifteen at the time."

"I'm only ten," Audrianna commented, adjusting her towel as she stood alongside Olivia. "And I know better than to kiss someone that doesn't want to be kissed."

"Maybe so," Olivia remarked, breaking off a long, thin stick from the log they had been sitting on. "But do you know better than to frown at someone who doesn't want to be frowned at?" Audrianna spied the switch in Olivia's hand. She knew there was no negotiating with the former Lady in Waiting. The princess turned her back to Olivia and leaned against the log. Olivia hid her smile at Audrianna's acceptance of her consequences. With two quick strokes, she swatted the princess's rear. Audrianna winced, then turned to face Olivia again.

"Under the circumstances," the princess replied, "your story was worth the switching." The two smiled at each other. From there, Olivia checked to see if the princess's clothes had dried. Finding them ready to be worn again, she helped little Audrianna put on her underwear, then her full-length undergarment. Olivia then helped her pull her dress over her head and laced it up the front. After that, she slipped the outer apron over her dress and tied it in the back. The two of them returned to the farm house, holding each other's hands.

The next day, after the morning chores were completed, and breakfast was eaten, Audrianna took it upon herself to practice her dagger tossing. She was so excited at sticking the knife in the target the day before, she didn't want to lose the chance at doing it a second time. As she threw one dagger after another, the princess began to peg one out of five throws.

Olivia, finished with cleaning up after breakfast, came to check on the princess's progress. Making several suggestions regarding her stance, and holding the knife, Audrianna began to peg one out of 'three' throws on the target. Elated with her progress, Audrianna began to push herself at perfecting her dagger tossing to the best of her ability. After an hour, though, Olivia led the princess from the back side of the barn, to the clearing on the front side, where Balen and Henry were practicing their sword skills. Olivia and Audrianna watched for several minutes as the two men began to spar intensely. Henry eyed the princess watching him, her hands folded and resting on a fence post, with her head resting sideways over her hands. Henry tried to show-off on behalf of Audrianna, using fancier footwork while sparring with Balen. Stepping back a bit, Balen looked for an opportunity to take advantage of Henry's antics. As Henry did a half spin with his feet, Balen put his foot out to the side of Henry, to which the prince tripped and fell to the ground on his back. Balen pointed his sword in Henry's face. "Don't let your wife become a distraction," he warned.

"She is not a distraction to me," Henry insisted. "I may have gotten a bit cocky while we are training, but I would never let that happen in the heat of battle." Balen reached his arm out and helped the prince to his feet.

"I don't just mean that you might be distracted with her watching on. But if you ever find yourself in a situation where Her Highness is either in danger, or calling out to you, you must stay in the moment with your opponent. You will not be able to rescue your betrothed if you become distracted, and run through, by the enemy."

"Okay, Okay," Henry replied. "I understand."

"I think it is time for the two love birds to spar for once," Olivia announced. "What birds?" Audrianna asked, raising her head from the post.

"You and Henry," Olivia clarified.

"We're not in love," Henry remarked. "We're just betrothed." Olivia and Balen both put a hand on one hip and glared at each other.

"That is possibly the saddest comment I have heard in quite some time," Balen responded to Olivia. Olivia nodded in agreement.

"Do I have to fight Henry?" Audrianna asked.

"You are not fighting him," Balen corrected. "You are sparring with him. The point is to hammer out each other's weaknesses, not to kill each other."

"But he is so much older, taller and more skilled than I am," the princess pointed out. "How am I expected to spar with him?"

"Your job is to deflect his advances," Olivia replied. "That is all we will worry about today."

"I'll go easy on you, little mouse," Henry teased, taking his stance, and tossing his sword from one hand to the other. Audrianna picked up her new sword Olivia had given her, from the rack on the barn wall.

"I'll try and keep myself from killing you, Horace," she said, taking her stance opposite Henry. "I'll need you later to spar with again." They both grimaced at each other and growled.

"Remember, Your Highness," Balen coached, "quick, fluid strokes. Let him come to you, don't reach out to meet him."

Henry circled the courtyard, with Audrianna mirroring his stance, circling to stay in front of him. Henry would half thrust his sword, causing the princess to swing her sword in defence, but missing his sword.

"He's testing you, Anna," Olivia commented. "He's trying to see how quick your reflexes are before he strikes. Don't give in to his pranks." They continued to circle the courtyard.

"Your hair looks good today, dear," Henry remarked to the princess. "It's growing out nicely. And you still smell like a garden of lilacs."

"Are you flattering me?" Audrianna asked. "You know I am above that, right? Don't play the flattering game with me, little boy." The two continued to circle the yard, Henry hesitating to strike at the princess.

"Are you two courting, or sparring?" Balen asked. "Let's see what the two of you got."

Finally, Henry gave a full thrust of his sword towards Audrianna. The princess quickly deflected his sword away from her. She regained her stance expecting him to come at her again. They both circled opposite of each other. Again, the prince thrust his sword at the princess, she again deflected it, to which Henry brought the sword around and swung at the blindside of Audrianna. Realising the sword was coming back around to her, she instinctively held up her sword to block. When the two swords contacted with a chiming CLANG, Henry's countenance dropped with surprise. Without looking, Audrianna jabbed her sword at Henry who frightfully deflected her attack with a TWANG. Balen and Olivia shot a look at each other.

"Did you see that?" Olivia asked.

"Amazing," Balen excitedly replied. "Stop you two! Everybody stop!" Henry and Audrianna raised their swords to their shoulders. Balen walked straight up to the princess.

"When did you learn to counter attack, Your Highness?" Balen asked. "Counter attack?" the princess asked.

"You were supposed to only deflect my attacks, Ree," Henry complained. "But instead, you blocked my advance, then immediately took the offensive when you immobilised my swipe."

"I'm sorry," Audrianna answered, looking down at her feet. "I don't know why I did that."

"I know exactly why you did that," Balen responded. Everyone looked at him. "But you need to stop apologising unless it becomes obvious that what you did was wrong, not out of character."

"You have a gift, Anna," Olivia announced. "You saw Henry's swipe even though he was swinging towards your blindside, and you blocked it without looking in his direction. That is an advanced skill."

"Has anyone taught you to do that," Balen asked, "or did you do that without thinking?"

"I didn't think about it," Audrianna replied. "He swung at me and I did what seemed natural to protect myself."

"Amazing," Balen repeated. "You have a sharp instinct for sword fighting." "Instinct?" the princess asked.

"That means you know what to do without having to think about it," Balen explained. "Let's have you two do some more sparring." Henry and Audrianna looked back at each other. They took their stances again.

"Here we go, little mouse," Henry teased again.

"If I do kill you this time," Audrianna remarked, "understand I didn't mean to. It was just my—instinct."

For several minutes, the prince and princess exchanged advances and deflections. Twice more, Audrianna displayed an uncanny ability to anticipate and predict Henry's trick advances, and took evasive actions to avoid them. She dodged one by shifting her small frame, and blocked the other in the same fashion as she had done before.

"That's incredible," Balen exclaimed. "To be so young, and so gifted." Henry showed displeasure in his face as the two royals lifted their swords to their shoulders.

"Well," Audrianna casually replied, "I am brown-haired, green-eyed, and left- handed." All three stared at the princess, not understanding the implication of her statement. Audrianna had taken what Rupp had told her as the absolute truth. However, right after the words escaped her lips, the thought suddenly occurred to her that Rupp had embellished the significance of her physique for the purpose of encouraging her.

For the rest of the day, the four went to work at catching up on much needed farm chores. Henry was assigned to the cow, which desperately needed milking, and was highly temperamental. Balen went to work feeding the surviving chickens, that excitedly pecked at the feed which was thrown down for them. He then to work at mowing the small hay field which needed to be cut, to have feed for the cow. Olivia worked at weeding the vegetable garden, pulling out weeds and spoiled vegetables.

On top of that, Olivia had become upset with how much work needed to be done cleaning the house. Audrianna was given the task of sweeping and dusting, which seemed to her to be an impossible task. With the constant breeze coming in through the windows, the dirt on the floor and furniture was never fully eradicated from the house. As frustrated as the princess was, Olivia felt it to be an acceptable task to keep the little girl busy and out of the way. Whenever Olivia would stumble over Audrianna, she would immediately send her to sweep or dust in another room, knowing it always needed to be done.

As the day was spent, and supper being ended that evening, the four of them walked outside to cool off from the exhausting work they had accomplished by nightfall. Audrianna, already dressed in her nightgown, sat under the night sky and admired the twinkling stars. She was excited at what the next day would bring. Mason had promised to arrive, along with over a hundred of his trained militia. They had pledged their loyalty to her—the future queen of Nadeau. And they were going to help her take back the castle. Henry would be king, and she would become the queen! Eventually.

As she excitedly looked up in the night sky, Olivia pointed out to her several local constellations. She told the princess the folk stories that whimsically, or superstitiously, went along with the starry pictures. Balen told the two of them adventure stories regarding the kingdom of Nadeau, and about battles he had fought in during the Andjety war.

After the third story, the exhausted little princess drifted off to sleep. As the angelic- faced child curled up in a ball, Olivia nudged Balen, who, in turn, nudged Henry. Henry picked up Audrianna and carried her into the house and softly laid her on the bed. With Olivia's help, they folded the blankets over the top of her, and Olivia kissed her on the forehead.

As Olivia began to lower the light of the lamp, Henry asked her to keep the light on.

He wanted to sit next to the princess for a few minutes.

"Why do you want to sit next to her?" Olivia asked. "She is not sick, and she is already asleep."

"That is correct," he answered. "But we have been through a lot of difficulties together and between us. I just need to sit next to her and sort all of this out in my head." "Don't be long," Olivia demanded. "It's not appropriate for a man to be in the room of a sleeping maid." She walked out of the room, leaving the door open behind her.

Henry pulled a wooden chair up close to Audrianna's bed. He sat in the chair and just stared at her for several minutes.

His mind raced through the past four months since he was first betrothed to the little girl. His eyes fixed upon the angelic expression on her face. So innocent-looking, yet so dangerous. So peaceful-looking, yet so unpredictable.

Henry took her hand in his as she continued to sleep. He knew, somehow, he needed to let go of all his resentment and anger towards her. He respected Audrianna, but there was still a part of him that felt like a large stone blocking a passageway. He couldn't resolve the fact that he felt trapped, betrothed to a little girl he couldn't marry, keeping him from becoming king. At the same time, he couldn't imagine sitting in royal court without her sharp judgment. He couldn't imagine taking on the Andjety without her. She somehow had become his lifeline, his security, during all this mess.

After bringing his thoughts full circle, he felt Lady Olivia standing at the door behind him, watching on. He turned his head slightly to catch a glimpse of her.

"You need to let her sleep, in peace," she calmly whispered. Henry nodded in agreement. He gently tucked her hand under the covers, then stroked her cheek with two of his fingers. He stood to his feet, and turned to leave. As he approached the doorway, Henry and Olivia exchanged glances.

"You're a fraud," she said accusingly. He stopped abruptly in front of her and looked her in the eyes.

"What do you mean?" he whispered, starting to get a bit huffy.

"You work so hard at pretending you don't care about anything or anyone," she replied.

"You should know just as well as anybody how selfish and self-obsessed I can be," Henry responded.

"Oh," Olivia remarked, "I know what the little boy I left back in Nadeau was capable of. But that is not the young man I welcomed into my house last week."

"And what kind of man do you think I am?" he asked.

"I have never before seen you become so protective and concerned over another person, like you are over Anna. And yet, I also see that she annoys you, but you shake it off like a woman would shake dust off a rug. You love her, yet you are unwilling to admit your true feelings for her."

"She is ten years old!" Henry exclaimed. "What kind of feelings do you think I could possibly have for a little girl?" Olivia began shaking her head.

"You are so used to women being objects, you don't know how to respond to one you genuinely care about. Henry, you are in love with someone that you can't be a lover to."

"I do not love her," Henry adamantly replied.

"Really?" Olivia asked. "In the morning, Mason will be arriving with over a hundred men that have pledged their lives to the princess. They will fight, and die, for Anna, because she is their symbol of future hope for Nadeau."

"So?" Henry countered.

"When we leave this farm, and go marching towards the castle, will you die for Her Highness? Or is marching against the castle merely about you and your throne? If it comes down to the moment, would you sacrifice your opportunity to become king for the sake of protecting the princess?"

Henry folded his arms.

"You ask a hard question, Olivia," he said. He thought a moment longer. "For me, I would die for Ree, not because she is the crowned princess, but because she is my friend." Olivia tilted her head towards Henry and raised her eyebrows. "I'm not in love with her, though."

"You need to stop thinking of love in terms of romance," Olivia responded. "You were once infatuated with me, remember? You longed for us to be lovers."

"I was fifteen, and insatiable," Henry Admitted.

"Exactly," Olivia replied. "But what you may not have known, was that I loved you. I loved you very much. But we could never have become lovers. Just because two people love each other, doesn't mean the world owes them the right to be together."

"What are you saying?" Henry asked.

"You and Anna care very deeply for one another," Olivia answered. "Stop thinking you don't have the right to love her just because you two can't be lovers. She deserves to be loved. So, Henry, love her."

Henry glanced at the open door to the princess, then back at Olivia.

"Tomorrow," Henry replied, "I will fight for the princess. But I cannot promise that I will die for her."

CHAPTER 21

The next morning, Audrianna was the first one awake and dressed. Usually, it took all three adults to rouse the little girl from sleep. But this morning, the morning that Mason and his men were to arrive, the princess ran to the barn to wake up her betrothed.

"Horace," she called out as she pounced on him and shook him. "Horace! Wake up!" "What's wrong, Ree?" he asked worriedly.

"Come spar with me again," she asked. "We need to spar and sharpen our skills some more."

"It is already morning?" he asked. "It still seems dark out."

"Come outside and see," she begged. "You'll see outside that the sun is up."

Henry rolled out of his haystack and dusted himself off. Audrianna realised that her betrothed was merely wearing his undergarments, which covered him at his waist and down to the middle of his calves. She shrieked and turned her back, blushing in the same manner Henry had at the sight of Rozelle in her undergarments.

Henry quickly pulled his outer garments on and followed Audrianna outside of the barn and into the courtyard. Henry could barely see the weapons rack against the side of the barn due to the absence of sunlight. The sky was still dark, with a tiny hint of sunlight peeking over the ridge of the Andjety mountains.

"I really don't consider this 'morning,'" Henry admonished. "We can barely see each other."

"That's okay," Audrianna replied. "Let's grab our swords, take our stance, and by that time, the sun will have fully risen over the mountains. Then we can start sparring."

Henry groped through the various swords hanging on the rack, until he was certain he had found his own sword. Audrianna quickly found her sword and stood opposite the prince. Within minutes, the sun fully peaked above the mountain range, lighting up the entire farm.

Without warning, Audrianna advanced towards Henry, who quickly blocked her strike and gave his own counter-strike. Knowing the princess was still rather a novice at sword fighting, Henry took things rather slow at first. But Audrianna gave every ounce of energy she had to perfecting her skills.

Multiple times Henry swung towards her blindside to see if she could still harness her instincts. Several times the princess failed to see his advance, to which Henry swatted her rump with his sword. The princess squeaked, spun around, and swiped his sword away.

After twenty minutes, the princess's skills began to warm up, and she started to excel with the same success she had the previous evening. However, even though her skills began to warm up, the princess's strength began to wear down. After blocking three of Henry's advances to her blindside, she raised her sword to her shoulder indicating she needed a break.

"I'm sorry," Audrianna replied, panting heavily. "I have to stop for a while."

"That was a good workout, Ree," Henry admitted. "You blocked several tricky swipes to your blindside." The princess smiled, bending over, and placing her hands on her knees. Sweat dripped from her face, and onto the ground.

"It's a bit early for sword practice," Olivia announced, walking from the house and towards the two by the barn. "The morning chores should be done first, then breakfast, then there will be plenty of time for practice."

"I just wanted to get as much practice in as I could before our army arrives to take us to the castle," Audrianna replied.

"Even when your special forces arrive, they will not be in a position to leave immediately," Olivia remarked.

"Why not?" Audrianna asked.

"Because we need to plan our strategy with them on how we plan to take the castle," Olivia answered. "Just because they know how to fight, doesn't mean they don't need a plan of attack."

"How long will that take?" the princess asked.

"I don't know the answer to that," Olivia replied, "but I do know it will be at least an hour to perform your various duties before breakfast is ready. Now, scoot you two, and get your chores done."

As the three others scurried around the farm like worker ants, Olivia prepared a large breakfast, intended to keep everyone well fed due to their rigorous training they were about to take part in. After the chores were done, and all four were seated, Balen was about to give the usual blessing over the food. Instead, Olivia piped up and asked Audrianna to bless the meal.

"Your Highness," Olivia asked, "Today is your special day. Your army of special forces are going to arrive sometime today." The princess beamed with excitement. "Would you please do the honours, and ask the Almighty to bless our humble meal today?" Everyone looked in Audrianna's direction. The princess swallowed hard out of fear. She had never been asked to do an "honour", like praying to God before. She may have interjected a small postscript to Balen's prayer a couple days earlier, but she'd never been asked to do the whole prayer. She thought nervously to remember how Balen's prayer would usually go. Then she prayed.

"Merciful Lord," Audrianna began, "We worked really hard to prepare this meal. You gave us land. Well, you didn't give me this land. I mean, it belongs to Lord Balen and Lady Olivia. But they let us stay here, and make us work. Not that we aren't willing to work. We are always willing to do our fair share. Although, I think the sweeping is a bit more than my fair share."

The three others, their hands folded and heads bowed, peaked one eye open and looked at Audrianna. Olivia softly cleared her throat to encourage the princess to conclude her prayer.

"Oh," Audrianna realised her prayer was becoming laborious for simply giving of thanks. "Sorry, Merciful Lord. I know You're busy up there. Thanks again for the food. For that, we are internally grateful."

"Eternally grateful," Balen corrected. "Amen," the princess concluded. "Amen," the other three chorused.

Audrianna looked up at the others rather embarrassed for what she felt was a poor prayer. Henry grinned and nodded his approval. Olivia lifted her head high, looked down at the princess, and waved her eyebrows in approval. Balen wasn't bothered, nor impressed by the prayer. He immediately reached towards the fruits and breads in an attempt to satisfy his anxious stomach.

As they ate, everyone's thoughts were preoccupied with the coming attack on Nadeau Castle that they all greatly anticipated. However, no one spoke to each other of their thoughts. They just sat quietly and ate, each looking down at their plate. They would look up only long enough to seize another parcel of food.

As they came to the end of the meal, the voice of a man could be heard from outside, calling to those inside the farmhouse.

"Hello?" the man called out the occupants of the house. "Is— is—is—is anyone at home?"

"Mason!" Audrianna cried out excitedly. "They are here!" She jumped to her feet and ran outside. The other three followed closely behind her. As they ran out the door of the house, Mason could be seen sitting on a horse, leaning on the front horn of his saddle. "Good morning, friends," Mason greeted. "I am here to present to you all, Princess Audrianna's Special Forces." He looked down at Audrianna and smiled. "You being the princess, correct?" The princess returned his smile by beaming a disarming grin. Mason slid off his horse and bowed to one knee before the princess.

"Where is your army, Mr Mason?" Audrianna asked, as the self-proclaimed leader of Her Highness's armed forces stood to his feet.

"They—they—they—they be not my army," Mason quickly replied. "They be your army, Your Highness." Mason pointed over his shoulder, to the road that he had travelled by. Everyone looked to the road. For as far as the pathway would let them, they could see a train of horses, wagons, and foot soldiers, in a line, coming up to the house.

The princess began to dance with excitement. It was her army, her armed forces, her special forces. An array of over a hundred men, geared for battle, to fight in the name of the future queen of Nadeau, paraded towards the house. As they approached and passed the princess, they removed their hats and bowed, and greeted her with the pleasantry, "Your Royal Highness!" Olivia and Balen directed the congress of wagons and horses to park on the far side of the barn. The foot soldiers gathered in the clearing next to the barn.

The wagons, filled with less mobile soldiers, unloaded the travel-spent men, who in turn, also unloaded an assortment of assault weapons and training equipment. There were broadswords, long swords, arming swords, claymores, and short swords. In addition to swords, there were spears, shields, maces, clubs, bludgeons, quarterstaffs, crossbows, longbows, daggers, portable archery targets, battering rams, wall ladders, and many other such equipment.

For the next hour, forty men took the initiative to set up training equipment, to quickly help remedial the skills of the inactive men and get them fit to fighting standards. As the men set up the equipment, and several of the leaders stood in the house, talking with Balen and Olivia, Henry and Audrianna heard another familiar voice from outside. "Ho, there!" the man called out. "Has anyone seen a little girl, about this high, going by the name of, Ree?" The prince and the princess cautiously walked outside to see Jaako sitting on an unbridled donkey.

"It's the 'dirty dog' himself," Audrianna called out, referring to what Jaako had called himself at the pub. She was uneasy with the old man's appearance at the farmhouse. She didn't like him, and hence, didn't trust him, either. Jaako dismounted his donkey, removed his large-brimmed hat, and then bowed low before the princess.

"I am at your service, m'lady," he replied to Audrianna.

"First off," Audrianna announced, "You must address me as 'Your Royal Highness'. That is the proper protocol, which I am certain you are aware of. Secondly, I thought you had said you were not a loyalist, and cared nothing for the crown. So, what are you doing here, Mr Jaako?"

Jaako was startled by the princess's response.

"I—er—uh…" he stammered. Olivia walked up behind Audrianna and placed her hands on the little girl's shoulders. "I am here to fight alongside the other elite swordsmen of the king."

"These are not the king's elite swordsmen," Olivia announced. Jaako glanced at the over-aged, past-their-prime, and hunched-over soldiers.

"They certainly are not!" he exclaimed. "These men can barely hold themselves up, much less a broadsword."

"These men are Princess Audrianna's Elite Special Forces," Olivia proclaimed. "They have come to help take Castle Nadeau back from the Andjety." Jaako turned to face the crowd of elderly soldiers, then looked over his shoulder at Olivia.

"They definitely are a special elite force," he replied. "Tell me, when charging the castle, do they require a nap halfway through the seizure?"

"They have plenty of fight left in them," Audrianna responded. "And they are loyal to the crown."

"Whose crown?" Jaako asked, turning to face the two ladies. "The king's crown, or the so-called crown of the unwed princess?"

"The king is dead," Olivia emphatically stated. Jaako shook his head.

"No, Lady Olivia," he replied, walking towards her and Audri-anna. "No, he is very much alive!" He then walked past the two of them, and ventured inside the house. Olivia and the princess looked at each other in astonishment. What did he mean?

Inside the house, several retired strategists stood at the table alongside Mason, Balen and Henry. On the table was a large, half-scrolled map of the castle and surrounding city of Nadeau. They all contributed their ideas as to how best to sneak into the castle and storm it from the inside. Jaako wandered past each of the men at the table, peeking in between them to view the map.

"What we need to be mindful of, is the fact that the War Witch has most likely replaced all the Nadeau guards with her own Andjety guards since killing the king."

"I'm telling you," Jaako angrily interjected, "the king is not dead. Why are all of you having a difficult time believing me?"

"Mainly because I saw Zymjai stick a knife into his back," Henry impatiently remarked.

"Also, because you are the one who continues to repeat that the king is alive," one of the strategists said. "That, in itself, lends to its incredibility." Jaako sneered.

"You will see, when we take Nadeau castle, that the king is alive and well," Jaako assured the men around the table.

"If there is a man depicting the king," Henry replied, "he is an imposter. The first thing I will verify is the fact that the king is not my father from whom I inherited the throne. The Witch killed him, and I am going to avenge his blood." The men surrounding the table barked their approval. Jaako turned and stormed out of the house.

Walking outside, Jaako decided to inspect the remedial train-ing for the over-aged soldiers. He noticed that several men could barely walk on their own, and some even still, used canes to walk over level ground. Jaako shook his head in disbelief. There was no way that this group of antiquated degenerates were going to be successful in taking the castle. As he walked by the temporary archery range, his eye caught three old men painstakingly loading their crossbows with darts. Their hands trembled as they held up the crossbows.

"I hope you don't hurt yourselves with those crossbows," Jaako muttered. "It's been a couple decades since you old crows fired one of those things. They can be rather…"

The three men turned their heads from the targets, looked towards Jaako, and lifted their bows. Then, without looking back, pulled their triggers. The arrows zipped towards the targets, each one landing somewhat off-centre from the bull's-eye. Jaako's countenance fell. "Well," he said to the three elderly archers, "you fellows are still old crows."

By this time, Mason left the farmhouse, and began reviewing the makeshift training camp. As he made his way past the barn, he stumbled upon Olivia and Audrianna practicing their sword skills. He stood watching for several minutes, impressed with the princess's proficiency. He witnessed Olivia intentionally swipe at the little girl's blind side, who raised her sword to block, then advance towards her sparring partner. As they brawled with their swords, Balen came walking up behind Mason to join him observing the ladies.

"Did-did-did-did you notice the princess favours her left hand?" Mason asked Balen. "Oh yes," Balen replied. "She said that Rupp, the Captain of the King's Guards, told

her that she was gifted because she is left-handed, brown-haired, and green-eyed." Mason nodded in agreement.

"That could be true," Mason remarked. "If anything, her-her-her-her green eyes and brown hair make her-her-her appearance enchanting. But I am most curious about her left-handed abilities."

"In what way?" Balen asked.

"Hand-to-hand fighting," Mason answered.

"I thought the broadsword was already hand-to-hand fighting," Balen replied. "Well," Mason reasoned, "the length of the broadsword keeps your opponent at a

distance. But knife fighting gets you up-close and personal with your assailant."

"And you feel Her Highness would excel at hand-to-hand knife fighting?" Balen asked.

"Those who are left-handed excel at hand-to-hand."

"Unless they are four-foot-seven," Balen commented. Mason looked up at Balen, who towered over him more than a foot in height.

"We'll see," Mason responded, turning to watch Olivia and the princess finish sparring. After a few minutes, Audrianna lifted her sword to her shoulder and raised her hand for the two of them to break.

"Excellent work, Anna," Olivia commented. "I am anxious to see how skilled you will be by your sixteenth birthday. Providing you keep up with your training."

"Do you think I will be skilled enough to best Henry at sword play?" the princess asked.

"I think you have the potential at besting him by your twelfth birthday," Olivia remarked.

"That's only fourteen months away," Audrianna replied.

"Well," Olivia reconsidered her estimation. "Perhaps by your thirteenth birthday." "Lady Olivia," Mason called out to the princess's Lady in Waiting. "May I make a

recommendation?"

"A recommendation?"

"Well," Mason answered, "more of a re-re-re-request."

"What request would that be, Mason?" Olivia asked.

"I noticed that Her Highness is left-handed," he replied. "Yes," Audrianna proudly admitted.

"I men-men-mentioned to your husband," Mason explained, "that it would be apropos to train Her Highness in the art of hand-to-hand fighting. Perhaps beginning with the skill of disarming an ass-ass-ass-assailant with a knife."

"That is an important skill to learn," Olivia replied, "especially before going off to battle." Olivia turned to Audrianna. "Would you like for me to teach you, Anna, how to disarm an adversary with a knife?"

"Really?" the princess asked with enthusiasm. "I would love to learn that." "Pardon, your ladyship," Mason interrupted, removing his hat, and holding it in his

hand. "But I was suggesting for-for-for me to teach Her Highness to fight hand-to-hand." "I beg your pardon," Olivia snapped. "What makes you think you should teach her

instead of me?"

"Well," Mason answered, nervously looking down at his hat. "Teaching knife fighting is unbecoming of a young lady, full of grace and beauty." Olivia looked at Mason in surprise. After a moment, she stepped back.

"Very well," Olivia responded, taking her stand to the side, next to Balen. "You may teach the princess her skill in hand-to-hand fighting." Mason eagerly reached towards the weapons table and picked up a training knife. Balen turned to his wife.

"Why did you abdicate?" he asked. "Hand-to-hand combat is your specialty." Olivia looked at Balen and shrugged.

"I decided to be a young lady today, full of grace, and beauty."

Mason led the princess to the side of the barn. He showed her the training knife, and how it was shaped like a knife, but it wasn't sharp, nor would it cut if you rubbed the blade against your skin. He then took the knife from the princess and held it in his own hand, as if he was going to jab and stab at her.

"Okay, Your Highness," Mason declared, "If a person comes at you with a knife, they most likely will be holding it in their right hand, like I am."

"I understand," Audrianna replied.

"So-so-so-so, when they attack you, they will expect for you to defend yourself with your right hand, because that is what they are used to. That was how they were trained. Do you see?"

"Yes," the princess answered.

"However, because you are left-handed, you have the advantage of taking them by surprise. Instead of grabbing at the knife with your right hand, at an angle, you can grab the knife from your attacker straight across with your left hand. They won't see it coming, and you will have the leverage to take the knife from them."

"How will I take the knife away from them?" Audrianna asked.

"Simple," Mason answered. "You-you-you-you grab the knife with your left hand, press down with your thumb, then twist their hand out, away from their body. They will have no choice but to release the knife. Then you can either take the knife away with your right hand, or-or-or-or shake the knife out of their hand and onto the ground."

Mason handed the knife back to the princess to demonstrate what he meant. He instructed her to strike with her right hand. As she jabbed at him, he reached straight across with his left hand, and quickly twisted her hand outwards, causing her to drop the knife. The thrust of his twist sent a sharp pain up the princess's arm.

"Ow!" she screeched. "You hurt me!" They both looked towards Olivia. Audrianna for emotional support, and Mason for approval. Olivia simply folded her hands in front of her, and slightly raised her chin. The two looked back at each other.

"Now-now-now now you try," Mason encouraged, taking the training knife away from the princess, and holding it out in a gesture to stab at her. Audrianna reached with her left hand to snatch the knife from Mason. As she tried to grab it, Mason poked her with the tip of the knife, causing her to involuntarily retract her hand from fear.

"Don't be afraid of the knife, Your Highness," Mason instructed. "If I was to cut your hand, or arm, even though it will hurt, it is still less dangerous than what would happen if I stabbed you in the heart."

"How do I grab hold of the knife, though?" the princess asked.

"Hold-hold-hold-hold out your right hand as a distraction, then when your enemy lashes at it, grab his hand with your left.

Got-got-got-got it, Your Highness?"

"I understand," Audrianna answered. The two of them faced-off in a hand-to-hand stance. Audrianna held her right hand out to bait her instructor. Mason lunged at the princess, while she grabbed hold of his knife with her left hand. As quickly as she grabbed it, she twisted his wrist, just as he had shown her.

"Whoa, whoa, whoa," Mason screamed. "That's a mighty strong grip you have for a ten-year-old." Audrianna reached over with her right hand, and retrieved the knife from Mason's compromised grip.

"Her Highness has trained rather vigorously at her swordsmanship," Olivia expressed. "She has advanced to a steel blade in her training."

"Impressive," Mason remarked. "This lesson must come rather easy for you, then." Audrianna beamed.

"Nothing comes easy at my size and height," she commented. "But I do give every lesson my absolute best effort."

"Indeed you do," Mason complimented her. "Let's go at it a few more times. But, try not to break my arm, if-if-if, if you please."

The two sparred a couple more times, with the princess being able to disarm her instructor a little easier each round, regardless how determined Mason was at not letting her take the knife. After the fifth successive retrieval of the knife, Audrianna held the knife up and dangled it in front of Mason.

"Mr Mason, what am I supposed to do with the knife once I take it away from the other person?"

"Simple," Mason declared. "You plunge it into their chest, and give it a twist." "What?" Audrianna asked in astonishment, dropping the knife to the ground. "That's right," Mason answered.

"You expect me to kill whoever I am fighting?" the princess asked repulsed with the idea.

"Your Highness," Olivia responded, "we haven't been training you to fight with swords and daggers if we weren't expecting you to kill your opponents." Audrianna looked down at the fallen dagger, placing both hands over her mouth. Up to this point she had seen sword fighting as a sport, not a battle to the death. All of her training suddenly sent a streak of terror up her spine. She had never killed anyone in her life. She went out of her way to keep from stepping on grasshoppers.

"I don't think I can do that, Mr Mason, sir," she replied with a pained expression on her face. Mason took her by both her hands and knelt in front of her.

"Your Highness," he remarked, looking sternly in her eyes, "sooner or later you will find yourself in a life or death struggle, where your enemy will stop at nothing to kill you. You have to decide now whether you are willing to take life to save your own."

The princess looked down at her feet, then back up at Mason.

"I guess if they are intent on killing me, I will do what is necessary to protect myself."

"And what if they beg for mercy?" Mason asked. "Then I will give them mercy," the princess replied.

"NO!" Mason yelled at Audrianna, startling both her and Olivia, and causing the princess to pull away from Mason, though he held firmly to both her hands. "Do not, do not, do not give mercy to one who once was intent on killing you."

"Why?" the princess asked. Mason pulled the princess close to himself and looked her square in the eyes.

"Your Highness," he answered, "Even the most hardened soldier and murderer will plead for his life when he realises he is about to die. But if you show him mercy, he will turn on you, and kill you in retaliation. Remember, a soldier's creed is, 'Kill or be killed'!" Mason looked up at Olivia. "Do you agree, Lady Olivia?"

"Yes," Olivia answered. "When fighting for your life, it is always best to finish the job. It may sound heartless, Anna, but that is the price of war." Mason looked back at the princess.

"Promise me you will always finish what you've started," Mason requested of the princess. Audrianna gave a pained expression, but she understood what the two were asking of her.

"I promise," she answered. "But why do I need to twist the knife? That's rather heartless, don't you think?"

"Not-not-not-not at all," Mason defended. "I think it is more humane. Depending on where you stab someone, it could take hours for a person to die. One-one-one-once you have the knife in your enemy, twisting it causes greater trauma to the body, and hence— almost instant death. You finished your job, and they don't have to linger. Understand?" Audrianna wasn't sure how she felt about this new level of training. She knew sword fighting, and fighting hand-to-hand meant someone was supposed to die. But up to this point, everything was about sparring, and learning the craft. But now, on the precipice of attacking the castle, she realised that she was going to have to play for keeps. She may have to decide whether someone was going to live or die. And she was going to have to live with her decision the rest of her life.

"I understand," Audrianna answered Mason as they concluded their training together. As soon as the words she spoke had finished echoing throughout the courtyard between the barn and the house, the princess heard Henry call out for her.

"Ree?" the prince called a second time. Audrianna ran towards the road where she heard her betrothed call for her.

"Here I am," Audrianna answered him. Across the road from the farmhouse stood Henry, holding the reins to a tall, dark horse.

"Look what I have, Ree," Henry proclaimed with a smile. "It's a horse, just for you." "It's my horse?" she asked excitedly. "My very own horse?"

"Yes, Your Highness," Henry assured her. "You will need a horse when we go into battle."

"It's a battle horse?" the princess asked.

"Yes," Henry answered. "You need a horse to help you remain visible to all that are fighting on your behalf. Even if you are remaining at a distance, the men will be able to see you on your horse and fight for your honour."

"Wow," Audrianna replied. "I never thought about that before."

"Not only that," Henry added, "if the battle doesn't go so well, you will need a strong horse to carry you far away from Nadeau, as fast as possible."

"You just ruined my excitement," Audrianna responded.

"At least try and sitting on the horse," Henry suggested. "Let's see how regal you look in the saddle of a royal horse."

Audrianna lifted the front of her farm dress and placed her left boot in the stirrup. She tried to hike her right leg over the seat of the saddle, but couldn't lift her leg high enough. She decided instead, while elevated to a standing position in the stirrup, to try and reach the other side of the saddle with her arms and pull herself up to the top of the saddle. She reached over the saddle and grabbed a hold of the opposite side with both hands, and slowly wiggled her way to the top of the saddle. She then lay sideways, her feet dangling on one side of the horse, and her head and hands dangling on the other.

Henry, still holding the reins, peered on the other side of the horse. Audrianna lay across the horse, limp for a moment, then poked her head up and looked at Henry.

"I need a little help," she suggested.

"If you would like," Henry offered, "I could show you the special foot hold on your saddle that was specially made for you to be able to mount the horse all by yourself." Audrianna nodded, then pushed against the saddle and slid off the horse, to the ground, and landed on her rump. Henry reached down and helped her to her feet.

Henry then showed the princess to place her right foot into the stirrup, rather than her left. He then showed her a special horn on the saddle halfway up the saddle strap, to which she could hook her left foot, then easily hike her right leg over the horse, and take her seat on top of the saddle.

"Now that you are properly mounted," Henry replied, "do you know how to ride." "I believe so," Audrianna announced. "I paid attention to what you did when we first left Nadeau. To get the horse to go, I just kick its sides." After saying that, she kicked both feet into the horse's sides, to which it jumped into a full gallop, down the main road, with the princess hanging on for dear life. Henry called out to her, but he knew she had no idea how to stop the strong horse.

Turning around, he spotted two old soldiers sitting atop their horses, witnessing the incident. They both pointed at themselves, gesturing that they should pursue the runaway horse and rescue the princess. Henry pointed towards the galloping princess with his whole hand and arm, to which the soldiers took off in a hard gallop to retrieve to two runaways.

Olivia, not seeing what transpired, calmly walked up to Henry. "Do you know where Anna might be," she asked.

Henry turned around to face her. "About five miles in that direction," he answered, then walked away.

"What?" Olivia asked incredulously.

"Don't worry," Henry responded, "I've got my top two horse-men in pursuit to bring them back."

CHAPTER 22

For two days the Princess's Elite Special Forces trained and planned for the taking of the castle, and restoring the throne of the princess. Jaako insisted that it was a waste of time because the king was still alive, while Henry and the Special Forces leaders maintained the opinion that Henry witnessed the king's death, and the so-called 'king', 'prince', and 'princess' were nothing short of imposters. The men also planned for the contingency that the castle guards were Andjety, and not impressed Nadeau guards.

The opening plan of approach to the castle included Olivia and Audrianna riding the princess's new horse close to dusk, while several of the archers remained behind the overgrown tree line. With lowered light, the two ladies would draw the castle guards towards the archers, and the archers would pick them off one at a time. Once the guards in the outer perimeter were successfully picked off, the ladder brigade would approach the castle walls at night, with grappling hooks and rope ladders.

Once the walls were scaled at precise locations, the men who were able-bodied to climb the ladders, would infiltrate the castle, overpower the tower guards, then open the main doors for the rest of the army to storm the castle. Henry and Balen planned to make their way to the royal suite to seek out the witch, and perhaps face the imposters and expose them as frauds.

The princess and Olivia planned to make their way to the city prison. Audrianna believed in her heart that Rupp and her ladies-in-waiting were still alive, thrown into prison for their loyalty to the crown. If there was any chance they were alive, Audrianna wanted to free them.

These were the main objectives of the small band of loyalists. If executed correctly, they would win the castle back. Henry was confident the plans that he and Balen, as well as the retired strategists, would win them the castle back. For another two days they journeyed from Pachenthou, down the winding path towards the city of Nadeau. Several scouts rode on ahead, to look out for patrols as they ventured closer to the city.

It was the middle of the day when the company arrived at the camp site Henry and Audrianna spent the first night of their flight from the Witch. Olivia and Balen divided the assembly into smaller groups, and established multiple camp sites, each site responsible for a different area and time to stand guard and watch. A designated leader would report hourly to Balen to account for their safety. Olivia assigned each camp site a different responsibility to prepare food for the entire company, and to serve it. Everybody responded to the couple's requests as if they had followed their orders for decades.

"I think I am starting to understand Lady Olivia a little bit better," Henry told the princess. "I know now why she is so no-nonsense of a woman. She used to organise the original Special Forces assembled by the king."

"Wow," Audrianna replied. "Both she and Balen really keep everybody on their toes and in line. If our army overtakes the castle, it will be because both of them kept Everybody organised and together."

"I think you are right, Ree," Henry agreed.

Within an hour, representatives from every camp site began serving an early supper meal. It wasn't anything special beyond several hot kettles of barley soup, containing carrots, celery, cabbage and radishes for vegetables. They had also brought with them an assortment of apples, berries, and other fruits, as well as walnuts, hazelnuts, and clay jars filled with honey.

Henry and Audrianna sat outside at a table that the crew had assembled for the royals to eat their supper. Balen sat at one side next to Henry, and Olivia sat on the other side next to the princess. As they ate, Jaako came walking up to the table with a lazy saunter.

"Your Majesty," he greeted. "and, of course, Your Highness."

"Jaako," Henry cautiously acknowledged. "Are you here to join Her Highness's Special Forces?" he asked. Jaako removed his large brimmed hat and bowed as he had a few days previous with the princess.

"I am here to offer my services and my military specialties." "What specialties?" Balen asked.

"Back when His Majesty's father had devised this menagerie of elite fighters, he appointed me as one of its captains. There were eight captains that commanded their battle strategies. The other seven are dead, so I am offering the privilege of hiring me for my experience and strategic gifts."

"And you are hoping to benefit from the princess's wealth, as well as her generosity," Balen interjected.

"A worker is worthy of his wages," Jaako replied.

"However, I am not the one to ask," Henry responded. "These people are under Her Highness's command."

"Perhaps," Jaako remarked, "but wouldn't Her Highness's forces benefit best from one who has seen his share of success and victory?" Balen and Olivia sat motionless. Henry was uncomfortable and silent. Audrianna wanted to look at the others to see if their faces reflected her same thoughts, but the months sitting in Royal Court taught her that each royal, and every throne, sat as an individual judge. To look to another royal would diminish the authority of that throne.

Audrianna sat up straight and squared her shoulders.

"I need less experience, and less talent," the princess declared. "What I need most, is loyalty. But you are not a loyalist. You, yourself, stated that you care nothing for the crown. This tells me that your loyalty is up for bid. I cannot afford to allow you to lead in such circumstances. I would rather have leaders who are less qualified, if they are loyal, than one who is ten times as gifted, but not loyal." Jaako bowed his head in shame. "I regret many of my words I spoke at the pub that night, Your Highness," Jaako replied.

"Will you pledge your loyalty to me?" Audrianna asked, holding out her hand. Jaako gazed at her extended hand.

"I'm sorry, Your Highness," Jaako answered. "I can't bring myself to make a pledge.

A part of me died during the Andjety War."

"Well then," the princess replied, "fight for my honour, and you might be given an opportunity to finish what you started."

As the sun hit its highest point in the sky, Olivia and Audrianna mounted the princess's steed. Olivia sat comfortably in the saddle, then commanded the princess to climb on in front of her. As Audrianna sat in front of Olivia, the Lady in Waiting draped her long flowing cape around the two of them, like a mother hen with her chick. Balen walked over to horse, and took the princess's hand and kissed it.

"God's safety, Your Highness," he encouraged her. He then looked over at his wife. Olivia leaned down, to kiss her husband. As she did, Audrianna was pushed forward against the horn of the saddle. She playfully rolled her eyes back, and stuck out her tongue, to let everyone watching know that she was being squished by her sworn protector. Olivia leaned towards Balen as they exchanged a long loving kiss. It wasn't a sensual or passionate kiss, as much as it was an endearing one. Balen took hold of her hand as well, as Olivia leaned back and straightened the hunched-over princess.

"Until the next adventure, my sweet!" he said.

From there, the two ladies rode slowly towards the castle. It took a little more than an hour, at a fast gallop, for Henry and

Audrianna to ride from the castle to the camp site. Now, Olivia and Audrianna would allow for several hours, walking the horse down the well-worn road, allowing for their militia to follow from a distance, and under cover.

Four and a half hours passed as the horse carried the two down the trail until they came to the edge of a hill, overlooking the castle. The sun had begun to descend towards the Andjety mountain range. Olivia stopped the horse as they both took a deep breath. This was the moment Audrianna was waiting for. But now, instead of excitement, her stomach turned with apprehension.

"Ready?" Olivia asked the princess.

Audrianna again took a deep breath, then sighed. She leaned back into Olivia's arms petitioning an assuring embrace. Olivia squeezed her arms against the princess, still holding the horse reins, then gently kissed the back of her head. Audrianna regained her courage, sat up straight, squared her shoulders, and lifted her head.

"You may proceed," the princess instructed. Olivia smiled.

"Yes, Your Highness," she answered the princess. She softly kicked the sides of the horse to command the beast to continue walking. They journeyed another half hour, not knowing where the militia was, but believing they were nearby.

As the light of the day began to turn grey, and the sun started to sink behind the mountains, out of nowhere, three soldiers came riding up the trail towards the two of them. The soldiers wore Nadeau uniforms, but their complexion and facial features gave them away as foreigners. Audrianna held her breath as she felt Olivia sit up straight and tense her muscles.

"Stops where you are!" the first soldier demanded.

"Andjety!" Olivia whispered over Audrianna's shoulder. Olivia brought the horse to a full stop while the three mounted men lined their horses in front of them.

"Who be you?" the man asked. "Why be you headed to Nadeau?" "That is where we live," the princess informed them. "Who are you?" "Shut up, child!" another one of the men yelled.

"Does you have a pass?" the first man asked.

"A pass?" Olivia asked. "Since when do citizens of Nadeau need a pass to travel home?"

"Since last two weeks ago," the third man announced. "If you doesn't have a pass, then I doesn't believe you are truly citizens of Nadeau. That would make you be spies!" The first two men jeered in agreement. "Does you know what happens to beautiful female spies we finds along the road?" the man asked suggestively, smirking at the two travellers.

"They get switched?" Audrianna asked. All three men paused. They didn't know what she meant. Suddenly, three arrows came flying passed the princess and her protector.

ZIP—ZIP—ZIP!

Without another word, the three Andjety men fell limp from their horses, and onto the ground.

"Well," Audrianna replied, turning to look at Olivia, and shaking off her anxiety. "That was quite a switch!" Olivia looked back from whence the arrows originated. Squinting her eyes at the darkening shadows, she could see a faint silhouette of one of their archers.

Regaining their composure, the ladies continued to ride along the path as it disappeared due to darkness setting in. As they came close to the Nadeau Bridge, they could see the lamp-lit city, flickering about like thousands of lightning bugs. The city bridge never before had a checkpoint station, but now, at least five large Andjety soldiers stood by waiting to see every citizen's pass card that wanted to go to and from the city. Large torches, stationed up and down the city entrance, illuminated the checkpoint.

"What should we do?" Audrianna asked, looking straight ahead at their next challenge.

"The same as we did before," Olivia answered. "Remember, we are the bait, not the hook."

The horse slowly made its way to the gate of the soldier's checkpoint. A large, imposing Andjety officer, also dressed as a Nadeau guard, grabbed a torch, and walked up to the travellers.

Before saying a word, he seized the horse's bridle.

"Please do not handle my horse," Olivia requested. "It is a rather timid creature. And soldiers make him uneasy."

"I cares nothing about your beast, stupid female," the guard lashed out at Olivia. "All I wants, is to see yours pass to gets into the city. Now, where be it?"

"Pardon me," Olivia replied, "but from what part of Nadeau does your accent come from?" Upon asking her question, two other guards rose from their seats. Grabbing torches of their own, they sauntered towards the ladies.

"Gets to him your pass, stupid female," one of the other two guards demanded. "Gets to him your pass, or you be throwed in the iron bars."

"Stupid female?" Olivia boldly asked, hoping her archers would soon be within range. "Do you know what I think is stupid? I think having to have passes to come and go from your own home city is as stupid as the Andjety military. And that's a lot of stupid!"

By now, all five men were standing, torches in hand, and began to surround the horse in a circle. The first checkpoint guard demanded the two dismount. Olivia refused. One guard grabbed Audrianna by the arm, and pulled her off the horse. The other Andjety men came to assist in restraining both Olivia and the princess.

With Audrianna off the horse, two men rushed to grab Olivia by the arm and pull her off as well. Olivia quickly slid off the opposite side of the horse. One of the men grabbed the princess around her middle, and held her tightly against himself, facing out. As she squirmed, the guard threw his torch down, and pulled a knife from his belt, intent on cutting her throat. Audrianna reached up with her right hand, grabbed his wrist, and tried to twist it outwards. She did not have the proper leverage, though, to disarm the imposter guard. The princess tried to wiggle free, but the guard tightly held onto her with his other arm.

As she firmly held onto his wrist that held the knife, she felt another presence come running up behind them. She heard the sound of flesh being cut, then a gurgling sound. Her attacker fell limp to the ground. She stepped forward, then turned around to see what happened. With the torch on the ground, all Audrianna could see were the legs of the dead guard. An arm reached out from behind the curtain of darkness and picked up the torch. Lifting the torch from the ground, the face of Henry was illuminated. He held a bloody knife in his left hand.

"Are you left-handed," Audrianna asked him.

"Only when it becomes necessary," he responded, returning his knife to its scabbard. "Are you right-handed, too?"

"Only when it becomes necessary," she answered. "But, I'm not very good at it."

Audrianna looked towards the other four fallen guards, whose torches had not fallen to the ground. Holding the torches were Balen, Mason, and two other younger mercenaries of Mason's. The princess reached down and picked up the fallen knife of the dead guard, and tucked it in her belt.

"What happened to your archers?" Olivia asked Balen.

"The tree line is too far away, and we did not anticipate they wouldn't be able to see very far in the dark."

"As soon as we realised the predicament," Henry added, "the five of us came running to dispatch the guards ourselves." Olivia looked up at Balen.

"You, dear," she asked. "You ran all the way from the tree line?"

"I can run," Balen defended himself. "I run from the barn to the house every time I smell you baking raspberry fig pie. And you're far more important to me than any ol' pie." Audrianna watched as Olivia kissed Balen on the cheek. She then turned to Henry.

"So, you're only loving and caring when you have to be," she commented. "Correct," Henry playfully replied, placing his hand on her shoulder. "But, I'm not very good at it."

The men dragged the bodies of the dead guards out from sight, while Olivia replaced the torches to their stands so as to make the checkpoint look normal from the tower of the castle. The men quickly reassembled with the rest of the Special Forces. Olivia and Audrianna made their way into the city, in search of the prison, to see if Rupp and her ladies could possibly still be alive.

From the elite fighters, four old men were selected to approach the walls of the castle and set up rope ladders. They were armed with one crossbow, one longbow, and one conventional bow. Two of the men carried arrows tied to grappling hooks. Once they shot the hooks over the castle walls, side-by-side, they would pull on the chords, causing the rope ladder to climb the wall like a flag on a rigging. They would then tie the ropes off at the bottom, and scale the wall. Once over the wall, they were to find their way to the main entrance, and open the doors for the army, and seize the castle. Everything was now dependent on the success of these four men.

The old men slipped through the maze of city streets, trying to avoid any Andjety guards, or any informing eyes. They finally arrived, unnoticed, at the exact location on the wall the prince had designated for them to scale. One of the men pulled his longbow from off his shoulder, then placed the arrow in the bow, prepared to shoot the grappling hook over the wall.

"What are you doing?" the second man asked. "What do you mean?" the first asked.

"You can't use a longbow with a grappling hook. You've got to use a short bow." "No, you can't," the first man declared. "The short bow is not powerful enough to send the hook over the wall."

"It will, if you pull it far enough back," the second man insisted.

"Like an old warthog like you could pull a short bow back that far," the first man accused.

"A longbow is overkill," the second man suggested. "You'll overshoot the wall." "Isn't that what we are supposed to do?" the third man replied. "Shoot it over the

wall, not at the wall?"

"What do you know, you old crust of bread?" the first man asked.

"I know a lot more than the two of you," the third man boasted. "I've shot grapplers over castle walls years before you two were born."

"You're a lying, senile, old goat," the first man accused.

"Am not," the third man replied. "I've climbed castle walls since I was seventeen years old."

"They didn't have castles back when you were seventeen," the second man surmised. "They had caves."

"This isn't going to work, no matter which bow we use," the fourth man griped. "I suggested we bring a tower ladder. That has always proven effective."

"How do you expect to get a tower ladder rolled through town without everyone in the kingdom, from here to Pachenthou, noticing?" the third man asked.

"I don't know," the fourth man replied. "I'm just saying, its fool proof."

"Except by the fool who suggested it," the third man said. "Hand me the grappling hook. I'll use my crossbow."

"You can't use a crossbow with a grappling hook," the first man scolded. "It's not designed to be used with a grappling hook."

"I can make it work," the third man defended his idea.

"Just give me the grappling hook," the second man demanded. "I'll show you that a short bow can make it over the wall."

"We don't have time, nor opportunity, to try and show-off," the first man declared. "Just let me do it with the longbow."

"No," the second man answered, holding the arrow away from him.

"For goodness sakes," the third man complained. He held up his crossbow and fired the first grappling hook over the wall. He then tugged on the chord until all the slack was taken out, then he tied it a stake he'd already hammered into the ground.

"See?" the first man remarked. "A short bow could never accomplish that." "Yes, it can," the second man responded, raising his voice.

"We are going to get caught for certain," the fourth man replied.

"Give me your arrow," the third man demanded, grabbing it out of the second man's hand. He then placed it in the shaft of his crossbow, and shot the second arrow over the wall.

"We should have all brought crossbows to begin with," the first man declared. "You were the one insisting on longbows," the second man argued.

The third and fourth men hoisted the ladder up the chords until they reached the very top of the wall. They then tied them off at the bottom. The third and fourth men started to climb the ladder.

"You stay here and keep watch," the first old man said to the second.

"I'm not staying here, you wrinkled bald bat," the second man declared to the first. "No one said someone needed to stay back and keep watch."

"Don't need to," the first man replied. "Just rather not have you join us." The two men started to climb after the third and fourth men.

Once all four men made it atop the wall landing, they scurried towards the staircase That spiralled down to the main courtyard. All four were careful to remain in the shadows, hidden from the light of the torches, as well as the light of the partial moon.

Meanwhile, Olivia and Audrianna made their way to the city prison. Several guards were stationed at the entrance to prevent anyone from getting out, or breaking in to set the prisoners free.

"How are we getting past the guards?" the princess asked.

"We will use our clandestine abilities as women," Olivia replied. "What do you mean?" the princess asked.

"The prison relies heavily on peasant women to carry food and water to the prisoners, in exchange for a copper coin or two," Olivia explained. "Let's change into peasant maid clothes, rub soot from the furnaces over our bodies, and they'll give us access to the prison, thinking we're poor simple peasants. Once we're inside, we can search for Rupp and the ladies."

Audrianna and Olivia ran back across town to a seamstress shop that, by that time of night, had locked its doors, and closed its window shutters. Olivia pulled a hairpin from one of the princess's tiny braids, and used it to unlock the front door.

"Wow!" Audrianna exclaimed with excitement. "Where did you learn to open a locked door with a hairpin?"

"I'm not proud of all my gifts, Anna," Olivia remarked. "But even some of my darkest talents come in handy now and again."

The two searched for chamber maid outfits. They were usually a greyish-blue colour, a simple design, and made from low quality material. Audrianna was the first to find an outfit comparable to her size. It took Olivia a few minutes longer to choose the correct size, due to how the dress was cut. The design did not fit well to her proportions. At least not how she preferred her dresses to fit.

They tucked their regular clothes under their arms and scurried back to the street where the entrance to the prison was. Hiding their regular clothes and weapons in baskets, the two ladies rubbed coal dust and grease from the furnaces over their faces, arms, and dresses, to give the appearance of being homeless street folk.

The two soot-clad ladies walked up to the entrance of the prison.

"Slow down, and keep your shoulders hunched," Audrianna whispered to Olivia. "Street urchins have very little dignity, so they meander with a shameful, hopeless posture."

As they approached the prison entrance, Olivia took point at talking their way through the doors.

"Is there any work for two cold and hungry ladies, to ease your burden, and give us a coin or two?"

"We don't wants no people here when the sky is black," the first Andjety guard declared.

"We wanted to help you with the food or water," Olivia explained. "Is there something we can do to earn a few coins?"

"No," the other guard snapped. "Comes back when the sky is light." Olivia looked down at the princess and waved her eyebrows.

"I'm sorry, little Anna," Olivia loudly replied to Audrianna, so the guards could overhear. "There will be no supper again tonight for my precious hungry baby girl."

"No, mama," Audrianna responded, cocking her head to one side. "We needed to work tonight. I can't go to bed hungry again! If I close my eyes tonight, without entering the prison, hauling water and food, and thus earning a copper coin and buying a few morsels of food, I will never open my precious emerald green eyes again." Audrianna fluttered her eyelids at the guards.

"What's do we care if you starve to death?" the guard declared. "One less annoying child and her ugly mother." Olivia, who during the entire time they talked was hunched over, stood up straight and tall.

"Ugly mother," she responded. "You think I'm an ugly mother?"

"He called me an annoying child, too," Audrianna added, tugging at Olivia's dirty dress. Olivia took several steps towards the Andjety guards.

"Any woman who carries a child inside her for nine months, and retains the slender figure you see before you, without gaining a single grey hair during the ten years she's been raising her, is not an 'ugly mother.'" The first guard sneered at Olivia.

"Any woman over fifty be ugly to me," he snapped.

Olivia's eyes opened wide with astonishment. She was only forty-five years of age. She took several more steps towards the men, then pulled the sides of her dress up to her knees, and took her offensive stance. The men looked down, gazing at her exposed lower legs. Then, like a wild dog that suddenly went rabid, Olivia began kicking and punching, twisting, and scratching. One by one, Olivia hurled each guard to ground. Within less than a minute, all four guards were unconscious, sprawled across the ground.

"Whoa!" Audrianna exclaimed, not saying another word.

"Come, Anna," Olivia said, straightening her dress, then taking the princess's hand. "Mama feels better."

CHAPTER 23

As the giant doors to the castle began to slowly creak open, Princess Audrianna's Special Forces quietly crept over the bridge and made their way towards the main entrance. They brought no torches with them, so they would not be seen from the sentries on the towers. They were also careful to not be spotted by the moonlight, beaming down on a cloudless night.

The doors fully opened, revealing the dark corridor inside the castle walls. As they passed through the door, their eyes began to adjust to the darkness, and the men could see the four archers they had sent to scale the walls and open the doors, waiting for them. As the militia entered the castle, a large, heavy cage door dropped behind them. Torches were suddenly lit, like a band, around the corridor, revealing the fact that they were all trapped in a giant cage. It was a trap!

"What is this?" Henry demanded.

"When we came to open the main doors," the first archer explained, "we were met with an unexpected surprise."

"You mean, the cage?" Balen asked.

"No," the second archer answered. "An even more alarming surprise." "What surprise?" Henry asked the archers.

As Audrianna and Olivia made their way down the dark, dank hallway leading to the main prison cells, they were both met with someone unexpected. It was Drake, the regular jailer of the prison. He was the first familiar Nadeau guard they had come across since entering the city. Both Olivia and Audrianna recognised him. Audrianna had seen him from time to time, standing in Royal Court, but Olivia knew him on more friendly terms. They were trained for swordsmanship at the same time under Balen's instruction. "Drake!" Olivia exclaimed. "I was afraid everybody had been replaced by Andjety soldiers."

"They are on the outside," Drake replied. "But no Andjety wants to be down here in the dark. They're too afraid and superstitious."

"Superstitious of what?" Olivia asked.

"Too many prisoners get sick down here in this waste pit," Drake replied. "They get sick and die. Andjety are afraid of the dead, something awful." Olivia looked suspiciously at Drake.

"Did they come up with that conclusion themselves," she asked, "or did they have help?" Drake gave a knowing grin.

"I might have dropped a hint of two," Drake answered. He looked back and forth between Olivia and the princess. "I might have also exaggerated a bit on how many die each day."

"Mr Drake, sir," Audrianna interrupted, "do you know what happened to my three ladies-in-waiting, or perhaps Lord Rupp?"

"Ah," he answered. "The political prisoners. The Witch ordered them to be executed due to their loyalty to Your Highness, the princess." Audrianna hung her head.

"They're dead," she replied.

"No," Drake clarified. "I said they were ordered to be executed. When they are executed is yet to be determined."

"Where are they?" the princess enthusiastically asked.

"That was the question you should have led with," Drake answered, grabbing a lit torch from the wall. "Follow me."

As the trapped men of the Special Forces pushed their arms through the spaces in between the iron bars, the four archers explained to Henry, Balen, and Mason how they came to be ensnared.

"We had just finished climbing up the wall, when we got a bit turned around as to where the main gates were to the castle," the first man explained.

"I knew where the gate was," the second man protested, "but no one wanted to listen to my opinion."

"You did not!" the first man argued. "Hold on," Balen commanded.

"It wouldn't have mattered," the third man added. "We were gonna get caught one way or another."

"Says who?" the second man asked.

"Wait just a moment," Balen broke in again.

"That's right," the fourth man confirmed. "They was waiting for us to spring their trap."

"Stop!" Balen demanded.

"My goodness," Jaako interjected. "These four would argue hair off a dog!" "Who was waiting to spring their trap," Henry asked.

"I sprung the trap," a familiar voice echoed from the darkness. Everybody in the cage abruptly stopped, all eyes looking in the direction from whence the voice came from. Out of the shadows stepped Rolf, Henry's new armour-bearer.

"Rolf," Henry exclaimed. "You filthy traitor!"

"He's not a traitor," another familiar voice could be heard from the other side of the cage. Everybody in the cage turned their heads in the opposite direction to see who was talking. Stepping into the light of the torches, Zymjai now stood before Henry and his compatriots.

"What do you mean," Henry asked. "He betrayed the crown."

"Oh," the Witch replied, "he betrayed your crown, but he has faithfully followed the instructions given him since before he became your armour-bearer."

"He was a plant," Balen remarked.

"In a way," Zymjai agreed. "But since the prince ran off, we needed someone to play the part, so the kingdom would continue, especially under Andjety control."

"You replaced Nadeau guards with Andjety guards. You replaced the royal family with imposters. What are you up to, Zymjai? What are you intending to do?"

"Imposters?" the Witch asked, with a puzzled look on her face. "I'm not using imposters. I am using nothing but bonified, true crowned royals. Rolf is a crowned prince, and his betrothed is a crowned princess. And, of course, there is the king."

"The very imposters I am speaking of," Henry replied. "Are you sure they are imposters?" the Witch asked.

"What else could they be," Henry inquired. "You stabbed my father in the back. You killed the true king."

Zymjai smiled a devious grin as she stepped towards Henry, and placed her hands on the bars dividing the two of them.

Drake led Olivia and the princess deeper into the prison chambers till they came to a dark cell at the end of one of the corridors.

"Rupp is here," he said to the ladies, then called out. "Rupp!" "Lord Rupp, come forward. You have a visitor."

The sound of tinkling chains could be heard approaching the door to the prison cell. An unrecognisable face came poking through the bars. The man's face looked weathered and tired. Hair had overgrown over his entire head.

"That's not Rupp," the princess declared.

"Your Highness?" Rupp called out in his familiar voice.

"Holy maggots!" the princess recanted. "It is Lord Rupp. What happened to you, Rupp?"

"Praise the heavens you are okay," Rupp answered. "But what are you doing here, Your Highness?"

"Lady Olivia and I are here to get you out of prison," the princess answered. "We are here with an army of loyalists."

"I'll stay here and free Rupp," Olivia said to Audrianna. "You and Drake go find your ladies-in-waiting."

"Right," Audrianna replied, anxious to check on her ladies' health.

Drake led the princess down another corridor to the prison until they came to the end. To the right sat a steel door with no window. Drake reached out his hand and pulled open the door without using a key. The door let out a rusty squeak as it slowly opened to where Audrianna could enter.

"Thank you, Mr Drake," the princess remarked.

"Hold on, there, Your Highness," the jailer replied. "You need to be prepared for what you might find in there."

"What will I find?" she asked.

"Prison conditions are, at best, deplorable," Drake answered. He then handed her his torch. "Go ahead and take this with you." Audrianna quietly slipped into the prison cell, and waved the torch around to shift the light throughout the room. She spotted the three ladies huddled in the corner. Their faced were covered with their matted dirty hair. The dresses they wore were dingy, and the same they had on the night of the invasion.

"Rose?" the princess called out. Rozelle lifted her head when she heard the princess's voice call her name. "Cassie? Ethel?" The other two ladies turned their heads towards the light.

"Your Highness?" Rozelle responded. "Your Highness, is that

truly you?" All three ladies attempted to stand out of respect to the princess. Rozelle made it to her feet, while Castalia and Ethlyn fell back to a seated position. Their legs had become dependent from weeks of inactivity in the small, dark prison cell.

"Yes, it's me," Audrianna assured her three ladies.

"Oh, Your Highness," Rozelle excitedly replied. "We were told you were dead. We had lost all hope."

"Who told you I was dead," the princess asked, helping the two ladies to their feet, one at a time.

"The Witch," Castalia announced.

"Yeah, and that horrible witchlet she toted with her," Ethlyn added. "Witchlet?" Audrianna asked.

"An ugly little Andjety girl, around Your Highness's age," Roselle remarked. "The witch claims the little girl has been coronated as the new crowned princess."

"That would only be possible if the king himself crowned her," Audrianna replied. "He has," Ethlyn stated.

"Has what?" Audrianna asked.

"The king," Ethlyn answered. "The king did coronate the little girl as the new crowned princess."

"You mean, the impostor king?" the princess asked.

"There is no imposter king," Castalia answered. "Only King Malcolm. The very king that coronated you."

"What are you saying?" Audrianna asked Castalia, lowering the torch down to her side.

As Zymjai and Henry stood inches from each other, with only the bars of the incarcerated Special Forces separating them, and Rolf standing on the other side of the giant cage, a third figure walked into the circle of light. Everyone turned their heads to look at the man that stood before them. It was King Malcolm. Not dead. Not a ghost. Malcolm, in the flesh.

"What?" Henry asked, shocked by what he saw. Shocked by who he saw, standing in front of them all.

"Father," Henry responded. "You are alive?"

"Yes, my son," The king answered. "Of course I'm alive. Why would you think any different? Where have you been? I've been worried about you since you kidnapped the princess and ran away."

Everyone turned to look at Henry.

"I didn't kidnap the princess," Henry replied. "The princess and I escaped the Andjety invasion. The Witch was about to kill the two of us. Rupp and the three ladies- in-waiting to the princess helped us escape before Zymjai got a hold of us."

"No, my son," The king replied. "That is not what happened." All the men of the special forces began to look at each other with confusion. Had they just attacked the castle without actual provocation? Were they now traitors to the crown for going against the king, thinking that they were avenging the blood of their fallen monarch? What was going to happen to them?

"Tell these men the truth," The king demanded. "They once fought valiantly on behalf of the kingdom, and for me. They deserve to hear the truth." Everyone turned to face the prince. What was the truth? What were they truly fighting for? Had been misled to believe Prince Henry and Princess Audrianna escaped for their lives, or did they come to Pachenthou to raise up a coup for Henry to take the throne from his father by force?

A conflicting thought also flashed through their minds as to why the Andjety were in control of the castle, and why the Nadeau soldiers had all been replaced by Andjety. Why was the Witch standing next to the king as an equal monarch, when they had been suffering for several years with her orchestrated raids throughout the land?

"They know the truth," Henry answered his father. "At least as true as I was aware of. I saw what I believed was the Witch stabbing you in the back. I had no idea it was another clever ruse to wrestle the throne from me." The king shook his head at Henry with a disparaging look.

"Oh, Henry," The king replied. "That is not the truth, now is it? You know what truly happened a few weeks ago."

"What happened, Your Majesty," Balen broke in. "Tell us what happened the night he and the princess disappeared."

"Yes, tell us," the elite fighting men echoed.

"Yes," Henry also responded, "tell everyone your side of what took place." The king stepped closer to the bars, while several of the men standing near, stepped back. Everyone stopped talking or whispering amongst themselves to listen carefully to the words of the king.

"The night that Henry ran away, I had called Zymjai to come and talk over the issue of the untimely death of Henry's armour-bearer, Pitt. Henry had claimed that Zymjai had killed him. So, in the presence of Henry and Lord Rupp, Zymjai graciously appeared to nullify the accusation. She had offered sufficient evidence to prove, not only had she not been responsible, but that Henry killed Pitt himself to force Nadeau to go to war with the Andjety."

"That is not true!" Henry screamed. "Pitt was my best friend! I would never have done anything to harm him!" Henry's face turned bright red from his fury over the accusation.

"Henry looked that night exactly as he does now," The king explained. "He took up his sword, ready to kill Zymjai. Lord Rupp opposed him, to which they began to fight with drawn swords."

"The fact that I am alive is proof that didn't happen," Henry replied with a chortle. "Henry did find himself outwitted with the sword," The king explained. "So, he ran as fast as he could towards the royal bedchambers, killed the princess's ladies, and took her prisoner. Luckily, we found the princess abandoned on the road, ten miles outside the city, towards the east."

"Ah ha," Henry responded. "That is where your lies expose you for a fraud. I did not kidnap the princess, we escaped together under duress. I did not abandon her along the road, because she has been with me the whole time. And everyone here in this cage with me has met her." The Princess's Special Forces began to nod in agreement and whisper acknowledgements.

"I don't know who the little girl is, nor where she came from," the king declared, "but Princess Audrianna is safe in her bed chamber up in the royal tower."

"What happened to Lord Rupp?" Balen calmly asked. "You said the princess's ladies were killed by Henry. If he is still alive, where is Lord Rupp, that we might consult with him?"

Audrianna, along with her three ladies, re-joined Drake in the corridor. They retraced their steps back to the cell where they left Olivia and Rupp.

"We've got to get out of here immediately!" the princess exclaimed to Olivia.

"We do indeed," Olivia replied. "Rupp has just informed me of what has been going on in your absence." Audrianna looked at Rupp, who nodded in agreement.

"We are all in danger," Rupp replied. "Rozelle, Castalia, Ethlyn, and myself should already be dead. At least, that's what the Witch believes. If it weren't for Drake hiding us in the inner prison…"

"We need to find the men before the Witch and the king has them in their clutches," Olivia interrupted. "They are trying to take back the castle, when the castle never left the hands of the king. This means that your elite Special Forces are committing treason, and are subject to hanging."

"If they followed the plan that Henry and Balen devised," Audrianna stated, "they may already be in their clutches."

"More than likely," Rupp replied. "The king had a trap set for all of you, the moment you stepped foot in the castle. Luckily for you two, neither the Witch, nor the king, counted on your sentiment towards the four of us."

"We need to release the men immediately," Olivia said with an anxious tone in her voice. "If what you are saying is true, they won't wait long to execute the men." Rupp shook his head.

"It's too late for that," Rupp responded. "What we need an alternate plan to expose the king and the Witch to the people." Olivia stopped and grabbed Rupp by the arm.

"Too late?" she angrily replied. "Too late for the prince? For my husband? For the hundred plus men who pledged their lives to Nadeau and the princess?" Rupp put his hand over Olivia's and pried her grip off his arm.

"Lady Olivia," he answered, "I have every intention to save the men who came to rescue the castle and fight the witch. But it will do no good to go against King Malcolm the Merciful unless the people are prepared to accept his downfall." Audrianna watched as she witnessed Olivia, for the first time since they met, lose all control over her emotions. Olivia had continually been a tower of strength and support. Now, with the threat of death looming over her husband and the prince, the former queen's Lady in Waiting had no more reserve of strength. She buried her face in her hands and wept. The princess stepped closer to Olivia and leaned against her. Not saying a word, but letting her presence be known to her surrogate mother.

"What shall we do, then," Rozelle asked, starting to regain her composure.

"I'll tell you one thing that should be done," Drake answered. All eyes turned to look at him. "Get rid of them Andjety," he said. "You can't do nothing till they are all gone. They are the meanest, most ignorant soldiers I've ever come across." Audrianna frowned at Drake.

"How did the king ever justify bringing Andjety soldiers in to replace Nadeau guards after Henry and I escaped?" the princess asked.

The men 0f the Princess's Special Forces hung on the bars of their cage as they awaited the king to answer Balen's request.

"If Rupp is still alive," Balen demanded, "then bring him in to testify to what you are saying." The king shook his head.

"I wish I could," the king responded. "I sent Rupp and over half my army to find Henry the next day. Not one returned. I can only assume he had somehow ambushed the captain, killing him and the castle guards."

"With a sword and a ten-year-old," Henry sarcastically remarked.

"Zymjai heard about the incident," The king continued, "and

she offered to supply the castle with a regiment of Andjety soldiers. They are sworn to protect the best interests of the kingdom."

"That would all depend on what your interests involve," Henry replied. "Are you intending to form an alliance between the Andjety and Nadeau?"

"Yes," the king answered bluntly. "It's time we stop fighting, and time we start getting along with each other. We once all owned this land. Why can't we share it?"

"I ain't sharing with no Andjety," one of the men responded. "Me neither," said another.

"You've got to be crazy!" "No way!"

The king raised his hand to silence the murmuring militia.

"I have the utmost respect for what you men did, all those years before, acquiring unused land from the Andjety people, so we could expand our farms and become a much more prosperous nation. But times have changed. And we must change along with it. It is time that we give back to the Andjety what was rightfully theirs, and we all become one strong nation, from the valleys in the east, and the sea to the west, and all the mountains to the north."

"That is why you betrothed me to the little princess," Henry remarked. "You were buying time to figure out a scheme to take the throne from me permanently. You have been bent on removing the burden of Nadeau law that says you must abdicate the throne after your heir reaches his twenty-fifth birthday."

"You are no longer my son," The king quickly replied. "I am your only son," Henry asserted.

"Not anymore," Rolf broke in. "I am the new crowned prince of Nadeau." Henry turned around and glared at Rolf. The armour-bearer folded his hands with a smirk.

"What do you mean?" Henry demanded.

"I officially adopted Rolf as my son, and made him the heir of Nadeau," The king answered. "I coronated him, just a couple weeks ago, as the new crowned prince, and gave Audrianna as his newly betrothed bride." Henry turned to Rolf.

"May your life with Audrianna, be as full as mine has been," he said.

Drake quickly led the five ladies and Rupp through the maze of prison tunnels until they came to the main door leading to the city streets. He pointed everyone out the door, indicating he was staying in the prison.

"We need you with us," the princess requested.

"I'm sorry, Your Highness," Drake replied. "I have a lot of other prisoners that need me to take care of them. My place is not on the outside, but on the inside. But I promise that if you, or your men, end up in the prison, I will personally take care of you."

"Thank you, Drake," Rupp said, shaking his hand. "I am alive because of you." The three ladies each came and hugged the jailer, giving him a kiss on his dirty, greasy face.

"Thank you, so much," Castalia said.

"I'll never forget what you've done, Mr Drake," Ethlyn said. "May God be with you, Drake," Rozelle said.

All six stepped through the door, one after the other. Upon exiting the prison, they stumbled over the unconscious guards, still sprawled across the ground.

"What happened here?" Rupp asked. Audrianna looked up at Olivia. "Age discrepancy," Olivia answered.

They all stepped past the guards and made their way down the street, and found their way to the backside of the castle walls. At the very edge of the walls, where the wall met the solid rock of the mountain, Olivia revealed a secret entrance that neither Audrianna, nor her ladies were aware of.

"A secret door?" the princess asked. "Where does it lead?"

"Luella and I used to sneak in and out of the castle a few times, dressed as commoners and buy dried figs from the marketplace. Luella had quite a fancy towards dried figs."

"But where does it lead?" Audrianna asked again.

"Directly into the breakfast room," Olivia answered, "across from the large bay windows."

"Isn't that a bit of a public room to do a bit of sneaking," Audrianna asked. "Not during the day," Olivia remarked. "Mainly only at morning breakfast."

The six of them scurried through the secret entrance and through the dark unlit passageway. Before long, they all emerged inside the breakfast room, and quietly made their way towards the grand staircase. At each doorway, Rupp would cautiously peer around the corner to make sure the room or hallway was clear from guards or other people who might give them away.

"We need to make it to the courtyard where the weapons are kept," Rupp advised. "With any luck, the Andjety haven't raided every closet of its wares."

"Do you think my crossbow will be there?" Castalia anxiously asked.

"It could be a possibility," Rupp answered. "Andjety soldiers tend to be simple- minded sword users. Now, from here on out, we must remain silent. Assume there are guards at every turn."

The six of them slithered close to the walls to be less noticeable. A couple times, as people walked by, they hid behind the large curtains against the walls on either side of the full-length windows. The largest challenge was the long hallway leading to the training courtyard. There were multiple windows, and no curtains or furniture to duck and hide, in case an informant might walk in on them.

As they slowly and carefully made their way down the hallway, an Andjety soldier came walking from the other direction. Looking shocked at seeing them, the soldier started to turn and run, shouting for help as he ran. Rupp looked around for something to throw, hoping to slow the informer's flight. Looking down at the princess, he spotted the Andjety dagger tucked in her belt near the small of her back. He quickly grabbed it up, and flung it at the fleeing soldier. Piercing him square in the back, the screaming man fell forward on his face. Dead.

"Hey," Audrianna quietly responded. "That was my dagger."

"Your dagger?" Rupp asked. "It was covered with Andjety

markings." "Well," the princess admitted, "I took it away from an Andjety guard earlier."

"And I just returned it to its rightful owner," Rupp said. Audrianna drew her mouth to one side of her face with a smirk, and playfully glared at Rupp. He winked as everyone started to scurry down the hallway, towards the courtyard.

As they made their way towards the courtyard, they saw several Andjety soldiers strolling the perimeter of the yard. The princess and her companions kept to the shadows that the lanterns and torches failed to illuminate. Rupp led the party to a weapons chest nearest the entrance. He quietly opened the chest only to discover it had been raided. He then led the others against the darkened wall which had all its weapons taken. From there, they made their way, as silent as possible, so as to not attract attention from the Andjety. As they approached the far west side of the courtyard, Rupp opened a side door that housed other weapons. Everyone quickly slipped in and closed the door behind them. The room was exceptionally dark, absent of any windows.

"How are we going to find anything in this place without a torch or lamp?" Ethlyn complained.

Immediately after she spoke, a loud squawk responded through the room. "Luella?" Ethlyn exclaimed. "Is that you, my beautiful lady?" Another squawk

responded. "Oh, I am so happy you are okay. I was afraid someone might have hurt you." Ethlyn stumbled towards the sound of her falcon, groping in the dark trying to make her way to the bird's cage. In the process, Ethlyn knocked over several shields, a rack of spears, and a wooden case off a table housing three sizes of daggers. All of which hit the ground making CRASH, BANG, CLANG sounds. Reaching the falcon, she shushed her for making her loud squawking.

"Ethlyn!" Roselle scolded in a whisper. "It's not the bird that's drawing attention to our whereabouts. Watch what you're running into."

"If I could see," Ethlyn defended herself, "I wouldn't be knocking anything over in the first place."

"I found the sword cabinet," Rupp softly declared victoriously. "Who wants a sword?"

Rozelle, Olivia, and Audrianna all chorused their interest in one. Rupp began placing swords into every hand that reached for a sword in the darkness. He began to place a broadsword into the princess's hand until he noticed how small the hand was that grasped the hilt.

"No, Your Highness," he said to the princess. "That's too big of a weapon for you to handle."

"Is not," she declared. "I've graduated to a steel sword." "From whom?" Rupp asked.

"I taught her," Olivia vouched. "But I think Your Highness should try using a short sword. That would be most appropriate for your size and strength."

"I'm getting stronger, though," Audrianna protested. "And you and Balen both said I have a gift for sword fighting."

"Having the gift, and being equipped to fight the Andjety with a broadsword, are not the same thing," Olivia pointed out.

"Lady Castalia," Rupp called to in the darkness. "Have you a sword?" "No, sir," Castalia answered. "I am not proficient with a sword." "Hold out you hand," Rupp commanded.

"No, sir," she protested. "I am no asset with a sword."

"Please give me your hand," Rupp repeated, patiently, but determined. Castalia reluctantly reached towards Rupp, expecting a sword to be placed in her hand. Instead, she felt a heavier, bulkier object. It took Castalia a few seconds before she realised what Rupp placed in her hand.

"Oh, my!" she exclaimed. "My crossbow!" "Shhh!" both Roselle and Olivia hushed her.

"Okay," Rupp called everyone together, "three of you ladies have swords, Lady Castalia has her crossbow, and Lady Ethlyn is armed with her falcon, Luella. Or Lu, for short."

"Armed with a falcon?" Olivia questioned.

"Oh, she's a weapon," Audrianna assured Olivia. "Take our word for it."

"Let's go back into the castle," Rupp suggested, "and see if we can find a place to hide tonight while we rest."

"I want to hide in my own room," Audrianna suggested. "They won't look for us there."

"It will be dangerous for us to sneak into the royal tower," Rupp replied. "But I think that is the best idea."

"I had better leave Lu here if we're going inside the palace," Ethlyn decided. "She will make a ruckus, and give us away. I'll just make sure she has plenty of food and water."

Rupp and the ladies stealthily made their way from the tiny weapons closet, back through the courtyard, then into the palace. Audrianna led everyone towards the grand staircase, then up into the royal tower. Once on the second floor, she made her way to her room. She pulled on the door, but discovered it was locked.

"Why is it locked?" she asked. "This is my room."

"Not anymore," Castalia stated. "It belongs to that witchlet. Remember?" "Witchlet?" Olivia asked. The princess banged on her door.

"A little girl, my age, pretending to be me," she answered, banging on the door even harder.

"Quietly," Roselle reminded. "Andjety guards are everywhere!" Audrianna lowered her white-knuckled fists, then looked up at her ladies. A few seconds after, the door unlocked from the inside. As it swung open, Audrianna peered into the room to see a little girl, close to her age, close to her height, with brown hair tied in a long braid, and brown eyes.

"Who be you, and whats does you want?" the strange girl asked accusingly. Audrianna reared back and punched the girl in the face, knocking her to the ground. The girl fell on her back holding her face with both hands. She started to scream and violently kicked her feet. Audrianna straddled the little girl on the floor and continued to slap and hit her on both sides of her head. Audrianna's ladies watched in amazement as Rupp pulled the princess off the flailing Andjety girl.

Rupp sat Audrianna in a chair as Olivia grabbed the imposter by the arm and stood her to her feet. Blood trickled from both nostrils, and tears rolled down her cheeks. Olivia sat the girl in a chair on the opposite side of the large bed. Castalia took a spare sheet from the cabinet and used it to restrain the child to the chair. She then took a small pillowcase and stuffed it in the Andjety's mouth to keep her quiet.

"What do we do with her now?" Ethlyn asked.

"Keep her tied up and gagged, and stuff her inside the hiding place of the bed," Audrianna demanded. The little girl glared at the princess and grunted her opposition through the pillowcase.

"I think being tied to the chair is acceptable for now," Olivia recommended.

"Yes, and since we have the occupant of this room incapacitated and bound," Rupp suggested, "we can hide here tonight and see what happens first thing in the morning."

Within the next half hour, everyone started to bed down. Rupp sat himself in a chair, and leaned against the wall in a reclined position. The ladies-in-waiting all traced down their sleeping mats, and happily bedded down in their usual spot, while Olivia and Audrianna both shared the princess's bed.

At first light, the large doors to the castle entrance slowly swung open as Andjety soldiers led the Special Forces men out of the cage one-by-one. As they exited, Rolf and several other soldiers stripped the mercenaries of their clothes, gave them a canteen of water, and sent them walking down the road, out of the city. Soon enough, the entire militia could be seen walking in a line back towards Pachenthou, without weapons and without clothes, except for their sandals and a canteen. As they walked, the entire Andjety army, lined along the road also, would point and laugh at the naked, embarrassed men.

Henry, Balen, and Mason watched in horror as the last of their elite fighters were led away, shame-faced and head down. No one looked up, nor did they turn and look from whence they came.

"What a disgraceful thing to do to our men," Balen commented.

"It was this, or have them all executed for treason," Henry remarked.

"It is the king who is the real traitor to the crown," Mason also commented. "He can't be a traitor to the crown, when he is the crown," Balen pointed out. "Do you men believe what he said about me, and Ree?" Henry asked.

"Not one word," Balen answered.

"Neither do the men," Mason added. "They pledged themselves to the princess, and they will remain loyal to the princess." Balen and Henry looked at Mason. "But, not without clothes," Mason clarified.

As the naked men walked through the city, with nothing to cover themselves, they began to murmur amongst themselves again.

"I can't believe we attacked the castle to avenge the king's blood, only to be going

against the king," one of the archers remarked.

"Who would have thought that the prince could have been taken for a sap by that horrid Witch," another also resounded.

"I would never have guessed the king to still be alive," a third replied.

"Really?" Jaako asked. "You mean NOBODY warned you?" He began to use a mocking tone. "That's right! We won't listen to Jaako. He's just an old, senile drunk that doesn't know anything. Jaako couldn't possible know that the king was still alive, just because Jaako's credible friends witnessed the king make a public proclamation and inaugurate the new crowned prince. We don't need to listen to Jaako warn us not to attack the castle with the king still alive! Jaako would NEVER be right!"

One of the mercenaries walked up and put his arm around Jaako as they strode past the checkpoint, and out of the city.

"That's okay," the man said to Jaako, "we forgive you." Jaako glared at his fellow mercenary.

"Unhand my naked body," he said as they continued walking down the path towards the east.

The large doors to the castle closed once again. Only Henry, Balen, and Mason remained, along with The king, the Witch, and Rolf, the newly crowned prince. The men faced the king and his two new royals.

"What will happen now?" Henry demanded to know.

"Now," the king said, motioning to several of his guards, "you will be taken to the tower dungeon, bound by chains, and kept there under guard until we are able to set a public execution. You will be condemned as traitors, and hung by the neck until dead."

"We don't have a tower dungeon," Henry argued.

"We do now," the king declared. "Your room has had all of your personal possessions removed, bars put on the windows, and an iron door in the place of your old wooden one. It has everything you could need, except your freedom."

"And what about my men that you just sent home on foot?" Mason inquired. "Nothing will happen to them," The king answered. "Their lives are spared to demonstrate once again that I am, and shall always be, 'Malcolm the Merciful.'"

"Your Majesty," Balen implored the king, "I came here in good faith, believing that you had been brutally slain, and I desired only that I might avenge the blood and the crown that I've had nothing but the utmost respect for. Please do not tarnish that memory by doing this horrible thing."

"Horrible thing?" Zymjai asked.

"Yes," Balen answered. "Your Excellency, the Witch has beguiled you. Somehow, she has gained control of you, convincing you she deserves to partner with you and share your throne. But, Your Majesty, this Witch is an evil, ruthless woman!"

"Evil?" the Witch asked indignantly. "I am doing the king a great favour. My soldiers are keeping the kingdom safe from raiding mercenaries, much like the traitors under the authority of Mason. Am I correct?"

"Only because the prince was misled to believe you had killed the king," Mason pointed out.

"And you believed Henry?" the king asked Mason. He then

turned back to Balen. "You are telling me that you believed such a story from the young man who forced himself upon your wife, what was it? Ten years ago?" Henry folded his arms and spun around to face the wall.

"Don't worry too much," the Witch declared. "You'll have plenty of time before your execution to make peace with God. Guards! Take them to the tower!"

"What would you know about peace with God?" Balen asked.

The soldiers marched the three men into the palace, then towards the grand staircase. They led them up the stairs, then down the hall to where Henry's room once was. Opening the heavy iron door, the men were led inside. There was no bed in the room. No chairs. No furniture of any kind. The closet was empty of any clothes.

The men were taken to the wall opposite the large window. On the wall were several sets of chains bolted into the stone. The three men's arms and feet were shackled to the wall. The chains were long enough for the men to sit on the floor, but not to freely walk about the room. The soldiers then left the room, and locked the iron door behind them. There was no latch on the inside to try and open or unlock the door.

All three men sat on the floor cross-legged, leaned against the wall, and folded their arms. There was nothing they could do. It was over. They only had hanging to look forward to. Henry shook his head. A month ago, he was crying because he had lost the kingdom. Now he was angry because the kingdom, he thought he lost, had betrayed him. And now he was going to be punished for being betrayed.

Suddenly, as if lightning flashed from the sky and struck him in the head, his thoughts quickly shifted to Audrianna. Oh, no! The princess and Olivia were in the city, somewhere. They went to look for Rupp and her ladies-in-waiting, an effort he thought to be less than productive. Whether she found them or not, would not change the fact that they were in grave danger. The moment they were spotted, they most likely would be killed, or imprisoned as he was, awaiting their execution. It was only a matter of time! How Henry wished he could send a message to the princess to warn her of their predicament.

Upon hearing the soldiers march past the princess's room, Audrianna and Rupp poked their heads out the door. Once the soldiers cleared the hallway, the captain and his protégé made their way to Henry's door. They tried to remain as quiet as possible, to not invite Andjety guards in their direction. Audrianna tried to open the large heavy door, but it was locked. Without saying a word, Audrianna motioned to Rupp to give her ideas as to how to open the door. Rupp shrugged that he had no idea. Remembering that Olivia knew how to pick locks, she motioned to Rupp for him to follow her back to the room. They carefully tiptoed back to the princess's chamber.

"Lady Olivia," the princess called, "I need you to come with me and use some of your darker talents on Henry's door." Olivia and Audrianna quietly made their way back to the hallway.

Henry sat closest to the door, with his back to the other two men. He felt personally responsible for their situation. As he sat there, a familiar aroma wafted in his direction. It was the scent of lilacs.

"Mason," he quietly and softly called over his shoulder. "Your Majesty," Mason quietly replied.

"Do you smell that?"

"I smell a lot of smells, Your Majesty," Mason declared. "What specific smell are you wanting me to notice?"

"I smell lilacs," he answered. "Like the perfume you gave to Ree." From the other side of the door, Audrianna could just scarcely hear Henry's observation.

"I smell lilacs too," she whispered through the door. "I think it's me." "Ree?" Henry inquired.

"Horace," she answered back.

"Ree, you've got to get out of here," Henry commanded. "Find your horse, and you two ladies ride as fast as you can, back to Pachenthou. Do you hear me?"

"Not without you," Audrianna protested. "And Balen," Olivia

prompted.

"And Balen," the princess added. "And Mason," Mason added.

"And Mason," Henry repeated.

"And Mason, of course," Audrianna agreed.

Olivia pulled the hairpin from her hair, the same one she had pulled from Audrianna and unlocked the dress shop. She wrestled with the lock of the heavy iron door. She couldn't get the hairpin to turn the internal latches of the lock.

"The pin it not sturdy enough to unlock the iron door," she announced. "We need the actual key."

"The Witch wears the key around her neck," Henry responded.

As the ladies talked to the men through the door, they heard the marching feet of guards coming down the hallway. Olivia grabbed the princess by the arm and dashed behind a long tapestry hanging on the wall. They stood motionless as the Andjety stomped their feet as they walked by. A few moments after the sound of the marching guards subsided, the two ladies emerged from behind the tapestry.

"Drake was correct," Olivia observed, "we have to do something about the Andjety soldiers before we can even begin to help rescue the men."

"We can't fight all of them off," Audrianna replied. "They're too many, even if the six of us gave it our all."

"That is true," Olivia confirmed. "It would be best if we could either draw them away from the castle, or chase them away."

"Chase them away?" Audrianna asked, bringing her hand up to rest her chin on. "Chase them away," she reiterated. "Yes. That Is what we can do."

"What are you thinking, you devious child?" Olivia asked the princess.

"Balen told us that the Andjety are easily started and scared," Audrianna recollected. "That's right," Olivia said. "They are exceptionally superstitious." The princess began to laugh out loud. He giggled a sort of maniacal giggle, then stopped, and looked straight at Olivia.

"Come with me," she commanded, with a look of menace in her eyes.

CHAPTER 24

It was too early in the day to put the princess's plan into action. Instead, Audrianna and Rupp spent the better half of the day, carefully choreographing her ideas among the two of them, and the four women. They rehearsed each step they would take, timing everything as close as they could. The only variable they had to contend with, was where the Witch and the king would be and how they would respond.

As the night drew on, lamps in the hallway were lit, as well as the torches in the courtyard. The first order of business, was for Ethlyn to slip back down to the courtyard and find her falcon, Luella. They were the first act of the princess's scheme. While making her way down to grab Luella, Rozelle and Castalia were to creep to the kitchen and snatch as many fireplace bellows as they could find. Olivia made use of some of the extra bedding, especially the sheets, as well as some of the princess's wardrobe accessories.

As the time came for their plan to be put into action, Ethlyn went first. Down the hallway, to the grand staircase, she quietly slinked. Down the stairs, past the main ballroom, down the hallway, then out the door to the courtyard. Several times she needed to stop and hide to avoid Andjety guards. However, she had several hiding places planned and anticipated.

Soon enough, she made it back to the small room where her falcon, Lu, was waiting. Although the falcon wasn't part of the plotting, she seemed to have an instinct as to what she was supposed to do. Ethlyn perched her feathered friend on her gloved forearm. A cap was over the head of Lu, to try and keep her from being distracted.

Ethlyn quickly retraced her steps, but instead of going upstairs, she turned towards the breakfast room, through the dark hidden passageway, and outside the walls of the castle. There by the walls, hidden in the shadows, they waited.

Meanwhile, Rozelle and Castalia had very little trouble arriving in the kitchen without being spotted by Andjety soldiers. Their greatest challenge was convincing the kitchen workers to let them have the fire bellow. The kitchen servants put such high value on their fire bellow, that one would think the bellow was all they used to prepare food.

Olivia and Rupp stole away, waiting in their positions for the plan to go into full scale action. They knew the signals they made for each other, and they knew in what order everything was supposed to happen. They waited, hidden in the hallway shadows. Audrianna guarded the imposter princess. While she kept her eye on the girl, she paced back and forth, hoping their plan would come to fruition, and that it would work the way they all hoped it would.

As the princess waited for Roselle and Castalia to return, the little girl began to groan, and squirm, kick her feet.

"What's the matter?" Audrianna asked her. She groaned at the princess through her gag. Audrianna reached towards the girl and pulled the gag from her mouth.

"I gots to use a bucket," the imposter princess declared. "You need what?" Audrianna asked.

"A bucket," the little girl repeated, fidgeting and kicking her feet wildly. "Gets to me a bucket. Gets to me a bucket."

"You mean," Audrianna asked, "you need a chamber pot?" The girl stopped kicking and looked at the princess bewildered.

"What's be a 'chamber pot'?" She asked. "A pot to pee in," the princess answered.

"Yes," the girl said. "Gets to me a 'chamber pot.'"

"Okay," Audrianna replied, "but I have my sword with me," she declared, pulling her short sword from its sheath. "If you try and fight me, or run away, I'll run you through." The little girl nodded in compliance as Audrianna untied the sheet that bound the girl to the chair.

Audrianna led the little girl to the side of the bed, then bent down to pull the chamber pot out from under the bed. The little girl watched Audrianna closely as the princess moved to the side of the bed, to give her prisoner some privacy. The little girl squatted out of sight from her captor.

About that time, Roselle and Castalia returned with several bellows in their arms. "Where's the Andjety girl," Roselle immediately asked. Audrianna pointed towards

the far side of the bed.

"She's using the chamber pot," she said. Roselle walked over to get a full view of their prisoner.

"janikaa wanakee tookie," the girl screamed in protest. Roselle wasn't sure what words she was saying, but she did understand that the girl did not appreciate being watched while doing her business.

"That's too bad for you," Roselle replied. "I've watched Her Highness use the chamber pot many times. I have every reason to keep my eye on you." The Andjety girl scowled at Rozelle, and angrily slouched on the pot.

"Everything is in place," Castalia announced. "We're waiting for Ethlyn and Lu to begin, then everyone else will do their part."

"Good," Audrianna replied. "Once we distract the soldiers, it will give us a better chance at taking down the king, the Witch, and the imposter prince, Rolf."

"Oh!" Castalia angrily sneered. "That horrid pretender to the throne! That opportunist! I can't wait to show him what I think of him!"

The little Andjety girl stood up from the chamber pot and adjusted her clothes. Instead of moving forward, though, she stepped backwards towards the wall near the headboard.

"Come this way!" Audrianna ordered. The girl stood still, silently staring at the princess with a determined look. "Come this way, towards me," Audrianna repeated, motioning with her hands. The girl stood motionless. Audrianna walked around the corner of the bed towards the little girl. Just as the princess came around the bed and stood in front of her, the girl took two giant steps and kicked the chamber pot, with all its contents, towards Audrianna. Audrianna ducked to one side, and fell to her knees, holding her sword up in the air. The contents of the pot partially sprayed Rozelle, catching her left arm and part of her hair. Roselle yelled, Castalia screamed, and the little girl wrestled the short sword from the princess's grasp.

Audrianna jumped to her feet, and retreated to the middle of the room. The girl swung Audrianna's sword wildly at her. The princess knew she needed to disarm the girl of her sword, before one of them got hurt. She took her defence stance, just like Mason taught her.

"You're not a real princess," Audrianna remarked. "The real princess is left- handed." The girl tilted her head, not understanding what she meant.

Audrianna raised her right hand as bait, pretending she was going to go for the sword with her right hand. As the Andjety girl swung towards her right hand, Audrianna grabbed the girl's wrist with her left hand. She twisted it outwards, causing her to release her grasp. The little girl screamed in pain. Audrianna grabbed the sword with her other hand, then let go of the girl.

The Andjety girl whirled around to run, but Audrianna caught her by her hair braid. She thought about what Mason said she needed to do with the sword. The sword was razor sharp. Audrianna pulled the little girl towards her, intending at first to plunge the sword through the girl. But at the last moment, Audrianna brought the sword up to the little girls braid, and sliced off her hair.

The remainder of the girl's hair draped around her head. The girl placed both her hands on her head, and felt her short, jagged hair.

"Now you look like a princess," Audrianna declared, dangling the severed braid out in front of her. The little girl turned to look at what the princess had done.

"Neggit harkoo!" the girl exclaimed in Andjety. Neggit harkoo, which meant, "not my hair". As she screamed, she ran wild circles around the room, until Rozelle latched onto her and sat her back in the chair. Castalia then grabbed the sheet and tied the girl securely.

"Neggit harkoo," the girl continued to exclaim as she softly wept.

"Think that's horrible?" Audrianna remarked as she stood in front of the restrained girl. "Wait until you're consummated."

The girl stopped chanting and looked at the princess with another bewildered look. "What do you know about 'consummated'?" Rozelle asked. Audrianna simply shrugged.

"I've learned a lot since being gone," she said.

Ethlyn sat outside the castle walls, holding her falcon, Lu. She gently stroked the bird's well-groomed feathers, and quietly talked to her as the falcon's talons gripped the leather glove on Ethlyn's hand. She suddenly realised that the time was right for her to send Luella to do what the group had talked about. She discussed the plan with Lu, and even though Ethlyn knew she was just a bird, somehow, she believed Lu knew what she was supposed to do.

Ethlyn stood to her feet, and held Luella up until the falcon spread its wings out majestically. Removing the falcon's cap, she then made a clicking sound with her tongue, a signal for Lu to take flight. Lu zoomed straight up in the air, then spiralled back down towards Ethlyn, then zipped across the side of the wall, and up to a nearby window. Luella looked inside the window, squeaked a few times, then flew to another perch. Several times she did so, as if she was looking for someone specific.

After flying from one window to the next, Luella finally perched on a window with light coming out from it in the master tower. Ethlyn watched as her prized falcon disappeared.

Inside the lighted window stood King The king, Zymjai, Rolf, and half a dozen Andjety soldiers. The group were discussing how soon they could hold a public execution of the Prince and his two comrades. Suddenly, Lu zipped past the back wall, and landed atop a torch stand containing no torch. Zymjai was a bit startled at first, not knowing what movement had just taken place in the room.

"What was that?" she demanded. The soldiers looked at each other in bewilderment, not noticing the entrance of the falcon.

"What was what?" Rolf asked. As soon as Rolf spoke, the begrudged falcon let out a frightening squawk. Everyone from the King to the soldiers jumped from fear. Lu, still remembering how Rolf had slapped her while training, lunged from the torch stand, towards Rolf.

"Oh no!" Rolf screamed. "It's Luella! Luella has returned to get me." The falcon landed on Rolf and began mercilessly pecking and clawing him while he screamed for help. Rolf thrashed about, flinging droplets of blood upon the soldiers.

The startled soldiers misunderstood what Rolf meant by saying, "Luella has returned". They thought he was talking about Luella, the dead queen. They immediately believed the attacking falcon was the queen reincarnated to exact vengeance on the invading marauders. As Rolf fled from the room, several of the Andjety soldiers fled as well, leaving the King and the Witch alone in the room.

Seeing the Andjety flee from the council chambers was the signal for Rupp, Castalia, and Rozelle to take action. Armed with bellows, the three of them stationed themselves next to statues of royal armour in three locations, each a different level of the castle. Using the bellows, they forced air through the face plates, causing the armour to make a loud ominous howling noise. All over the castle, the superstitious Andjety guards were alarmed by the sound, not knowing where is was coming from, and fearful for what to might be.

As the noise of the howling armour reverberated through the castle, Olivia put phase three into play. Dressed as an apparition, her face and hair powdered white, her clothes made from white bed sheets, and a string of bells wrapped around her waist, Olivia ran through the halls of the castle. The fearful Andjety, upon seeing such a sight, and hearing the echoing noise, scattered in all directions. As everyone ran, they bumped into each other, causing the hysteria to grow.

Olivia ran from the backside of the castle, towards the front, going up and down flights of stairs, herding the soldiers towards the front of the castle.

"Get out, or lose your soul," Olivia would scream. "I am hungry for Andjety souls." The soldiers scrambled down the hallways, and flights of stairs, tripping over one another to leave the castle as fast as they could. Soon, every one of the Andjety soldiers and guards were outside the castle walls, still running as fast as they could for the mountains. Rupp ran towards the main doors, and shifted the lever that dropped the heavy iron gate, closing off the entrance. Except for the King, the Witch, and wounded Rolf, the castle was now in the hands of Nadeau again. Now, the final step that needed to be taken,

was to release Henry, Balen, and Mason from the castle dungeon.

Audrianna left the Andjety girl in her room, and made her way down the hall way to try and open the large iron door to Henry's room. There was no handle on the iron door, only a keyhole.

"Horace," she called through the door. "Ree?" he asked.

"We took over the castle," she exclaimed. "The castle is ours." "Really?" he asked. "How did you do that?"

"Horatio," she replied. "Pardon me?" Henry asked.

"Horatio, the castle ghost scared them all away. We then locked them out." "Ingenious," Henry responded, "you scheming little mouse." Audrianna giggled. "We still have to find the

Witch and get the key from around her neck," she remarked.

"Leave that to Rupp," Henry ordered. "That's too dangerous for you to be involved in."

"Don't worry," the princess replied. "Rupp is already…"

As Audrianna was speaking, she was suddenly cut off, and was unable to finish her statement. The sound of a struggle, and heavy footsteps were heard leading away from the it in door.

"Ree?" Henry called. "Ree, are you okay?" Silence.

"Ree?" Henry repeated. Silence.

"What happened to her?" Balen asked.

"She's gone," Henry answered. "Someone just took her."

CHAPTER 25

It was early morning before Rupp and the ladies could open the large iron door, and free the men from their shackles. By that time, there was no trace of Princess Audrianna. Neither was there any trace of where the king, the Witch or Rolf escaped to. After searching the entire castle, Henry became panic-stricken. Audrianna was gone. Where did they take her? Which direction did they go? Was she safe? He was determined to track them down and rescue her, as 'she' had rescued 'them' from being executed.

On top of that, when the ladies-in-waiting returned to the room, they discovered the little Andjety girl missing as well. Either she had escaped on her own, or the Witch had rescued her, too. The castle was in the hands of Nadeau, but with the king still alive and in partnership with the Witch, the kingdom was still under Andjety control.

Henry was joined by Balen, Olivia, Mason and Rupp in the Royal Court council chambers. Along with the five of them, Audrianna's ladies-in-waiting also stood to the side, observing. While normally the Highness's ladies were not at liberty to speak in Royal Court, Henry was more interested in rescuing his betrothed, than maintaining appropriate protocols.

The eight of them together attempted to figure out where the Witch and the King escaped to, and why they might have taken the princess. On top of that, they needed to bring the king back to Nadeau, to stand before the people, and be tried for his treacherous activities.

"The king is at liberty to do as he wishes, and to enter into whatever treaty he desires," Rupp pointed out. "Just because the Andjety have been a sworn enemy of ours for decades, does not give us levity to undergo a takeover."

"Understood," Henry agreed. "However, we also need to consider the lives that were taken by the Andjety. Hundreds of Nadeau soldiers and guards were killed the night Ree and I fled. How can we allow the king to brush such atrocities aside as if their deaths are for a greater good?"

"Right," Balen answered. "Men and women who swore their lives to protect the king and royal family, only to be victims of a plot by the king, to senselessly have them all murdered."

"Why would the king do such a horrid thing," Rozelle asked. "Why not just establish a treaty with the Andjety without causing such bloodshed to Nadeau? He's the king after all."

"Because," Olivia answered, "according to Nadeau law, the king is required to abdicate his throne upon the prince's twenty-fifth birthday, and marriage. It wasn't enough for the king to gain another six years through Henry's betrothal to the princess."
"He wanted to remain king until his death," Henry replied, "and expand his kingdom

to include all of the Andjety land, and who knows how much more."

"So, what's our next move, Your Majesty?" Rozelle asked. "How do we get Her Highness back?"

"We first need to figure out the king's true motive for taking the princess," Henry answered. "My father is not one to hold hostages just for collateral. He has another purpose in mind for capturing her."

"I'm sure he expects us to come looking for her," Balen remarked. "Perhaps he is using her as a bargaining tool."

"Right," Henry replied. "Holding her is his way of attempting to remain at an advantage. But something tells me that he's up to something bigger than that."

For the rest of the morning, the Crowned Prince and his most trusted friends discussed a multitude of ideas where the king, the Witch, Rolf, and the Andjety girl could have escaped to.

"I believe there is a cave on the other side of the Andjety mountains," Balen informed Henry. "I have heard the Witch has equipped it as a palace."

"Do you know how to get there?" Henry asked.

"No," Balen replied, "but I know someone who does." "Who?" Henry eagerly asked. Balen shook his head. "You're not going to like the answer."

"Who?" Henry cautiously asked, turning his head away from Balen, but looking at him through the corner of his eyes.

"Let's just say," Balen answered, "he's a bit of a 'dirty dog.'" Henry looked straight at Balen.

"No!" he exclaimed, looking from one face to another. "No! I am not tracing my steps all the way back to Pachenthou, find Jaako, only to come all the way back in search of Ree. I'd rather head out straightway and hope to find another way."

"True—true—true—truthfully, Your Majesty," Mason stated, "the men may not be as far as you think. They were sent off yesterday morning wearing nothing but sandals and a scowl. I estimate they made it no further than the campsite."

"We could take clothes with us," Rupp suggested, "along with wagons and horses, retrieve them, and be back here tomorrow morning."

"Ex-ex-ex-excellent idea," Mason agreed. "Let's collect the supplies, and head out straight away."

Henry, Balen, and Rupp rounded up horses and wagons from the city stables. Olivia and Mason gathered clothing, food and weapons. Within a few hours, the five of them began driving a wagon, each pulled by several horses, and weighed down with resources. The three ladies-in-waiting also rode along in Olivia's wagon.

By nightfall, the horses and wagons had caught up with the naked travellers, sitting around the campfires, attempting to keep warm. As they approached the camp, Henry called out, "The castle belongs to Nadeau!" Upon seeing the train of wagons, horses and clothes, all the men stood to their feet and cheered. Accustomed to their lack of apparel, the men swarmed the four wagons, pulling the men off and hugging them. As a group of naked men swarmed Olivia's wagon, Castalia and Ethlyn covered their faces out of propriety, while Roselle looked on and chuckled. Olivia silently raised her hand in protest, which persuaded the men to refrain from swarming them.

After all the men were once again comfortably clothed, Olivia began the task of preparing meals. As everyone ate their supper, Henry and Balen drew everyone in a circle while they explained everything that had happened after they were sent away.

As Henry described what Audrianna had done to chase the Andjety out of the castle, the men of her elite special forces cheered. They were so proud of their ten-year-old leader. She was their princess. Their hero.

However, when Henry told them how she was stolen away while talking to him through the door, the sound of anxious murmurings wafted over the camp. Upon that revelation, Jaako stood from the crowd, dressed in clean apparel for the first time in months, due to the king ordering his own clothes stripped off his body.

"We must leave immediately and rescue Her Highness," he yelled, turning to face the crowd. "The longer we wait, the less likely she will be unharmed when we reach her." Everyone sat motionless while staring at the one who claimed to not be a loyalist. "Come. We must go," Jaako urgently repeated.

"Hold on, Jaako," Balen responded, attempting to calm the dirty dog down. "We are all together with the notion to rescue Her Highness. But, His Majesty is concerned that the king has an alternate motive for taking the princess that we need to figure out first." "We don't need to wait," Jaako exclaimed, his voice crackling, and his eyes beginning to water. "We can't afford to wait! The princess is in danger! We need to go—right now!"

Balen, Mason, and Henry were all surprised to see Jaako become emotional over the capture of the princess. They had never expected such a response to come from him. He had behaved disrespectful towards her up to that point, offended that he should follow a female into battle, and a child at that.

"She will be alright for now," Henry declared. "The king will not kill her, until he can use her to bargain with." Jaako walked directly up to the prince and stood face-to- face, inches from him.

"There are worse fates than death," Jaako replied, a look of fear gripping his face. "If you have something to tell me," Henry responded, "now is the time to speak."

"I will show you where the Witch's palace is," he replied. "Providing we leave in the next hour. If not, you will have to follow from a distance."

"If you must leave immediately," Henry countered, "then I and Rupp will go with you. The rest of the camp will follow under Lord Balen and Lady Olivia's direction."

"If you are going to free the princess," Rozelle interjected, "then I am coming with you."

"Oh no," Jaako responded. "I'm not taking any women with me. You'll just slow us down."

"Really?" Rozelle replied. "I am Her Highness's sworn protector. Her Lady in Waiting. You three men are not traipsing through the mountains, with a maiden, without an appropriate chaperone."

"Chaperone?" Henry asked. "You weren't too concerned with chaperones when you tossed her out the window the night of the Andjety siege." Rozelle realised that her reasoning wasn't winning her the right to tag along.

"Please, Your Majesty," Rozelle begged, softening her tone.

"Let me come with you.

I promise to not slow your journey."

"Well, then," Henry answered, "all you had to do was ask. I respond better to requests than demands."

"I would like to come too," Castalia replied.

"I," Henry hesitated, seeing the scouting party getting a bit large.

"You men are not traipsing through mountains," Castalia remarked, "with a Lady, without an appropriate."

"Oh, stop it!" Henry interrupted. "Just be ready within the hour."

It was early that morning when Audrianna awoke from her sleep. Although her eyes were open, she laid still in the bed, in between the satin sheets, and under a think woolly blanket. The palace of the Witch was at a higher elevation than the Nadeau castle, so the room was draughty and cold. Tears rolled down the sides of her head, and dripped off her ears, onto the pillow.

Audrianna wore a beautiful silk nightgown the king presented to her the night before. King Malcolm was being so nice to her, yet she couldn't understand why he suddenly changed from the loving, understanding, and merciful king, to a power-crazed maniac. Had the Witch somehow cast a spell upon him? Henry told her she was called the War Witch due to her evil behaviour, and not because she cast spells. However, she couldn't help but wonder why the sudden change.

As she lay in the bed, the door opened without anyone knocking. The princess popped her head up to see the king appear, then plopped her head back on her pillow.

"Good morning, Your Highness," The king expressed. Audrianna didn't respond.

"I trust you slept comfortably," He inquired. "Were you warm enough in your nightgown and heavy blanket?"

No response.

"Perhaps you are hungry," he offered. The princess looked in his direction.

The king carried in his hands a tray bearing a full breakfast. Although Audrianna wanted to dismiss anything the king offered her, her stomach reminded her that it had been almost an entire day since she had last eaten. On the tray were breads, fruits, cheeses, but best of all, several types of meat. Audrianna's mouth watered as the aroma from the meat permeated the entire bedroom. Without any protest, and without consideration, the princess automatically stood to her feet and sat at the tiny table in the centre of the room. The king set the food tray in front of her. She wanted to devour the food right away, but for the past several weeks Balen and Olivia had conditioned her to pray before eating a meal. To The king's surprise, Audrianna folded her hands, closed her eyes, and recited an adaptation to the usual prayer.

"Merciful Lord," she prayed, "I have walked hard for the food set before me. You gave us land. You gave us food. You gave me a crown. And, you gave me a husband that is going to hunt down these murderous, thieving, hateful Andjety cowards, rescue me, and end their lives. For that, we are eternally grateful. Amen."

The king felt a lump form in his throat after hearing the ten-year-old pray to the Almighty regarding his downfall.

"I suspect you might be a bit resentful over what has happened the past several weeks," the king responded. Audrianna began to aggressively eat her food, ignoring anything The king had to say. "I want you to know that I have no intention to bring you any harm." Audrianna raised her eyes and stared at the king while tearing flesh with her teeth from a baked leg of lamb. "I have the utmost respect for who you are," he said, "and what you've accomplished." The princess fiercely chewed her food, swallowed hard, then stuffed more breads and cheeses in her mouth without saying a word. Her mannerisms indicated to the king she was upset with him as well as her circumstances.

"Please understand," he continued, "I have done everything for a greater purpose than what you can see or understand."

"Oh, I undathtand." The princess responded, her mouth full of food. "But I dunt thing you wealyth wut you dune." She choked down her food, then grabbed another piece of bread and held it in her hand. "You can't use bad actions to bring about a greater purpose. As my father used to say, 'Bad parents make bad kids, but good parents make great kids.'" The king looked at the princess with a puzzled expression. "Of course," she answered, "I'm not totally certain what side of that coin he was claiming."

"What do you mean?" the king asked the princess.

"You killed a bunch of Nadeau soldiers," Audrianna recounted, "and you've joined our kingdom with the evil War Witch, all in the name of making the kingdom better? It won't work! You'll have a bigger kingdom, but not a better one."

As they sat at the breakfast table, the door opened once again, revealing the Witch, Zymjai. Only this time, the Witch wasn't wearing an Andjety military uniform, but rather a beautiful dress. Her face was clean, and her hair was nicely brushed and pinned. Although Audrianna had reason to be afraid and hate her, Zymjai was a beautiful woman. Instead of wearing a frown, Zymjai wore a smile.

"And how is everybody today?" the Witch softly and politely asked the two at the table. "Did you enjoy your breakfast, my dear?" Audrianna looked back and forth between the Witch and the king.

"Am I your dear, or is he?" she asked. The Witch let out what seemed a genuine laugh.

"Why, you, silly," Zymjai answered. "You are my dear." Audrianna placed the rest of her food on the platter, then folded her hands in her lap.

"What are you two up to?" she asked.

"We are not up to anything," the king answered. "We are simply glad we could rescue you from the traitorous prince before he could harm you."

"Horace?" she asked. "Horace wouldn't dream of hurting me. He took good care of me while we were on the run."

"Who is Horace?" the Witch calmly, and somewhat playfully asked. The princess realised her mistake.

"I meant Henry, not Horace," she answered.

"At any rate," The king replied, "I tried my best to raise Henry to be a good king someday. But it seemed he chose to go a different path than what he was taught."

"You're lying, Your Majesty," Audrianna argued with The king. "I know personally from Lady Olivia that after Queen Luella died, you gave no consideration towards Henry for most of his upbringing."

"That's not true," The king replied. "Why would she say such lies about me?" "No, dear," the Witch calmly answered, shaking her head at the princess.

"It is true," Audrianna answered. "Henry told me himself how you would never praise him for any of his accomplishments, not tell him that you were proud of him, nor ever showed any interest in holding so much as your own son's hand."

"Enough!" the king angrily called out. "You are basing your estimation of me on the word of a spoiled resentful child." Audrianna leaned back slightly in her chair, alarmed by the king's anger. The king stopped yelling, recomposed himself, and dropped his tone to a soft one. "I brought you here, not to make you a prisoner, but to show you that I have been grossly misunderstood."

"For what purpose?" the little girl asked, crossing her arms. The king took a deep breath and let out a sigh.

"Because I value you," he replied. "You are a brave intelligent young lady. You are wise beyond your years. It would be a shame to no longer have you part of loyal court." The king reached both his hands out and grasped a hold of the princess's. "When I get my kingdom back, it would be an honour for you to continue serving as the crowned princess. And maybe soon, as the Queen."

"And marry Rolf?" Audrianna asked. The king let go of her hands and folded his own in his lap.

"Soon enough, both Nadeau and the Andjety, will be one nation," The king announced. "When that happens, we won't have to contend with Nadeau traditions."

"What traditions?" the princess asked.

"You dearly remind me of the dead queen, Luella," the king replied. "Nadeau law prohibits me marrying anyone as young as you. But I think you will enjoy being the new queen, ruling the new empire, and sitting by my side." Audrianna's eyes widened with disbelief.

"You want me to marry you?" she asked, horrified. "Now, before I'm sixteen?" She stood up from the table and took several steps backwards towards the wall.

"I think you are mature enough," The king answered, looking up at her from his seat. "And I can think of no one better to help link our two nations together." Audrianna took a few more steps backwards until she bumped into Zymjai behind her. Zymjai placed her cold hands over the princess's shoulders.

"No," Audrianna responded, shaking her head. "Why marry me? Why don't you marry the Witch? She's closer to your age. And she's pretty. Why not marry her?"

Zymjai and The king exchanged glances, then looked back at the princess. They both smiled and began to laugh.

"Marry him?" the Witch asked.

"Marry her?" the king asked. "That would never happen." "Why not?" the princess demanded to know.

"Let's just say," the king answered, "that you are far more suitable."

"That's why you brought me here," she realised. "You plan to marry me, and not wait six years."

"I know you will be a beautiful woman someday," The king replied. "But, it's a shame to wait that long for us to be lovers."

"No," was her soft reply. She could not believe what she was hearing. "What was that, my pet?" the Witch asked.

"NO!" the princess shouted. "No! No! NO! I will not marry the king! I will not marry anyone until I am at least sixteen! That is the law! Nadeau law is in place to protect me, not deprive me. I have the right to wait!" The king stood to his feet and took a few steps towards the princess and the Witch.

"You are not in Nadeau," he remarked. "I can marry you whenever I want." He reached out to stroke the princess's face with his right hand. Audrianna quickly grabbed his hand with her left, and twisted it as if she was trying to disarm him. She turned his hand. And turned it. And turned it, causing him to scream in pain, and kneel to the floor on one knee.

The witch, who had been holding Audrianna by her shoulders, reached down and wrestled the princess's grip from the king. Now the princess was closest to the door, with neither of them standing in the way. While the Witch helped the hurting king to his feet, Audrianna darted out the door and down a very narrow passageway.

"Stop her, you idiot!" the king screamed at Zymjai.

As the princess ran down one corridor after another, she could hear the feet of the Witch behind her, gaining on her escape. The princess was completely unfamiliar with the Witch's palace, and not certain which direction to run. Before long, the princess mistakenly turned down a blind corridor that ended up being a dead end.

Audrianna raced to the stone wall and slapped her hands against the smooth wall, half wishing the wall would've opened up for her to escape. The Witch caught up with her and grabbed her by the arm and neck. The Witch's sharp fingernails dug into the skin on the back of her neck as Zymjai led her captive back to her assigned room.

The king stood in the middle of the princess's room, still nursing his injured wrist. Standing next to The king was Rolf, who had recently entered the room ahead of the Witch and the princess. Rolf's face was bandaged around his forehead and over one eye. Multiple lacerations were still evident around his face, ears, and down his neck.

"Oh, my," the princess shrieked at the sight of Rolf. "What happened to you?" "As if you didn't know," Rolf replied.

"Luella?" the princess asked.

"That malicious falcon scratched me all over my face," Rolf angrily answered. "She took a chunk off the tip of my right ear, and gouged out one of my eyes!"

"Holy maggots!" the princess exclaimed.

"If I ever see that bird again, I'll ring its neck," Rolf threatened.

"Bring her over here," The king ordered the Witch. Zymjai led Audrianna to a chair to which Rolf bound her wrists to the arms of the chair, and her ankles to its legs. The king and Rolf dragged the chair against a far wall, and parked the princess facing the wall.

"This is a lot more secure than how we tied up that Andjety girl who pretended to be me," Audrianna commented. "Say, whatever happened to her?"

"She will be rewarded for her diligence during the Nadeau overthrow," Rolf answered. "I am her betrothed husband. She and I will be married soon as the crowned Prince and Princess of the United Nadeau-Andjety kingdom."

"You call that a reward?" Audrianna asked.

"Rolf," the king commanded, satisfied that the princess was properly bound, "stay with the crowned princess, and make sure she doesn't escape."

"Yes, sir!" Rolf responded, snapping to attention.

"Stay alert," the Witch warned him. "I'm sure the prince will come looking for her, and try to rescue her."

"I will stay alert," Rolf promised.

"We have other business to attend to," the king announced. The two cohorts left the room, leaving Audrianna alone with Rolf.

Rolf sat in a chair, on the other side of the room, watching the princess as she sat facing the wall. For a long time, the princess sat silently. But after a while, her audacious mind began to come up with a variety of brazen comments to throw at Rolf. She would turn her head in the direction of Rolf and say things like, "Hey, Rolf! Let's run away together. Untie me, and I'll go first."

"Hey, Rolf! Didn't the Witch tell you to keep both eyes on me? Oh! That's right..." "Hey, Rolf! Do you hear that? Sounds like an angry falcon!"

For the most part, Rolf just ignored her jabs at him. He picked up a dish full of pistachios, and started eating them to keep himself occupied. As Audrianna jabbed at Rolf, he would fling the pistachio shells at the back of her head, until a pile of shells accumulated around her chair.

Meanwhile, Jaako led Henry, Rupp, Rozelle, and Castalia up the steep mountainside towards the secret location of the Witch's palace. Not used to the high elevation, nor the frigid temperatures, the scouting party was forced to stop frequently and rest. The first village they came across within the borders of the Andjety land, Jaako acquired warm clothes and coats for the entire group. The hooded coats almost completely covered the faces of the ladies, although they gave no complaint to that fact. The higher they climbed up the Andjety mountain, the stronger the cold wind blew against them. While the ladies promised they would not slow the group down, it was Henry that continued to announce they needed to stop and rest.

"I knew we shouldn't have brought the men along," Castalia teased. "They just can't keep up with us ladies."

"True," Roselle remarked. "But they begged us so sincerely, it was hard to say no." "Alright," Henry responded. "I admit I'm not as fit as I thought I was. But I've been half starved these past few weeks, being fed only vegetables from Balen and Olivia's

garden. Not even cooked or roasted vegetables. Just, straight from the garden."

"Maybe so," Roselle countered, "but the rest of us, except for Jaako, have subsisted on gruel. Not much nourishment there." Jaako walked over to the group and sat in between the two ladies. He tucked his arms behind and around their shoulders.

"I've survived these past fifteen years on nothing but bread and ale," he bragged, trying to get a reaction from the women. "Maybe every once and a while, some stale cheese."

"Oh, my," Roselle said, mocking Jaako's boast. "You are the answer to a maiden's prayer. I've always wanted a drunk that would take advantage of my moral integrity, and ruin my life." Jaako retrieved his arms and glared at Rozelle.

"Why is the kingdom filled with so many insolent women?"

he asked.

"Why, Mr Jaako," Castalia remarked. "Have you used that same bread and ale line before?"

"With similar results," he replied.

"And what leads you to believe the problem lies with the women?" she asked.

"I don't believe it does," Jaako answered, leaning into Castalia. "That's just the explanation I claim."

"I think that is enough rest," Henry remarked, standing to his feet. "Where do we go from here, Dirty Dog?"

Jaako grinned at the prince, and stood to his feet as well. Their guide pulled out a spy glass from a purse tucked inside his heavy coat. He pushed back the hood covering his head and surveyed the top region of the mountain. He then pulled out a small handwritten journal, and thumbed through its pages.

"We follow the trail to the right," Jaako said, pointing towards the highest peak of the mountain. "Another fifteen kilometres or so, and the trail will narrow. We will encounter ice and snow, so watch every step. You do not want to fall from the height we've already reached."

For several more hours, the five of them slowly walked up the steep trail, pushing themselves against the strong wind. True to Jaako's word, the trail began to narrow. Both ladies held each other's hand as they gingerly scooted past a precipice, with the path not being much wider than they were. The only benefit from that part of the trail was the absence of the strong, cold wind.

"How in the world did the king manage to make it up this mountain trail with a little girl in tote?" Rupp asked in astonishment.

"They most likely went up the other trail," Jaako replied. "It's a much easier climb." Everybody stopped and slowly turned their heads to look at Jaako.

"Well," he explained, "This way is much faster." Everyone remained still, continuing to stare. "You want to catch up with the Witch and king, or not?" Jaako asked. The group shook their heads as they finished sliding past the steep canyon.

Rolf sat slouched in his chair, his back to the door, but facing the princess. Audrianna had stopped talking to Rolf, and bowed her head from sheer boredom. It was cold in the room. In fact, the entire palace was frigid. The princess entertained herself by playing with the fog her breath caused while exhaling. However, facing a bare wall with not so much as a painting to stimulate her had taken its toll on the little ten-year-old.

Rolf had finished off the small jar of pistachios, and had become rather rigid as well. He leaned back in his chair and stretched his arms and legs and gave out a loud yawn. As he leaned back, Rolf was startled at first by the presence of the little Andjety girl whom he was betrothed to.

"Oh," Rolf exclaimed. "You startled me, dear." The little girl placed her arms over Rolf's shoulders and leaned against her future husband.

"Why does you gets to be here all day?" the little girl asked in broken Nadeau. "I have to be here to watch over the prisoner," Rolf explained.

"Is you enough warm in here?" she asked.

"I have a coat if I need it," Rolf answered. "But I am warm for now." "You gots to be here alone all day?" she asked.

"Oh, don't worry," Rolf pacified her. "We will be married in a few days. You will belong to me, and I always take good care of my belongings." He reached over and took her hand, then kissed it.

"No one gets to be here too?" she asked.

"Nope," Rolf said. "Just me, watching the helpless princess of Nadeau." The Andjety girl nodded, then stepped back a few steps behind him.

Audrianna, who for the most part ignored the two Andjety's conversation, suddenly was alerted to a loud CRASH! Popping her head up, and turning it to the left as far as it would turn, she saw Rolf crumble to the floor unconscious. She could not see where the Andjety girl disappeared to until a razor-sharp blade was held up to her neck from her right side.

"Why didn'ts you run through me?" the little girl asked.

"You mean, 'run you through'?" Audrianna asked. "Why didn't I run you through

with my sword?"

"Yes," the girl said, nodding. "You saids you were going to run me through if I didn'ts do whats you say."

"I know," Audrianna answered. "And I am trained to kill. Especially once I take a weapon away from someone trying to kill me, I am supposed to run you through."

"Then, why didn'ts you kill me?" the Andjety asked. Audrianna sighed, then shrugged.

"I guess because I saw me in you," she answered.

"You sees you in me?" the girl asked, stepping around to where they could both look in each other's faces. The girl still held the tip of the blade against Audrianna's neck.

"Yes. I sees me in you," she mimicked the little girl, without mocking. "How come?"

"Well," the princess explained, "I never asked to live in Nadeau castle. I never asked to be betrothed to the prince. I never asked to learn how to kill another person. But I was taken from my home, without my consent, and forced to endure all of that." The Andjety girl slowly pulled her dagger from Audrianna's neck.

"I guess, when I look at you," Audrianna continued, "I see a little girl, trapped and betrothed, just like me. When it came time to kill you, I decided instead to cut off your hair, just like mine was cut off." Audrianna pointed to her own short hair. The girl dropped the dagger to her side.

"You and me be lots alike?" she asked.

"Indeed," Audrianna remarked. "Our lives are so much alike, you could consider us sisters." The Andjety girl's eyes widened with surprise. She then squared her shoulders, and pointed the dagger at Audrianna again. She wore a determined look on her face.

"No!' she exclaimed, thrusting the dagger towards Audrianna. The princess closed her eyes and winced, thinking the girl was about to plunge the knife into her heart. Instead, the Andjety girl sliced off the ropes from Audrianna's right arm. She then leaned over and cut the ropes off her right leg. Walking to the other side of the chair, the little girl cut the ropes off the princess's left side as well."

"Now, we be like sisters," the little girl exclaimed. Audrianna smiled and stood to her feet. The Andjety girl bowed her head and handed Audrianna the dagger. Audrianna took the knife, then took hold of the girl's arms, causing her to become frightened. She then drew the little girl into an embrace, something the girl was completely unaccustomed to.

After holding her for a moment, Audrianna stepped back and looked at the little girl. "We need to get out of here, before Rolf wakes up," she exclaimed. They both ran towards the door, then carefully peered around the corner into the corridor. "Which way do we go to get out?" the princess asked.

"You follows me," the Andjety commanded. They quickly scrambled in a different direction than where Audrianna attempted to escape the first time.

"What's your name?" the princess quietly asked. The Andjety girl glanced at the princess while they quietly strode down the corridor.

"I don't have a name," she said.

"What do you mean?" the princess asked. "Everybody has a name. What do they call you?" The Andjety girl shook her head.

"They calls me 'Koofay'," she answered. "Which more is a number, than is a name." "What does it mean in Nadeau?" Audrianna asked.

"It means, 'two after five'."

"Well, if we're going to be sisters," Audrianna replied, "then I need to give you a name." The little girl looked at the princess and beamed her first smile.

"Whats will you call me?" she asked.

"Hmm," Audrianna thought. "What do you think of the name, 'Gertrude'?" The girl nodded enthusiastically.

"I likes the name," she said excitedly.

"No," Audrianna chortled. "I was just teasing. That is a horrible name." They both stopped at the end of the hallway, and looked both ways down the new corridor. The Andjety girl slowly turned down the passage to the left, then motioned to Audrianna that the way was safe. Again, they briskly walked together.

"If we're both princesses," Audrianna explained, "then we both should have royal sounding names." Audrianna thought long and hard. As they turned down another corridor, Audrianna suggested another name.

"How about 'Janessa'?" she offered. "That kind of has a royal sound to it. What do you think."

"I guesses," the little girl replied. "Do you thinks it sounds like I be a princess?" "Well," Audrianna answered, "I don't know if it is all that regal, but my mother's

name was 'Janessa.'" The little girl abruptly stopped walking, then looked at the princess. "You be naming me after you mother?"

"Yes," she answered. "Why not?" The little girl stared at Audrianna for several seconds, wanting to say something, but having nothing to say. Her eyes began to sparkle. All of a sudden, the Andjety girl wrapped her arms around Audrianna, then kissed her directly on the lips.

"Thank you, Sister," she responded. "I wants to be called, 'Janessa'!" Audrianna wiped the moisture from her mouth the little girl left on her lips.

"Okay," she confirmed. "Janessa it is." The girl took hold of Audrianna's hand, smiled, then pulled her down another passageway.

"Just to be clear," Audrianna remarked to Janessa, "That did not count as my first kiss."

CHAPTER 26

Rolf awoke on the ice-cold floor, next to the fallen chair he had been sitting in. As he lifted his head, a string of drool followed him from the floor, until it snapped and hit him in the chin. Wiping off his chin with one hand, he held his head with the other, discovering a large painful knot on the back of his scalp. As his head began to clear, he realised the presence of the king and Witch standing next to him.

"Where is your prisoner, Prince Rolf?" the Witch asked. Rolf looked over to where the princess had been tied up, only to find an empty chair, and shredded ropes.

"I… I… I don't know, Your Highness," he answered. The Witch bent down and picked up broken pottery lying next to Rolf's chair.

"It appears as though someone ambushed you with a vase to the head," Zymjai concluded. "Any idea who might have done that?" Rolf's head was still rather dazed as he traced back to his last conscious thoughts.

"My betrothed was here right before I blacked out," he replied.

"The slave girl?" the king asked.

"Two-After-Five," the Witch answered. "She's freed the princess."

"Why would she do that?" Rolf asked. "The Nadeau princess punched her in the nose, and chopped off her hair. Why would she free her?"

"I don't know," the Witch responded, "but I am certain that is what happened. Alert the palace guards. Find them immediately!"

"Where do you expect them to go," The king asked. "They will never survive outside without proper clothing." The Witch spun around and pointed her finger in the king's face.

"Don't underestimate that little girl," she said. "She seems to have an uncanny ability to become quite bothersome."

As Audrianna and Janessa quickly made their way down a darkly lit hallway, the sound of a ram's horn echoed through the palace.

"What is that?" Audrianna asked.

"They knows we be running," Janessa replied, frantically pulling on Audrianna's arm. "Hurry, hurry, hurry!"

As they scurried quickly near the end of the passage, the sound of running guards could be heard coming in the opposite direction. Both girls stopped dead in their tracks and looked for an alternate passageway. Janessa spotted a door a little further to her right.

"Gets with me in here," she quietly exclaimed. The two girls scrambled inside the door and shut it behind them. They both leaned against the inside of the door while the sound of the guards faded away.

"Shoo!" Audrianna sighed. "That was close!"

"Whats do we do now?" Janessa asked. The two girls looked to see what was in the room. Except for another door, the room was completely bare.

"It's be very cold in here," Janessa observed. "It's be colder here, than in the hall." "Let's see where this door leads," Audrianna suggested, grabbing a hold of the door handle and opening the door wide. Before the princess could fully assess what was on the other side, a large wrapped package fell forward, knocking Audrianna to the ground and pinning her to the floor.

"Help!" Audrianna screamed. "Help me! Get this big bag off me!" "Shush!" Janessa responded. "You needs to become quiet."

"If you don't roll this thing off me," Audrianna warned, "I'll be quiet forever in a few seconds."

"Janessa pushed the large wrapped package to one side, allowing Audrianna to gain enough leverage so she could help push it off her the rest of the way. Straddling the top of the heavy bag, Audrianna panted heavy, making steam clouds with her breath."

"That's be a not-light thing," Janessa remarked in broken Nadeau.

"You're not kidding," Audrianna replied. "It feels like a giant rock. Like a statue." "Be it a statue?" Janessa asked. Audrianna shrugged.

"Don't know," she said. "Let's see."

The princess tried to peel away the fabric wrappings from around the top of the package. The wrappings seemed to have been sealed together with some kind of sticky glue, making the unwrapping a gruelling task. Finally, Audrianna ran her fingers down the top of the so-called rock, to see if she could find a loose band on the wrapping, to pull and tear the packaging free. Finding a spot in the wrappings, the princess yanked open the bindings to see what was inside.

"Holy maggots!" she screamed. Janessa gazed past Audrianna to also see what was inside the wrappings.

"Where be the maggots?" the Andjety girl asked.

Henry and Jaako led the rest of the scouting party to the top of the ridge. As they peered over the top of the summit, the two men spotted the large mouth of a cave. It was Zymjai's palace. They both laid on their bellies while studying their next challenge. The cave had several pillars that were built up in the front, along with a stone front to close off the cave from the elements, and to secure the palace from intruders. There was no way to tell from the outside how extensive the interior of the palace was. Several Andjety sentries stood guard near the entrance to the witch's palace.

"Okay, Captain Jaako," Henry said, "What's our next move?"

Jaako took out his spy glass and surveyed the entrance, along with the Andjety guards. Rupp and the two ladies caught up with the two men, and sat alongside them. Lowering his glass, Jaako stroked his beard, thinking over their options. As he sat, silently contemplating, the sound of the ram's horn blared from inside the palace cave. All the sentries turned around, and ran inside the palace entrance.

"I would say our next move," Jaako declared, "is to follow the guards inside, and see what all the squaller is about."

"Whatever it is," Henry said, "I guarantee Ree is at the centre of it."

All five scouts scrambled to their feet and ran towards the palace doors. Upon entering, there was no one to be found past the entrance. Everyone but Castalia drew their swords as they passed the entryway. Castalia loaded a dart in the shaft of her crossbow. Carefully and slowly they made their way down one passageway, and up another. Several minutes went by without being spotted by any guards, officers, or the Witch.

As the elite forces of Audrianna's elite special forces searched for the captured princess, they all heard a little girl cry out, "Help! Help me! Get this big bag off me!"

"That voice sounds familiar," Henry whispered.

"From which corridor did it come from?" Rupp asked. They all listened intently, hoping for her to cry out again so they could figure out which direction her voice originated.

All was quiet.

"Are you sure it was Her Highness that shouted?" Jaako asked. "Holy maggots!" her voice echoed again.

"Oh, yeah," Henry replied. "It's her!"

"Down this way," Rozelle called, pointing to a door halfway

down an adjacent corridor. Henry walked up to the door, looked back at his armed compatriots, then burst through the door.

Inside he found Audrianna standing across from the little Andjety girl, with a large bundle laying in between them.

"Ree?" Henry called out.

"Horace!" she answered, running up to him and hugging him around the waist. "I'm so glad you're okay."

"Me okay?" he asked. "I came here to rescue you."

"Well," the princess replied, "I didn't get to see you escape your room in the castle." She hugged him again. "I was worried."

"Well, if it isn't the imposter princess," Rozelle announced, holding the blade of her sword up to Janessa's throat.

"I nots an imposter," Janessa called out. "I be her sister. We be sisters now." Rozelle lowered her blade.

"Sister?" she asked the princess. "What does she mean?"

"She means, she helped me escape," Audrianna explained. "I know what's going on.

I know that the king is not who he claims to be." "What do you know, Ree?" Henry asked.

"Look-look-look!" Janessa excitedly chanted, pointing to the wrapped bundle in between the two girls. The rescue party stared down at the opening of the wrappings that Audrianna had torn free.

"What on earth?" Jaako responded. "It can't be!" Henry remarked.

"Oh my," the two ladies chorused.

"There in the space of the opening of the wrappings was a face. It was the face of King Malcolm, the Merciful. The true king. The real Malcolm. He was dead, and his body was frozen, due to the frigid temperature within the castle—especially in the cold closet the girls discovered him in."

"If this is my father, who I witnessed the Witch kill," Henry deduced, "then who is the king that overtook Nadeau castle?"

"Look!" Rupp called to the others, pointing inside the closet that Malcolm's body was stored. Everyone walked to the closet and peered in. Inside the closet were several valuable trinkets and keepsakes. But most noticeable was a large painting sitting on the floor and leaning against the wall.

"Who is it?" Audrianna asked, poking her head past the others. "Grandfather Albert," Henry answered.

"Albert?" Audrianna asked incredulously.

"Yes," the imposter king answered from the hallway. Everyone in the room jumped. "And now that you know the truth, now you will pay the price." From behind the imposter came six guards, armed with spears and swords. Each guard grabbed one from the Nadeau group and bound their hands behind their backs.

"Take them to the palace dungeon," the imposter ordered.

The Andjety soldiers led the Nadeau captives down several corridors, each corridor colder than the last. Finally, they came to an iron door, similar to the one installed on Henry's room at Nadeau castle. Everyone, except Audrianna and Janessa were chained to the wall.

"Didn't I already dance this jig," Henry asked as they clasped the shackles to his wrists and ankles. Rupp was chained on his left side, while Jaako was secured on his right. Rozelle was chained on the other side of Jaako.

Audrianna looked at the four chained captives. Henry, Jaako, Rupp, and Rozelle.

Four.

"Um, Horace," Audrianna began to ask.

"Let it go, Ree," Henry replied, knowing exactly what bothered the princess. She nodded, then looked away.

Audrianna and Janessa were dragged to the front and stood before the false king.

"You will be my wife in the morning," the false king said to Audrianna. "And you," he said, pointing at Janessa, "you worthless, traitorous, slave girl. I will demand Lord Rolf beat you within an inch of your life. You will be wed to him, the day after tomorrow, and never see outside the palace walls again, for the rest of your life." Janessa's head dropped and her shoulders hunched. Tears began to drop to the floor and her body began to shake for fear.

"You are not the king," Audrianna shouted. "You are nothing but a fraud! You have no right to threaten my friend. My sister!" Janessa's head remained lowered, though her eyes looked up into Audrianna's, searching for courage and hope.

"Sister?" the Zymjai inquired, walking into the room from behind the false king. "Sister? There is only one person in this room who has a sister," she declared. "And it is not you." Audrianna scowled at the Witch, who by now had changed back into her Andjety uniform. Zymjai walked past the captive Nadeau rescue party, and stood directly in front of the princess.

"Who has a sister?" she asked the Witch. "I have a sister," the false king announced.

"Care to guess who?" the Witch asked Audrianna. The princess folded her arms and pursed her lips.

"You," she answered.

"That's right, my little caterpillar," the Witch congratulated.

"But how is it that you two are related," Audrianna asked, "you being Andjety, and 'make-believe Malcolm' looking so much like the true king?"

"I know why, Ree," Henry interjected. The Witch turned and walked over to the prince.

"Have you figured it out, Henry?" she mocked. "Do you know the truth, you worthless and spoiled child of privilege?"

"Yes," he calmly answered. "Not only are you two related, but, so am I?"

Everybody in the room began to look at each other, making puzzled faces at one another.

"Your Majesty?" Rozelle asked. "Go on," Zymjai prodded.

"Up until a few moments ago, I was still in the dark," he admitted. "But then, Ree uncovered the body of my father, the true king. Then, Rupp pointed out the stash of mementos in the closet, including the portrait of my father's father, King Albert the Aged."

"And?" the false king sneered from behind the Witch.

"And everybody in the kingdom knows that King Albert was a womaniser, something fierce. It is strongly believed that he fathered children with multiple maidens from multiple nations. Judging from the age of my half-uncle here, he must have started back when he was young and still a prince."

"True indeed," the Witch confirmed. "Your father Malcolm was merciful to his own people of Nadeau, but he had stolen almost half of the most fertile land from the Andjety. For the past several years I've built up my step-father's forces to try and one day overtake Nadeau, and restore what was once rightfully ours. However, not very many of our fighting men wanted to follow me into battle. I am young, and a woman. So, I sought an alternate plan. As fate would have it, I discovered Vynjoi, here, ploughing a field with a cantankerous donkey. Noticing how much he matched the appearance of king Malcolm, I investigated his origin, only to find out we were both related to King Albert. Therefore, I unhatched the plan right on the spot, and he agreed to help."

"So where do I fit in on your scheme?" Audrianna asked the Witch.

"Neither one of us are Nadeau," Vynjoi answered. "In order to legitimise our takeover of your country, I must marry a crowned princess, otherwise it's all just a ruse." "But you didn't count on Malcolm betrothing me to a ten-year-old," Henry replied. "No," the false king answered. "It definitely complicated the whole plan. We had to either wait six years for the princess to mature…"

"Or change the circumstances to where her age wasn't an issue," Rozelle interrupted. "Exactly," Zymjai responded. "Tomorrow morning, Vynjoi will marry the little princess, consummate their bond, and thus giving control of Nadeau over to the Andjety."

"What's about me," Janessa softly asked, her head still bowed. "Why does I have to marry Lord Rolf? What does that do?"

"Nothing really," Vynjoi confessed. "You and Rolf were merely decoys to draw the prince to attack the castle and thus commit treason. As far as marrying Rolf, well, he prefers his lovers to be young and tender. Something about them being more manageable."

"You people are sickening!" Henry angrily bellowed. "You would destroy a child's life for your own purposes and pleasure?"

"Don't lecture me about destroying a child's life," the Witch countered. "Training a ten-year-old to swordfight and kill is robbing the innocence from them just as much as marriage."

"Where is Rolf, anyway?" Rozelle asked.

"Laying down in his chamber room," the Witch answered. "He seems to be nursing a migraine from a head wound." Audrianna and Janessa exchanged glances, causing both to grin mischievously.

"Come ladies," the false king commanded. "You must prepare for your morning nuptials." A separate guard grabbed each of the little girls forcibly by the arm and pulled them out of the room, and down two adjacent corridors. They soon came to a flight of stairs leading up to a second level of the cave.

"Take these children to their room," Vynjoi ordered, "and 'both of you' stand guard.

Keep a sharp eye out. These girls are devious to the core."

"As you command, Your Majesty," the guards complied. The imposter king turned and quickly strode up the flight of stairs. The guards then pushed the two captives to the end of the corridor, then turned to the right. As they turned, Castalia emerged from the shadows, pointing her crossbow at the men.

"It's important for you to know that my crossbow can pin a fly to the wall at fifty paces." The guards froze. "At this range, my accuracy is nothing but impeccable." The men released their grip on the girls, who quickly ran behind Castalia. "If you please," she commanded, "I would like for you barbarians to take me to free the prince and my friends." The men raised their hands, turned towards the dungeon, and led the ladies back from whence they came.

"Does not the prince be one of your friends," Janessa asked.

"Not really," Castalia remarked. "But he comes with the package."

As they marched down the passageway, they passed the flight of stairs, from which Vynjoi, the imposter, appeared.

"Here now," the false king cried out, "Where do you men think you're taking those children?"

"Gets you away, Your Majesty," one of the guards yelled. The false king darted up the stairs as Castalia shot her crossbow at him. The dart missed Vynjoi, who ran up the stairs and out of sight before Castalia could reload her crossbow. One of the guards disappeared down the corridor, while the other pulled a dagger from his belt intending to stab the Lady in Waiting.

As the Andjety lunged towards Castalia, Audrianna grabbed hold of the man's wrist and tried to disarm him. However, the soldier was much stronger than the little princess, and they stood facing each other, wrestling with the dagger back and forth. Castalia took the butt of her crossbow and struck the Andjety on the back of the head. The soldier let go of the knife and fell unconscious upon the floor.

"Look, Cassie!" Audrianna exclaimed, holding up the Andjety weapon. "I've got another dagger!" The little princess tucked it in her belt, at the small of her back, like the one before. From the direction the first guard escaped, came the sound of approaching soldiers.

"Time to go!" Cassie declared, placing her hands on the backs of the two ten-year- old girls, and gently prodding them to run. As the Lady in Waiting led them towards the mouth of the cave, the approaching army ran closely up behind them, shouting and cursing, like a raging torrent of water. Still several meters away from the entrance, it appeared the Andjety were going to overtake them.

Suddenly, several arrows came zipping through the doors from the outside, and striking the attacking Andjety. The Witch's army ceased their attack, as they watched their prisoners escape to the outside.

As Castalia, Audrianna, and Janessa ran out the door of the

palace, everyone cheered to see the princess once again, alive and well. A flank of her Special Forces swarmed, protecting them from the attacking Andjety. Several old men were armed with warm coats and blankets, which they used to bundle the girls from the elements.

Multiple groups of Andjety soldiers came teeming out the mouth of the cave. As far as the Nadeau Special Forces, the swordsmen, under Balen's command, came charging in front, followed by spearmen, then the archers. Castalia joined the ranks of the archers and directed them to pick off the most valiant of the Andjety soldiers, giving the retired, feeble swordsmen a fighting chance. When too many Andjety swordsmen began to horde the front lines, Olivia commanded the spearmen to thrust their spears past Balen's swordsmen, keeping the enemy at a safe distance.

Prince Rolf came bounding out of the cave and took charge of the Andjety fighters. With only one eye, he had to stand at an angle so as to see what was happening on the front lines. However, his torn and bandaged ear, was on the opposite side of his head. When he needed to hear better, he had to turn the other direction. A young man stood next to him, and held him upright, in case all the turning made him dizzy.

As the battle waged on, Ethlyn released her falcon to distract the enemy forces. When Luella would hear Rolf shout commands, she would swoop down and ruffle him.

"Somebody kill that stupid bird," he screamed. Several arrows were launched in her direction, but through the entire battle, Luella remained unscathed.

Audrianna and Janessa had been ushered back behind the ranks of the archers. The princess led Janessa to a nearby ledge from where they cheered the Nadeau fighters on. The fighting was brutal, and many Nadeau fighters suffered mortal wounds. However, Audrianna's elite fighters fought with valiant honour as the Andjety began to be defeated. From a hidden opening above the cave appeared the Witch. She had a sword and sheath belted to each hip, and carried a crossbow in her hands. Intent on singling out a courageous warrior to kill with her crossbow, her eyes fell on Audrianna, standing above the teeming armies. Knowing her plans had been grossly thwarted, she decided to take vengeance on the unsuspecting little girl. Just before the Witch could shoot her deadly dart, Janessa spotted the Witch pointing her weapon at them. Looking about, Janessa couldn't see anywhere that she could push her friend out of the way of the impending dart. As the Witch pulled the trigger, Janessa hugged Audrianna, and turned her body, exchanging places with the princess. In a split second, the dart pierced thc little girl in the back. Audrianna quickly placed her arms around Janessa, and slowly lowered her to the ground.

"Sister!" Janessa cried. "It hurts! It hurts! It hurts!" Audrianna immediately began to weep over her friend.

"Just lie still," she ordered. "Be still and I will find someone to help." Janessa laid on her side on the rocky ledge they had previously cheered the Nadeau army. Audrianna knelt next to Janessa and put her head in her lap. The princess stroked her friend's short hair as she softly talked to her, gazing into her frightened face.

From down below, Balen noticed Audrianna kneeling next to the Andjety girl. He didn't know about their kindled friendship, but he could see how upset the princess was. He quickly made his way up to where they were. As he approached, Audrianna looked up at Balen with tears streaming down her face.

"Help her," she begged. "Please. She's my friend."

Balen grabbed hold of the princess and moved her out of the way. He examined the wound and the amount of blood the Andjety girl had lost. Janessa's eyes began to slowly close. Balen looked up at Audrianna, standing beside him, wearing a fearful expression. "You need to leave, Anna. Right now!" he ordered so firmly, he seemed angry at Audrianna. She took several steps back, but continued to watch on, until Olivia walked up. Before Olivia could scold her, Audrianna turned around and looked up at the hidden ingress above the main entrance to the palace.

Anger gripped her heart. She clinched her fists. No one else was going to die! She was determined to return to the dungeon, free her husband, and her other three friends. She was determined to bring an end to everything the Witch had started. Kidnapping. Slavery. Child marriages. Bloodshed. It all had to stop! It was all going to stop!

CHAPTER 27

As Audrianna entered the secret door atop the main entrance to the palace, she found herself on the second level of the palace. Torches lined the halls, lighting the path from the door, to the stairs leading down to the dungeon.

She had no sword to fight with, only a dagger she had wrestled free from an Andjety guard. She was smaller than anyone else and weaker. But she was green-eyed, left- handed, and her brown hair had already grown out a bit. Although nobody believed those features made any difference, the fact was—she was different.

She was different than she was the day her parents died. She was different than she was the day she was coronated. She was not a helpless and weak ten-year-old child. She was a highly-trained killer. A devious little mouse. The crowned princess. Audrianna, the tenderhearted.

As she marched her way towards the dungeon, head up, shoulders squared, four palace guards spotted her. Pulling out their swords, they made their way towards the princess. As they approached her, she announced her intentions.

"Take me to my future husband, Vynjoi," she commanded, looking the guards directly in the eyes. The guards stopped, startled by her demanding tenacity. Grabbing her by the arm, the guards led her down the stairs, then down the passageway, to the large iron door of the dungeon. After knocking three times, the iron door opened, and the four guards brought the princess inside.

There on the east wall was chained Rupp, Henry, Jaako, and Rozelle. The chains they were shackled to had been shortened, forcing them to remain standing, with their arms above their heads. Facing them was the false king, Vynjoi, as well as the Witch, Zymjai.

"Look what fortune has brought me," the Witch declared.

"Fortune brought you nothing," Audrianna replied, her shoulders still squared and a scowl across her face. "I came on my own."

"And why did you come?" Zymjai asked.

"You killed my friend," the princess replied. "And my parents, my family. You've taken my betrothed, and chained him to the wall. And you intend to execute him. Am I right?"

"Indeed," the Witch responded. "It is all true." Audrianna nodded her head. "You've taken everything away from me," the princess replied, "including the

kingdom of Nadeau. I am empty. I have nothing more to give, and nothing else to lose."

"That is not true," Vynjoi remarked. "You still have your life to give. We can still kill you."

"But you won't," Audrianna replied.

"Really?" Zymjai asked. "What makes you so certain I won't take my sword and strike you down, right here and now." The Witch pulled her sword halfway out of its sheath.

"Because," the princess answered, "You want control of Nadeau. I am the only key you have, to get it."

"Ree," Henry scolded.

"If you kill me," the princess continued, "the Nadeau army will stop at nothing until they hunt each of you down and kill you."

"Possibly," the Witch agreed, her face displaying no fear.

"But, if Vynjoi marries me," Audrianna offered, "then no matter how much they protest, Nadeau and Andjety will be one united nation. So, which choice will you make?"

"Ree," Henry scolded again. "Your Highness," Rozelle begged.

"This won't end well," Jaako proclaimed.

Audrianna walked up to Vynjoi and took his hand. The imposter king withdrew his hand from the little girl's grip.

"Don't you dare twist my hand again, naughty child."

"I'm not," Audrianna announced, bending down to one knee and holding up her hands in compliance. "I am offering myself to you, in exchange for my friends' freedom."

"No, Ree," Henry commanded. "Don't you dare hand yourself and the nation over to these ruthless fiends. Our lives are not worth the exchange. My life is not worth the loss of our people's freedom. Let me die! But do not give Nadeau over to the Andjety." "Please," Audrianna begged, "Your Majesty." She then bowed her head, and began

to softly cry. Tears trickled down her cheeks, and on down her neck. Vynjoi looked on as the princess raised her head, showing that she was completely earnest.

At that moment, an Andjety soldier came bounding into the room. His face was flustered, his clothes were saturated with sweat, and he had several superficial wounds on his arms and face.

"Your Excellency," he called out.

"Yes," both Zymjai and Vynjoi chorused. The soldier looked back and forth between the two, then looked directly at Vynjoi.

"Our army is retreating, sir." he reported. "The Nadeau forces are pushing their way inside the palace. We are trying to keep them outside, but they are determined."

"They are after the princess," Vynjoi remarked, turning to look at his half-sister. "They won't stop!"

"Then," Zymjai commanded, "You—STOP—them!" Vynjoi walked towards the messenger, then looked at the guards.

"Come!" he ordered the four guards. "I'll show you how to defeat a bunch of old, obsolete, Nadeau swordsmen." Vynjoi and his soldiers briskly charged out the door.

Zymjai walked closer to Audrianna and placed the tip of her fingernail under the princess's chin. Lifting the girl's head so they could look into each other's faces, Audrianna turned her head away from the Witch's fingernail, bowed her head, and began to cry.

"Don't be sad, little one," the Witch replied. "You are doing what is right. Offering yourself in exchange for the lives of your friends."

"Please don't hurt them," the princess wept, "I've lost everybody who is important to me. Please don't take them away from me." She began to wail, tears streaming down her face.

At first, Henry thought that Audrianna might have been pretending, like she did multiple times while they were on the run. However, her tale that she was play-acting was that she would cock her head to one side and look at you out the corner of her eyes. But this time, Audrianna looked straight into the Witch's face as she wailed. The Witch herself knew that she had the princess under her control.

"Poor little Audrianna," the Witch replied. "Why would you care about any of these horrible people?"

"I love them," Audrianna answered.

"You love them?" the Witch asked incredulously. "How can you love those that snatched you from your home. Betrothed you to a monster like Henry who cares about no one but himself. He spanked you with his scabbard, then cut off your beautiful hair. Your ladies-in-waiting took care of you merely to get rewarded. Lord Rupp took away your childhood innocence and trained you to be a killer. Even your friends, Balen and Olivia used you for their own purpose of returning to the castle, and even Olivia beat you with a switch." Audrianna stared straight into Zymjai's face, tears still streaming down her cheeks.

"How do you know that?" Henry asked the witch.

"Poor Audrianna," the witch repeated. "So mistreated. And only ten—years—old!" The princess sniffled as the tears from her eyes mixed with the mucus running from her nose. She wiped the salty mixture from around her mouth, not once taking her eyes off the Witch. "Don't worry about them," she told the princess. "What have they done for you?" Audrianna began to nod her head.

"Nothing," she softly replied.

"That's right," Zymjai reiterated. "They've given you nothing. They've left you empty."

"And I'm only ten," the princess said, staring blankly into Zymjai's eyes. "Ten years old."

Henry, Rupp, Jaako and Rozelle all looked on with dismay. The Witch had her. She had beguiled the princess. She was under the control of the war empress. They watched helplessly as Zymjai reached behind her back, and slowly pulled a knife from her belt.

"Ree," Henry shouted. Zymjai quickly brought the knife around to her front. But, before she could plunge it into Audrianna, she herself felt a sudden sharp pain radiate from the lower middle of her chest. She and the princess had not taken their eyes off one another, and Audrianna continued to stare, flat affect.

Zymjai looked down, and saw an Andjety dagger partially thrust into her middle. She then looked back into the princess's face. Audrianna's widened-eyes narrowed, and her flat expressionless mouth began to smirk. Where did the princess get that knife?

The Witch quickly grabbed hold of the dagger's hilt to prevent the princess from plunging it deeper. But, Audrianna was just short enough to have the right leverage and lean into the Witch and push the knife deeper into her body.

"No!" the Witch angrily scolded. She grabbed Audrianna's wrists attempting to pry her hands free. But the months of intense training strengthened her arms, and her hands, and her fingers. The princess pushed the blade even deeper. The Witch felt the knife penetrate a vital organ inside her. Her arms froze. Pain shot from her chest, down her arms, and down to her feet.

"No!" she pleaded. "Please, no!" Her face went pale. A look of horror swept over it. Audrianna's immediate instinct was to stop hurting her. But her mind raced back to what Mason had told her. She couldn't stop. Zymjai was exactly who he was referring

to. If she was to yield, the Witch would quickly turn on her and kill her.

Audrianna's mind then raced back to Janessa. Then to King Malcolm. Then to Pitt.

Then to her own family. No, she couldn't stop. She had to finish what she started.

Sliding the blade of the dagger up to the hilt, the princess reached up and grabbed the Witch by the leather strap slung across her body. She pulled the fearful Witch in her direction until their faces almost touched one another.

"I may only be a little girl," Audrianna remarked, grabbing the sword's handle with both hands. "But I'm still—a bitch!"

She immediately twisted the dagger for all she was worth. Zymjai—the war Witch— fell limp to the ground. Dead.

"Your Royal Highness!" Rupp and Rozelle shouted in victory. "Holy maggots!" Henry exclaimed.

"That's our warrior princess!" Jaako called out.

Audrianna leaned over the Witch's dead body and yanked the set of keys from around her neck. There was a key for the dungeon door, and a smaller key for her friends' shackles.

Running to the door, she slammed it with a loud, CLANG! She then stuck the large brass key in the keyhole, and locked the door.

"Quick, Ree!" Henry shouted. Audrianna turned to face the prince, and saw him lift his foot against the wall, making a step from his knee. The little girl ran towards her betrothed, put one foot on his knee, then stood on his leg with both feet. She wrapped her arms around his neck, looking in his eyes, face-to-face.

"I am so proud of you, Ree!" Henry said. "You defeated the Witch!" Audrianna beamed a wide grin.

"I have something for you," she announced.

"What do you have?" he asked. The princess leaned in, close to Henry, and kissed him on the lips. Henry's eyes bugged open, but he couldn't push her off with his hands chained in the air.

"My first kiss," she answered, beaming and blushing at the same time.

"You sweet little dear," Henry smiled. Audrianna immediately leaned in and kissed him again.

"Okay," Henry replied urgently, "Use the Witch's keys and unlock our fetters." Audrianna leaned in a third time and kissed him again.

"Stop that!" he scolded. The princess giggled as she brought the key up to Henry's wrists. At that moment, three loud knocks were heard, coming from the opposite side of the door.

"Uh-oh!" Audrianna exclaimed.

"Quickly," Henry commanded her, "unlock Lord Rupp's shackles first."

"Lord Rupp?" she asked. Three more knocks resounded from the other side of the door.

"Hurry," Henry directed. Rupp raised his foot from the floor to the wall, also creating a step from his knee. Audrianna stepped from Henry, over to Rupp. The sound of banging, rattling, and arguing could be heard from the other side of the iron door. Audrianna quickly unlocked the shackle from around Rupp's right wrist, then swung over to his left wrist and unlocked that shackle. She then jumped down and removed the restraints from around his ankles.

"We need weapons," Jaako declared. "We have no swords to defend ourselves." Immediately, the large iron door of the dungeon unlocked with a CLANK, and the door swung open. Rupp shook the blood back into his wrists from being elevated for so long. "You want a sword?" he asked, walking towards the open door, "I'll get each of you

a sword." The four Andjety guards looked around the room and spotted the Witch, dead on the floor.

"What's happened?" one of the guards asked. "Dids you kill our queen?"

"Nope," Rupp answered. "We had our ten-year-old kill her. That's how insignificant we find your kingdom."

One of the guards pulled his sword from its sheath. Rupp opened his arms wide and presented the fact that he was un-armed. Undaunted, the angry Andjety thrust his sword at the Nadeau captain, who dodged the sword, but caught the man by the forearm and quickly disarmed him. Kicking him out of the way, Rupp used the newly acquired sword to deflect the sword from the second Andjety. After clanging their blades a couple times, Rupp slashed him in the heart, and took his sword. Audri-anna hurriedly unlocked the fetters and shacles from the others while Rupp continued to fight the guards. The third Andjety thrust his sword in Rupp's direction, to which Rupp slashed him as well. Having floored the third assailant, Rupp kicked the sol-dier's sword in the air and caught it in his right hand, now having a sword in his left hand, and two in his right. The fourth soldier rushed Rupp from behind, and swung his blade at Rupp's head. Rupp ducked and thrust his left sword into the man's chest. As the final soldier fell dead to the floor, Rupp grabbed the sword from the Andjety's hand. Rupp stood up straight, each hand bearing two swords.

"Your Majesty," Rupp declared, tossing a sword in Henry's direction. He then tossed a sword at Jaako, who examined the blade and hilt of the Andjety weapon.

"He's the Captain of Your Majesty's guard?" Jaako asked the prince. "Indeed, he is," Henry confirmed.

"Excellent choice," Jaako conceded. Audrianna finished un-locking Rozelle's shackles, then stood before the four Nadeau leaders, her hands behind her back. Her face was dirty, and blood from the Witch covered the front of her clothes. She wielded the dagger in her hand like a warrior, rather than a little girl.

Jaako stepped in front of the princess, then fell to one knee. He bowed his head low to the ground and held out his hand in a gesture to ask for Audrianna's. She held out her hand, to which Jaako took it in his, kissed it, then touched it to his forehead. He then lowered himself to a kneeling position and looked into the princess's face.

"I will be loyal to you, Your Highness," he said, "till the day I die."

CHAPTER 28

Henry and Rupp peered out the door of the dungeon, looking both ways down the corridor. Jaako and Rozelle came bounding out behind them, with Audrianna in the rear. As the princess pushed her way past Jaako and Rozelle, her lady-in-waiting grabbed her by her stubby braid.

"You need to stay in the back, Your Highness," Rozelle reprimanded. "I can fight," Audrianna replied. "I'm not afraid."

"Of course you're not," Jaako responded. "That's why we need you in the rear. We need you to watch our backs." Audrianna grinned at Jaako, then spun around and swung her dagger back and forth at imaginary assailants. She wore a determined look on her face, keeping an eye on the corridor behind them.

The five former captives scurried through the passageways of Zymjai's Palace, making their way towards the outside. As they rounded the corner, close to the exit leading outside, the Nadeau warriors came face to face with Vynjoi and four Andjety soldiers.

"The Witch is dead!" Henry announced. Vynjoi's eyes widened with fear, and his countenance dropped. The soldiers gripped their weapons tightly.

"Honour your queen's memory," Vynjoi commanded. The soldiers rushed the Prince and his comrades. As the four Nadeau adults engaged the soldiers, Vynjoi turned and ran down another corridor. Audrianna quickly ran past the sword fighting and pursued the fleeing Andjety noble.

"Ree," Henry called after. "Ree, STOP!" The princess ignored his scolding and continued pursuit. "That girl listens to no one," he remarked to the assailant he was fighting.

"What's do I care of a stupid child?" the soldier asked. "I hopes she gets dead." A look of anger shot across Henry's face.

"You first," he replied, thrusting his sword a few more times until he could counter at the Andjety's blindside. Slashing his opponent through the heart, Henry ran towards the corridor that he saw the princess disappear down. Turning around, he reviewed the success and progress of the others. Roselle had dispatched the guard she was fighting and started to make her way towards Henry. Jaako over-matched his opponent, but he made great sport at harassing him. As Rupp slashed the Andjety he was fighting, he walked past Jaako.

"Come on, Dog," he said. "Either run him off or run him through. We need to assist Her Highness." Jaako nodded his head, then grabbed his opponent's sword-bearing wrist.

"Friend," Jaako remarked, "I hope you kiss your woman better than you fight. I could have killed you five minutes ago. Maybe you should just run home to your mama." Still holding the Andjety's wrist, Jaako swatted the man's rump with the blade of his sword. The young soldier yelped, then ran out the door of the palace, leaving his sword with Jaako.

"Not everyone is cut out for sword fighting," Rozelle commented. The four of them hurried after the princess in hopes of catching up with her before Vynjoi harmed her.

As they made their way through the labyrinth of passageways, two corridors converged on each other. Sitting atop an unlit torch sat Ethlyn's falcon, Luella. Rozelle pointed out the falcon to the others.

"If Lu is in here, that could only mean one thing," Henry observed. "That Ethlyn is nearby?" Rozelle asked.

"Well," Henry replied, "That too. But I was meaning Rolf. Lu seems to be intent on hunting that poor soul down until she sits on his cold grave."

"It's true," Rupp added. "Which means we need to be doubly careful. With the Witch dead, they will feel as if they have nothing to lose."

"They don't," Jaako replied. "It's over for them. We need to find Her Highness before they do. They will take vengeance on her the moment they lay eyes on her."

Rozelle tried to coax the falcon to leave the perch and come with her. However, Luella was not interested in leaving without her true handler. Before the four of them could get beyond earshot, though, Ethlyn's tongue clicking could be heard. The falcon leaped from her perch, and flew back down the adjacent passageway.

"Ethel?" Rozelle called down the dark tunnel. "Are you alone?"

"Rose!" the answer echoed back. "Cassie and I are headed your way. Along with Lu."

"Hurry," Rozelle shouted. "Her Highness is in danger." Both ladies-in-waiting emerged from the shadows and into the light of the torches.

"What else could she be?" Castalia asked. "That's the theme of her life."

Ethlyn wore a heavy leather glove on her right hand, along with Luella perched atop of it. Castalia carried her crossbow in her hand, with a quiver slung across her back. There was evidence of fatigue in the faces of the ladies, due to the battle they had just left.

"Is Rolf somewhere in these caves?" Rupp inquired.

"Yes," Ethlyn answered. "As the battle was winding down, and the remaining Andjety fell to their knees and surrendered, Rolf took off as fast as he could. I released Luella to track him and help us find which way he went. This is the direction she led us."

"The princess is down this way too," Rupp announced. "We need to find her before Rolf or the false king do."

The six leaders of the Nadeau forces hurried as fast as their eyes would allow them. The torches that lined the walls of the tunnels became sparser the further they made their way deep into the cave.

Henry again became anxious for fear that Audrianna was missing, running ahead of them.

"Ree!" he called out with a desperate voice. "Ree, where are you?" Silence.

"Your Highness?" all three ladies chorused. Silence.

Soon the group rounded a corner of the tunnel only to find that the rest of the passage was absent of any torches, or any light. The group briefly discussed whether they should retreat a bit and acquire one of the torches they had already passed. But Henry was frantic that Audrianna had gotten herself into trouble once again, and unwilling to retrace his steps.

As the rescue party felt their way down the darkened tunnel, a light flickered in the distance. As they approached the light, they began to realise it was the glow of a campfire. It was still quite a distance away, but Rupp encouraged the group to unsheathe their swords, and for Castalia to load her crossbow.

"I'm not sure if we will find Vynjoi, or Rolf, or both," Rupp warned, "but be prepared for anything. Okay?"

"Okay," Castalia and Ethlyn chorused. "Right," Henry and Rozelle answered. "Got it," Jaako responded.

"Me too," resounded the voice of a little girl. "Ree?" Henry called out in the darkness. "Horace," she answered.

"Where have you been, young lady?" he asked, once again mimicking a responsible parent.

"Shh!" Audrianna hushed Henry, indicating he needed to lower his voice. "I've been right here, waiting for the rest of you to catch up," she softly answered.

"Did you hear us call you?" Henry asked.

"Yes, but I couldn't answer back, or the Andjety king would

hear me." "He's not a king," Henry scoffed. "He's an imposter."

"Alright," Rupp replied. "Is everybody ready to nab us a fugitive?" Everybody quietly gave their affirmative responses.

"Yes."

"Ready." "Let's do this."

The group slowly and quietly made their way closer to the glowing light, to what appeared to be a small room in the very far end of the cave. The sounds of arguing could

be heard. Perhaps Rolf and Vynjoi were both there. Vynjoi could be heard muttering profanities and curses against the Nadeau people, but especially against the Prince and Princess. As the group finally made it to the mouth of the secret room, they peered in to find Vynjoi pacing back and forth in the room. In the centre of the room was a large bonfire. The room was comfortably warm compared to the rest of the cave, the palace, and the general climate of the area. On the far side of the room was an opening to the cave. The opening led to the side of the Andjety mountain facing Nadeau castle.

Vynjoi seemed to be talking to no one but himself, and arguing about how their plan went awry. Henry looked back and motioned for the group to follow close after him.

"It's over Vynjoi," Henry declared. "The six of us have come to take you prisoner." "And what?" Vynjoi angrily replied. "To be taken back to Nadeau and be hanged? I would rather die in my own cave, then hang in your miserable country."

"If that is your choice," Henry countered. The Prince entered the warm room, pointing his sword at the imposter of his late father. Rozelle bounded in the room and circled around the other side, attempting to come at Vynjoi from behind. As Henry and Vynjoi clashed their swords together, Audrianna and the other four raced into the room. The princess tried to attack from the front left of Vynjoi. As she thrust her sword towards the false king, Vynjoi grabbed her wrist and pulled her into his arms. Both Henry and Rozelle looked on helplessly. Vynjoi walked backwards towards the mouth of the cave. "Maybe once we rid ourselves of the pesky child, we can get down to business,"

Vynjoi commented.

"That girl is my business," Henry replied. Vynjoi grinned as he turned to the side, and tossed the princess over the side.

"NO!" Rozelle screamed. Both she and Henry raced to the edge and to see what happened to Audrianna. About five meters below the precipice, a rapidly flowing stream of water rushed by, and off a shallow falls. Nearly a hundred yards from the cave, the falls spilled into a pool of freezing water.

As the two surveyed the situation, Rupp, Jaako, Castalia, and Ethlyn engaged Vynjoi in battle. Vynjoi turned to a bundle laying to the side of the cave, and extracted a large wool blanket. Throwing the blanket over the fire, the imposter jumped on top of the blanket and stomped out the fire. Immediately the cavern went dark.

Henry realised any chance of saving Audrianna depended on him jumping into the stream, following her over the falls, and retrieving her from the frigid pool of water below. He looked back at Rozelle, then turned back and jumped into the streaming water. Rozelle quickly followed after him. Back and forth they both bounced against the rocks as well as the shallow bottom of the stream. Within seconds, the two of them plummeted off the falls and into the pool of frozen water.

As for the ones facing off with Vynjoi, smoke billowed from the campfire, choking their breathing and stinging their eyes. Vynjoi, wrapping his face in a cloth, was impervious to the stinging of the smoke. Drawing his sword, he began to swing at the blinded Nadeau party. Rupp was the first to be struck, slashed in the arm, then in his leg. He fell back and called Jaako to relieve him.

"Over here, Dog!" Rupp called out. "The imposter is in this direction. Jaako stumbled in the direction of his voice, his free arm covering his eyes to reduce the amount of stinging. As he blindly swung his sword, Jaako made contact with Vynjoi with a TWANG, but missed him when he tried to strike a second time. Vynjoi thrust his sword towards Jaako and sliced him in the side, causing him to retreat towards the wall of the cave, tripping over Rupp."

"I'm down," Jaako called out. Both Castalia and Ethlyn realised that Vynjoi had an advantage, already taken down two skilled swordsmen. Neither one of the ladies were anywhere close to being skilled with a sword, but Ethlyn knew that Castalia had one more skill Vynjoi had not counted on.

Henry landed in the pool and immediately started to search for the young princess in the dark and cold waters. Rozelle also landed near Henry and made her way to dry ground. Thrashing about the water, Henry at first could not find Audrianna, until he spotted a huddled mass clinging to a large rock. Not being able to distinguish if it was the princess or not, Henry waded through the frigid water towards the dark image. His hands began to go numb. As he reached the huddled mass, he pulled it towards him, unable to feel what it was or who it was. But indeed, it was Audrianna as he suspected. She was alive, and awake, but so cold, she was unresponsive.

"Ree?" he shouted at her. No response.

"Look at me, Ree!" he commanded.

No response. She laid in his arms shivering. Her breathing laboured and shallow. "Stay awake, Ree," he demanded. "Listen to me, and don't fall asleep."

Vynjoi slowly walked towards the corridor leading to the maze of caverns. It was where he last saw Ethlyn and Castalia. As he walked closer to them, he swung his sword against the jagged rock wall of the cave, creating sparks with a loud CHING!

"Where are those tender ladies?" he mocked. CHING! "They couldn't possibly know how to wield a sword, could they?" CHING! CHING!

"Cassie," Ethlyn replied.

"I can't," Castalia answered. "I don't want to hit the other men."

"Rupp. Jaako," Ethlyn announced. "Call out for Cassie!" Castalia raised her loaded crossbow, one hand under the shaft, the other on the trigger. The end of the crossbow pointed straight in the air.

"Here," Rupp shouted.

"Here," Jaako answered, not certain why Castalia needed a roll call.

"Come here, Cassie," Vynjoi sneered and jeered. "Come and I will show you how to die like a man."

As he taunted the Lady in Waiting, Castalia isolated the echoing from the cave, and where her comrades reported their whereabouts. Her eyes stung, and the smoke choked her. She thought she had located where the king's half-brother was standing, but needed him to speak one—more—time.

"Do I frighten you, little maid?" he asked.

Castalia immediately dropped the end of her crossbow and fired. The sound of the dart zipping through the air was suddenly stifled with the sound of the dart entering flesh and meat. A gurgling grunt was the last sound Vynjoi made as he died.

"No," Castalia remarked. "I'm not frightened in the least."

Henry slowly climbed from the frigid water towards Rozelle. He cradled the little princess in his arms. Her lips had turned blue. The tips of her fingers were blue. Her breathing was less laboured, but shallower.

"Help me, Rose," he begged. "Help her!" Rozelle grabbed up Audrianna from Henry's arms and carried her a few feet from the water's edge and laid her on the ground. Henry climbed out of the water, his feet also numb from the icy water.

"We've got to get her warm," Rozelle said. "Warm clothes and a warm fire. Neither of which we have."

"Then we'll keep going until they become available," Henry desperately replied. He picked up his shivering betrothed and raced down the steep embankment, hoping to come across a village or farm. A house. Any house. They would have clothing, or blankets, a stove, or a fireplace. Whatever they could find would be a thousand times better than what they had.

Both Henry and Rozelle made their way down the side of the mountain, complicated with the fact that Henry could barely feel his feet, much less the lower half of his legs. He stumbled a few times, falling to his knees on the rocky terrain, but protecting Audrianna in his arms. With great difficulty, the Prince wrestled back to his feet, then carried his betrothed down to the edge of a valley.

In the distance, the two spotted flickering lights faintly through the trees. Where there was light, there was fire. Fire meant warmth, and warmth came with blankets. Hopefully.

A mile passed. Two miles.

The feeling came back to Henry's feet as he raced towards the house. Faster and faster he ran, looking down at Audrianna to make sure her eyes had not closed. Rozelle ran behind him, trying her best to keep up, but halfway through the second mile, she lagged behind.

As Henry approached the Andjety farmhouse, he looked down into Audrianna's face. Her eyes shut right.

"Ree, wake up," he called. He shook her as he ran. "Ree! Open your eyes! Ree, you need to open your eyes and stay awake!"

No response. Her breathing had all but stopped. She stopped shaking or shivering.

Henry ran for all he was worth towards the front door of the house. Every ounce of energy he had was given to entering the house and warming his friend. As he stepped on the small porch, instead of knocking and asking to come inside, he briskly walked up to the door, and kicked it in. The thin fragile door broke in half. Startled, an old man jumped from his chair to confront the intruder.

"I am Prince Henry of Nadeau," he announced. "Forgive my abrupt intrusion, but my little girl fell into icy cold water, and is dying. I need to warm her beside your fire, and I need warm blankets immediately."

"Nadeau?" was the old man's response.

"BLANKETS!" Henry shouted. "Gets to me blankets!" The old man quickly ran into the next room. Henry knew the princess's wet clothes were preventing her from warming up, so he immediately started to strip all her clothes off. Rozelle should have been the one to undress the princess, but she had fallen behind, and the princess's life was hanging in the balance. There was no time for social propriety.

As the old man returned with several blankets, he also handed Henry several wash rags. Henry took them in his hand, not sure what the man expected him to do with them. As he stared at the rags in his hand, the man reached above the fire, and removed a hanging kettle. Inside was hot water. The man took one of rags from Henry and dipped it in the hot water and placed the rag back in his hand. The man then silently motioned for Henry to rub the hot cloth over Audrianna's body to warm her.

Henry rubbed the cloth over her face until it started turning pink again, then rubbed her chest and stomach. He dipped the rag a second time and rubbed it over her back, then her arms and then spent considerable time warming her hands and fingers. The prince, having removed her cold, wet pants, rubbed her legs, feet and toes. The old man then held up a blanket against the heat of the fire. As Henry finished undressing and warming the princess, the man walked over and wrapped the little girl in the blanket, the warm side against her body. Henry sat on the floor in front of the fire and held Audrianna in his arms.

By this time, Rozelle had made it to the farmhouse. Seeing the dilapidated door hanging in the doorway at the front of the house, she knew she had arrived at the correct place. Walking straight inside, she startled the old resident again.

"Prince Henry?" she hesitantly asked. The old man pointed towards the room with the fireplace. Lady Rozelle entered the room to see Henry holding the quiet princess in his arms. He rocked her back and forth in his arms, like a mother would rock her baby. Periodically, he placed his hand over her mouth to check her breathing.

Rozelle, reached her hand into the blanket and felt Audrianna's temperature. Although she wasn't as cold as she was when Henry fished her out of the pool, her temperature had not yet risen to a person's normal temperature. Rozelle held out her arms to take the princess from Henry, and relieve him from holding her.

"No," he answered. "I want to hold her." Rozelle was taken aback by his response. "I want to be the one she sees when she opens her eyes."

"Why?" she softly asked, looking straight in his face.

"Because," he answered her, hesitating before fully allowing it to spill from his mouth. "She's my friend. I love her." Rozelle smiled, then scooted herself beside Henry. The Lady in Waiting presumptuously put one hand on the prince's shoulder, then reached around and rested her other arm around the princess. The three of them huddled in front of the fire, while the Andjety resident quietly returned to his seat behind them.

CHAPTER 29

Castalia and Ethlyn nursed the wounds of Rupp and Jaako before leaving the cavern room. Castalia worked at stopping the bleeding in Jaako's side. Having no bandages, she grabbed hold of Jaako's shirt sleeve and tore it off his arm. She then proceeded to apply the sleeve directly against the wound, then tucked his shirt around it.

"If I would have known you were going to remove an article of clothing off my body for each wound I acquired, I would have fought more valiantly," Jaako remarked. "Maybe by the time you bound every wound, we could have had something to talk about."

"Don't kid yourself," Castalia remarked. "It would have taken more wounds then you could survive, for me to remove anything of interest off your body."

Ethlyn bound the wound on Rupp's shoulder, then buttoned up his shirt.

"Thank you, m'lady," he gratified. "My shoulder feels better already. However, I don't know how we are going to prove to the kingdom that there was an imposter king ruling for a time, and that the real king was killed by the Andjety months beforehand."

"We need to take Vynjoi's body with us," Ethlyn replied, "so that the kingdom might see and understand what took place under their noses."

"Yeah," Jaako responded. "Who's going to carry Vynjoi's body all the way back to the battlefield?"

"Don't have to," Castalia answered. "But we can reduce the load we do need to carry."

"Reduce?" Jaako asked. As soon as the question escaped his lips, Castalia picked up Jaako's sword, and with both hands swung it to the ground, where Vynjoi's body lay. As the sword came down with all of Castalia's strength, Vynjoi's head was severed from his body, and rolled towards Jaako. Jaako leaped to his feet and pressed himself against the cavern wall.

"You are one sick, crazy lady!" Jaako exclaimed.

"There," Castalia responded, with cool resolve. "I reduced the carrying load one- tenth."

Everybody watched her in disbelief as she wrapped the head in a smaller blanket that Vynjoi had not thrown over the fire. She wrapped it, then slung it over her shoulder, like one would field dress a downed deer. As soon as everybody regained their composure, the group headed back towards the battlefield on the other side of the palace.

It took Rupp, Jaako, Castalia and Ethlyn more than an hour to walk all the way from the cavern room, back out the front side of the palace. As the four heroes emerged from the front of the palace, the Special Forces had camped themselves on the battlefield in several camps, complete with fires. Each camp spent time binding the wounds of their wounded, and wrapping their dead casualties in burial wrappings to be transported back to Nadeau for proper burial.

A couple of the camps took responsibility to process the surrendered enemy soldiers by writing down their personal information, disarming them, feeding them, and binding any wounds they also might have sustained. Then they were sat in a corner of the field to be released the moment the Nadeau camp broke to return to Nadeau.

Upon approaching the camp, Rupp announced to the camp, "The Witch is dead. Vynjoi is dead." The special forces cheered, then asked two questions. First, who was Vynjoi? And second, what happened to Rolf?

The four heroes sat down in the centre of camp and explained what transpired while Rupp and Jaako were chained. As they explained that the princess uncovered the body of Malcolm, and that Vynjoi was the king's half-brother, Castalia unravelled the blanket that held the head of Vynjoi. She held his head up by the hair and offered for anyone to examine it to see if what they said was true. Everybody accepted their word. Castalia then sat the head of Vynjoi on the ground near the Andjety prisoners. She turned the head so it faced them. Every one of the Andjety scooted close to one another, and pressed against the side of the mountain to stay as far away from the severed head as possible.

The four then explained that Vynjoi tossed the princess over the side of the cave, and how Henry and Rozelle jumped off to save her. Because it was dark, nobody knew the outcome, nor where the three had ended up. Balen and Olivia stepped forward and suggested forming a search party to scour the area and see if they could uncover the Royal Family's location. Rupp, Jaako and Castalia were spent from fighting and walking from one end of the cavern to the other, and back again. They verbally bowed out and abdicated to anyone willing.

Mason was the first to volunteer, along with two of his younger members of her Highness's Special Forces. Next to volunteer were three of the archers. The six of them stood to their feet, walked over and faced the Captain of the Royal guards.

"We are prepared, sir," one of Mason's men announced, "to depart immediately and scour the area in search of Her Highness, the princess."

"You men have just finished expending your energy defeating an entire army of Andjety," Rupp replied. "Are you prepared to search the rest of the night for the missing royals?"

"We are prepared," the men chorused. Rupp shook his head.

"If you are prepared, who am I to stop you?"

"Luella and I will go with them and help," Ethlyn added. "Lu might be able to find them more easily from the air."

"We—we—we—we are honoured to include a heroine in our search party," Mason replied. Ethlyn blushed and turned her head to the side.

"I'm no heroine," Ethlyn humbly responded.

"A thousand pardons," Mason replied, "but I was referring to your falcon. She did all she could at injuring the traitorous Rolf. It gave us an edge while fighting the Andjety forces." Luella let out a loud squawk.

"Don't be smug," Ethlyn scolded her feathered companion.

As Henry watched over the princess, Audrianna began to cough uncontrollably. Her eyes opened briefly, looking up into Henry's face, then shut again as she coughed once more.

"She's got the coughs," Rozelle declared, a shot of worry spreading across her face. "That is bad."

"What can we do to get rid of the coughs?" Henry asked. Rozelle shook her head, looking down at the wrapped princess, and wiping sweat

"I've heard that some doctors cut the wrists and bleed the sick person until all the bad blood pours out," Rozelle answered. "But I don't know the difference between good blood and bad blood."

"How does that help get rid of the coughs?" Henry asked.

"It won't," a voice uttered behind them. Both Henry and Rozelle turned to look at the Andjety, still sitting in his chair behind them. "It's not bad blood that ails her," the man said, leaning forward in his chair towards the three of them.

"I didn't know you could speak Nadeau," Henry remarked. "You acted like there was a language barrier between us."

"So did you," the man replied with a wink. "Your little girl doesn't need to be butchered to get well. She has trouble breathing. You need to fix her breathing problem first."

"And how do we do that?" Henry asked. The old man leaned back in his chair and smiled.

"I might have some medicine that should cure her breathing problems," the man answered. "If you feel inclined to trust me." Henry shot a look at Rozelle who shrugged in agreement.

"What kind of medicine is it?" Henry asked.

"It's an old remedy that I acquired from a doctor who practiced many years in Europe." The man stood and walked over to a cabinet, opened the small door, and extracted a stout opaque bottle filled with fluid. He pulled the cork from the top of the bottle and poured some of the fluid into a tin cup. Toting the bottle and the cup back to his chair, the man handed the cup to Henry and sat the bottle on the floor next to his chair.

"See if she will drink this," the man replied. Henry propped the weakened princess up in his lap, then brought the cup to her lips.

"Ree," he softly whispered, while gently shaking Audrianna to open her eyes. "Ree," he repeated, "you need to drink this. It's only half a cup." Henry tipped the cup to her mouth, to which the princess received the drink the moment she felt the liquid touch her lips. Downing the entire drink, the princess laid back in Henry's arms, her eyes still shut tight. The Prince handed the empty cup to the Andjety, who leaned forward to take the cup, then peered at the princess waiting to see a reaction.

Within half a minute, Audrianna's eyes popped open, and she lunged from Henry's lap, out of the blanket, and rushed to the ash bucket, sitting next to the fireplace. The princess vomited up a large amount of fluid, much more than what she had ingested. She then sat back on the cold wooden floor, only to realise she was totally naked.

"Oh, my!" she exclaimed, realising her predicament. Rozelle took the blanket from Henry and held it open to the princess.

"Does Your Highness care to return to the blanket?" Rozelle asked. Audrianna scrambled to her feet, and rushed back inside the comfort, warmth and covering of the blanket.

"My chest is on fire!" she declared, taking deep clear breaths.

"What was in that medicine of yours?" Henry asked the And-jety man.

"Liquorish and Comfrey," the man answered, picking up the bottle next to his chair. "And, of course, a high concentration of rum."

"Rum?" both Henry and Audrianna exclaimed at the same time.

"Yep," the man answered. "Drink it twice a day, and I never get sick." He lifted the bottle to his mouth and took a large sip. Audrianna glared at Henry.

"What's with you letting people give me rum drinks all the time?" she asked. "I did not know there was rum in that drink," Henry argued.

"In the drink?" the man asked. "Rum is the drink!"

"Well," Rozelle observed, "it doesn't seem Your Highness is still coughing. At least the drink was able to get rid of the coughs." The man grinned and began to laugh.

"There's enough rum in that drink to kill most poisons," he bragged.

The six-man search party, along with Ethlyn and Luella, traipsed through the tunnels and corridors of the late Witch's palace caverns. They eventully came to the cavern where Vyn-joi's headless body lay. Stepping past the body, they popped out the other side of the mountain. The sun began to break over its peaks, lighting up the valley near the bottom. The search party slowly climbed down the treacherous steep slope, down to the edge of the rapidly flowing stream. There was very little evidence of either Henry, Audrianna, or Rozelle, sliding down the shallow stream to the small pond near the bottom of the mountainside.

However, as they began to descend the steep slope, Ethlyn released her falcon, giving her the command to search for any human activity. As the group gathered at the edge of the icy pond, Luella circled near a cluster of trees and squawked.

"Something has aroused her curiosity," Ethlyn announced. Everyone quickly hurried past the pond, and down into a valley. The cluster of trees that Luella circled were premised by a large plain of tall g[______]t of the searchers, they could see that the grass had been recently trodden down by travellers.

"That—that—that—that must be Prince Henry and Princess Audrianna's tracks," Mason said.

"And Lady Rozelle," Ethlyn added.

The group quickly pushed through the overgrowth, towards the cluster of trees that Luella continued to circle. As they made their way to the edge of the forest, the smell of burning wood caught their attention.

"I don't see anything yet," one of the searchers commented, "but I smell what seems to be a fireplace."

"Or a campfire," one of the other searchers chimed in.

"No," the first searcher said, "a fireplace has a distinct aroma that is different than a campfire. I can't explain why, but it does."

"Look!" Ethlyn cried out. "Through the trees, I see a cabin." Everyone doubled their pace as they made their way towards the cabin that might hold a clue to the royals' whereabouts.

As they approached the cabin, the group noticed that the front door had been broken in two, and an attempt was made at propping it up in front of the doorway.

"This must be the place," Mason muttered as Luella landed on Ethlyn's gloved hand. "This has Prince Henry's sig—sig—sig—signature written all over it." Two of the men moved the broken pieces of the door to one side, while the group cautiously entered the cabin, in search of the missing Nadeau leaders. Ethlyn covered Luella's head with her blinder cap, then set her on a stool on the front porch.

As they entered, they found Henry and Rozelle laying on the floor, with a bundled Audrianna snuggled in between them. All three were fast asleep, with the Andjety still sitting in his chair watching over them.

Before the Andjety man knew it, seven dirty, battle worn, and tired searchers, stood behind him looking on the three in front of the fire. Sensing a presence behind him, the man turned, saw the new intruders, and stood to his feet facing them.

"Don't be alarmed," Mason assured the man. "We came looking for the three keeping your fire warm."

As Mason spoke, Henry was startled and sat up, careful to not disturb Audrianna. "You three look awfully cosy," Ethlyn commented. Rozelle was next to be startled. "We…uh…er…" Rozelle stammered.

"We fell asleep looking after the princess," Henry announced. "Princess Audrianna is very ill, and was close to dying. Lady Rozelle and I have been nursing her back to health, disregarding our own fatigue and need of rest."

"Shall we assist in hel—hel—helping to nurse her?" Mason asked. Audrianna gave a fearful look.

"No," she said. "I would rather stay right where I am." "With Prince Henry and Lady Rozelle?" Ethlyn asked. "More like, under this blanket," Audrianna answered. "Why is that?" Ethlyn asked.

"Because," Rozelle explained, "her clothes are laying over the hearth. Drying." "Which clothes?" Mason asked.

"Every stitch of clothes," Audrianna answered. "This blanket is my only covering." All the men of the search party took a step backwards.

"Maybe we should step outside," one of the men suggested, "and let Her Highness make herself more presentable, and not so—'unembellished.'"

Henry, Mason, and the other men of the search party waited outside while Rozelle and Ethlyn helped dress the princess. Halfway through the process, though, Rozelle popped her head out the door and called for Henry to come back in the house.

"The Princess is not doing well," she declared. "We were able to get most of her clothes on her, but every effort at dressing, seemed to drain Her Highness's energy."

"The men and I may need to go back to the camp," Mason recommended, "and bring back horses, wagons and provisions to transport the princess back to Nadeau."

"Yes," Rozelle stated, "the sooner we get her back to Nadeau, the sooner our physicians will be able to treat her."

"How fast can your men make it back to camp?" Henry asked. Mason turn to look at his men.

"How fast can you men run?" he asked them.

"Run?" two of the archers argued. "You mean, uphill? Up the side of the mountain?" "Run, walk, crawl, or climb," Mason replied. "How—how—how—how long will it take you to return to camp?"

"Most likely a couple hours at least," one of the men answered. "But once we team together the horses to the wagons, and gather the necessary provisions, it will take the remainder of the day to travel around the other side of the mountain and make it back here."

"Then I—I—I—I suggest you get going right away," Mason replied. "Be back here by nightfall." The men looked astonished at his request, but quickly turned and started running towards the mountain from whence they came. Every so often they would look over their shoulder to see if Mason meant the request he gave.

Soon enough, Rozelle allowed the two men to return inside the cabin. Audrianna, though fully dressed, continued to lay on the blanket, in front of the fire. Although her breathing had improved, it was obvious her health was compromised. A wet cool cloth lay across her forehead, and her skin seemed quite pale. Ethlyn sat cross-legged on the floor beside her, while the Andjety man, still sitting in his chair, tried to get Ethlyn to try a sip from his jug of "medicine".

As the day wore on, everyone waited with anticipation for the arrival of their wagons. Henry sat undaunted next to the little princess, checking to see if he needed to change the cloth over her forehead. Even though he knew very little of what to do to take care of Audrianna, he was determined to do whatever might help her condition.

As night settled across the valley, and no sign of the wagons appearing, Mason and the two ladies decided to watch from outside on the porch. Mason entertained the two maids with fanciful tales of fighting battles during the reign of Malcolm the Merciful. The Andjety man retired to his bedroom and shut the door.

Henry sat next to his betrothed, his back to the low burning fire. As he did their first night on the run, he watched the shadows from the fire dance about the room. He thought about how Audrianna had completely transformed his life over the course of the last eighteen weeks. He thought about the brazen saucy comments she would make that would completely flabbergast him. He thought about how she dared him to spank her, to which he did. How she jumped out her bedroom window and became tangled in a tree by her hair. He chuckled to himself when he thought about how she went to the pub with him and Balen, only to become intoxicated, dancing on the table declaring herself the new queen of Nadeau.

Call me Ree, she would say. I'm a little farm girl. He would call her Ree, then she would smile at him and immediately respond by calling him the atrocious name, Horace. He thought about how she would cock her head to one side and look at him through the corner of her eyes as she would spin some wild yarn she knew he would never believe.

Now Henry looked down at the quiet, weak little girl. There was no smile, nor any reminiscence of her angelic face. She was dying. How could he go on without her? How could he live if she died? She brought so much light to his world. Now as the fire behind him began to dim, so did the light in Audrianna. He quickly grasped her hand as if he was restraining her from being pulled down into the grave.

"Ree," he gently whispered, bending down close to her ear. "Ree, can you hear me?" The little girl turned her head in Henry's direction, but did not open her eyes, and showed no expression on her face. Henry removed the cloth from atop her forehead, then stared into her face as he took her hand once again.

"Ree," he repeated, this time in a louder, but soft volume. "I know you can hear me, even though you are too sick to answer. Perhaps you're too sick to understand, but I still want to tell you what you've meant to me these past four and a half months." Henry paused to see if there was any sign of comprehension evident on her face.

Nothing.

"I hated being betrothed to you because I thought your tender age would undermine my influence and authority. I believed people would think I preferred children, seeing me as a child myself. I hated the fact our engagement meant I had to wait another six years, because I believed I was ready then. But I wasn't."

"When the Andjety seized the castle and chased us away, I was terrified. Completely lost. I had no hope and no ideas. No motivation to fix the broken kingdom. But you, Ree. You never lost hope. You never let our circumstances, or your circumstances, dampen your spirit. You still chose to laugh, and to love, and to spin yarns. I had never seen the like my whole life. And I've been around fifteen years longer than your ten."

"What I'm saying is, I need you to get better. I need you to survive. If you die, I will die. I can't rule the kingdom without you, even if we aren't fit to be married. Just to know you are somewhere in Nadeau helps me to believe the kingdom will be strong, and go on. Please, Ree! Audrianna! Your Royal Highness! I need you to live. I need you in my life. I love you. I love you from my heart to my head."

Henry began to softly weep. He drew her hand up to his cheek and held her cold hand next to his warm face. As tears began to stream down his face, one of his tears dripped off his cheek and trickled down Audrianna's arm. The princess began to stir.

"I want a taller throne," she replied in a coarse and raspy voice. Henry chuckled, tears still streaming down his face.

Slowly, Henry stretched himself prostrate on the floor, his head next to hers, their bodies perpendicular to one another.

There, he slept. Her spirit was still alive. He knew she was going to be okay.

By morning light, the entire company of the princess's elite special forces arrived at the cabin. Olivia was the first to jump from her wagon and run after Audrianna. Inside, she found Henry, Mason, the two ladies-in-waiting, as well as the Andjety man sitting in a circle on the floor eating porridge. Audrianna sat propped up in Rozelle's lap, also eating porridge.

"How is Her Highness?" Olivia asked. "I heard she was gravely ill."

"She was," Henry commented. "Up until late last night. Her fever broke, and she became as arrant and mouthy as always."

Olivia looked at Audrianna.

"They're feeding me porridge," the princess responded. "As if I was a peasant farm girl. No veal, no cheese, nor bread. Just—porridge!" She stuck out her tongue in protest. Olivia put both hands on her hips, then nodded in agreement at Henry.

"I'm glad you are better, Anna," she replied.

"She's still very weak," Rozelle said. "She will most likely be bedridden for at least two weeks."

"Two weeks?" the princess exclaimed.

"Longer, if it would keep her out of trouble," Henry remarked. Audrianna wrinkled her nose at Henry.

"She frowned at me," he said, looking at Olivia and pointing to the princess. "Did you see her frown?" Audrianna turned her face away.

"Anna frowning at you is your problem," Olivia responded to Henry. "I only handle belligerence that is directed at me. You're going to be the king soon. Handle your own discipline."

Henry looked about the room until his eyes met Rupp's, who had just entered the house.

"Off with her head!" he playfully commanded. Rupp smiled, looked at the princess, then back at Henry.

"Good luck finding an executioner that will carry out that

order," Rupp answered.

Audrianna giggled and squirmed in Rozelle's lap.

"Eat your porridge, Your Highness," Rozelle encouraged. Audrianna stuck out her tongue again in protest.

"Well, if you won't eat your porridge here," Olivia replied, "then you'll have to wait till we get back home to eat. And that might be all day."

"Home?" Audrianna asked. "Who's home?" "Our home," Olivia answered.

"But I live in Nadeau castle," the princess argued, "not Pachenthou."

"But you're not well enough to be in a draughty castle," Olivia said. "Staying with us will guarantee you will recover rapidly. Don't you agree, Your Excellency?" Olivia asked Henry.

"I do believe they will take excellent care of you, Ree," he answered. "Once you are well," Olivia offered, "you can return to the castle."

Audrianna wanted to frown, or stuck her tongue out in protest. But that would illicit a response from Olivia that she didn't wish to happen. Not only that, as with Henry, she thoroughly believed that her chances of recovering were greater with Olivia and Balen.

"Besides," Olivia added, "you're not the only sick person that will be recovering on our farm."

"What do you mean?" she asked, pushing on Rozelle to sit up higher.

"Maybe you should come and see who else is in the wagon with Balen," Olivia suggested. Audrianna tried to scramble to her feet, but could not even fully sit up without assistance. Henry walked over to her and picked her up in his arms. He then carried the little girl outside, to the wagon, in which Balen sat on the bench holding the reins to the horses. Henry then proceeded to carry her towards the back of the wagon, so she could peer inside to see its passenger.

Wide-eyed, the princess looked to see who else could be going home with Olivia and Balen.

"Sister," the voice of a familiar little girl rang out. "Gets up here in the wagon with me. We gets to gets home with Olivia and Balen!"

"Janessa!" Audrianna exclaimed. "I thought you had been killed!"

"Me toos," Janessa stated. "Buts I woke up here in the wagon, with Lord Balen takes caring of me. And now I'm better!" The little Andjety girl cupped her hands as if to whisper a secret, but spoke loud enough for everyone to hear. "I just only lay here so they will takes me home with them." Balen turned to look at Janessa and chuckled.

"So, do you want to go home with us, or go back to the castle?" Olivia asked. Audrianna looked at Olivia, then at Balen, then at Janessa, who patted an empty space next to her.

"I'll go back to Pachenthou until I get better," the princess resigned. "Or rather, until both of us get better," including Janessa in her decision.

"Very well," Henry replied. "Shall I help you get settled?"

"Oh, yes," Audrianna responded with a broad smile. "I would love you to come along."

"I meant, settled in the back of the wagon," Henry clarified. "Oh," she said, her smile dropping.

"But I would be honoured to help escort you to the Royal Farm in Pachenthou," Henry offered. Audrianna smiled again.

"Royal Farm?" Balen replied. "Are you talking about our humble farm?"

"Any farm that is the residence of the crowned princess, and a Lord and Lady, is a royal farm, not a humble one," Henry declared.

"You can call our farm whatever you want," Balen replied, "just as long as you understand that it is our farm."

Henry laid Audrianna in the back of the wagon, to which she crawled towards Janessa. As she positioned herself next to her friend, Audrianna reached around to hug Janessa.

"Whoa! Carefuls," Janessa replied. "I be still mighty tender."

"I'm sorry, Sister," Audrianna replied. "I'll be gentle with you, but I won't stop hugging you. You saved my life!" The princess laid next to her and took her hand. The Andjety girl smiled and squeezed Audrianna's hand.

"Well," she replied to the princess, "if I hads to choose over again whether to takes an arrow in the back for you…"

"You would do it again?" Audrianna asked.

"Nots a chance!" Janessa exclaimed, her voice cracking. "That arrow hurted! I used to gets beaten almosts everyday as a slave. Lets me tells you, that arrow hurted me much, much more!" Audrianna let out a giggle. "I was goings to say," Janessa continued, "I would pushed you off the ledge."

"Push me off the ledge?" the princess asked incredulously.

"You wouldn't haves gotten hurted as bad as me." Janessa grinned and squeezed her new sister's hand.

Henry walked back to the cabin and gave instructions to Rupp concerning the return to Nadeau, and rewarding those who fought against the Witch's army. He also gave instructions regarding the safe return of King Malcolm's body to Nadeau, as well as planning for his funeral upon Henry's return. Rupp informed the crowned Prince the demise of Vynjoi, as well as Castalia severing his head.

"What did you do with his head?" Henry asked.

"As far as I know, it's still sitting in front of the Andjety prisoners, keeping a watchful eye on them," Rupp answered. Henry shook his head in disbelief.

"Bury the head, release the prisoners, and bring my father's body back to Nadeau." "Yes, Your Majesty," Rupp replied, giving an official bow.

"I will be in Pachenthou no longer than two days," Henry announced, "then I will return home."

"Will His Majesty be traveling alone?" Rupp asked. "I can provide a safe escort for Your Majesty."

"No need," Henry answered. "I have the safest escort in all of

Nadeau." "Your Majesty?" Rupp asked. Henry laughed.

"Her Highness's ladies-in-waiting," he replied.

"Your Majesty will be traveling alone with three royal maids across half of Nadeau?" Rupp asked.

"Don't worry," Henry answered. "They're not afraid of me."

Olivia and Balen sat at the very front of the wagon, Balen controlling the horses' reins. Olivia sat next to him, her arm over his closest shoulder. Henry, the crowned prince, sat in the very back of the wagon. He sat with his back towards the rear, and facing the two girls. Rozelle, Castalia, and Ethlyn followed the wagon on horseback. They rode towards Pachenthou as fast as the wagon and the girls could allow. Audrianna and Janessa snuggled down on fresh straw. The jostling of the wagon was painful for Janessa, but she bravely tolerated it, knowing the wagon took her to a new home, and a new family. Audrianna laid as still as possible in the straw. Any attempt at fighting the motion of the wagon drained her energy. Balen turned around every so often to check to see how the girls were fairing. Henry was left to the bare wood of the wagon. He grabbed a hold of one side of the wagon and held on tightly the entire journey to the Pachenthou farm.

Upon arriving at the farm, both girls were physically spent. Balen carried both of them, one at a time, into the house, laying them together on the bed Audrianna had previously used.

Olivia returned Audrianna's nightgown to her, while Janessa was given one of Balen's farm shirts to sleep in. Olivia prepared a light supper for the entire group. As the children, Henry, and the ladies ate their supper, Olivia prepared sleeping quarters for the ladies in the main room of the house. After everyone ate their fill, and the ladies assisted in cleaning up the kitchen, Henry retired to the barn, to the exact place he slept before.

The next morning, Henry and the three ladies showed themselves to be rather useful in bringing in vegetables from the garden, cutting them up, and serving them to the set table. Neither Audrianna nor Janessa were strong enough to sit at the table.

After the adults finished eating, Henry volunteered to take

food into the room for the hungry girls. Although it was painful, Janessa sat up right away to receive the offered food. Audrianna, less impressed with the plate of assorted vegetables, took extra coaxing to get her to sit up and eat.

As they ate, Henry told Audrianna that he needed to talk to her concerning an important matter. The princess sat up, taking interest in any issues of state.

"You know the way Nadeau law is written," Henry explained. "The law prohibits me from being king unless I have married a maiden to sit by my side and help me rule with justice and mercy?"

"Yes," the princess answered.

"Without a wife, I can only be a crowned Prince. That is why my father betrothed me to you, was because he wanted me to not be king for at least six years."

"I know," Audrianna replied.

"Well," Henry stammered, "this whole ordeal with Zymjai and Vynjoi, being half- siblings to the king through King Albert's prolific womanising. Well, it caused me to realise that there are possibly more out there that could seize the opportunity to wrestle away the throne. Which means, I need to get married and seize the throne for myself."

"That would be wise," Audrianna replied, "but how are we to marry if I'm not eligible due to me being too young?"

"Well," Henry continued, "the king is dead, which means his claim to our betrothal can be considered dissolved." Audrianna's countenance dropped, as did her head. She knew where Henry was going with the conversation.

"But, Horace…" she started to reason.

"Now, Ree," Henry interrupted, "I've got to be king. And as much as I love you, you're still a little girl. And you deserve to be a little girl."

"But…" Audrianna tried to chime in.

"Now, Ree," Henry scolded. "You deserve to grow up naturally, with a sister, and two parents. I think Olivia and Balen will make a great mama and papa for you. You deserve to get a switching when you need it, and a piece of pie when you earn it."

"Horace, please!" she interjected, tears starting to stream down her face. "I know everything you told me is true. You need to marry an adult so you can have the throne. I know I'm too young to be your queen. I know. Believe me, I know."

"I'm sorry, Ree."

All three of them sat on the bed in silence, no one speaking, with only Janessa eating her plate of food.

"I just want you to know," Audrianna remarked, breaking the silence, "that I love you! I love you with all my heart. I may only be ten, but if I lived to be a hundred, I will never love another person as much as I love you!" Henry put his arm around the princess and pulled her close to him.

"Ninety years is a long time," he replied. "Don't limit better opportunities because you are unwilling to part from what never will be."

Audrianna looked up into Henry's eyes. She suddenly realised that his eyes were tearing up also.

"Do you love me, Henry?" she asked, calling him by his real name. Henry, still having one arm around her, brought his other hand up and gently stroked her soft cheek with the back of his hand. The familiar scent of lilacs wafted through the room.

"From my heart, to my head," repeating what he said to her while still recovering.

Audrianna smiled. Janessa snapped a carrot in her mouth. "Do you think you will forget about me?" she asked.

"No," he answered. "That is not possible. I will always remember you, and possibly think of you often."

"Then," she said, "if you will not marry me, please do one last thing before you leave."

"Whatever you ask," he promised.

Audrianna leaned her head backwards against the headboard of her bed, and looked straight into Henry's eyes.

"I want you to kiss me," she said.

"Kiss you?" he asked. "You and I have kissed before."

"No," she replied. "I kissed you. I gave you my first kiss. But you were chained, and unable to willingly comply. I don't want that kind of kiss." Henry continued to stare into the little girl's face.

"Please, kiss me," she asked again. "Kiss me like you're my husband."

Henry shot an uncomfortable look at Audrianna. Janessa looked away from them both. If she had the strength, Janessa would have crawled out of the bed, and hidden herself under the mattress.

"Ree… I… er…," he wasn't sure what to tell his precocious adolescent friend. "Please," she said. "In honour of all we've been through together." Henry stared at her for a moment, then sighed.

Without saying another word, he withdrew his arm from behind Audrianna's back, and cradled her head in his hand. With his other hand, he guided her chin to position her mouth at the best angle. He then leaned in and placed his lips against her lips.

It wasn't a passionate kiss, nor an erotic one. Their friendship would not dictate such a superficial experience. No, this kiss went beyond a kiss of friendship, or companionship. Beyond a kiss between two lovers. Similar to the kiss Olivia and Balen exchanged, theirs was an endearing one. It was a kiss that forgave all transgressions, yet validated all their personal joys together. It sealed their friendship, yet released each other from any obligation or expectation. All of that, and it only lasted a few seconds.

As Henry slowly pulled away from Audrianna, still staring into her face, he felt Janessa tug at his coat. Henry looked over at the girl who remained quiet throughout their encounter.

"Can I gets to kiss you goodbye too?" she asked.

"No," Audrianna scolded. "He was my betrothed, not yours." Janessa grinned.

"It don't hurts nobody to ask," she responded. Henry leaned

over and kissed Janessa on the forehead.

"That was for saving Ree's life," he replied.

"Yeah," Audrianna added, "and not pushing me off the ledge." Henry stood from the bed, then gave an official bow to Audrianna. "Your Highness," he remarked.

"I'm not a princess anymore, remember?" she resigned.

"No," Henry answered. "You will always be the crowned princess. You just will never be the queen without marrying the king."

"Really?" Audrianna asked.

"Yes," Henry answered. "And you are welcome to the castle anytime you wish. Your royal chamber will always be yours."

"So if you gets married quick," Janessa pipped up, "and haves a son, and he grows up, she cans marry him and still be the queen?"

"I'll be an old lady by then," Audrianna replied. "You only wills be thirty-five." Janessa stated. "Yeah. Old!" Audrianna exclaimed.

"I think it's time for me and the ladies to leave for Nadeau," Henry declared. "Goodbye, little mice."

"Goodbye," both the girls chorused.

As Henry left the room, Janessa took hold of Audrianna's hand as they both laid back in their bed.

"What be it likes being a princess for real?" Janessa asked. Audrianna sighed a long hard sigh.

"Four different meats at every meal, seven types of cheeses, multiple grains of bread, sweet breads, and pastries." Janessa's eyes grew wide as she nibbled a parsnip from her plate. "Also," Audrianna continued, "tight fitting clothes, which you have to change several times a day. Horrible bustiers! Sitting in royal court for hours, listening to people complain and make excuses." Audrianna let out another loud sigh. "Sometimes it's just not worth it."

They both lay quietly on the bed.

"Sister," Janessa broke the silence of the room. "Yes, Sister?" Audrianna asked.

"Just so we be clear, I gets to gets the next Prince that comes along."

They both giggled.

EPILOGUE

Rolf never did surface again in Nadeau. Many people began to circulate rumours that he ran off with a woman that had big ears and three eyes, to compensate for the one eye he lost and part of his ear. A reward was set by Henry for the capture of the former armour- bearer, but no one claimed it.

Henry returned to Nadeau that very week. Within a few days after his return, the nation mourned the death of King Malcolm the Merciful. Although Henry knew he needed to take a bride to become king, it was several months before the nation celebrated his union in matrimony.

Before being wed, Henry spent many Royal Court days alone on the throne. Throughout each royal court session, as well as sword practice, and every meal he spent alone, he would reminisce concerning the scent of lilacs that Audrianna would smell like every day. When the season became available, Henry ordered lilacs to be planted throughout the castle and in the city of Nadeau. Before long, one could smell lilacs from one end of the city to the other, as well as throughout the entire castle.

Audrianna's birthday was declared a national holiday in honour of "the hero of the Battle of Zymjai Palace". The story of Audrianna slaying the Witch was retold in narrative as well as in song. Girls who were ten years old on the princess's birthday would traditionally have their hair cut short, and every pub would serve mugs of sassafras drinks, void of any shots of rum.

Henry proved to be a good and gracious king. He was shown to be wise in his judgments, always erring on the side of mercy and empathy. It was because of this that the people of Nadeau desired to call the king, Henry the Honourable. However, not wanting to ever forget how Audrianna the Tenderhearted transformed him from what he had been, King Henry insisted that he continue being called Henry the Horrible all the days of his life.

As far as who Henry chose to marry as the new queen of Nadeau, and what became of Princess Audrianna…

Well, that is a different story!

The End